LOST BOY

DEAN HAMID

LOST BOY

First edition. December, 2022.

Second edition. May, 2024

Copyright © 2022 Dean Hamid.

Written by Dean Hamid.

Lost Boy

Dean Hamid

Dean Hamid LLC Presents

Lost Boy
By
Dean Hamid

LOST BOY©
COPYRIGHT @2022 LOST BOY

By: Dean Hamid

Editor: Dean Hamid LLC PUBLISHING SERVICES

Cover Design: Dean Hamid LLC

Acknowledgments

Big shout outs go to my people in the Chuck, Charleston, South Carolina keeping it real! The people...the flavor; Walterboro, and the Low Country Dirty South.

That brother that be writin' all the time, you know him! *~Dean Hamid~*

Dedication

Dedicated to all the ballas, trapaholics, gangstas and tricks in South Carolina exclusively! Keepin' it hard! I ain't mad at cha', and of course, Devario.

Prologue

Some cats...actually a whole lot of them always seem to be on the wrong side of the street when shit is going down, falling short, stuck in time in their own vain, selfish desires. They do good for a while then fall flat on their faces, even after trying their damndest. The utmost pure intentions and all that crap always trying to make some sort of trick work...suckers...all of them. But, you know, the crazy part of it all is that they still get the fuck back up, wipe all the filthy grime and sludge off, then insanely start the process all over again. It's crazy losing it all for days, months, even years and then suddenly, just like that they disappear looking for an out, healing...help!

Many get caught up with bumping their heads five times a day, even more, in prayer, constant meditation, and repentance, looking for some sort of guidance and reassurance that seemingly in the midst of it all leads only to desperate, distraught lives that they loathe. While others cry out to a savior looking for a response from some mysterious voice that everyone's sold you on. That you're supposed to hear. Ya know jumping from churches to churches trying to find some inner sound twitching at your earlobes. Deep inside never really evolving then, they're back to the same old bullshit again.

The muthafuckin' Joneses, the Tom's and the Bob's. People you've looked up to in admiration all your life, unwittingly idolizing them, telling your dumb naive ass that it was so easy for them that you can do it too. But you know what they never put you on their team, dudes get caught up all the time-waking up out of their sleep hollering in the dark for answers...tired of that shit, too, ya know.

I want to make it to Heaven. I just don't want to die one way or another not knowing that blissful, peaceful type of vibe, no, not me. But you know what? It's real simple, it always is, it just has to be. Some of us were just made for the Hellfire! All of us are...how they say it in Charleston: *~Lost Boy~*

Chapter One

T-Black stepped out onto the enclosed porch of his mother's house and sat. Lounging deep into the worn, outdated patio sofa he pulled out a Newport from his shirt pocket, then fumbled around into his equally worn pants pockets and pulled out a lighter. He glanced briefly up the street before lighting his cigarette at a house that sat on a corner peeping halfway out in front of his, about a block and a half away. Hustler by the name of Riko his family's home, but T-Black wasn't too concerned with the residence as he was with Riko's young sister, Cleo.

Riko's family was the well to do type, both parents owned businesses downtown Charleston while T-Black grew up poor and alone, especially after his old man got locked up for a robbery. Eventually, and not too long after he was killed in prison, Central Correctional Institution.

His drug-addicted mother ended up trying to raise him and his oldest brother, Bobby alone. Bobby was later killed in a botched liquor store holdup in North Charleston, leaving T-Black by himself and his mother to fend for both of them by tricking. As a result, he grew up introverted and bullied in school. When he got tired of it all, he just quit going.

His size mushroomed from a scrawny awkward kid to a tall muscular, man-child and he ended up becoming the bully, stalking the streets of Liberty Hill. Eventually, he became a pick-up man for the dealers and the number takers, while Riko and his sister went to school downtown at some of the best academics available to rich well to do kids.

He'd go by their house after their mother got a liking to him, considered him to be one of her college social type experiments of sorts, and tried to foster him into a quote-unquote good home. He was real big on the adoption thing. Maybe there was going to be change in his life, after-all he figured. He ended up staying with a couple she'd found for him. He even went on a family outing. A camping trip with just him and the father one weekend.

He told T-Black it would make him more of a man. The cops later found him alone, lost and shaking from the damp cold in the thick of the dense woods. Soon, after investigating they came upon the trailer they were staying in and found his foster father dead. He'd been stabbed numerous times in the chest with a buoy knife. He'd made the mistake of trying TBlack, sexually. Things just went south from there. He ran the streets much harder than before and became estranged altogether from Riko's parents.

Riko and Cleo would later do what every other kid in America did and start running the streets. Cleo was instantly kicked out of the house for being sexually active. Her mother cited her behavior as rebellious saying, *the devil got in her.* She stayed with T-Black's mother for a minute, when she wasn't wandering the streets, and she and T-Black became lovers. But he wasn't the pretty-boy, dope dealing type that the young, bright-eyed, naive girl craved. He was blue-black, with shiny, bright white teeth and yellow, constricted eyes. Though he was perfect physically standing at six-foot-two and weighing two-hundred and ten pounds. He was just too much of a raw brute for her. He was something she used to scratch the itch between her legs. A habit she was getting accustomed to more and more.

T-Black continued to be a bully but dope boys were his main targets now. He learned how to finesse other playas from out of town, having them front him dope and cash to set up shop in the lucrative drug heavy hoods. It worked for a while, but his face started becoming too Notorious. So, he needed another front...Riko. That only worked for a short period of time, because Riko had other motives. He saw this as his opportunity to get back at Hulie, a merciful, ruthless, up and coming hustla who was pimping his sister hard on the track and at times beating her senseless.

Hulie couldn't quite finger Riko, but he knew T-Black was involved in the flam they ran on him. He felt like he was being played for a sucka and wanted revenge. Riko worked it so that T-Black was kept out of the loop. It was through his ignorance that Riko would set in motion his plans to set Hulie up, snatch his dope and money, then eventually Liberty Hill.

T-Black had a premonition that things weren't going to get any better for him. So, he stashed a nice sizable amount of cash and made plans to skip town in case he needed to. But now as he contemplated on this half-baked scheme Riko told him about over the phone, getting out was seriously not an option anymore. At least, not yet. He stared up the street reminiscing, hoping maybe Cleo was thinking about getting out of the game and getting her life together, too. From the money, he had stashed and this lick, a fifty-fifty split between him and Riko, it might work out. They could make a run like they used to talk about when they were young lovers.

He outed his cigarette and smiled sitting in the quiet of the darkness that engulfed him. Thinking real hard about the idea. A fantasy at best and thought out loud to himself after he was convinced. That it could all be real.

"This is my time," he said, the only thing breaking the silence stilled around him.

Later, that evening, T-Black stood in front of Riko's trap watching bodies creep about in the darkness as the flickering of lighters flicked on and off like fireflies around the busted out, glass window panes. Homes that were at one time halfassed decent, but still showed signs of breaking and entering on the backroom windows or mostly plain old breaking. Most owned by parents who's now grown children came back to the nest only to become drug addicted, scavenging, crackheads that stole from them every chance they got.

T-Black could only somewhat relate to that. His own mother would come home herself geeking, but she usually stowed away enough dope from her tricks to not have to worry about stealing, especially from the house, just from the tricks. She didn't have much, but she'd rather trick than sell anything she bought into the home. She always said that that was working backward. She never once considered herself a hustla', just an opportunist of sorts. When the situation presented itself, which was most of the time. T-Black considered himself to be the apple that didn't fall too far from the tree.

Unlike his mother, he didn't get high, the furthest he went was cigarettes. Even when circumstances presented itself, he never got caught up into it sniffing cocaine, rolling or smoking off what his mother would say was *the glass dick*. His biggest addiction was money. He loved to stow money, plenty at times. He'd offer his mother money, but she'd refuse, telling him to put it up for a rainy day. He did, he buried a lot of it in holes around his backyard with a Pitbull posted guard, but that was soon short-lived once word got out, and he damn near terrorized North Charleston getting his money back. So, he came up with a better spot. A stash that even he had to pat himself on the back for.

He checked his watch, Riko was late. He didn't see anyone in his spot when he searched around the house. It was strange, no tricks, no smokers...nothing. He called out his name a couple of times, and there was no answer. It didn't make sense to him. Whoever heard of an empty crack house? Coming towards him was a truck. It looked familiar, but he couldn't quite place it. The gleam from the headlight beams made it difficult to decipher. The truck pulled into a space up the street from him. Maybe it was Riko and the marks they talked about. It was that time anyway he thought as he stepped towards it, then reached into his pocket.

Damn, how could he forget his gun? Feeling some sort of way, he didn't sweat it, though. He figured there shouldn't be any trouble tonight, anyway. They'd just agree on the lick, then set a date for later according to the plan, Riko had put down. Besides he was in his hood, and no one would have the balls to try him in, Liberty Hill, so he relaxed.

Riko got out the truck. "Yo, wassup, son?"

"Wassup, where's the mark?" T-Black asked as he peeped inside the windows.

"They'll be here in a minute," Riko replied as he opened the lock to the bricked, gated fence. T-Black started to walk through and he stopped him. "I'm just gonna be a sec. I need to get something. Wait out here so they'll see you if they pull up." He walked up the walkway to the steps.

T-Black walked back out the fence, then Riko yelled back out at him. "Hey, uh, close the gate. You never know when five-o might roll up."

T-Black did, after all, he was right. The gate being closed meant he would have no connection to the trap at all if they did. He'd tell them he was out walking or something. He shut the fence back and fastened the lock behind him. Riko made it up the steps, opened the door and closed it behind him. The light on the front porch came on, T-Black was mused maybe that was the code for the smokers. It was a code, but not for the crackheads, though.

Hulie peeped up his head and looked at the light as it blinked on. He stood, shaking Jabari and Rip out of their doze. "Yo...it's that time," he said.

Jabari stood up and stretched letting out a loud yawn. Immediately Hulie put his hand over his mouth. "Shut the fuck

up! we don't want him to know we're coming." Shrugging him off, Jabari said, "Alright!"

He helped put the chairs on the back porch, silently. Right after he was on his heels as they crept through the bushes towards the street. They could now see the dude that he had told them about. Didn't recognize him, would have remembered if they'd seen him before. He was the big boy type. Tall and pretty damn muscular, bigger than Hulie. No wonder he needed help putting the timdown, but damn, where was that dude, Riko? They could see the light on at the trap, and Hulie's truck out front.

Hulie tipped slightly towards him and pulled out his gun tucking it tightly to his side. Old boy was smoking a cigarette with his back turned away from them. Hulie then motioned to Rip and Jabari to fan up the street and look out for the police. Just like the plan they did.

Hulie then stepped in front of him and hollered. "Yo, Busta, remember me!"

T-Black now recognized the truck and the man who stood in front of him from the last flam that he and Riko had done. He glanced up at the porch for Riko and suddenly the lights went out. The door locked and there were no lights on in the house either. He put it all together, he'd been set up.

"Yeah...yeah, I remember you partna," he said as he backed up slowly away from him looking for some room and an out.

"Where's my muthafuckin' money!"

T-Black pointed towards the building. "You mean, you've been riding with that dude and you don't know." He laughed trying to buy some time, bullshitting. "Damn, I thought you was built better than that. A big boy..."

Hulie swung, and the pistol cracked him in the mouth. Blood slung out and stained the windshield on the truck. "I don't wanna hear this shit! I'll deal with his ass later. You the one I want right, now," he yelled.

T-Black wiped the blood from around his lips. He knew Hulie's rep and he also knew he'd have to straighten this mess up, then deal with Riko's sheisty ass later. "Look, man, I ain't got your money."

"Where's it at then!" Hulie asked as he pointed the gun at him and stepped closer towards him.

The one mistake T-black hoped he'd make. "It's in the trap. Damn, Riko didn't tell you that shit...he played you, too."

Hulie paused, glancing behind him at the door of the dwelling, then T-Black sidestepped him and swung, catching Hulie square on the chin. He damn near knocked him out as Hulie fell to his knees. The gun dropped out of his hand and slid underneath the truck. T-Black dove for it. Hulie grabbed his leg and bit down. T-Black hollered out in pain, then reached back and punched him in the forehead causing Hulie to crash to the ground.

Jabari and Rip heard the yell all the way up the block. They looked up and saw them scuffling. Rip said. "Let's go."

Jabari reached into his pocket and pulled out his pistol then hauled ass with Rip up the street. T-Black looked up and saw them coming. He kicked Hulie who still hung onto his leg and scrambled desperately for the pistol underneath the truck.

Rip got there first. For some stupid ass reason, he grabbed T-Black by the neck and tried to put the yoke on him, with his gun still in his hand. T-Black flipped his light ass off his feet and he went sprawling to the ground. He hit, and the gun went off. The bullet whizzed past Jabari's head and he gave Rip a look that said *you dumb muthafucka*. Cause he got the hell outta the way. Jabari was pissed but managed to still stay focused as he aimed at T-Black.

"A'ight, stay the fuck where you at!" he yelled.

T-Black froze and looked over at him, searching his face trying to figure out if he knew him or not. Then he looked over at Rip who was now just getting off the ground. He didn't flinch or shake, but he knew Jabari was serious as hell. One false move and he was shot, if not dead. Hulie had gotten his ass off the ground, but he backed up and stepped in front of T-Black in between them and bent over reaching for the gun underneath the truck. Jabari gasped, damn, this muthafucka' was crazy as all hell.

T-Black smiled momentarily, then raised up his foot and kicked him dead in the ass, Jabari jerked up the gun as Hulie came tumbling down on top of him. T-Black broke for the gate. He jiggled at the lock, but it wouldn't open. Then he backed up and jumped at the seven-foot wall and started climbing over. Hulie had finally gotten the gun, and he and Jabari both got off the ground and went after him. Rip had already hopped over and was on the other side already.

"Freeze, muthafucka!" he yelled, on some old police shit.

Hulie nodded at him. He figured they had him, but just as he climbed over the fence making his way over. Rip turned his head away from T-Black and tried to shine. "You see,

Hulie, I got 'em." Rip never saw it coming.

T-Black bulldozed him to the ground wrestling the gun out of his hand. Rip grabbed at it and they wrestled some more. Jabari and Hulie had just made it over the fence when they heard the gun go off. They just stood there motionless in their tracks. T-Black was on top of Rip who was laid face down in the dirt. They couldn't make out what was what.

Jabari couldn't take it anymore and yelled out.

"Rip...Rip!" He didn't answer, but he heard a faint groan.

T-Black moved and turned his head towards them. Then started crawling in the dirt. Quickly, he scrambled to his feet sprinting towards the doorway. Hulie took off after him.

Jabari ran over to Rip and shook him. "Rip, talk to me!"

It was no use, the hole was small, but the blood that stained the opened fire burnt hole in his shirt spoke volumes. He felt for a pulse, but Rip was already dead. He hyperventilated losing his breath. Then he got angry and all he saw next was red. He looked up at Hulie as he chased T-Black up the stoop. Where it all came from, he didn't know, but he raised the gun. He yelled out because Hulie stopped dead in his tracks, turned and dove to the ground. The recoil shook Jabari's body as the 9mm spit two rounds. The first one ran wild and struck the side of the door jab, but the second one met its mark.

T-Black dropped in his tracks, then tried crawling, but Hulie got back up catching up to him. He grabbed the back of his shirt, threw him to the dirt off to the side of the stoop, and started yelling at him. Jabari couldn't make out what he was saying. He was still in a state of shock as Rip laid bleeding out in his arms, blood coming out the little hole in his chest.

Thick, and at times it squirted in spurts. It was too much for him. He let him down gently, got up, and stumbled out his daze towards Hulie who now stood over T-black with his gun pointed at his chest. He had his foot on his neck screaming at the top of his lungs.

"It didn't have to be like this! Where's the fuckin' money!"

T-Black's breathing was shallow. He took deep labored breaths. The bullet tore through his back and must have ripped through a lung. He coughed up blood as he tried talking.

"Riko set you up..." He coughed some more. "He told me the money was bribe money...said you took payments from some broad downtown..."

Jabari tried to understand and make sense of what he was trying to say, but Hulie looked his way all the time mean mugging. He couldn't quite concentrate. Then T-Black looked his way also. "You mean, this ain't have shit to do with Riko..." he asked.

Hulie told Jabari to knock on the door and get Riko. He looked back at T-Black as his eyes begged him not to go.

"Brother...get an ambulance...don't let him kill me..." "Go 'head, muthafucka get, Riko!" Hulie yelled.

"Who the fuck you yellin' at!" Jabari barked back. "You can get it, too!"

Hulie bit his tongue. Jabari had been through enough shit with his ass today. All the shit that went down didn't come with the package. He turned around looking at Rip's body as it laid on the blood-soaked ground. Yeah, Riko had better let him know what was up.

He started up the steps and T-Black pleaded with him again. "Don't leave...he's gonna kill me..." He said still coughing up blood.

It was no use Jabari's mind was made up until he said. "The lady works downtown at the court..." That's when Hulie shot him straight in the chest.

"What the fuck was that for?" Jabari hollered. "Now, how are we supposed to get the money?"

Jabari grabbed at his head, shit was all fucked up now. He spun around as he tried to figure it out, then he banged on the door.

"Riko...Riko! Get your punk ass out here!" No one answered. "Damn!"

Hulie stood over the body with the gun still smoking in his hand. Then they heard sirens in the background sounding like they were just around the corner. Five-o would be here in minutes. They had to go. Jabari grabbed Hulie. "Come on
man, let's get the fuck out of here."

Hulie started muttering something under his breath Jabari couldn't quite make out until he got closer. "My money...where's my money..." He was shot-out.

Jabari grabbed him and dragged his ass to the fence. He tried to go back, but he wasn't going for it, so he put the gun to his head, and said, "Give me your gun!" Hulie hesitated. "Now!" He placed it in his hand. "Climb over the fence." He stepped back and jumped, and they both started over what seemed to be a mountain instead of the seven-foot wall they'd just scaled over earlier.

Before they climbed the wall, Jabari looked over at Rip and shook my head. He'd definitely have to explain this mess. Finally, he made it over, and Hulie must have come to his senses. He was already in his truck starting it up. Jabari thought maybe he was going to dip on him, but the passenger side door opened, and he said, "Get in!" He dove in and he skidded off up the block to Montague Avenue speeding towards Rivers Avenue.

As he was just about to turn the corner Jabari glanced back over his shoulder and looked towards the house. The light had come on. Riko was in there the whole time. What kind of game was the rat bastard fuckin' playing? He rubbed the dirt and sweat off his gun on the palm of his hands and

said to Hulie. "I'ma get your boy..." "What?" he asked. "Your boy, Riko, his ass is mine."

Hulie started to say something but stopped short when he looked over at him as he wiped the gun down with his shirt, drenched with Rip's blood all over it. He just mumbled

under his breath. "I hear you...I hear you."

Jabari glanced at his watch. They were only more than a few hours into this so-called plan, and he was already tired of it. He stared at the sun as it drifted east into a sunset, and his mind wandered back to how the hell he got involved in this mess, anyway.

EARLIER THAT DAY...

Jabari remembered Dondi saying that morning, "Don't y'all got something to do, somewhere to go?"

She was right, Rip came up with a plan that Jabari bought into. He'd been hanging around Spruill Avenue and overheard some hustlers talking about a robbery gone bad, and they needed someone to run interference. They couldn't get their own hands dirty, so Rip volunteered for the job. He was baited, he was always in someone's business. They put it out there and he bit.

The money itself was good, and the job didn't seem too rough. The only thing Jabari was supposed to do was ride shotgun. At least that was the plan. Dondi stared at the aluminum foil on the table fidgeting, while waiting for them to be finished so she could get hers. Her eyes excitedly looked at the stem as Rip lit it then blew out the thick cloud of smoke he'd inhaled. His eyes exploded as his body twitched, fixated at Dondi as she stared up at him.

Dondi was five-foot-four and a former dime piece that got hooked on crack back in the early 90s. Soon after she turned her taste to methamphetamines and ecstasy pills after an all too brief stint at sobriety. She tried the club life and stripping, but it didn't work out too well for her. It was hard making money cause her looks had gone downhill. Her teeth had started to turn and became plague-ridden, as she continued smoking excessively. She still had coke bottle curves that probably were her downfall more than anything else. She tricked exclusively to the dealers when that went sour, she prostituted heavily on Rivers Avenue. Mostly, with white boys smoking meth out of cans.

Jabari stared at her round, plump titties as her nipples poked unmercifully hard beneath the t-shirt she was wearing. His dick was getting a rise. She had that good pussy, wet and warm, with curly pubic hairs that tickled his nuts. Rip was thinking the same thing as he reached over and pulled her closer to him. He fumbled with his zipper and finally pulled out. She resisted at first, but it didn't work. She figured just as soon as she took care of him, he'd finally put the stem down and she could finish off the rest of what was in the package by herself.

Dondi grabbed it and started stroking when he rose, she glanced over at Jabari and looked down at his crouch. He was getting an erection, too. He smiled knowing he was next, and she was right. As soon as she sucked them off, they were gone.

A BLACK DENALI SUV was parked inconspicuously in a cut over by a ho-track. Inside peeking around were two men, Hulie and Riko. "You think dude will show up, or what?"

Hulie asked.

"He should," Riko said as he looked down at his watch. "Any minute...after all, he's thirsty."

Hulie peeped out the tinted windows of the big-bodied truck they sat in by a Chinese restaurant. They'd just copped a bag of migraine from a dude named Lil Zeke in front of a store by the name of P&Ms.

"Well, anytime now. By the way, how did you get these guys anyway?" he asked

Riko reached into his jacket pocket, pulled out a chocolate blunt and sniffed it. Reaching again he pulled out a gold plated lighter, flipped the top, then put the blunt to his mouth. "It was easy..." He lit it and let the blue flame flicker for a moment as he pulled on the cigar. "I knew he was one of

those nosy muthafucka's anyway..."

"Aw, man...he ain't no snitch, huh?"

"Naw...he's straight like that, but he's just one of those goffer types. Always wanting to hustle up something for a hit, ya know."

Hulie reached for the blunt as he passed it, cut his eyes, then said out the side of his mouth. "Yeah, I know the type."

"Hold up, what do you mean, *you know the type*. You implying something, huh?" Riko said as he turned facing him, then faked putting his hand inside his jacket like he had a gat. Hulie paid him no mind and that pissed him off. "Don't fuckin' ignore me, bruh! You got something you wanna say, or what?" Riko propped his back against the driver's side door. His upper lip twitched as he wriggled his hand underneath his jacket.

Hulie didn't know why he was trying him like this, after all, the weed wasn't that damn good, and he really didn't feel like this shit today. So, he laughed him off. "Go on with the bullshit!"

Riko's eyes narrowed. He was heated and felt dissed not particularly because of what was said, but because Hulie paid him no mind, didn't take him seriously at all. "You think, I'm

playing! You think I'm playing, muthafucka..."

In one swift move, Hulie spun towards him gritting his teeth and grabbed his arm that was supposedly holding the pistol. He squeezed his mammoth, python-like hands causing Riko to grimace in pain. "You got one more muthafucka left in you..." with his other hand he reached inside his jacket pocket, pulled out a black steel, Smith & Wesson, 9-millimeter Glock and pointed it towards his chest. "And, the next time you pump fake a pistol you'd better be serious." He

cocked it. "Dead serious, ya hear."

Riko snarled his lips. "Yeah, yeah...calm the fuck down. I was just bullshittin', that's all."

Hulie pressed the nose of the gun to his chest causing him to flinch. "I wasn't."

"C'mon now, Hulie. You're blaming all this shit on me. It wasn't my fault."

Hulie's mind flashed back to the crap that cranked this whole thing up, because as far as he was concerned. If it wasn't for the dumb ass move Riko had made, he'd be at the crib knee deep in some pussy instead of being stuck in a Denali with a pistol thrust to his chest. "You know, you should have checked that dude out before you put any product in his hands."

"Aw man, Hulie. We've been through this shit a thousand fuckin' times already."

"And, I still ain't got my money!"

Riko slowly eased up his hands towards the gun, gently and very carefully pushing it aside. "Calm down, man..."

Hulie looked him square in his eyes. It wasn't over for him, just yet. "You said you knew he was from across town.

And then, the split he wanted..." He lowered the gun, pulled it back, and holstered it inside his jacket sling. "A key...a couple of grand? C'mon, that alone made me fuckin' suspicious."

"I didn't think that much about that...or him!" Riko eased back up and squirmed underneath the steering wheel. "He was fuckin' my sister, and..."

"Riko, this is business. What the fuck your sister got to do with anything? A muthafucka lay some pipe on your slut-ass sister, and you think they're cool enough to do business wit'!

Hell, if that's the case..."

"What!"

Hulie's lips curled into a half-assed grin. "All the pipe, I put down her throat...heh...heh." He snickered.

"Fuck you, Hulie, fuck you!"

"All that muthafucka did was scheme on people. He was never about shit. You gave him a play because he finessed you. Admit it...and now. I got to be the one to pay for it. Well..." Hulie pulled the blunt from out of the ashtray and lit it back up. "Either, you pay me back my loot...or hand over that cat. After all, you sent him to me!" He blew smoke his way causing Riko to cough, and roll the window down halfway searching for air.

Hulie laughed at him as he puffed away at the weed getting his head right. Then looked up across the street watching the two figures that b-lined directly towards them. Riko tapped him lightly on the shoulder. "I think that's them...coming towards us."

"Yeah... I see 'em."

"HOLD UP, RIP."

"What?"
"Just hold up, man."
"What the fuck is up with you, now?"

"I'm not really feeling this. It seems too easy. In and out, when's the last time that ever happened? And, why the hell we got to meet then over here...on Spruill Avenue? Who does any real business on Spruill except for hoes and runners? Hell, even they stay in the cut. Rip, you sure you got this whole thing worked out?"

"Jabari." Rip turned in protest. "Don't start this bullshit now!" He stomped over towards him and grabbed him by the collar, then shoved him hard against the side of the building. Chips of old plaster and paint from the weathered wall showered the ground. "This money is too easy!"

Jabari wrestled him from off him and said. "No such thing!" He had already heard about Riko and his sheisty ass dealings. Also, the other dude that was with him, Hulie he knew from Downtown and he wasn't shit.

He used to be half-ass alright before he met up with some gangbangers from New York. The gaudy gold jewelry he wore, the cars and trucks he drove. Then, there was this bike. A money green, Suzuki, GSX R1000 made him a beast on two wheels. The sparkle off the chrome from the shiny, seventeen-inch, Assassin wheels and fast boy Pirelli tires made the other dope boys take notice as he dipped in and out dropping off baby bricks from a saddle bag draped across his shoulder.

Picking up money, he also dished out heaps of pistol whippings for shorts at the same time. Male, female, young or old.

It didn't matter, and all that was on a good day.

He'd done two bids in the Feds, but never really talked about it, and no one asked either. He was a private dude and very suspicious of others. Why in the world would he want both of them to take care of some business for him? It just didn't sit right, and the more the dope wore off, the questions continued to pop up for me, at least, for Jabari. "Rip...what are we really supposed to do?" he asked.

"Damn." He reached into his coat and pulled out a wrinkled pack of Basics. He patted the back of a cigarette, then lit it. "All we gotta do is put the tim down on some dude, and that's it."

Jabari straightened up his coat, and reached for the cigarette, taking two drags off it, then gave it back. "Suppose this dude has a gun?"

Rip shoved his hands into his pockets and peeped around the corner looking for them. "Don't worry about all that. They got our back for sho' okay. Damn...where the hell are, they?"

The big-bodied Denali glided down Chicora Street and dipped the corner on Iris Street pulling over across the street from us. "There they go," Rip said as we watched Riko jump out the truck.

Riko was a redbone, short and light in the ass. About a buck fiddy soaking wet. Every bit of five-foot-five, with a lot of mouth to boot, and when that didn't suffice. The .40 Caliber he carried backed him up. At least that's what he always says he has even though no one's seen it as of yet.

He had the reputation of being one nasty, no good muthafucka and everyone knew it. No one liked him. The passenger side window rolled down, and a lump came to Jabari's throat as he stared into the face of the other occupant. He could barely hold eye contact as he beckoned them over to the truck.

"Damn Jabari. You see, we done fucked up already." Rip said under his breath.

Jabari didn't want to look like a busta'. Rip already made them look weak as it was. So, he stood tall and did his best crimp walk towards them.

He stuck out his hand real cool towards Riko and said. "Wassup." He looked down at it, then spit on the ground beside me. Never taking his hands out his pockets.

Least until Rip came over suckin' up, fuckin' shit up. "What the fuck y'all turn around for, Rip? Something going on that I should know about!" He glanced Jabari's way, checking him out.

"Naw." Rip said as he peered over at him, too. "Just my man over here got a little sick, that's all."

Hulie laughed as he gazed over at him. His eyes were red and glossy as the high started to seep in on him. He'd recognized him. "Damn, ain't you, Tangie's brother?" He said it like he knew her like that, but the fact remained he once fucked his sister. Let her tell it, he was the one who really got screwed. "Yeah...that's me."

"Damn...you hooked on beans..." He eyeballed him in disgust, and Jabari felt offended.

Never thought it would come down to this. Not in his wildest dreams. Shamefully he lowered his gaze and kicked rocks on the ground. As was his habit he chewed on his bottom lip. Hulie knew he'd touched a nerve and even perhaps found a weakness he could exploit later.

He called over to Rip, and Riko as they rapped about bullshit, and told them all to get in the ride. "Let's go across town and kick it."

"Where?" Riko asked.

"I don't know...past Rivers Avenue, somewhere..." "Cool." He responded as he cranked up the truck.

Jabari and Rip hopped in the back seat and the truck cut a U-turn in front of traffic on Spruill heading towards Reynolds Avenue, past the rough end of North Charleston.

The Makin'!

Chapter Two

They didn't go too far. They ended up parked near the front of the old Winn Dixie parking lot near Rivers Avenue. Riko scanned the area before pulling out a sack and rolling a blunt. He lit it up and passed it Jabari's way. He exhaled it's sweet, vaporous fumes into his nostrils and let it swim throughout his brain as he leaned back to let it mellow.

He then noticed, Hulie staring at him.

'*Now what?*' he thought and immediately tensed up.

He didn't want to give him anything that would make him think he was slacking, or even jeopardizing the lick. Still, he kept his eyes beaded on him. Jabari passed him the joint.

"My bad...here you go."

He nodded his head, no, so he tapped Rip on the shoulder, and he greeted it eagerly. Jabari leaned back wondering what was going on with Hulie, and it didn't take long before he let him know.

"So, uh...what's been up with your sister, lately?"

He didn't see why he was asking him some shit like that. Jabari hadn't seen Tangie in a while. Last time they kicked it, they argued. "Couldn't tell you, haven't seen her in a minute."

"I hear you," Hulie said as he leaned back, and finally reached out for the blunt as Riko passed it back his way. "Remember, when we used to date...right?"

30

"I was a little dude, then."
"Yeah." He blew smoke his way. "You was, wasn't you."

Hulie passed him the blunt, then kept watching him making Jabari feel uncomfortable, and he knew it. Jabari started tapping his feet, and he could feel the palms of his hands getting a little sweaty. Trying to stay cool, but it was like he'd been trying him since the minute he walked up to the truck with Rip. "Is everything alright?" he asked. "Yeah, everything's cool."

He damn sure hoped Hulie wasn't on some old bullshit.

Thinking he might try him, cause he kept eyeballing him. "Your sister is one hell of a girl...high powered..."

Jabari looked over at him. He knew good and damn well she was. "Hey, uh, you got something you wanna say?" That caused Rip and Riko to turn abruptly his way as if to say, '*Are you crazy?*' "I mean hell, you can speak your mind..."
"You're right, I can, and I will. Look, this the muthafuckin' deal, a'ight! The shit we about to do is major, and I need to know if you can keep your mouth shut. How 'bout that?"

"I ain't no fuckin' snitch if that's what you sayin'!"
"Probably not, but maybe so if the right situation was to

come along. Like...your sister."
"Hell, you was the one fuckin' her." Jabari shot back at him.

"You damn right, and every time I put dick up in her, she sang like a fuckin' bird telling me all types of shit that was going on in her life."

Jabari knew it was something. He was sizing him up. He must have figured maybe the apple didn't fall too far from the tree. He wondered what all she told him. The family and all. What secrets did she yell out while he was pile driving dick up in her? And damn, why's he fuckin' wit my head! '*He ain't shit.*' Jabari thought.

"Yo, snap out of it! I wanna know..."

"What? I ain't never been about telling shit. 'Sides, if I was on it like that you wouldn't have never even bought me this deep into whatever y'all tryin' to do." Jabari looked at Rip, for confirmation. If it was that serious, they wouldn't have let me get this close. He pulled out a bluff card searching. "Matter of fact." Jabari reached for the door handle like he was getting out. "If you don't trust me. Well, thanks for the get high.

I'm fuckin' out, I don't need the drama, either."

He pulled at the doorknob, it wouldn't budge. Then the door popped open electronically from the front and swung open suddenly. Making him jump a little. He looked up at Rip and turned his head. Pussy muthafucka's he mumbled. Hulie kept his eyes trained on Jabari, then Riko's ass said what he was expecting him to say.

"Well, what the fuck are you waiting for?" Jabari started getting out. Hell, it was over with, as far as he was concerned. No biggie. Nothing lost, nothing gained. The bluff card was no good, he guessed.

"Yo...get the fuck back in the truck." It was Hulie. "Let me tell you something. Matter of fact, both you muthafucka's." Jabari got back in, and Riko locked the doors. The windows were rolled up, and the radio turned off. "If any of you muthafucka's say anything about what's about to go down. I'll kill you both, and your families my muthafuckin' self. Ya hear?"

This was big boy serious. Hulie wanted to kill families and shit. They were going to do something major. Something that needed them all to be quiet, forever. It was more than puttin' the tim down like Rip said earlier. That's why they were asking all the questions about Jabari's sister.

'Damn, Rip, what the fuck did you get us into?' Jabari couldn't help thinking. "What's the job?" Jabari asked. "Since you threatenin' my peeps. Then, I'll make my own decision, one way or another," he said, then looked Hulie square in his

eyes. He was on his own. "Cool?"

Hulie nodded his head, he was on game. He could do with or with or without him, and as far as Jabari was concerned, fuck his sister. She didn't have shit to do with whatever he did. As far as he was concerned Hulie could be holding pipe down her throat right here in front of him for all he cared.

"This is what's going down," he said.

Jabari listened closely to everything as Hulie laid down the plan, at least what he wanted to be done. It seemed simple enough but based on what he said earlier, just a little too simple. Snatch a muthafucka up, and pick up some money, that's all. Still, based on how he tried to handle him. Jabari really didn't trust him. He'd definitely have to watch him and keep one in the chamber for his ass.

It was all good though, Riko rolled up two more blunts, to celebrate. Everything was feeling good, shit felt right. Jabari figured he'd go check out Dondi after this before he called it a night. But then, the script twisted. Jabari, nor Rip was prepared for what Hulie said next.

"Oh yeah." They all turned his way and listened, figuring he'd missed something. "We do what we do...tonight."

It was going down. All the other shit went right out the window. Fuck it. They were all pretty fucked up as the sun set east, and they watched it fall. They sat in the truck smoking trees and drinking forties. Hulie jumped out of the truck for a piss giving Riko the opportunity to throw salt on him, talking big boy shit.

"This is a real, sweet money run, son."
"Damn sure wish we could do it tomorrow, cause I'm

'bout fucked up." Rip said as he rubbed sleep from his eyes.

Riko popped him upside his head. "Yo man, tighten up."
"I'm just sayin'."
"You see, that's your problem. I put you in the game and

look at you. All you wanna do is get high and fuck."

"What you talkin' 'bout, Riko?"
'Hell, where was all this coming from,' Jabari thought?
Riko glanced his way and pointed. "You see how he han-

dled, Hulie? That's what's up."
"Bari was bluffin'. He wouldn't have got out of the truck." Rip said looking his way for a response. He gave him none, Riko grinned.

Hulie hopped back in the truck and said. "Let's pull up

into the K-Spot and make this call."
Riko cranked up the truck and they dipped. They pulled by a bunch of pay-phones, then Riko and Hulie hopped out the truck and walked over to one. They were on some old secret-shit. Jabari tried to ear-hustle, but he was well out of range. He did know, that whatever it was it had to do with tonight.

Over by the phone, Riko asked Hulie. "So, we tell him..."

Hulie grabbed the phone out of his hand and said. "To meet you over at your trap house. You got something for him."

Riko dialed some numbers and leaned against the booth until he got an answer, "Uh, yeah, is T-Black there?" He paused, listening, then gritted his teeth. "Sorry, 'bout that, ma'am...Carl." He put his hand over the receiver. "He's there, she went to get him."

Jabari leaned up in the seat and said to Rip. "Must be going well."

"What?" Rip asked.

I knew more than him about how they were going to handle the plan. From everything they said so far, they were going to have to draw this guy out from wherever he was, or whoever he was with.

They didn't know what he did for a living, least from the way Riko was so hush-hush over the phone. Hulie stood off to the side. Then just like that they hung up the phone, dapped each other and started walking back towards the truck. Jabari leaned back playing it off like he didn't see a thing.

He asked. "Everything cool?"

Riko ignored him and didn't say a word as he cranked up the car. They pulled up behind some abandoned houses and parked. Hulie jumped out with Riko tight on his ass and walked into the back way of an old broke down row house, then motioned for everyone else to come in. Jabari got out and cautiously made his way past the splintered broke down door. Inside as he looked there were roaches everywhere. Towards the bedrooms, they could hear the sound of paneling being ripped off the walls. Rip walked in, and as Jabari peeped through the door slowly, he saw Hulie and Riko pulling out shotguns from a hole in the wall. Handguns were already scattered on the small mattress on the floor.

Riko glanced his way and asked. "You know how to handle these?"

Rip quickly snatched up a semi-automatic 9mm. Ignorantly, he peeped through the front of the muzzle, and Jabari snatched it away from him. He pulled back the slide, and damn sure enough there was one in the chamber. The gun hadn't been greased or cleaned, and dirt was already formulating inside the creases. Rip was lucky a hole the size of a baseball would have been blown between his eyes.

Hulie chuckled. "He knows what he's doing, but I don't know about his homeboy."

Riko frowned at Rip, picked up a .38, and tossed it over to him.

"Here, now don't kill yourself with this, a'ight."

Rip turned Jabari's way as he handled the gun, he took from him and admired his skill. Jabari picked up a full clip off the bed and shoved it into the butt. So, now each one of them had a gun.

Hulie shoved one of the shotguns he had back into the ripped hole in the wall. and placed the panels back over them. They loaded their guns and took extra bullets. They felt like they were going to war or something. All for one man. The bullshit kicked in high gear from there. '*Who the fuck are we going after*?' Jabari thought.

They made it back to the truck, pulled off and Hulie said. "Y'all need to forget this spot...a'ight."

Jabari looked over at Rip, they both hunched their shoulders. It was cool by Jabari because, after this, he was through fuckin' with Hulie, Riko, and even Rip. They got on Rivers Avenue going uptown and pulled a right into a dimly lit street going past the beer distributor.

Jabari scanned the area as he thought to himself. '*Damn, we're on our way to Liberty Hill, I bet.*'

Liberty Hill was one of those neighborhoods littered with traps, old and new. There were even generational liquor houses dating back

from the 30s and 40s. It was still one of those hoods in South
Carolina that bred shystas, hustlas, gangstas and thrived on dirty
money. Jabari wondered who the hell were they going to put the tim
down on over there? From what he knew of the area, if they weren't
careful, they would have the tim put down on them.

They got to the corner of East Montague Street near the railroad
tracks and Riko pointed up the street. Hulie nodded his head, they
pulled in front of a building. Looked like old, dry cleaners, then he
motioned for them to get out. He pointed toward the back, and they
walked around into a small wooded area.

Riko sped off up the street. "We walk from here," he said.
"It ain't far."

They walked up Nesbitt Avenue until they got to Lester Street,
and dipped behind a house into the backyard of another house. This
time a decent, steel fenced, ranch style home. Hulie again pointed
them across the street towards an old house, surrounded by a high
brick wall, with a fenced front...Riko's trap. That must be where it
was going down. He pulled out some lawn chairs from the back
porch and sat.

"Relax, they'll be here shortly." Those were the first words he
spoke since they got out of the truck.

He put the shotgun off to the side out of view and leaned back
crossing his legs. Reaching deep down into his pocket he pulled out
a small plastic bag with some brown pills. Adams,
Jabari hadn't seen them in a while.

"Want some?" he asked Jabari.

At first, it seemed like he started to say no. He even turned his
head away, but it was no use. He was addicted, and he knew it. He
grabbed at two and swallowed them whole. Hulie snickered, Rip
looked his way too wanting some also, but he pulled out a blunt and
tossed it his way instead.

'*Strange,*' Jabari thought.

He knew Rip meant nothing to him, but somehow, he felt like he wanted him for something. What, he couldn't quite put a finger on it. He had one hell of a role to play, he guessed. He believed he was about to be set-up for one hell of a performance in this twisted scenario. The pills had just started to kick in. There was no turning back.

THERE WAS NO MORE TURNING back for Jabari. For him now, it was what it was. The here and the now. They didn't say a word to each other. It was like ice inside the truck as they slowly drove Rivers Avenue to Charleston Heights or *The Heights* as it was called. They watched car after car of police speeding off to where they'd just come from. Someone must have called in shots fired into a dwelling because they were jetting up there like it was that big or something.

Jabari couldn't quite figure it out, and he didn't try to anymore. He was too busy thinking about Rip. He couldn't believe he was dead. His mind wrestled with the thoughts that they were supposed to be getting fucked up right about now. Laid up in a Days Inn, knee-deep tricking their asses off. Just the two of them. He remembered the last thing he'd said to him. Talking something about getting Dondi's hair done with his end of the money.

Damn, it hit him. '*Was he catching feelings for her?*' Come to think of it, he did use to look at him funny whenever he messed around with her. '*He shoulda said something.*' Jabari rationed, he would have respected that.

She needed to slow down anyway. After all, at her age with no diseases, and a little fixin' up she could still be worth something.

Maybe not a dime piece, but a good nickel for sure. Rip needed something like that in his life.

'*It was time we all slowed down*,' Jabari thought.

He peered over at Hulie, he was fixed on the road in front. He started to say something to him, but he could tell he was heavy in thought. It wasn't the time, but he had so many questions he didn't know where to begin. Like, how was he going to explain this to Dondi? She was the last person to see them together. He knew the police would be coming to see her once they identified the body. A known drug user and thief, who was associated with him. He was sure they'd come looking for him, too.

But hell, that damn Riko, his mind couldn't get away from it. What was his take on all this? '*Was he the one that called the police?*' He wondered.

T-Black was saying something to Hulie, but he shot him before he finished. What kinda mess did he get himself caught up in? Jabari knew he needed to go somewhere and collect his thoughts. Try and figure out what he was going to do. His anxiety had kicked in overdrive.

Okay, Jabari rationed, after Hulie gave him his money and dropped him off. He might as well ask for Rip's cut, too and give it to Dondi. Then try to find his people, so they could bury him right. More than likely he would probably double back and stay at the room they got earlier. He was sure Dondi was still there. He'd let her know what was up. Out of nowhere, the truck started skidding. He braced himself and looked over at Hulie. He had the brakes stomped.

He hollered at him. "What the fuck you doing!" Hulie didn't budge as he held onto the steering wheel of the out of control truck. It veered into oncoming traffic, and he jerked it back. Then, it shut off and slowly came to a stop at a curb.

It was a miracle it didn't tip over and flip. Jabari looked out the window around them, thinking luckily there was no one on the street.

Catching his breath, he started screaming at Hulie. "What the hell is the matter with you, you crazy or something!"

Hulie looked up from the steering wheel visibly shaken. Literally, he unglued his fingers off. He checked his head for bruises after banging it against the windshield, then slowly turned Jabari's way. "Sorry, 'bout that. But...I just can't let it go like..."

"Let it go, Rip is dead! The police are probably flooding Liberty Hill. Hell, somebody might have seen the truck! Then your boy, Riko, they know it was his trap-house. Don't think they don't know! They're looking for us. So, you do this crazy shit..." Jabari banged the dashboard, he couldn't help but spaz. "I can't even grasp this shit! Man, pay me and let me get the fuck outta here!" He turned his way with his hand out waiting. Hulie looked off mumbling something under his breath. "What?"

"I ain't got it."

"You ain't got it! What the fuck you mean, *you ain't got it*? Well, where is it? Let's go get it."

"I ain't got it. The money we was supposed to get from that dude, T-Black. I was gonna pay you from that."

Jabari grabbed at his head. The bullshit meter was off the chart. This was it. The last fucking straw, he reached over and grabbed him by the collar. "This wasn't part of the deal. You said all we had to do was put the tim down, then we'd get paid. That was the deal!"

"I know...I know!"

"*You fucking lied then*! You knew this crazy ass shit was going down from the jump. You, and that fucking slime-ball, Riko!" Jabari started reaching for his gun, but it was too late. Hulie already had his pointed to his chest.

He peeped around slowly for any witnesses on the street. Jabari just knew he was gonna kill him, then kick his body out in the gutter. So, he leaned back.

'Let it happen.' Then, he thought. 'To hell with this, I'm going out like a trooper. He figured he was already dead, anyway. He didn't have much more to lose.

Strangely enough, Hulie started easing back the gun. "Just hear me out..." He was trying to calm him down.

Jabari started to relax, a little while looking him square in the eyes.

He thought. 'This had better be good.'

Hulie knew exactly where his gun was, and once he fully pulled back his gun, he was coming out shooting. Fuck it.

"What's up?" Jabari asked.

"I didn't mean to lie to you. It wasn't supposed to go down like this." He turned and put the gun away. "Yeah, we was supposed to just go over there, put the tim down and he
was supposed to give us back the money, and dope."

"Then, why'd you kill him?"
"He was fuckin' with my head, trigger finger slipped..."
"You fucked up."
"Man, this shit is big."

"He said something about a lady downtown. What was that about?"
He flinched when Jabari said that, his demeanor changed. He guessed, that maybe he didn't catch it. He turned his way

straightening up. Jabari started to reach for his gun. He definitely didn't want no trigger finger's slipping on him. He knew it was going down as he reached into his pocket, but

Hulie just pulled out a card, then handed it to him.

"This."

Jabari reached for it and it read: *Sunshine Brown, Esquire,* 9th *Circuit Solicitor-Charleston, South Carolina.*

"What the hell she got to do with anything?" It was a dumb question at this stage, but Jabari knew he had to ask.

"Trust me and don't get it twisted. We're in danger, but I can't do nothing without the money."

Somehow as he spoke, Jabari knew what he was saying was real. He sighed. "Okay *but trust me and don't get it twisted.* It's not we! You fucked up, not me. Now, what's the deal, this time...tell me the truth?"

Hulie nodded his head and leaned over his way. Jabari hoped this had better be good. Still, he would have to take it all with a grain of salt. He didn't trust him as far as he could throw him.

"He stole some money from some people I know, and I was sent to collect."

Jabari's face twisted. "And."

"What I'm saying is that, if we get the money, I can pay you. That's what you want, right?"

"Hold up, you're saying a whole lot that don't add up. What was up with the broad? The card you showed me.

Where does she figure in at?"

"The people that want the money say if I don't get it,

they'll blackmail me. Tell her some shit to get me fucked up."

Jabari leaned back in the seat and digested what he'd told me him. It all sounded like one big lie. There was no money at least, from what he could see. Either that, or he just didn't want to pay him.

"I'll tell you what. How 'bout I get out right here, and we cut our losses and ties, okay?" "A hundred grand!"

Jabari was just about to turn for the door to get out.

"That's the number...for what?" he asked.

"That's what we were going to pick up, ninety-six stacks, and twelve keys of cocaine."

That caught his attention, he was curious now, so he got back in to see where Hulie was going with this. "Let me get this straight. T-Black owed you damn near one-hundred stacks, and twelve keys. Okay...okay, what does Riko have to do with this?"

He started to look off instead of at Jabari. A sure sign of lying, but he humored him anyway. "Riko tried to set me up and keep the money."

"Where is this...so called money, anyway?"

"T-Black's house, it has to be there. We...uh...*I* thought he would bring it, but he didn't. I just know it has to be there."

"Where's that at?"

Hulie reached into his pocket and pulled out a paper with some numbers on it, then tossed it over. "His mom's crib, he stayed with his mother."

"So, you're sure? I mean, this shit sounds crucial. What is his mom supposed to do, just give us the money? Hell, does she even know that her son is dead? And on top of that...you killed him!" Jabari chuckled. "Man, you're fucking crazy. You're out your rabid-ass mind. We suppose to just go over there, ask for ninety stacks...twelve keys and she just goes and gets it?"

Hulie banged the steering wheel. A honk went off and echoed across the quiet night causing the yelps of stray dogs in the distance. Jabari guessed he was looking for a reaction, but he was used to his shit already. He got nothing but a stern look.

"I didn't say it was going to be easy." He turned facing him and started fidgeting with his hands. "Look, if we get this money. I'll give you thirty grand and three...no, four keys.

A'ight?"

The sweat poured from his head as he spoke. He was desperate and scared. *For what*? Thirty grand sounded good and with four keys he could easily sell two and give the money to Rip's people. Then still have money and dope to make a run and lay low for a while. It didn't take long for Jabari to agree with it.

"One thing," Jabari said.
"What?"

"You gots to keep your cool because she just might not know where the money is. We might have to go searching
through the house. No bodies, alright."

Hulie nodded head, then put his hand out towards him.
"Agreed."

"Now, where does she live?"
"Back up in Liberty Hill."

This time it was Jabari who banged the dash. "It's flooded with police! We'll be taking a chance, it's too risky. Let's do it another time."

"No, my ass is in deep shit, I gotta get it tonight!"

"It's your ass, Hulie. Not mine, and...if I do this tonight.

It's gonna cost you half."

"*Half!*" Hulie screamed. "A'ight...half, then."

Jabari knew he was going to renege on the deal, so he'd already made up in his mind that he was going to have to kill him once they got the money. He looked over at him, he was quite sure he was thinking the same thing.

T-BLACK'S MOTHER, NIKKI, picked up the remote control to the widescreen plasma T.V., then swung her feet up on the coffee table. She flipped through a bunch of channels until she settled on one in particular. A romance-mystery, she prepared a cup of smoothing, mocha coffee and gently blew the hot steam smoldering from off the top. Taking a sip, she curled underneath a blanket. She was trying to concentrate on the movie, but her mind couldn't help but wander off to the conversation she and her son Carl a.k.a T-Black had earlier.

She'd been begging him to stay home this evening. He'd been running himself ragged lately, and she took notice. He'd almost agreed until he got a call, but he didn't say from who. All he said was that he'd be back later, and they'd talk. She thought about all types of things as he worried. The biggest being, was he thinking of leaving? She feared that the most. At her age, all she had was him, even though she didn't want to seem like she was smothering him. She didn't want him to leave either. Like her husband...his father did.

He'd gone out one night telling her the same thing. *He'd be back later.* A couple of weeks later he was looking at a fresh fifteen. She played the role of the good wife. There for him as much as she could, establishing phone contact right off the muscle.

'It was unbelievable,' she thought, as she reminisced.

Talking to his sons over the phone got him stabbed in the back...killed. That took a lot out of her. A good while passed before she'd gotten over it, then Bobby, the oldest started running the streets. He'd tell her tales of how he wanted to be a tough guy like his old man, Big Willie.

But when she tried to tell him that his father wasn't no real tough guy. That he didn't have a choice when he robbed the liquor store. That pressure bust pipes, rent was due. It was hard and the only thing that was tough was the times. Bobby wasn't trying to hear that. He needed something to replace his father. So, he lived off a rep that wasn't there. One he created for himself...*an illusion.*

It was too much for her when she answered the door that evening. The police came right out and told her he was dead. On top of it all, she couldn't even claim the body. He had to be identified by a victim in the robbery. After being shot dead, he laid in the morgue for a week. She turned to drinking and smoking reefer, trying to take her mind away from the reality, the pain. She socially tried cocaine ignorantly thinking it would suffice, but instead it took her deep into the seedy, underworld life of freebase. When that well ran dry, she turned to crack-cocaine.

Crack had flooded much of the hood, and she fell right in line with it. At first, it was an entertaining type of high, but after getting raped a couple of times by the dope dealers that gave her the drug freely. She gave in and started tricking to get her own. She would become one of hundreds of crack whores that flooded South Carolina in the nineties. Now, she was getting older, and ready to give it all up. Rehabs after rehabs wasn't cutting it for her anymore. She was sick and tired of sucking young boy's dicks for dope. Boys no older than her own sons. She was tired of it all, the game had changed, they had no respect.

The dope hadn't affected her weight much. She was naturally good looking for her age. A ripe thirty-six, a statuesque, five-foot-ten, and she carried her one hundred twenty-fivepound frame well. She had big round titties and a plump ass with a youthful swagger that kept her pussy busy. But these days she didn't have no man for herself. No real friends to talk to. It took a toll on her, and she kept to herself.

She started dozing off when she heard a light tapping sound at the window. "Carl?" she called out, but no one answered back.

She got up hesitantly, and cautiously tipped over to the window, then peeped out. *No one.* The wind was blowing, and tree branches crashed against the cold window. It was late, and she was in for the night. She still had a couple of rocks left in her purse. Maybe, she'd take a hit, or two then finish watching the movie, but first, she needed a shower.

Nikki walked into her bedroom and rummaged through some drawers. She found what she was searching for. A nineinch dildo that was shiny and gold metal, three inches around. She smiled pleasingly. She was going to get off tonight in the shower, her own way, fuck anyone else. She did think about calling one of her trick-girls over, Bebe they could get down with each other and freak. Yeah, she grinned, that was a plan. Carl wouldn't be home for a while, anyway.

'*He's probably out fucking one of them, young girls that flock around him all the time,*' she thought.

There were always girls playing with his dick. Trying to get money out his pockets. She peeped out the window one more time to make sure he wasn't coming. Catching her eye was the house up the street where his childhood sweetheart lived, Cleo. She wondered how she was doing lately. She hadn't seen her on the track lately, or even running the streets. Carl wanted to talk to her about something. Maybe, she was it.

She closed the curtains uptight, then cut off the front porch light, went into the bathroom and started running the water. She took off her clothes and stepped in after testing the water with her toes. She liked it hot, especially for what she wanted to do. Once she got in, she tried the batteries out on the shiny dildo, then wet it down slick with some K-Y, getting it right.

Slowly, she slid it up her gap-opened legs and welcoming pussy. She pushed it in and out, pulling slowly so that it grinded against her now throbbing, and fattened clit. As she pushed it further, she hit what she was looking for, her Gspot. She moaned, the pleasure caused her to nearly slip in the tub, but she braced one foot firmly on the bath knobs and continued pushing until it became dripping wet. She could smell the pussy juice coming off the heat of the mechanical dick. Her juices were dripping down her leg into the tub, foaming up into a lather as the water gently washed it down the drain.

She slowly adjusted her body so that the soothing hot water ran down her back to the crack of her ass from her long silky, shoulder length hair, letting it drip into her pussy. She gyrated her hips and started to thrust it inside of her faster and harder. A foam worked up between her legs, it wouldn't be long now.

Her body started to spasm, her asshole tightened. She squealed in delight, tensed up, then shouted. "Oh, my fuckin' God! Ooooohhhh..." She'd come and was still coming when she bent over and rammed the still wet stick into her ass. She pulled it out back and forth, circling it around, while with the other hand massaging her clit until she fell to her knees exhausted. Her body rocked in convulsions as she braced her hand on the tub's railing, moaning loudly.

The dildo slid slowly out her asshole and floated on the button of the tub. She picked it up, turned it off, and tossed it outside the tub. Opening her eyes, she turned over and sat as the soothing water drenched her like rain from the showerhead. She curled herself up into an almost fetal-childlike ball and started crying.

LOST BOY 51

It was all too much for her, she was tired, she was lonely. HER MIND, HER BODY, and her soul.

Chapter Three

They slowly drove back towards Liberty Hill, coming through the front end of Montague Avenue. As opposed to the backside of the hood near the beer factory. They knew *ball* which, is code for police would be deep looking for any suspicious activity, mainly the shit they were doing. As they drove through, they were right, ball was all over the place. They turned to Lester Street and drove down Nesbitt Avenue, figuring they'd come up the street, so the truck would be facing towards Rivers Avenue and a fast get-away.

It was crazy, but dope was still being smoked openly. It seemed like everyone said fuck the police. Tricks, prostitutes, and fiends looked at them like nothing happened. The only thing though, no one crossed the avenue to the other side. The ones that tried were immediately pulled over, questioned and subsequently harassed. Good for their dumb asses. There was no expression on Hulie's face. His breathing was heavy like he had bronchitis or something. He drove carefully, this time on purpose, paying attention to the speed traps along the way.

As he came to a stop where 'ball' sat, he smiled but all the time rubbing his gun along his thigh like he had a nervous tick. Jabari thought about what his sister would say. It would be some ole slick shit. She'd just told him something bad was

52

going to happen if he didn't change. She'd asked him for his social security number and if he knew where his birth certificate was just in case, he died, or something happened? Man, she'd hit it dead on the head. That's what started the damn argument.

Jabari cursed her ass out so bad she cried in the street like a lost baby. Jabari knew he was wrong for that shit. After all, he loved his sister, but they were just on separate roads. Jabari still wondered what she saw in Hulie's ass, he wasn't shit. To Jabari, he seemed bigger than life when he really didn't know him. But now he was just a quick-tempered thug who really didn't have no more than the drugs allowed to him. Given another environment he would be an average dick-head joe.

'I can't believe fuckin' Rip got himself killed. I'd have to explain this shit to Dondi, to everyone. Hell, I haven't had the chance to come up with a good lie yet. But what would I tell the cops?' All this ran through Jabari's mind.

He knew they would come looking for him asking questions. Dondi saw them leave together, she knew something was going down but maybe she wouldn't say anything. Yeah, fuckin' right. That bitch would sing louder than Beyonce if given the chance. Jabari's mind wouldn't stand still for shit. He wondered what T-Black was trying to say. Why did Hulie shoot him in the chest if he needed to know where the money was? The bullshit he fed him about all this money. Was it real? Jabari was about to get trapped off.

"Yo' man, that's the house," Hulie said pulling Jabari out of his thoughts if only for a moment.

He pointed up the street to an old wooden house that sat deep inside a fenced-in lot. It was well kept but the screen was dark and dirty. You really couldn't see on the porch. Jabari looked around the sides as they drove by and no lights were on in the front, but one shone bright in the back. It looked like the kitchen or something there was an old Beamer sitting in the yard off to the side on blocks. The hood was halfway open like somebody was doing work. Bushes sat off along the three-foot leaning fence with crabgrass running wild along its bottom.

They turned the corner and came up the other block on the back side and parked in the darkest spot they could find.

Hulie checked his gun and reloaded it.

"Is there going to be that type of trouble?" Jabari asked.

"You never know," Hulie answered.

He was right, so far, the night hadn't gone according to the plan. Jabari checked his clip and replaced the bullets he'd used earlier. Jabari looked over at Hulie than put one in the chamber.

"I'm ready," Jabari said.

They got out quickly and silently and snuck into the wooded area behind the house looking behind our backs up and down the street making sure there were no cop cars in the vicinity. They peeped over towards the next couple of blocks where they'd just left earlier. They were all over there and an ambulance had just left. Jabari wondered if T-Black's moms knew what was going on? They'd better handle this before the cops came because they would be over once they got people to ID the bodies. Then shits fired, oh yeah, they'd be over. They pushed our way through the thick prick filled bushes into the back of the house. Something was different, kid's bikes were pulled up in the back, that was strange. Hulie pulled out his gun and started towards the porch.

Jabari grabbed him by the shoulder, and he looked back at me and snarled. "What!"

Jabari pointed next door. "This is the wrong house. We're supposed to be over there."

He looked around at the yard and realized Jabari was right. They quickly beelined toward the bushes to the fence and looked in the other yard. An old boy kennel and the gates were open. Jabari picked up a small rock and threw it. There was no dog, at least Jabari hoped it wasn't. Jabari looked around for fresh dog shit making sure and saw nothing. They hopped the fence and stayed low making our way to the back porch. The back porch was also screened in and they slowly opened the door and peeped in.

An old washer and dryer sat on the back with dirty linen and big laundry bags scattered about on the floor. Jabari guessed the washer must have worked and it looked like they still had to dry clothes elsewhere from the condition of the dryer. He glanced across the yard and spotted the clothesline. Hulie snapped Jabari out of his trance and pointed to the window. Jabari ducked...it was her! T-Black's mother, she looked so familiar. He knew he'd seen her somewhere before. She tricked on the tracks downtown around Romney Street.

She opened the window, looked around, then called out. "Carl! Carl, you out there, baby?" she looked around the yard.

They hugged the ground in the shadows beneath her and stopped breathing. They panicked somewhat and made a little noise, but if she saw them, she would have screamed. Between the dogs barking and the sound of her screaming, the cops would have been here asap. She shook her head, checked her watch and shut the window. Jabari couldn't get her face out of his mind. She was pretty as hell. She was fine on the block and all but up close, her face was flawless. Her lips were full, and her eyes were slanted, bright and mysterious.

One thing about her she didn't just jump in and out of cars. She had certain people she dealt with from what he saw they were mostly old skool ballers. Every now and then a young boy or two would come up with the nerve to get at her, but it would cost them big. Jabari never knew that would be T-Black's mother. *Damn...T-Black why would you let your own mom trick and be in the streets like that?*

They got back up slowly and opened the gate to the porch, crept up the steps and slowly tiptoed our way to the back door. Hulie braced himself against it.

"Hold up!" Jabari told him, then checked the doorknob to see if it was open...it wasn't.

He braced up against the door and signaled to Jabari that he was going to count off then they'd hit it together. They had one good shot, that was all, and they were lucky she sat in the back of the house. Jabari peeped back in one more time and she sat at the table with a bathrobe on. Her long, shapely legs were exposed and as Jabari strained his eyes, he could see a slight glimpse of pink between her thighs and that was enough to make his dick tingle. He felt like jacking off right then and there. She was reading a newspaper and smoking...smoking crack. That fucked the whole picture up. A minute ago, he was horny as hell. Now all he wanted to do was get high, too.

As if he'd read Jabari's mind, Hulie dug into his pocket and pulled out some pills.

"Where the fuck he getting that shit from?" Jabari asked himself.

He had no clue, but Hulie took one and offered Jabari one. Jabari quickly snatched it out of his hand. He needed to be good and high to do this shit.

Hulie held up his hand and his fingers, then counted down. "Five...four...three...two!"

"One...ahhhh, shit! Damn, that shit hurt," Jabari said.

They bounced off like rubber bands. It felt like there was a solid bar of steel or something midway around the door. All they did was manage to crack it and as they gawked and held their arms in pain that's exactly what was holding it, a steel bar bolted across the middle.

T-Black's mother looked up at them, turned and started to haul ass. Hulie pointed to the screws that held the bar and they hit it one more time. The door burst off the hinges and Jabari fell and scrambled to his feet. Hulie fell against a huge metal refrigerator collected himself and dived at her. She tripped, fell and desperately crawled trying to get up to her feet. It was too late, Hulie was holding her foot. She kicked at him repeatedly, at one point catching him in the face. He swung at her and started beating her backside like a drum.

Jabari ran over trying to hold her down. Hulie continued to swing and he held up his hand.

"I got her!" Jabari yelled. "I got her!"

Hulie paid him no mind. Jabari turned her underneath him and Hulie's punches made their way to his back as he shielded her, then turned slightly.

"That's enough, calm the fuck down!" Jabari yelled out.

Hulie stopped, but T-Black's mother continued to struggle. Jabari held her tighter and motioned for Hulie to grab a chair. Then he picked her up and sat her down.

"Where's the money, bitch?" Hulie questioned after catching his breath.

"Mi-nuh...kna-wah...em-de-raj dem tak 'bout!" she said.

At first, it took Jabari a minute to digest what she was saying. It was straight geechie and right now she was spittin' raw Gullah.

"You know!" Hulie slapped her.

Too bad for her, Hulie had been in downtown Charleston and his Mama and Auntie bought him up on fish and rice. He understood every muthafuckin' word she said. She closed her eyes for a second absorbing the sting. Jabari could tell she didn't like that shit at all.

"The money he stole from me!" Hulie yelled.

She spit some blood from her mouth and looked back up at him. "Who?"

"Your son, T-Black!"

She shook her head, it started to register for her now. It was a stickup. After all these years she was being robbed. Who would have the nerve? They had to be from out of town or something. Hulie slapped her again.

"Unuh, haff ta ask him!" she hollered back.

Hulie snickered, it was like he was waiting for this moment all his fuckin' life. He stood up and smiled. "I would...but, he's dead!"

She turned her head towards Jabari, and he looked off. He couldn't look her in the face. All Jabari saw was pain as wells of water formed in her eyes and she broke down. Hulie wasn't shit, he could have at least let her have her moment, but he slapped her again. This time she didn't move or nothing. She continued crying, bitterly.

Hulie shouted at her. "*Tell me where the money is or you're dead, too!*"

She looked up at him and said softly. "Mi-nuh care...kill me den."

Hulie clutched her face with his hands tightly. "That's how you want it, huh?"

He walked over to Jabari and told him to start searching the place. He said he was going to try and get some info out of her. Shit sounded too corny, so Jabari paid him no mind and started in the front room. He looked up in the ceiling and found nothing. He pulled back the carpet and stomped the floorboards looking for an opening. He rummaged through

closets and drawers thinking, 'It's got to be here!'

He walked into T-Black's room, he could tell it was his. Black label shirts and outfits, Timbs, A PlayStation 3, Air Force Ones and Jordan's and a closet full of Dickie outfits gave it away. Jabari checked his dresser and came up on a jewelry box full of rings, chains, watches, and other shit. He grabbed what he could and stuffed them in his pockets. He scattered everything on the desk and then noticed a small black and white picture. He picked it up and looked at it, it was of two kids and some older dude that looked like him. It must have been his dad. Jabari smiled wishing he had pictures like that. He threw it down to the floor and flipped over the bed, checked the mattress and then dipped into the next room, which was his mother's.

It was decked out like one of those five-star hotel suites that he'd seen in magazines. It had a king size bed, a silk linen bedspread, and sheets. He rummaged through the closet and threw brand new outfits to the floor still with the price tags on them. Brand new stilettos in boxes and then he looked up and spotted a panel that was slightly cocked. He pushed at it and it fell, jumped and pulled himself up. He spotted a box, grabbed it, pulled it down and peered inside it. It was cash, bundles of cash, it wasn't ninety grand but it was something. Jabari tossed it aside, flipped over the mattress then stopped in his tracks. It was weird, there was a big ass gold metal dick, still wet at that.

'Damn you mean to tell me as fine as this chick is and with this kind of money. She can't find a real dick?' Jabari thought shaking his head.

To top it all off her crib was laid, she had new plasma flat screen T.V.s that were thirty-two and fifty-six inches. A brand-new carpet and state of the art appliances. Why did she have to sell pussy anyway? Was Jabari's next question. But if this is what it got her, it must be some good pussy and he wasn't mad at her. He didn't dwell on it too much longer. The room was empty other than some jewelry she had laying around. He left it alone, he had enough shit in his pockets. He stuffed what cash he could in his socks and briefs then left out of the room and went into the kitchen and tripped.

"What the fuck did you do?"

Hulie stood over her straightening his pants then turned away from Jabari and said, "I had to punish her." He laughed.

Jabari looked at her, her face was damn near unrecognizable. All that beauty she had was beat into a bloody pulp. Her robe was pulled open and bite marks bled around her breasts. Her legs were gaped open and blood oozed out of her pussy.

This muthafucka was sick. He walked over to a cabinet and pulled out a bottle.

He held it up. "This outta finish her off." He stalked over to her grinning.

Jabari stepped in front of her. "Did she at least tell you anything?"

"Naw...that's why she has to be punished. Her bitch ass son stole my..."

This wasn't about her, it was about T-Black. Jabari couldn't just let him do her like that. He looked down her and thought she was dead. Hulie started to raise his arm and Jabari stopped him.

He pulled his gun out. "You want some too?"

"I think she's dead, yo." Jabari turned away from him, picked her body up and carried it over to some clothes that were piled up near a room by the back porch. It was a linen closet or something.

Hulie kicked her. This nigga wasn't shit, her body flinched slightly, and he saw it.

"She's still alive!" he said. "We need to torture her ass and find out..."

"No, that's enough. We gotta get the fuck outta here."

Jabari advised.

"Did you check the house?" he asked.
"Yeah."
"Did you find...anything?"

Jabari tried to conceal the bulge in his pockets, but it was too late. Hulie saw it but didn't say anything. He put a towel over T-Black's mother and started to stand and confront Hulie. Shortly after that, he felt the stinging of a bottle on the back of his head and glass shattering all over the place. His head throbbed as he tried to turn, all he felt next was a hard thud to his jaw. Stars and blackness started to overcome him. Jabari fell on top of T-Black's mother and felt Hulie going through his pockets and talking shit. He didn't search his pants leg at least he hadn't felt anything, but he was numb anyway. He would have never known. Jabari tried to stay conscious and collect himself.

He heard Hulie going through some boxes on the back porch. He came back in and ran through the house. He sprinkled some wet shit on them. It stunk, it was gas, this nigga was gonna burn them up.

"Yo' what the fuck you doing?" Jabari asked.

"She's seen our faces," he replied.

"Help me up..." Jabari pleaded struggling to get to his feet.

Hulie kicked him back down. "No, you gotta go too. You just tried to steal from me. What makes you think I can trust you now? You might tell your sister and shit. Oh, hell no!"

He kicked him in the chest. "Now take it like a man!"

He pulled out a lighter and Jabari heard him run into the living room and the others kicking doors open like a maniac. Jabari could hear a whoosh from the flames as he lit the gas. He ran back into the kitchen squealing in delight like he was possessed and flicked the lighter. It wouldn't light, he played with it and Jabari mustered everything he had, got up and jumped on him. The can with the gas in it spilled all over the place and it made a trail to the fire. Hulie tried to run but the flames made its way to his arm and cried out in pain.

He bolted for the back door. The fire had gotten worse, it was already making its way to the kitchen. Jabari tried to make his way over to T-Black's mother, but it was useless, the smoke, the fire in between them, blocked any attempt to reach her. He could hear the faint sounds of sirens in the distance. Jabari looked over at her and she started moving and coughing. Maybe she would get up after all, but he couldn't take it no more. It was just too damn hot. Jabari dived through the door and hit the ground rolling. He got up, fanned the fire off and groggily made it across the fence.

The pricks on the bushes cut through his face and chest. He could see the lights at the other houses on the street coming on. He made it through the cut they came through and spotted Hulie's truck. Hulie was already inside cranking it up. Jabari waved at him and started running towards him, then he skidded the wheels and took off.

"He left me," Jabari mumbled.

Jabari was in pain; the burns made his arms welp up and this bitch ass nigga had left him. Jabari looked behind him and all he could see was the orange glow from the house. He looked back and saw someone run up the street.

He was seen. "Hey...hey you!" someone called out.

Jabari ran back into the darkness and slipped into the woods cursing Hulie's ass out. "I'm gonna get that muthafucka if it's the last thing I do...I swear!" Jabari said running as fast as he could through the darkened woods trying to escape.

ALL NIKKI COULD SEE as she awoke from her pain inflicted stupor was thick, white smoke and fire flickering from behind it. She coughed and wheezed as her throat burned trying to grasp at whatever cooling air she could find. Instinctively she started to get up and run, but the sharp pain in her now fractured ribs prevented her from doing so. Perhaps it was a good thing because it made her stay low. She obeyed that inner voice now and crawled around on the floor looking for an escape from the unbearable heat that ate her flesh.

She had to get her bearings, so she looked around for a fix and she spotted the bottom half of the kitchen table chairs and right behind them the bottom of the kitchen cabinets. Across directly from them was the oven, it glowed crimson red as the flames worked steadily on it. She knew to stay away. The door to the back porch should be directly behind her she remembered. She turned and was met with kindling in her face coming from off the expensive oak table she'd just bought, burning out of control to the ground. The tile started to buckle and melt beneath her hands and knees and she crawled knowing she only had moments before the door would eventually catch fire also.

The top part of the doorway was torched, and she couldn't see her way clear from all the flames.

"Damn, I'm stuck," she said to herself.

It was at that point she seriously thought of dying. It was so damn hot, just give the fuck up. Something made her glance up at the refrigerator by the doorway to the pantry, an expensive and huge appliance her son had just brought into the house. She complained about it at first.

"It's too out of place. The house's too small. It's gonna eat up all the electricity like crazy. How much food we gon put in it anyway," she had whined.

Now as she glanced up, she was glad they kept it and damn sure glad he ignored her. Now if she could only open it and get some ice, that was the only thing her mind wrapped around, right now. She crawled over and touched it cautiously. It was still cool to the touch, but just barely. It would soon look like the oven in a matter of time, she had to act fast. She grabbed at the side of the door and the rubber seal around it burnt her fingers. She cried out in pain but still managed to get it open. The frost and cool air coming from it drew the flames like a moth to a candle. She started lifting herself up by the shelves inside and was almost successful until they collapsed from her weight.

She fell down onto the heated floor cursing as her head was beat down from the food and bottles of juice that fell on top of her. She could hear the sizzle from the containers of liquid that were consumed into the refrigerator sucking up whatever air she could and shuddered when she heard the windows to the house explode from the heat. Scared, she squeezed herself up into it some more trying to shield herself from the glass that was slung throughout the air like missiles. She was safe now, but for how long?

"The fire trucks should be here any minute," she told herself, as she heard the once faint sirens grown louder in the distance.

The sound of cracking underneath her suddenly caught her attention, she looked down to see where it was coming from. The floor beneath her was starting to give and the refrigerator started teetering forward slightly.

"Damn!" she screamed. "Now what?"

The floor wouldn't support the weight if the huge refrigerator anymore. The support beams underneath the house were loosening and shifting. The fire was destroying the small home completely. It was ready to give up and collapse. The fire was just too much for it. She wrapped herself up into a ball and braced herself trying to prepare for the impending impact. It fell forward slowly at first then hard with a bonecrushing thud and the whole back side panel of the refrigerator fell on top of her.

She waited a second before she made any moves. It was dark but she could hear and feel things falling on her. It was plastic and papers of some sort. She wiggled around on her back and picked up the refrigerator slightly by using her legs and tried with all her might to turn it towards the door. Almost as if it sensed opportunity the flames jumped on top of it attacking the cool air that escaped from it. The bottom of her feet stung like hell from the heat. She figured if she could just ease it towards the door using it as a shield, she would be alright. She managed to move a couple of feet but got stuck on some trash that came down from the ceilings, probably burnt up insulation. If she could just muster enough strength to clear a hole to the back porch. Yeah, that was the plan she was going with, but the reality of it all was clear as she felt the crusted-up blood that had hardened on her inner thighs and her pussy was swollen and bruised.

It was going to be hard, Hulie's brutal assault made her sick to her stomach. It also made just angry enough to push the metal tank-like object around and lift it ever so slightly and she could see an opening on the back porch. She knew it was going to be tough, but hopefully, she'd make a dash for the door to safety. Keeping that in mind with all the force and strength she could muster, she tried pushing the refrigerator up off of her. It was much heavier than she thought. She did manage to push it up and aside exposing her to the flames even more. She pushed the panel that fell on top of her and looked around at the trash that came out of it.

She did a second take, it wasn't garbage, but bundles of money and plastic wrapped around white looking bricks. She knew immediately what it was kilos of cocaine or even heroin.

She gasped almost losing her breath.

"What the hell?" she mumbled. "This is why Carl wanted that damn thing in here. He was stashing money!"

She grabbed at one of the bundles of money and looked at the wrapper, one thousand. She backed away slowly and glanced inside the refrigerator and money was still dropping from the hidden panels inside it. The next thing she knew she heard the sounds of the firetrucks even louder in the background. They were there and the house was on its last leg. She did a double take at the money than the dope.

"Damn, I can't just leave it here to go up in smoke," she said.

Her mind was made up, she looked over at the linen closet next to the pantry by the side of the door and spotted some laundry bags.

"That should do it!" she said.

She crawled over, grabbed one, came back and started stuffing all that she could grab inside of it.

"There's too much money," she kept telling herself. "What the hell did, Carl get himself into?"

She grabbed at the white plastic wrapped packages gingerly. They were singed from the heat, but they were sealed, and nothing leaked. She continued stuffing two-five-eight, then crawled back over to the refrigerator an grabbed the rest, eleven-twelve. She looked frantically and there was no other money or dope left that she could see. Her body was still sore, her eyes were puffy, and it felt like her pelvic bone was broken. Now she had a new life, new energy. She heard the banging on the door as the firemen tried busting their way in.

It was time to go, she crawled through the door dragging the weighted bag behind her trying to dodge the hot smoking kindles in her path and all the trash that dropped from the ceiling. Something jumped on her neck and it burned, but she had to grin and bear it long enough to get outside. Halfway through the doorway, she heard a faint hissing sound that came from underneath the oven. She crawled faster because she knew what it was, the gas line. She was too close now, she fought through the pain and almost black out as she dived for the back door of the porch and tumbled down the steps making her body hurt even more. She was out, she gulped down some cooling air into her lungs and started rolling around on the dirt and grass putting out the fire on her back. Then she remembered the gas line. She grabbed at the bag got up and ran as fast as she could towards the back part of the yard near the edge of the woods. She ducked down when she heard a voice yell out.

"Go around back!" the person said.

The firemen would be in the back yard momentarily and the would spot her easily. One naked ass, burnt, black woman dazed and standing in the mud, of course, they would rescue her. She'd have to explain the satchel of money she was dragging, the dope and the fire. That would make for a very long, difficult day and she'd probably get committed. Then just like that, suddenly, the house exploded sending a cloud of ash into the night sky. She shielded her eyes and peeped. It was a blessing in disguise as she looked at the collapsing house, but at the same time, a feeling of sadness for the memories lost that went with it.

She struggled to her feet with both hands now grabbed the bag, pulling it off into the dark escape of the woods. She hunched down behind a tree as the firemen ran towards the burning structure with hoses and axes in hand. She made it finally, they didn't see her yet, but the cops wouldn't be that far behind them, snooping. Her mind stayed fixed bitterly on Hulie's face as the pain throbbed throughout her aching body.

She remembered Jabari's face if just faintly.

"Why didn't he stop him?" she questioned. "Bastards they killed my son!"

She needed to find a place to lay low for a while and get her mind together. Get her body healed and get herself a plan, with the ninety-six grand and twelve keys she had in a satchel.

She'd have her day and her *revenge*!

Chapter Four

The sun rose high over the Cooper River Bridge as light raced into the cracked windows of the two-story condo in the upper-class section of Mount Pleasant exposing the voluptuous, sexy, ass freckled face, red bone sitting on the side of her bed. She'd been wide awake now for a while watching the sun come up as she sat impatiently by the phone. She closed the blinds slightly as the bright morning sunlight flooded the room causing her to shield her eyes momentarily then grabbed for a pair of shades and tossed them on. Her long, thick eyelashes fluttered as they adjusted to the light.

She reached over to her bedside dresser searching for the pack of cigarettes she could have sworn she'd just bought before she came in last night. She got up and grabbed the cashmere sweater slung across the top of the closet door and dug through the pockets. She pulled out a half-broken cigarette then sucked her teeth and threw the garment across the room. She lifted her shades and adjusted them on her silk, flaming red hair, then crossed her legs trying to piece it together. To hell with the promise she'd made to stop smoking...*fuck that shit*. She wet her full, rose-colored lips and lit it, sucking all the smoke her lungs would inhale then fell back dizzy on the king size bed.

71

"When is this muthafucka gonna call?" She sighed staring over at her glossy, black Samsung scanning it for texts.

Not seeing anything new she looked around the room for an ashtray then it dawned on her that she threw them all away. She'd been since reneged a while ago on that crazy ass New Year's shit she was on, drunk at the moment it was just one of a dozen promises she slurred on and on about. Glancing down to the floor, she spotted a brand-new pair of pink Jordan's and picked one of them up then flicked the ashes from the cigarette inside.

"It's just ashes it shouldn't hurt anything," she convinced herself.

She propped up some pillows and leaned back staring up at the ceiling fan spinning round and round and started thinking out loud. "Why do I fuck with this shit anyway?" As she took another long drag of the cigarette the answer shot back at her like a light. "It's too easy bitch!" She continued talking to herself as she went over it again for the hundredth time. "Damn, girl, it was only a week or so ago and still I

haven't seen any of my money."

A knucklehead ass balla got himself knocked off on some ole bullshit, tricking. According to her people, he spent crazy money on crack hoes and cheap hotels. Picture that, she giggled at the thought. As much loot as he had at his disposal at any given time. He'd rather spend it playing Russian Roulette with HIV and Hepatitis. He was a fuckin' sucka who deserved this shit, she said then flicked some more ashes into the sneaker.

His ass was easy to find, hell, everyone knew his business. Really it was just a matter of time anyway before the streets woulda got him. Her snitch told her where he'd be and all it took was a couple of calls to some crooked ass cops, she'd grown up with and boom, his twisted, crazy looking ass was in the county jail. Immediately she had his ass processed, thrown into an interrogation room and hidden away. It would have to go down quickly, they worked him physically and mentally. They told his dumb ass he was going away for life. That this was a felony and a strike.

Fuck the Fed's, he'd do State time first, and at eighty percent. It didn't take long, he panicked and got scared. They'd picked the right muthafucka, she knew he'd wanted to become a snitch, but she had enough of them already. If she needed to, she'd play that card later after she was finished with him. After a couple of good cop, bad cop scenarios, slaps and brutal stomach punches were administered just like in the movies. It was suggested in no certain way that maybe he'd have to get himself a lawyer.

They convinced him that he'd have to pay a lot of money getting out of this shit. They were gonna put it down on him and set him up good. They were going to smack up a couple of his crack hoe girlfriends, blame it all on him and maybe throw in a little sexual assault, rape, or after a couple of black eyes, attempted murder.

"Why go through all that?" they asked.

Once again, they suggested that maybe he could get his own self out if things were right. Not even see jail time or court, but of course, they'd have to ask their people to make sure it was 'quote...unquote', legit. She liked this part of it, making it her business to go down to the count joint dressed in the tightest, tittie hugging, ass fitting mini skirt she could find. She glanced over at the walk-in closet and she had many outfits similar to it. Different ones for the many moods and roles she had to play.

"Whatever!" She giggled. "It worked."

When she got there, she let him know that yes, if he had the right money, he could walk away from all of this. She'd make this a simple matter and of course, the cops agreed, after all, they were in on it. But then he started second-guessing himself and shit, trying to figure shit out.

She picked up on the vibe. "Damn, this cat is really stupid."

She slightly pushed back the chair she was sitting in and opened her legs wide long enough to allow him to get a good glimpse and detail what was in between her panty-less thighs. Showing itself was reddish blonde pubic hairs, revealing a pink clit hiding behind it if you squinted just right. She closed her legs and really went to work on him. She pulled her chair up closer to him playing like she was opening a folder.

His eyes were ready, he had just dropped a pencil and caught one show. "God-damn, now what?"

She adjusted her cleavage and out popped a nipple, so-called accidentally, in front of him.

"Equipment malfunction." She laughed.

It was on, it didn't take two minutes. His dick was hard, and a god-damn deal was in the making.

It wasn't over with yet though. The good cop dude would come rushing in soon after whispering something in her ear, another part of the plan. Something about a stash house. He made sure he was loud enough so that he could hear. She looked up at him and smiled, suggesting once again that maybe if he had one of them stash houses, he might be able to go free today. You could see it in his face. If he told them about that he'd definitely have to deal with his partners later and it wouldn't be good. He didn't want to go with it.

Then on cue, the bad cop dude came in wrapping the steel cuffs around his knuckles shouting. "Fuck this shit, let's fuck his ass up. Then lock his ass down and throw away the fuckin' key!" She rolled her eyes at him letting him know what was going down if he fucked up and made the wrong move.

She got up and shook her fat round booty all the way to the door, opening it, then looked over her shoulder telling him she tried working with him. He'd never see her...again, ever. It's amazing what a hard dick and some common sense could accomplish.

He was completely punked and played.
"Okay, okay!" he yelled.

She nodded to the cop to get the address then winked at him. "I got you, baby, don't worry." Then she let him get a good eyeful. "See you around, huh?"

He damn near snatched his dick out through his drawers and started jacking right there, both the perp and the cop. This bitch dripped sex. She hurried back to her office calling her folks on the street about the address he'd given up. It was his partner's stash spot. He was supposed to be in charge of it. That's where he was skimming all the money to trick. She told them they had to get there before the cops did, she'd delay them a bit with warrants and paperwork.

"Just fuckin' get the money!" she screamed.

She was that girl, yep, that double-crossing bitch type. Her plan was set in motion. Rob the stash spot and when the cops came, they'd find scraps, a few thousand at best. Petty, of course, they would be pissed thinking that he'd lied to them, bullshitted them and renege the deal. Now they'd really punish him. Make sure he'd see jail time with busted ribs and shit. Life was a bitch!

She was smooth, she played it all too well. Her sweet Emmy award-winning, ghetto ass.

"Fuck it!" she told them. "Just split the money."

Of course, she'd give them the lion's share. They'd be happy with that. Whatever dope they found, which was always a couple of grams, she'd tell them to record it as evidence. A small-time dope bust, he'd get simple possession or and enough jail time for her to launder the real money and still keep tabs on him.

"Hell, give his ass a strike that'll work in my favor later," she said.

He would think somebody on the streets robbed him. Probably thinking one of those hoes he fucked with set him up. He'd deal with it as soon as he hit the streets, but he needed to disappear for awhile anyway. He needed time to explain this shit to his people. They were already on his ass about the tricking anyway. So, he needed to be safe for a minute and it never actually dawned on him that the actual thief was the one sending him up the road. That's how she did business, one muthafucka at a time. It was consistent.

Charleston, South Carolina the port city full of dope boys, dealers, ballas, hustlas, whatever, all she saw was dollars. With two Beamers in the driveway, fur coats in the closet, brand new outfits, and stilettos from New York to Italy, jewelry and of course anything she fuckin' wanted.

"Ouch!" she yelled as the cigarette burned her nails and snapped her back into the present moment. "Damn...now I gotta make an appointment."

She got up and walked to the bathroom then flushed the butt down the toilet and flopped back in bed. She pulled back the covers exposing the naked man who laid sleeping underneath and giggled as she started playing with his dick feeling its warmth and marveling as it stiffened between her fingers. She wrapped her hands tightly around it as it seemed to explode and swing uncontrollably. She stroked it and it calmed down. He wasn't circumcised, and she was entranced as she watched the foreskin slide up and down over his now enlarged tip. It freaked her out.

Her pussy started tingling, she felt it and it was hot and wet. She hoisted herself on top of him quickly and slowly thrust his dick inside of her then slid up and down its shaft until it was swallowed whole. She leaned forward and kissed the side of his neck, then sucked his nipples making his dick even harder inside of her. She sat deep, it hit her G-spot and she heard him moan as she grinded down on him. She rested her large titties on top of his face and his tongue reached out eagerly searching for her thick stout nipples and sucked them.

She closed her eyes and her pussy juices ran down her leg and tickled his nuts.

She stroked faster and faster until she worked up a lather and he couldn't speak. When he did it made no sense, but she had the cure for that. She started working her strong hips on his pelvis and whispered gently in his ear.

"What's my name, baby?" she asked.
"Uggghhhh..." he groaned.

She grabbed him by the throat. "What's my name, muthafucka?"

"Sunshine..."
"Sunshine what?"
"Sunshine Brown!"

She squeezed her pussy with all her might feeling his dick get fatter as his blood vessels thickened pushing the cum up inside of his balls to the top. Then, without warning, she came to a dead stop and slowly raised up. The tip of his head was the only thing left in her wet tightened pussy.

That fucked him up and he yelled out like a bitch. "Oh my God...oh my God!"

"No...not, God!" she said giggling as she started backstroking making her ass clap as he dug deeper into her pussy. "Not God, but who...who muthafucka?"

He grabbed at her and tried pulling her closer to get intimate. She wasn't going for it, she pushed him back down and he tried once more but slipped from the sweat that raced down her back. She could feel the precum build up and then grabbed him by the throat again and squeezed some more. He was defeated. She felt hot sperm shooting wildly inside of her like a hose.

She started draining the life out of him and yelled. "I said, what's my fuckin' name?"

"Sunshine Brown...Sunshine Brown!" he yelled out.
"Sssss...give me that dick! Sunshine Brown what?"
"Sunshine Brown...D...District Attorney!"

That's what she wanted to hear, that's all she wanted. That and the ninety god-damned grand and the dope she was supposed to flip. That's all she wanted as she leaned forward and whispered softly into his ear.

"And you know this...man!" she giggled, then raised up and adjusted her pussy over his face snuggling down on his mouth. "Now...let's see if you can get this promotion okay."

The young college law student that interned in her office lapped up her pussy eagerly and hungrily. Now it was his chance to shine for the now moaning and convulsing 9th Circuit District Attorney of Charleston, South Carolina, and part-time hood-rat Sunshine Brown!

IT HAD BEEN A COUPLE days and Dondi still hadn't heard anything from Rip or Jabari. She'd been expecting them at least that next morning after they left. Maybe she thought, and the idea even pissed her off a little, that they might have taken what money they made and went tricking out of town or the country. But now it was just too long, at the rate they got high it woulda only been a couple of days at best before they bought their asses up in here.

The rent was due, the hotel owner had come to see her twice already. She gave him what little she had but it still wasn't the rent. Her mind wasn't too bent on tricking, she wanted to stay close just in case they came back with money or even dope. She could use both right about now. She hadn't got high in a minute and hadn't been able to hit the streets.

That's what cost her, she paced the small hotel room mumbling. "Just wait until they get here!"

A couple of her so-called girls came through with the occasional trick-daddy but quickly left after he got a good eyeful of Dondi. Instead of losing them to her and in fear of Dondi getting all the money, they dipped. They probably took them way across town to West of Ashley taking the back way so the trick couldn't retrace his steps back to Dondi. She had that type of effect on men.

Something had to be done, though. She turned on the television and started flicking through the stations then heard a knock at the door. She ran to it and opened it wide. It was the hotel owner, Pasheeva or something, she could never get his name right for the hell of it. She stood in the doorway in her panties and wifebeater, bowlegged with her arms crossed.

He stood right in front of her with his hand out. "You got money?"

Her mouth dropped a little from the disappointment of seeing him and not Rip and also tired of him asking the same

shit. *'You got money...you got money...you got money?'*

"Fuck him!" she mumbled to herself, then sucked her teeth and turned around walking away from him.

She rubbed her arms trying to warm them from the cool draft that rushed inside through the open doorway. Her nipples poked out causing the hotel owner to stare.

He smiled. "Look you got money...or what?"

He followed close behind her after he stepped in and closed the door. She put on a pair of jeans, squeezing into the hip-hugging garment as he continued to ogle at her body.

"No, not yet. I told you by the end of the week..." she jumped slightly as he reached for her hand pulling him close to her rubbing his groin against her ass.

"Maybe we can work something out..." he said.

At first, she pulled away slightly, then said fuck it and started to go with it.

"Hell, fuck it!" she mumbled. "If that's all he wanted was a shot of ass then that'll work."

She figured he'd be easy to pull anyway. All she had to do was fuck his God damn brains out and he'd be bringing her money. She rubbed on his dick, it was getting hard as she pulled him towards her and sat down on the edge of the bed. He backed up and walked over to the window and looked out and around both ways then closed the curtains tight. He walked back over to her pulling his dick out of his pants and started stroking it in front of her face.

She looked up at him and said, "So...will this take care of it or what?"

"Sure...you give me some pussy, too!"

"That'll work!" she grinned. "But I don't want no shit or

I'ma tell your wife."

"No...no don't do that. No need for that!" He grabbed the back of her head. "C'mon, just hurry!"

She started to open her mouth and she caught something that popped up on the TV in front of her. A picture that flashed on the screen caught her eye. Some sort of special report.

"Oh my, God!" she said as she held the hotel owner's dick in her hand. She dropped it and pushed him aside.

He looked down beside. "What...what is it?" He tried shoving his dick into her mouth, but she just kept pushing it

away. "C'mon...before my wife gets back!"

She paid him no mind as she focused intently on the television. He turned and caught the headlines that read:

A man identified who was shot dead. His name is Mark Brown! He was found dead in the street at Montague Street and Nesbitt Avenue in the Liberty Hill section of North Charleston a week ago. Apparently, the victim of a robbery. If you have any information on the shooting call Crime Stoppers at..."

He recognized Rip from the shoddy mugshot they showed. He looked at Dondi who was sprawled out on the bed crying. His dick started to go limp, but not without thinking that maybe he should just take the pussy. He knew that now she had no one to look after her. Rip used to be there all the time and would help her out with the rent and even put the tim down on him from time to time buying her a couple of days in back rent. He straightened up his pants and grinned there'd be plenty of time.

He walked over to the door and said, "Uh...look, I come back later on today, okay!"

She didn't respond, she didn't have too. It was what it was, he opened the door and left.

Dondi laid crying hysterically on the bed for a long while after, but in between the sniffles, it suddenly dawned on her. If Rip was dead, where the hell was Jabari? She rubbed her eyes wondering did he have something to do with it? He would know what happened to him or was he dead too and just not found yet? She sat up staring into the TV screen at much of nothing.

Her mind filled with so many thoughts. *"What should I do? Should I claim the body? I need to find his people."*

She got up and went into the bathroom to straighten her face. She put on her best hooker outfit and ran out of the room. She knew just the place to find Jabari if he was still alive and she hoped he was. Then she'd find out exactly what happened.

On her way out, the hotel owner's wife beckoned her inside the office. She pointed her finger at her and said, "If you do not have the rest of the money by this evening, pack your stuff. If you are not here, we will."

Dondi peeped behind her and caught a glimpse of her husband coward behind in the back office. A red mark was visible on the right side of his face.

"He was slapped." She snickered. "Yeah right, if that happens...we might need to talk first." She straightened up her tight fitted top revealing her plump, mellon titties then winked at her husband. "I really don't think you want...uh, what's his name Pasheeva to get in any trouble. Now, do we?"

It was on, she'd play her completely out of the box. She'd run the bullshit about her husband. Tell her he used to take the pussy and eat her out. Hell, that right there would get her at least a couple of months or so of free rent.

'*Damn!*' she thought. '*Why didn't she think of this before?*' She zipped up her leather jacket and turned towards the door going out. "Not unless you want me to call...the cops."

"No, we don't want that...just go...just go!" she heard Pasheeva say from out the back room.

His wife's brown-skinned face turned red and she looked down unhappily at the desk. At first, Dondi felt sorry for her but this was the game and besides, she really would have thrown her shit out in the street.

"Look...I'll try to have something by the end of the week like I said." She opened the door and as it closed behind her, she heard shouts from Pasheeva in the background. Good for his stinkin' ass!

She stepped into the chilly, wind blowing street ass first and immediately a car stopped.

'My first trick of the day,' she thought.

Maybe it was some old man with his dick in one hand and money in the other. She looked up River's Avenue towards Remount Road and figured after she was finished with him, he could take her the back way into Liberty Hill. She grabbed the car handle and bent over to get inside the vehicle.

"Oh my..." She was snatched in and the car sped off. She rubbed her eyes, not believing what she was seeing. When she finally adjusted to the reality of what was going on, she started shouting. "Fuckin' Jabari! I thought you mighta been dead! What the hell happened to, Rip? Did you kill him...did you kill him!" Dondi started yelling, then grabbed his arm. "Why aren't you saying anything, Jabari? Talk to me...talk to me goddamnit!" She yanked at the steering wheel and Jabari swerved avoiding a car just to his left.

They were just approaching Remount Road a busy intersection and Jabari knew five-o always sat on the corner in front of the Quickie Mart. Jabari had to quiet Dondi down quick. He pulled into the parking lot of Piggly Wiggly right next to Highway-26 around back. Dondi was still hollering and acting out and shit, but Jabari understood. Jabari knew he should've gotten in touch with her earlier, but he needed to find a place and gather his thoughts and lay low. He managed to catch a ride that night to Dorchester Road over near Pepper Tree Houses.

Melissa took Jabari in without questions, didn't ask him shit about where he'd been. She just gave him some clean clothes, she'd put up from her old man. He'd just caught a bid for twenty years. She gave Jabari some quilts for a pallet and he fell out. He didn't remember what time he'd gotten there or even he'd gone. After gathering his thoughts, he knew exactly why he'd gone there. There was no bullshittin' it, he was in love with Melissa and would probably always be. She was his high school sweetheart. They were each other's first loves but had gone their separate ways after school.

He got caught up in drugs and she got caught up in dope boys and three kids. Jabari still managed to see her from timeto-time. They caught eyes whenever her old man would swing by the block and drop off some work. Jabari didn't even know he was up the road. He'd heard some things...but he really needed to talk to someone, and she was that one.

Sometime during the day, she'd woken up and asked him everything was alright. Did he need help or something? He told her that he needed to get his head together and asked if she could give him another day. She agreed, when he woke that following morning, he went to get and told her he needed to go on a run for a minute. She had just watched the news and knew something. Jabari could see it in her face. She cooked breakfast for him and told him to wait in the crib until she dropped the kids off at daycare. When she did, she hugged him tight and told him she loved him.

Then she dropped three stacks on the table and a set of car keys. Jabari felt obligated and started explaining rambling off at the mouth. Melissa shushed him, putting her fingers to his lips then planted a big wet kiss on his lips. She told him she still loved him too. Jabari helped washed the dishes then he got dressed and she walked him out to the parking lot. She pointed to a royal blue, 96 Nissan

Maxima and said that all he needed was gas. Jabari smiled, gave her a hug and was waving goodbye as he turned onto Dorchester Road.

It seemed like the news was on everything he turned the radio to. Everywhere he looked, he felt watched. He gassed up the ride and felt the money burning a hole in his pocket. He wanted to get high so fuckin' bad, but he had one thing left to do before he dipped.

"Calm the fuck down, Dondi!" Jabari yelled.

"Calm down...fuck you! Rip is dead, 'Bari...the news said he was killed in a robbery. I thought y'all was going to just put the tim down on someone...what happened?" Buckets of tears rolled out of her now puffed up, pretty doe-like eyes and Jabari felt so fuckin' bad. But he couldn't tell her anything because he didn't know nuthin' his damn self.

"Look, Dondi! We met these dudes and we heard them out. Then, when we got to the spot to do what we had to do it all just went fucked the hell up," Jabari tried to explain.

"What went fucked the hell up? Who did you meet?" Dondi questioned.

"I can't tell you all that, at least not yet, trust me on this." Jabari grabbed her by the shoulders and pulled her closer. At first, she resisted then broke down in his arms. "I know it's crazy! I wanted to come see you earlier, and let you know what it was up, but damn was hard. Rip was my friend, too.

Hell, Dondi, I don't even know where his people at!"

Dondi looked up into Jabari's eyes. "I know...that's fucked up! All this time together and we really didn't even know each other. All we did was get high. Damn..." She rubbed her eyes with the cuff of her sleeve and mascara smeared her face.

Jabari reached into his jacket and pulled out a tissue wiping her eyes. "I need to get outta town for a minute so that I can get shit together. We was fucked over and I'm gonna make sure some sort of way that we get ours."

"What happened, y'all got robbed? Tell me sumptin'!"

"Naw, we got set up."

"By who...who did y'all go see?"

Jabari wanted to tell her something, but he knew that the police would be coming to see her. Everyone knew about Rip and her and even Jabari. It would be easier if they had just split up. Jabari couldn't take her, and he knew she would want to come.

"I'm going in the country," Jabari informed her.

"Where...can I go?"

"Dondi...hear me out. The cops will be coming to see you sometime today, believe that. I wouldn't doubt it if they were already at the hotel waitin'. They gonna ask you a lot of questions and that's exactly why I can't tell you shit. You understand?"

She nodded her head, she finally started to come around.

"The less I know..."

"Yeah, the better." Jabari reached into his jacket and pulled out six hundred and fifty dollars. "I gotta lil' bit of money. Take this and give it to the hotel dude so he won't fuck with you."

"Don't worry I got that covered," Dondi said winking at Jabari. She crossed her legs kind of cocky and he knew then she was already on some dumb shit.

"No, take care of the business. I don't need his ass snooping around. Just do what you normally would do, but just nothing illegal."

"I can't hustle...get high?" Dondi looked at Jabari like he'd lost his mind.

Jabari grabbed his hand, deciding to go another route. He gently stroked it and with the other hand rubbed the side of her face.

"Dondi...for this to go right, you got to stay straight because I need someone to watch my back. I thought that it might just be you."

She cocked her head slightly like a little puppy and shit searching his eyes for any signs of the bullshit she was so used to encountering. "You want me to have your back." She found none.

"That's what's up."

"Okay, but I ain't never had no one..." she smiled. "Okay, you got it!"

"Cool, so I'ma drop you off and just chill a'ight. Order Chinese or something, watch movies but know this five-o will be there soon. If they're not already and they'll be watching you, so be careful."

Jabari hoped this shit wasn't going in one ear and out the other. Jabari needed to use Dondi as his contact, but if she fucked up then he'd know they'd locked her up, trying to get whatever they could outta of her.

"I got you." Dondi leaned over and kissed him on the cheek. "Be careful, Jabari."

"I will, I'll be in touch soon."
"Okay."

Jabari drove back to the hotel and dropped her off. He watched her go into the office and come back out. She was smiling so he knew she'd done the right thing. She waved and he peeled out into traffic. Jabari thought about it for a while, he finally made up his mind though. He would go someplace small where no one would know his face. Somewhere he could blend in, somewhere secluded. Summerville was the next town over, but he needed to go much further than that.

Not out of the State though, he had another school mate he knew. Not too many people knew they were friends, but they were.

cut grass was trimmed to a tee. It was fenced in from both sides, giving the impression of a quiet, ideal place to raise a small family, but it wasn't. Going inside the front door the living room was adorned with four, seventy-five-gallon fish tanks with exotic fish and eels. Over to the side sat a big sixty-two-inch flat screen, plasma TV. Three beautiful, scantily clad women sat over on a couch not far sipping on small glasses of brown-liquid, a bottle of Cognac sat in front of them half empty or half full. Tricks and hookers for some comfort for others depending on how you looked at it and who you talked to. Sitting off to the side with a laptop going through figures on the screen and yelling numbers into a phone was the bookie.

Back behind them was an archway that led into a kitchen. You could hear the sounds of loud voices coming from beyond it. The kitchen was blazing with the smell of fish and chicken being fried on the stove. A robust, older woman stood in front of it talking shit to two men that sat at a small, round table. As the bottle of scotch sat in front of them, they talked shit about politics and why Obama had his foot on their neck type of shit. Going past the kitchen was a spacious parlor with tables and a makeshift bar. The tables were setup with bid whisk and spade games, rummy players sat to the side and some serious skinning was going on.

A couple of people sat at the bar drinking while two bartenders ran drinks. The back porch was closed in and decorated with blinking Christmas tree lights and a jukebox pumped out music as old men grinded with young girls to *Clarence Carter's Strokin'*. This was indeed a bonafide grade A, down south liquor house.

The gentleman that ran it always sat in the back of the parlor with a girl, that was pretty and sexy sitting on his lap and rubbing on his dick. That's why he smiled all the time while keeping an eye on the money that moved. A short bugged eyed dude stood next to him rubbing his gut and crying, complaining that he should get his drinks free, but off to the side of him was a twelve-gauge, pump shotgun and on his waist was a .44 Magnum. He was security, the guy that sat in the chair told him he'd think about it, then smacked his hand away as he tried to feel on the girl. He called his name, Wood, short for Hollywood.

The owner had a reddish-brown skin color, with the straightest white teeth you'd ever seen on a man. He sported a low, cropped well-kept haircut and wore a Kangol hat tipped to the side. He maintained his weight at a strapping one-hundred and ninety-five pounds and stood at just five-ten or so. He treated his customers special, but when he was crossed which wasn't often, ass whippings were given out on the spot and he was at the front of the line. He never ducked away, he loved that shit.

He knew every damn thing that went on in Liberty Hill. He had his hands in all sorts of properties and other hustles except dope. He let others run that end of things. All he did was rent out trap houses. He was calm and muthafucking collected. They called him Blaze sometimes, even Country, but the name that stuck was Dirty-Red from Che-raw.

Nikki came through the back way of the festive parlor through the back yard. The porch was dark and dimly lit, and she crept easily by the man at the gate ogling over the girls who danced in the moon's glow. She walked through the curtain amid the action and saw the man she was looking for, Dirty-Red. Now all she had to do was get closer to him. Even though, she stood out with an oversized ball cap worn down over her eyes. Wood had spotted her already, he was on point.

He didn't recognize her, so he tipped closer and asked, "Hey, uh...I know you? His eyes fixed on the tight-fitting jeans she wore exposing her fine shapely body.

"You know me?" she asked as she turned.

"Nikki!" Wood grinned and started digging in his pockets looking around trying to be discreet. "Look...I got some money." He peeled off a fifty. "I know how you go, and you know, I, uh always wanted to..." he looked her up and down,

"...get with you!"

It humored her, he was right. Wood had tried for years and so far, had been unsuccessful. "Another place...another time," she said then pushed the money back towards him. "I need to speak to Dirty-Red."

Wood looked over his shoulder behind him. "I mean, you can see...he's busy, but I'm not." He pushed the money back at her and pulled out his knot. "If it's not enough, I mean...I heard you had that blazin' hot..." he rubbed her arm and she pulled away.

"Aahh..." she shrieked with a grimace.

"Damn, I didn't mean to hurt you."

"No...no, it's not you. Wood, sweetie please, I need to speak to Dirty-Red about something important."

"I hear you, but you know he don't like to be disturbed while he's fuckin' with them ole young ass girls."

She pulled off her hat and Wood turned his face slightly away.

"Damn, girl! What the fuck happened?" He turned, stepped over to Dirty-Red and whispered something in his ear.

Dirty-Red looked up and waved her over. "I've been hearing some wild shit about you. What the fuck is going on?"

She got closer up in his face whispering, "I need to talk to you, it's real important." She pulled the hat up.

Dirty-Red looked at her and shook his head.

"C'mon...follow me. Hey, Wood, make sure we not disturbed a'ight!"

"What about the girl?" Wood asked.

"Yo' baby, take care of my man. But make sure he pays for the kitty."

Wood smiled, as she grabbed at the fifty in his hand quickly and led him off to the bathroom. "Thanks,

Red...fuckin' thanks."

Dirty-Red entered a large bedroom that was decorated with a king-sized bed, covered in satin sheets, black curtains adorning the windows and plush carpeting. The musk fragrance coming from the incense lit the room up like a candle. He escorted her to a desk.

"I heard you was kidnapped. What up, gurl?" Dirty-Red said.

Nikki unzipped her jacket, took it off and tossed it over onto the bed. Dirty-Red gasped when he saw the burns and bruises.

"Damn, I saw the house. You made it out of there!" DirtyRed was shocked.

"God been with me!" Nikki commented.

"What the fuck happened with your son?"

She plopped down on the side of the bed and held her head in her hands. "I don't know, he left the house, said he was going to talk to someone."

"Who?"

"He didn't say."

Dirty-Red sat next to her rubbing her back. She cringed a little from the touch. She was still sore. "Did you go to the hospital?"

"I went to the doctor by the cemetery."

"Geechie Sam! A bootleg doctor, gurl? You need to go to a real hospital."

"I will...later. The police are looking for me and I have to get rid of some things before they find me," Nikki explained. "*Things?*"

"Two men came in that night and robbed the house.

Then burnt it down!"

"Aahhh shit...I didn't know that."

"They busted in through the back porch and said they was looking for my son. Said he owed them some money and shit. Hell, I didn't know what they was talkin' about. They didn't care, one looked around the house and the other..." Nikki paused reliving the gruesome attack.

"The other...what..." Dirty-Red asked hesitantly.
"*Raped me!*" Nikki cried. "Then beat the shit outta me.

He wanted to kill me, but other one didn't let him."

"You knew who they were...did you recognize em?"
"No...I didn't, but I remember their faces though."
"You need to tell the police." Dirty-Red got up and

reached for his cell phone. "You need to call..."
Nikki stopped him and pulled him back down on the bed. "I want revenge, fuck justice! They killed my only son left." She started sniffling and holding back a flood of tears that threatened to let loose at any moment.

Dirty-Red passed her a handkerchief. "I feel you."
"But...I got his money, all of it and it's a lot."
"How much?"
She wiped her eyes. "Ninety-six thousand dollars."

Dirty-Red pulled back. "Ooohhh shit, that's a lot of fuckin' money!"

"Also...twelve keys of pure white."

"Horse!"

"Un-cut!"

"God damn gurl!" Dirty-Red shook his head. "So, what you thinkin' 'bout doing?"

"I need some guns and shit...I'ma find them muthafuckas and kill em."

"Whoa...whoa hold up. What about your son's body?"

She looked over at him, she'd completely forgotten. "Oh, my Lord, I need to get him." She broke down in his arms.

"I got you, Nikki! Where you at, are you safe?"

"I'm cool for now."

"A'ight then, I'll go get your son's body myself and get it to the funeral home. Then we can go from there. Okay?" He lifted her head and wiped tears from her still soft, smooth, but worried face. "You always been straight up wit' me. You and your son T-Black, I got you!" "I'll give you something."

"Be cool, don't worry about that right now. You want to stay here tonight?"

"No...no, I'll come by tomorrow with the money and dope."

"A'ight, but just be careful. You want me to send Wood to come get you?"

"If I need him, I'll call." She got up and put on her jacket, tucked her long hair in her cap, then walked over to the door. "Dirty-Red...thank you!" She hugged him and kissed his cheek.

He walked her out the back door and watched as she disappeared into the darkness of the streets. He closed the door and walked swiftly to his room. He stood over by his desk still mulling over what Nikki had said.

'Ninety-six stacks and twelve keys, that's a lot of cheese,' he thought.

He could easily get a good twenty percent out of her, but first, he needed to find a man to flip the keys for him and someone to help Nikki plot out her revenge. He picked up his cell phone and scrolled through some numbers. He believed he knew just the man for the job. He stopped at a name pop-

ping up on the screen. It read: Diplite. "Yeah, he'll do it!"

"NAW, MAN...LISTEN..." Moonie G glanced at the line in back of him at least five deep in unit 1-B. He'd been on the phone now for thirty-two minutes and this was his third call. "No...the money got stolen..." He was trying to explain to his people why they was out a quarter of a million dollars in cash and dope. "It had to be the police, I tell ya. They were the only ones that knew..."

Moonie was a transfer from California only coming to South Carolina after hanging out with some bangers during a G-Unit concert tour. He fell out with the show's promoters and eventually was kicked off the bus. His boys told him he'd have to scramble up some cash quickly to make it back home. They fronted him some money and a dope connect they knew, and he went to work. After becoming the new face in the game, he soon became known as a hot boy, an offbrand. He was plugged into the loop making sure the money he made, made it back to his folks in Cali. He sat on thousands of dollars a week at times. He was doing it big, so he decided to stay in Charleston.

Involving himself in the local pussy business became a problem along with the money he tricked on them. He became complacent and started skimming from the stash. At first, it was just a couple dollars here and there, then it escalated to hundreds easily. He was confronted a few times by Jack boys and shots were fired, in clubs, on the block, even in supermarkets. Women started staying away from him after he was considered to be a very dangerous man to be around. They didn't want to become victims of one of his bad days or catch any stray bullets that were meant for him. He was left fucking around with the tricks that frequented the traps. That was easy pussy and his new thing.

He grew to be a trick daddy of sorts, staying in hotels and traps where his dope was moved until he got crazy paranoid and started smoking too. He had enough sense a couple of times to pay off some people that watched his back and kept him safe at least from the stickups, but not the game. He quickly became a mark and Sunshine had him in her snare because of it.

Now he was trying to get his lie straight. "Of course, I didn't say nothing to them."

He was given a deal verbally for three charges, all supposedly misdemeanors. The charges were simple possession, with less than a gram of crack, and less than a gram of cocaine. They would eventually be dropped once Sunshine and her people got ahold of the money and he would go free on a Disorderly Conduct, perhaps even Loitering or something. But the reality of it all was that he still had to explain the money being missing and the dope. he was scared shitless, he knew he'd fucked up. He needed time to make the money back. He had his own cash but not that much. He could do it in a couple of months maybe if they gave him the chance. That was the big problem, they had to give him the chance.

So, now, he literally begged for his life. "I could make it up, you know that. You know, I'm good for it."

The voice on the other end of the line wasn't too convinced. Already it was known even way out there that he was fucking up. The only thing that kept him plugged in was the connects he generated for them over the years, but now the new jacks coming up in the game could replace him easily without a problem. They were hungry and wanted to eat too.

"Okay...okay...I'll call later..."

People online in back of him were getting impatient. Charleston County had only one phone on the pods and the others were broke not looking at being repaired anytime soon. A tall, wavy-haired, dark-skinned brother they called 'Tree' pushed his way up front.

He'd lost whatever cool he had. "Yo' man...need to use the fuckin' phone, too!"

Moonie looked back at him. "I got you, just another minute..." Moonie was no slouch, he was big and brawly. He stood about five-eleven and weighed about two-hundred and forty pounds. He could hold his own.

"Man...fuck that!" Old boy snatched the phone out of his hand and hung it up, then pushed him off to the side.

Moonie fell up against the wall and charged back at him. He wrestled him to the ground and the guards came in and tackled them. One of the guards pulled out his spray and started aiming but they both stood down. No one was feeling their shit today. No windows opened from the inside and it would be pure hell dealing with pepper spray on this humid ass day.

Moonie got up off the ground with his hands in the air and walked off. "Sorry, 'bout that boss!"

He didn't need the headaches anyway and he knew he was dead wrong. He'd call later, his people had already told him to come back to Cali, but he just didn't want too. He was too scared for his life. They had already told him a hundred times already to stop fucking with tricks and get his mind focused on the business. He went to his cell and sat on his bunk. There was nothing else to do but wait. He'd be out soon, he hoped anyway according to what Sunshine had said.

He knew the address he gave them was legit and they should have gotten the money by now. A couple of days had already gone by, it had to be anytime now.

He was awakened from his nap by a call from the CO about a lawyer. He quickly got up and damn near ran to the booth where they sat. He was expecting Sunshine, maybe if he was lucky being that she got the money she'd let him get out today. He sat at the wide-screened plexiglass window and waited. The door opened, and he cocked his head to the side.

It wasn't her, but this chick was just as fine.

The public defender that was assigned to his case was a sexy, five-foot-seven and slim like a Tyra Banks lingerie model looking chick. She wore her hair up and you could tell it was long and curly. She had the type of eyes that you couldn't say no to, slanted and wide with thick lashes. Her full luscious lips screamed at you behind the gloss as she licked them. She sat down in front of him and he pulled himself together long enough to pick up the phone.

"My name is Tangie Singleton, I was assigned to represent you," she said.

"*Represent*!" Moonie repeated shocked.

"Yes, you have some serious charges and we could..." She looked through a folder with his mug-shot on the front.

"...possibly have to take this to trial."

"Trial...oh hell no! I was supposed to get a deal."

"A deal, really?" Tangie sat back and crossed her legs with a smirk on her face. The skirt she had on revealed her long tan, nearly flawless legs, and Moonie almost got distracted. "Who offered you a deal?" she asked.

"That god-damned, Albino chick!"

Tangie uncrossed her legs and leaned closer to the window. She looked around before speaking, "Sunshine...the D.A?"

"Yeah, that's her."
"What kind of deal did she offer you? Because right now,

there's nothing on the table."

Moonie's eyes grew wide. "I need to talk to her...now!"

He banged his fist on the desk and the officer peeped in.
Tangie waved him off. "Look you need to tell me exactly what they said."
"Naw...I can't snitch. That chick gave me a deal, she knows what's up."
Tangie shook her head and sighed. "Hear me out, right now, here on paper. You have no deal! You have a strike and you're looking at fifty years if you're lucky."

"But...she...told me..."

"To hell with what she told you. This is the lick right now. If you tell me exactly what she said then I can help you, but you gotta trust me."

"Why should I trust you? You all work together!"

"She works for herself. I know the shit she does, but I need someone to be man enough to confront her...bring her down."

Moonie knew even if he told her, he'd still be out of the money if Sunshine did get ahold of it. Then she could still drum up charges on him and he'd still get time. "I'll get up with you later, a'ight," he said.

"C'mon, now Mr. Moon, I can help you."

He got up. "I said later. I need to think this through." He slammed the phone down, then walked over to the payphone and got in line.

Tangie opened the files again and shook her head. He was another vick Sunshine got her hands on. She needed someone to go to bat with her, so she could take her down. "I'ma get your ass yet!"

Later that afternoon, Tangie stepped into her office, sat down at her desk and picked up the phone, then started pressing numbers. "Hello, it's Tangie Singleton. I need to speak with Sunshine Brown."

Sunshine was paged, she looked at the phone and after recognizing the number said, "Damn...now what?" before answering.

"Yeah, it's me."
"What you want, aren't you on some old save the world

type of shit? You ain't got enough cases?"
"Ha...ha, but I do. I have an ass load of cases. I have a trail and I want you to know it's just a matter of time."
"Damn, Tangie, you still sore with me after all these years? You always wanted to follow in my shoes, but you just
couldn't fit them, could you?"

"Fuck you!"
"Oh, is that what you want?"

"When I fuck you, you'll know it...trust me. And it won't be with no dick!"

"What you want, bitch? I ain't got all day."

"That's more like it." Tangie opened the files. "Moon Gregg, aka Moonie G. What's up with that? He said you offered him a deal."

Sunshine pulled the phone away from her face and banged her desk. She didn't need this shit now, and then with Tangie on her ass. "What deal? There's nothing on paper."

"I told him that, but he seems adamant about it. Expect a call from him soon."

"Look, I can offer him something. Let me get back with you okay."

"Hmm...you seem kinda jumpy about this."

"Tangie...I'm having a bad day, alright. I don't need this shit!"

"Yeah, well, let me tell you something. If I find out you've been giving people bad deals, 'I'ma nail your ass. You hear me?"

Sunshine giggled. "Please girl, you can't touch me. And you know this..." She giggled again. "...man!" Then she hung up the phone in Tangie's ear.

Tangie was pissed. She was tired of this bitch slipping through her fingers. Moonie had to be her ticket in. Her thoughts were pulled away abruptly when a detective came into her office. "Yes, can I help you."

He placed a photo on her desk in front of her. "Do you know him?"

She picked it up and sighed. "Yes! Now what?"

"We believe he was involved in a murder."

"*Murder*!"

"We want to know if you could get in touch with him."

Tell him to come in for questioning?"

She tossed the picture back at him. "I don't know where he's at officer."

"Well, you better get in touch with him, rather than us picking him up. If you know what I mean."

She looked up at him. *If you know what I mean*! What the hell was that about? Then it dawned on her, he was one of the investigators Sunshine used. He was right, they would probably kill him.

"I'll see what I can do," she agreed.

He placed his card on her desk and told her she could keep the picture.

"Thank you, I'll call when I find out something." She leaned back in her chair smiling. All the while keeping an eye on him waiting for him to disappear into the elevator. "Yeah, right!" She got up and threw on her coat, then raced out the door and yelled over to her assistant. "I'll be out of the office for a while. Set me up an appointment with Moon Gregg for this evening at the County!"

"You got your phone on you?"

She reached into her purse checking. "Yeah, call me if you need me." She pressed the elevator button impatiently while thinking to herself. '*What the hell did he get himself into now?*

Please, Jabari, just listen to me for once!"

MOONIE TAPPED HIS FEET impatiently while waiting his turn on the phone, wishing he'd copped the jack from the old head when he had the chance. Now, he looked around the pod for old dude figuring he could at least put a couple of dollars on his card easily if he could just get through to his people right now. He noticed a couple of inmates checking him out, sizing him up. He turned away from their stares, they noticed that he was that off-brand dude from California.

He was bumped intentionally by a short, dreadlocked, gold grilled G and he backed up looking him up and down waiting for some sort of an apology. If he didn't have to use the phone, he would've had to put something on his ass and let him know who he was fucking with.

"Yo' man, what's up?" Moonie asked.

"He stepped towards him and Moonie braced a leg up against the wall ready for the barrage of punches he was going to have to wall on him if he tried him, but it never came.

"Yo' man, I don't know you, but I'm tellin' you anyway. They checkin' you out. Watch y'o' back!" Then he walked off just as quick as he appeared.

Moonie looked back up at the steps on the top tier and they were gone. He looked around the pod and dude that had just approached him had disappeared too. He back up against the wall, beads of sweat began to rain down his face. He needed to get to the CO's booth quick. He stepped out the line out of sight and eased toward the desk, creeping slowly against the wall keeping an eye out for any out of the way motion towards him. As he got closer, he spotted a white shirt, a supervisor, coming through the door and he b-lined straight for him.

"Yo' Sarge...I need to talk to you, it's important!"

The sergeant read his body movements and looked into his eyes and knew it was serious. He escorted him out the door into the hall.

"What's the problem?" he asked.

"Yo' Sarge, there's a hit out on me. I need PC now! And I

wanna call my lawyer. I need to do this now..."

"Whoa, hold up, I just can't make no..."

"Please!" He grabbed his arms and the Sergeant's instincts told him something was up.

"Okay, but you got to go to your cell. I'll have the CO

lock you in, then I'll call your lawyer from up here, alright."

"Yeah!" He went back into the pod and the Sergeant whispered something to the CO.

He nodded his head as Sarge, walked out the door. He called Moonie over and told him to go to the cell he'd be right behind him to deadlock it. Everybody on the pod watched as it went down. Moonie didn't give a fuck his life was on the line. The next thing he knew all hell broke loose. Opposite the cell, a fight started, and a crowd had erupted, hollering and throwing chairs and shit. The CO picked up the red phone screaming for backup. Moonie stood by his door hoping the CO would pop the door quickly before the goon squad came. The CO waved him towards the desk but was suddenly distracted. Moonie turned toward him and all he saw next was darkness. Somebody had put a pillowcase over his head.

He struggled but it was no use they had a good yoke on him. He could smell the pepper spray that the CO unleashed as it choked at his nostrils, then he heard a voice that said in no certain way.

"You shoulda kept ya mouth shut!"

He could feel the stinging from the jabs and pokes at his abdomen from the searing hot blade ripping through his guts, liver, and kidneys. He sank to his knees and closed his eyes. Tears came gushing down his cheeks from the pain and all he could do was say a prayer. He realized he never should've gotten on that bus back in the day following his homeboys. He should have stayed home. He gagged and coughed, then felt the warm blood in his throat strangling him and fell over amid the stomps that put him to rest for good.

Sunshine flipped through cases on her desk with her assistant and was interrupted by the call. She excused herself and answered it. "Yeah...it's me!"

"It went down!"

"Good, you took care of that for me?"

"It's a done deal."

"Alright, check your books later."

"Hey, you gonna take care of my charges or what?"

"Hey...hey, not over the phone. I'll be in touch!"

"A'ight!"

"I might have something else for you to do anyway."

"What?"

"I need you to go sightseeing in the women's pod. You feel me?"

"Yeah...that's what's up. Who?"

"Later." She hung up the phone and walked back over to her meeting and picked up the folder with Dondi's picture on it, then tucked it into her desk.

Chapter Six

Tangie stepped out of the elevator into the lobby and ran straight into Clark Marshall. She was met by an intern in the District Attorney's Office. His face showed signs of alarm as he pulled her by the arm into an out of the way cubbyhole.

"There's something you need to know."

Tangie searched his face trying to figure out what was going on. The only thing she really knew about him was the fact that he was fucking around with Sunshine or at least she was using him. He wasn't bad looking at all, he stood six-feet-two, with the slim muscular frame of a basketball player and the feet to match. He was almost in a panic as he looked around to make sure no one saw them since Sunshine usually kept tabs on his comings and goings.

"What the hell is the matter?" Tangie asked.

"Look, there's some devious stuff going on." Tangie liked the fact that he didn't cuss.

How he got involved with Sunshine was beyond her. She was almost jealous. She tugged her arm away from him and backed up.

"Hell, you should know..." and it showed.

He sighed and put his head down, then took a deep breath and continued. "Yeah, yeah I know. One day I'll get it

113

together. I will, I just need a break that's all and she's my ticket."

Tangie moved closer and touched his hand. "You don't have to deal with that shit. It ain't right, she just can't handle you any way she wants.

"Ms. Singleton..."
"Tangie!"

"I'm on a scholarship, I don't have the type of money you guys have and I need a good job." He looked off. "I don't want to be locked up like the rest of..." his voice trailed off. "But, it's not about me, okay?"

"What's up, then?"

"I kinda peeped at Ms. Brown's notes and I came across something you should know about."

"C'mon wit it." Tangie stood against the wall with her arms crossed, looking up in his eyes.

She could tell that he was fed up with something and that this was indeed his last straw. She knew whatever he had to say was at least sincere but was it that serious because she was in a hurry.

"She has some stuff written down about you. Man, she wants your butt real bad...but, there was something about a girl that really ticked her off. Somebody by the name of Dondi, uh, I think it was Dondi Middleton or something. She had her picked up by Charleston PD this morning." He looked off from her and spotted some police officers coming in the building and shielded his face.

Tangie did the same until they want past. "I can't talk too long, somebody might see us." "Tell me quick and here..." Tangie reached into her purse retrieving one of her business cards. "...take my card and call me."

"Cool!" He took the card and stuffed it in the lapel of his jacket. "They got the girl upstairs and it don't look good."

"Whaat!"

"Yeah, they got her in one of those back rooms and it looks like they're gonna kick her...excuse my French Ms.

Tangie...ass, if not worse. You need to get her."

Tangie pushed past him on her way to the elevator. That was enough to let her know the seriousness of the situation, he cussed.

He caught her arm and said, "Please don't anyone I told you anything."

"No, of course not, remember call me!"

He dipped through the lobby and disappeared out of sight like he'd shrunk or something. She felt for him and made a mental note when he called to try to get him some help. She just hoped her motives were purer than Sunshine's. She pressed the elevator button frantically then remembered he never even said what room or floor they were on. But she did remember an old wing of the Courthouse that was roped off for repairs. Somehow, she knew it had to be there, she pushed four as she got into the empty elevator.

The fourth floor had indeed been roped off and the offices closed. Dust hung off the doors and the floor was full of it. She looked down and saw the fresh footprints that led to a room in the back. As she tipped slowly towards the office, she heard whispering then loud voices. She got closer and put her ear to the door.

"You gonna tell us what we need to know or else. You understand Missy?"

"Please, I don't know anything!"
"You said he came to see you, didn't he?"

"But he didn't say nuthin' to me about where he was going. I swear!"

The big-bellied officer stepped back and whispered something to the other officer and the man that stood next to them in a suit. He got closer then back-handed her.

"You know something!" he yelled.

"I...I swear to God, I don't know anything!" she shouted as she spit blood on the floor.

The officer started playing with the collar of the shirt she had on, rubbed his hands on her shoulders, then said, "I see,

you need some coercing, huh?" "Please...don't!" she cried.

He walked over to his buddies and snickered, making plans on who would go first. Taking that pussy was definitely where they were headed with this. She looked up at them and started crying, wondering why all men wanted to rape her so much? Her father, her father's friend, her whole life. These muthafuckas were no different from the men who picked her up on the street. Hell, she thought, all they had to do was get high with her and she would have just fucked all their brains out easily. She loved being a whore, but she let that thought go. It would be better anyway to fuck them than continuing to be beat. That would only get worse.

The cop and his other buddies moved in closer. One of them maneuvered around her and put his hands on her shoulders.

"Well, we do understand that you could fuck the shit outta anyone of us at any given time," the big-bellied cop remarked. "But..." He looked around at his comrades. "How about all of us at the same time? I mean, you can handle that, can't you?"

He snapped his fingers and the big, muscled, black cop stepped forward, reached into his pants and pulled out his dick.

"Ooohhh...my!" Dondi gasped.

It was rock-hard and huge, it had to be one of the biggest dicks she'd ever seen in her life. She tensed up, closed her eye and tears fell down her cheeks.

"Don't cry now... wait until he fucks you in the ass." He laughed out loud. "With no goddamned grease."

Dondi screamed as they threw her to the ground and started pulling her pants off.

"Then, while he's doing that you can suck my dick, huh. It ain't as big as his..." The white cop looked over at the big, muscled black dude snickering. "...but you can swallow all these white babies."

Dondi kicked at him, then a tall skinny, white cop with nerdy looking glasses punched her in the stomach and took the fight out of her. She stopped wriggling and closed her eyes.

"Do you..." Dondi said bitterly. "...but please don't kill me!"

"Then it better be some good ass!" the black cop said.

Tangie couldn't take anymore. She reached into her purse and pulled out the only weapon she had, pepper spray. She stuck it out with her blouse pulled over like she had a gun and charged into the room.

"Alright muthafuckas, enough!" She moved swiftly towards Dondi and grabbed her by the arm.

The cops moved back some, then one of them recognized

her. "It's that public defender bitch!"

"Damn!" the black cop said as he tried to hide his face. "If she tells..."

"Naw, she won't tell." The big-bellied cop slowly reached for his gun. He looked Tangie up and down and eased toward her. "Besides I always wanted some of that high-yellow ass anyway."

Both cops looked and smiled, one of them even replied,

"Yeah, me too."

Tangie pulled at Dondi and she got up then pushed her way towards the door.

"Go press the elevator," Tangie ordered Dondi.

Dondi hesitated at first, she didn't want to leave her by herself. Tangie however, had other plans, she pulled out and pointed in their direction, then pressed down on the pepper spray and held it tight. They gagged as the spray littered their eyes and nostrils. She ducked down, slid out of the door and bolted towards the elevator, just as they came to their senses and started running after her.

"Get that bitch!" one yelled.

Tangie and Dondi huddled close inside the back of the elevator waiting for it to close. Tangie still had her pepper spray in hand. Hearing the footsteps running down the hall they braced themselves for whatever, but the doors closed dead in their faces. They both let out a sigh of relief. Tangie hurriedly pressed two, thinking they would take the stairs. She knew enough to get off and hit the fire exit then make their escape to the back of the building and to her car.

They jumped in, she cranked up the bright silver Audi and pulled into traffic on East Bay Street hauling ass. She looked behind her up at Sunshine's office and she saw her standing in the window mean mugging.

She peered over at Dondi. "I don't know what you know

or don't know, but I gotta get you the fuck outta of town."
Dondi looked over at her puzzled. "Who the fuck are you?"
"Tangie Singleton! Would you believe I work back there?"
"Doing what?" Dondi shot back as she straightened up her clothes.

"Public Defender."

"Oh yeah, I heard of them but you're more like fuckin'

Foxy Brown or some shit. You something serious!" Tangie laughed. "And I'm looking for someone."

"Everyone is...who you looking for?"

"My brother."

"Your brother...who's that?"

"Jabari...Jabari Singleton!"

Dondi stopped fumbling with her clothes and stared her way. "So, you're the one...his sister?"
Tangie sighed. "Yeah, that's me. I'm sure you heard a lot about me, too. And a whole lot of it ain't been good, I bet."
Dondi pointed to a restaurant on Rivers Avenue and told her to pull around the back. "Look, before we go any further. You need to tell me what the fuck is going on...now! I'm not

sayin' nuthin' else until then. I'm tired of this shit!"

Tangie agreed, she went in and ordered them some food, then got back into the car and took a sip of the hot coffee she bought. Tangie put the coffee in a cup holder making sure it was secured before turning to face Dondi. Tangie took a deep breath and exhaled, then closed her eyes for a moment. Dondi caught her movements, realizing she was praying, Dondi also put her head down, then reached over and grasped her hands tightly.

After completing her prayer, Tangie said, "Amen!"

Dondi reached over for her cup, blew the steam off the top of the hot brew, and waited for every word to come off her lips.

"I want you to know that I love my brother with all my heart and soul believe me. But I had no control over..." She paused then looked off.

Dondi grabbed her hand again and squeezed it. "It's okay!"

Tangie smiled and continued. "I remember when we were little. Jabari was bad and all, but he was so small and chubby. My mama always had him in her tickling him and stuff, spoiling him." She grinned, her thoughts were all over the place along with her emotions. "Not that I was jealous or anything, hell, I tickled him all the time myself. He was just one happy kid."

"Excuse me...Ms...Singleton..."

"Please call me, Tangie!"

"Tangie, how old were you all then?"

"Well, I was about seven and Jabari was like, uh, let's

see...three. Yeah, he'd just turned three!"

"You remember way back like that?"

Tangie smiled and said teasingly. "C'mon, girl, I ain't that old."

"I'm sorry, I didn't mean it like that."

"I'm messing with you. Anyway, our father worked construction and my mom did secretary work downtown at an art gallery. She loved herself some art, she was always bringing home different prints or paintings she wanted us to see. My dad had his own business and was always busy, but don't get me wrong he always had time to be with us."

"Okay...so what happened?"

Tangie took a long swig of the coffee and started to chew on her bottom lip.

Dondi rubbed her arm. "That's what your brother would do when he was worried about something."

Tangie smiled again and a twinkle seemed to appear in

her eyes. "He got it from, mama."

"So, what happened?"

"Oh, yeah, everything was going well. I'd just turned ten and Jabari was a big old boy then. It happened so quick!" She rubbed the brow of her forehead. "All I know is I was at school and the principal came and got me and rushed me to his office. I thought I was in trouble or something. There were a lot of cops there. The nurse took me by the hand and told me something bad had happened." She started chewing on her lip again and caught Dondi staring at her.

"Sorry! They rushed me to the house and there were a lot of cop cars in front of the house. A crowd of people was also gathered around the house. I came through the door and saw my father sitting on the couch crying. I ran over to him, then I looked around and didn't see Jabari. I asked where he was, and he pointed to the kitchen.

I ran in and saw him sitting at the table with some men in suits standing around him. The next thing I knew they were taking him out the door. I remember him crying and hollering, looking back at us as they carried him off to a car and drove away.

"My dad didn't say anything...not a word. He just looked down shaking his head. I ran around the house calling out for my mother. I rushed to the bedroom and just before I opened the door someone grabbed my arm, trying to stop me, but it was too late." Tangie reached for a napkin and dabbed at the tears in the corner of her eyes. "Blood was all over the floor and the bed was soaked with it. I saw my mother lying face down. I screamed out for my mama as loud as I could, and she didn't move."

"Oh my, God," Dondi gasped. "Was she alright?"

"She was dead, but that wasn't all. A man laid naked over by the window. Blood was splattered all over his him and the all, he was dead too."

"Damn, Tangie!" Dondi reached for her. "I'm so sorry."

"My grandmother, my father's mother took me to her house, and I didn't see Jabari no more for years. I asked about him from time to time and they would always say the same thing. Something about him living somewhere else. They wouldn't say where, though. I cried all the time, my father, well he just went about his business as if nothing happened. I

didn't even see my brother at my mama's funeral."

"What happened?"

"I later found out, at least from my father's version. Evidently, my mother was supposedly cheating on him with one of his laborers. My father followed him to the house one day and caught them in bed together. Said the guy started shooting at him and he ended up shooting them both. The cops said it was self-defense. Said they found the gun he had with his prints. I really don't know... it didn't seem right to me then and it doesn't now. My father's people paid a lot of folks off.

That's how he would get his contracts."

"What happened to, Jabari, where did he go?"

"He never went to my other grandmother's house like I thought. He was sent to a mental hospital and then to foster care. My father said he was too sick or him to take care of, so he was bounced around from foster home to foster home. I never really heard about him except what my father told me,

and he always said he was sick...*crazy*."

"Oh my, God!"

"But the deal was this, Jabari had actually seen everything. The cops had him down as a witness. He said my father murdered my mother and set up his worker to take the fall. Said my dad was fuckin' around with his secretary or some shit.

Had to be true cause he married her ass right after that. And all the time I didn't know a damn thing." Tangie stared aimlessly out of the window, tears were running freely now. "I kept asking about him, but it was the same old thing over and over...he's crazy. I felt real bad for a while but my father's family...they had money. And one thing about money, enough of it makes a whole lot disappear. They sent me to all the good

schools, bought me a lot of...stuff."

"Did you ever see him at any time after that?"

"I remember this one time he came up to the school I was in. a real good well-off school. He came on the campus, he found me and flashed this real bright smile...like when he was a little boy. He tried to hug me, but I pushed him away. He was wearing these old clothes and looked scraggly. He'd been living at the shelter. I was around all my rich girlfriends and I felt ashamed...better than him. Would you believe that? I felt ashamed of my own brother!" she banged the top of the steering wheel, almost spilling her coffee and started sobbing heavily. Dondi sat silently, not saying a word and Tangie went on. "The look in his eyes, I'll never forget. He felt so unwanted. He tried coming with me to the house. He wanted my father to help him and bring him back home. But my father called

the fuckin' cops on him like he was nothing."

"Damn, Jabari...damn." Tears started forming in Dondi's eyes as well.

"He started doing drugs and I can't blame him. God knows what happened to him all those years in those shelters."

"God knows and...I know too. I know his pain, trust me!"

Tangie glanced over at her. "I'm sorry, I never should have..."

"Get it out, Tangie, you need to."

"When I got to college and became more aware. I guess you can call it that. I knew I was dead wrong, but I still didn't know where he was. The next time I saw him was when my father died, and he came to the funeral...drunk and high. I tried to talk to him, but he didn't want nothing to do with me or any of us. They tried to call the cops on him, and I wouldn't let them. When everyone left, I spotted him at the

burial site...pissing on my father's grave."

"Hmph...that's all, sorry, 'bout that."

"That's alright, you know my brother. You how he is, I tried to talk to him, and he looked square in the eyes and said, *That, bastard killed our mother and they let him get away with it!* I tried to talk to him, but he made it clear we were no longer family. He said he would see me in hell before he'd ever fuck with me again. He told me to kiss his ass and then just walked off."

"But, didn't he still see you from time to time? I mean, he would still talk about you."

"Yeah, but I'm sure it wasn't good. He'd cuss me out, but I never gave up on him...I never will." Tangie looked at her wiping her eyes. "Were you there when he threw me out in the street in front of the hotel?"

"Naw, but I heard about it. I cussed his ass out if it makes you feel any better. But, of course, he paid me no mind."

Tangie pulled herself together and drove to the hotel were Dondi was staying but not before she had her search around the block looking to spot any strange vehicles thinking maybe the cops had come after them or someone would be spying on them. After riding around they both came to the conclusion that there was on one. They both thought it was strange but Tangie knew one thing for sure that eventually things would blow-up once Sunshine made her move. They pulled into the hotel's office area and Pasheeva waved them down.

They stopped only after he ran out and damn near jumped in front of the car. "Wait...hold up, hold up!"

Tangie rolled down the window after Dondi gave her the run-down about who he was and what he was about. "Can I help you?" Tangie asked.

"The police came and searched through your room," he said.

"What! You let them?" Dondi shrieked angrily.

"What could I do? They had a paper that said they could." He shrugged his shoulders. "I locked the door, they left it wide open."

"Damn," Dondi said. "I wonder if they anything?"

"They looked like they weren't really looking for anything in particular, but the place is still torn up." He eased closer and closer until he was leaning on the door.

"Thank you, sir," Tangie said as she started pulling off.

He held on tightly to the window. "Wait, look...uh..." He stared over at Dondi studying her body, literally undressing her with his eyes. It made her feel uncomfortable and after all, she'd been through today she squirmed. Tangie quickly caught on.

"You...uh remember what we talked about, heh?" he said as he glanced back toward the office. Beads of sweat appeared on his forehead as he licked his lips lustfully. Tangie caught on to that as well. "My wife went to her relative's place, she won't be home till later." He started checking out Tangie's legs. "Maybe...the two of us can have some...fun!"

Dondi waved him off. "No...not now..."

"But you said so, I mean, it's a good time." He drummed up the nerve and reached in to feel Tangie's thighs. "The both of us can..."

Tangie rolled the window up on his arm and he screamed, then pulled him closer to the window. His face was mushed on the glass. "Look, whatever y'all two had planned...or discussed. "She pulled out her badge and showed it to the glass in front of his face. "It's over with!" She turned around to
Dondi. "Is the bill paid or what?"

"It's paid for the rest of the month," she said.

"Well, then...sir, if there's nothing else.' She let go of him.

Pasheeva mean mugged her but backed off slowly. He didn't want to scrap with Tangie today and the look in eyes confirmed it. "Bye." She gunned the gas and damn near ran

over his foot. "Now which room, Dondi?"

Dondi pointed to the room and she pulled into a spot, grabbed her purse and started getting out. Dondi reached over and grabbed Tangie's arm. "Look, my life is different from yours. I have to do what I have to do, at times, ya know."

Tangie looked at her and sighed. "Believe me, I know the feeling, but, right now, at least it's over. I need you to be

straight cause this shit is serious, alright."

"You sound just like your brother," she said as she got out of the car sucking her teeth.

"Yeah..." They walked to the door and opened it.

Pasheeva was right, the place was a wreck. Her mattress was flipped over and cut up. The drawers were pulled out and clothes were strewn all over. Dondi's, Rip's and Jabari's papers had been scattered over the floor.

"They were definitely looking for something, Dondi." Tangie threw some clothes off a char and sat down, then asked. "Now, do you know where my brother is?" It was getting late and she needed to get down to business. She still had to get up with Moonie G.

Dondi started picking up things and tossing them on the bed. "He didn't say where he was going."

"Hmmm...hell." She peeped through the blinds and looked around outside. "He could be watching us, right now."

Dondi paused for a second and looked her way. "Naw, he was definitely leaving Charleston. He wouldn't need a car, it'd be too hot for him."

"You're right, so...damn, where did he go?"

Dondi picked up some cards and stared at them, then scanned around and picked up a plastic blindfold. "Damn, here's Rip's wallet."

"Rip, who is Rip?" Tangie asked.

Dondi came racing over to her, showing her a photo.

"Rip, the one who was killed, he stayed here with me."
"Okay...I see."

She shoved his I.D. in her pocket. "I got what I need now. I can finally find his family, but damn, I need to go downtown and claim the body." She grabbed Tangie by the hand. "Take me...please!"

"Wow, you really liked this guy?"

Dondi sat on the floor next to her and stared at the picture. "I guess...I miss him."

"Pass me the phone."

Dondi did as Tangie requested, dialed some numbers, turned away then said something Dondi couldn't hear. "They're going to hold the body for you so let's clean up this mess and I'll take you down there," Tangie told her, scratched her head as she scanned the room, looking for a place to start. "I know some people that can find his family too. We'll make sure he gets a decent burial."

Dondi hugged Tangie. "Thank you, Tangie.
Tangie pushed her away a little and held her nose up.

"Girl, you need to jump in some water."
Dondi's face turned flushed red and she smelled under her arms. "Ooohhh...damn! So much has been going on." She searched the floor for some clothes and dashed into the bathroom.

Tangie picked up some papers then leaned on the bathroom door. "Dondi, was Rip and Jabari together that day?"

Dondi pulled back the curtain to the shower exposing herself. Tangie couldn't help but admire her shapely presence, curved body, and smooth chocolate skin.

"I'ma tell you, but you can't mention it to no one else. Yes, they left out of her together."

"You have to tell me something, Dondi, so I can help."

"Look, you saved my life, so I owe you something, but there's just not a whole lot I know. There's one thing though!" She got out of the shower dripping wet and walked past her.

Tangie was taken aback at her exhibition and even admired her confidence in her own body as she walked. She knew she was fine, and it showed. She reached for the vanity mirror over the sink, wriggled it and it came off its hinges into her arms. Behind it was a plastic bag, taped up on the wall holding some white, tarnish, powdery chunks in place. She laid the mirror down and reached for the canvas bag next to it.

"He gave me some money, here's what's left of it," Dondi said.

Tangie took it and counted what was there. "Where did he get this?"

"He didn't say, he just told me to lay low. And to use it to pay rent and eat. He told me not to get high or anything with it, but..." She pointed to the plastic bag. "I have my own stash."

Tangie grabbed it. "If he told you to stay clean, Dondi. Then that's what it is." Dondi grabbed for it back and Tangie scolded her. "Look, girl, you got too much shit going on already to be fucking with this shit. Aren't you tired of this bullshit?"

Dondi looked up at Tangie pouting like she was going to cry, like a big kid. But she conceded and stomped back inside the shower sloshing around.

"You're right, but just do this. Put it away for me because if shit doesn't work out. I'ma get good and fucked up." She reached out the shower curtain for a towel and Tangie tossed her one.

"Trust me, Dondi, things will work out." Tangie put the money and dope back in place and put the mirror back over it.

She didn't have no wins, hell, if Dondi was going to get high she could, easily. She picked up a shirt and wiped it down getting rid of her prints, then walked back over to her chair and sat down, fumbling with some papers she'd picked up along the way. She spotted a picture of Jabari. He was smiling like there was no tomorrow, like when he was a kid. He was standing side by side with Dondi and someone else.

"Cute guy," she said to herself.

He had curly hair and sported a close-cropped mustache. He was quite handsome Tangie was caught up in her own thoughts until Dondi came over and pointed to the guy.

"That's Rip, we was at the fair when we took this. Jabari used to say that we were his only family. Hell, I thought he was bullshittin', but I guess he wasn't, huh."

Tangie peeped up at her running her finger gently on the photo across his face. "Yeah...I guess."

Dondi walked off feeling sorry for Tangie and Jabari.

Chapter Seven

Sunshine stood staring out the window seemingly at nothing in particular. She'd just witnessed Tangie jump into her car and speed away. The one person that could jeopardize her career and it didn't sit well with her at all, but she had other plans. A backup, she smirked, Tangie was good for now. Dondi, on the other hand, didn't know anything anyway, she was just collateral damage. She'd get rid of her dumb ass in the mix one way or another, later.

The door swung open behind her, she didn't move or even flinch. She was expecting the person who entered the room.

"So, how did it happen?" she asked.

The man who stood in front of her desk opened his coat. The room was hot, stuffy and filled with tension. The shiny glistened of the badge he wore glinted off the window.

"Shit happens," he said sheepishly.

Sunshine turned facing him and shook her head, then giggled. "Somehow or another..." she pulled her chair back and sat down, then swung her legs up on the desk in front of him. She could see his eyes were now traveling up her skirt, so she obliged and cocked her legs open slightly. "...it had something to do with pussy, huh?"

132

He caught himself staring and losing his train of thought. He knew he had to be real cool and careful when dealing with her. "Oh, no that Public Defender chick had a gun."

"Tangie...Tangie had a gun?" She leaned forward, probing the lie he was telling.

"Yeah, and she just charged in. Hell, we thought she was gonna shoot. Didn't need no bloodshed in the building, ya know. I mean...it was broad daylight..." He started rubbing the back of his neck. The anxiety in his face spoke volumes.

She waved at him. "Get outta here, baby. You're telling me nerd ass, little old, Tangie Singleton came in with a gun and you all just let them get away?" She snapped her fingers. "Just like that, huh?"

"Yeah, uh something like that."

"Oh, that's just great. I'm sure you *tried* to stop them." She waved him over to the desk. "But...it must have been hard." She grabbed him by his tie and pulled him around the desk.

"With your pants down, huh?"

"Uh...no, I wasn't doing any..."

"No...it's cool." She had him around the desk in front of her now with him on his knees. "I understand, Chief." She grabbed him by his neck, thrust his head between her legs and squeezed down. "But you know what, I forgive you...ahhh...there you go right there. Aahhh...you knew you'd have to pay, now didn't you?" The Police Chief tried to get some air, he pulled back, but she squeezed tighter and wrapped her legs around his neck making him gag as he tried coming up for some air. "C'mon now, Chief, you know the lick already, just go with it. Maybe I won't be so hard on you. I know you like this shit." She leaned back and gyrated her pussy into his face as his tongue lapped up the hot cum that she sprayed into his mouth. "Oh...ahhh...by the way...baby, how's that pretty little wife of yours doing? Aahhh...yeah...stay right there." She loosened up a little and he looked up at her. "She's do-

ing...oh...shit, what the fuck!"

In front of her eyes was a small, handheld, Sony recorder she had dangling in front of him. He tried to push it out of his face, but she kicked him back away from her.

"What are you gonna do with that!" he hollered.

She smiled and licked her lips. "I'm sure that pretty little wife of yours wouldn't mind watching a nice video." He tried to grab it. "No, no, no..." She snatched it away then put her finger to her phone by the speed dial, straight to security. "I'm sure you wouldn't want no one busting up in here...seeing little old me in this vulnerable position, now would you?"

The Police Chief held his hand down. "What do you want, Sunshine?"

"Sun...what! Oh, hell naw, we ain't cool like that. Now, try again."

"Ms. Brown," he humbly replied.

"That's better." She pointed him to a chair in front of her desk and told him to sit down. "I'm gonna give you one more fuckin' chance. Find that bitch...both of them and take care of the matter, discreetly! Or else your pretty little wife, that daughter of a goddamned Senator will find this tape in the mail...her personal mail, too. You dumb muthafucka! I bet your dumb ass didn't know she has her own P.O. box?"

"C'mon, please, Ms. Brown. I just had a baby..."

"Fuck that! You should have thought about all that shit when you let those bitches getaway! Now get the fuck outta my office."

The Police Chief got up, turned towards the door and walked off. He shook his head, opened the door and exited making sure it was closed behind him. "Bitch!" he mumbled under his breath.

She heard him and smiled, then spun around with the camera in front of her watching what had just gone down.

"That's Ms. Bitch!" She started giggling.

JABARI DUG A HOLE THROUGH his pockets searching for some sort of relief. The ride had his mind racing once again and he didn't have any more pills to stop it. He did, however, stop long enough for him to buy a forty-ounce of Magnum that mellowed him somewhat, but he didn't want to be too bent on the road just in case a Trooper pulled him over. About thirty-five miles deep he made the last bend on the long-curved road into the country and off in a ditch he spotted the sign he was looking for. It stood off to the side, faded and was worn from years of weathered abuse and long-neglected service. Boonie Doone, a small, affluent, gated community, once a haven for slaves and one-time former plantation that thrived on rice paddies and tobacco money. Now overcome by shallow, elevated water and swamp.

Jabari's old man used to tell him that this was where hangings went down and as he looked off at the distant oak trees bent over with long whitened willows from years gone by, it all looked so surreal before his eyes. He could picture muthafuckas hanging off the limbs by their necks. Jabari drove further down the long winding road that was crowded with huge oak trees on both sides until it finally opened up into a clearing with three-story Victorian homes surrounded by six-foot tall, iron fences. Jabari drove to the security booth that stood sentry at the front and slowed down. No one was there so he eased in and made his way around to a road that threaded through very wealthy woods.

It had been a while but aside from a few taller trees here and there and a couple of hedged bushes he admired and newly configured, concrete driveways, it was all the same. Littered along the freshly cut, manicured lawns were Benzes, Beamers and F-150s, all new. Jabari stood out like a sore thumb as he crept through with his Maxima. He strained his brain trying to remember which house, was it brown the last time he saw it? He'd been there a couple of times before, but it wasn't clicking.

He'd met this dude at one of the many foster homes he'd been in, apparently, he'd been caught getting high with his friends in the garage one night. He swore up and down somebody ratted him out and Jabari believed him. How in the hell would DEA know to come into a gated community and bust into his garage at just the right time, while they just happened to be getting high and bagging weed. That wasn't the bad thing, though. They searched the premises and found one-hundred and fifty or so pounds of weed and some meth. DEA fucked around and busted everyone in the whole damn house. Come to find out his mom was fucking some Mexican dude on the side, who was part of the Cartel.

Hell, this guy was trafficking pounds of weed and growing shit in the woods behind the house. The Mexican figured who the hell would go way out there? He must've stepped on somebody's toes or fucked the wrong pussy cause they was on his ass. Anyway, after some questioning from ball to his mom's, old boy was busted and sent up the road real quick. Jabari's partner, Dunnington Doral or Double D as he was called, was taken from his folks for a while and put into foster care, with Jabari as his roommate.

At first, there was some bad blood between them. It was pretty much on some black and white, racism shit, but the common ground was dope. Eventually, they got past that and became friends. They both loved to get high, he still had connects and from time to time Jabari would help him move a pound or two. He wanted to go into the hoods and make money, so Jabari became his frontman, making sure he didn't get shitted on or robbed.

"Okay, there it go!" Jabari said finally finding the house.

The two-story home still looked the same, trimmed in white with a jazzy front porch, and bricked stoops, a garage off to the side with a white awning trimmed in black above it and right directly in the back was the small barn where they'd get lit up.

"Damn the memories!" Jabari said smiling. "I can't wait to see the muthafucka."

A Benz and a brand spanking new Cadillac sat in the driveway. Jabari peeped his eyes around the back and spied the in-ground pool and horse stables. Jabari parked behind the cars and that's when he noticed the front porch window curtains being opened slightly.

"Damn, I hope he still lives here. If not, I'm going to jail for trespassing...if not worse." Jabari said continuing to stare toward the curtains.

The curtains opened and kept closing, Jabari couldn't quite make out the face as he walked towards the frosted glass, enclosed door, very cautiously. He was not trying to get shot by some old, gung-ho, white man or woman. Jabari rang the doorbell and the door opened. Jabari thought the scene was similar to something you'd see on TV or movies. A black man ringing the doorbell and a white woman answering dressed in nothing but a bathrobe.

"Hey, Mrs. Davis," Jabari said.

There she stood in front of him with a pink, fluffy, terrycloth robe on, opened and revealing cleavage for days. The belt was tied tightly around her small, petite waist and her round shapely hips were supported by tanned, nearly flawless legs.

"Jabari!" she yelled, flying straight into his arms, puckering up her bright, red, glossed lips.

Granted when they were kids, she would this and they'd get a kick from it. But right now, Jabari was a grown man and his dick was hard as hell. He knew she felt it as he moved in closer to accept her kisses. He ran his hands through her long, thick hair that ran down her backside. Jabari had to keep his cool to keep from grabbing ahold of her ass. Her tongue slipped briefly into his mouth and he met it with his.

It seemed liked it was just about to go to another level as he pulled her closer towards him.

"Mrs. Davis!" somebody interrupted, calling her from the kitchen.

Jabari pushed her away slightly, not knowing what to expect. Was it, Double D? Because it damn sure didn't sound like him, the person sounded Spanish at best. Mrs. Davis grabbed Jabari by the hand and walked towards the kitchen. Jabari followed like a child hoping she'd cut to her bedroom and ignore it. They walked into the kitchen and there was a Mexican with tools in his hands working on the sink. Another was underneath the counter fucking around with the pipes. He stood in front of them with a monkey wrench observing the fact that they were holding hands. He didn't look too fucking goddamned pleased either.

"Mrs. Davis, uh, we need to cut off the water main," he said as he looked Jabari up and downsizing him up.

Jabari checked him out also, especially the pipe he held in his hands. Jabari didn't want no shit, so he backed up a little to the doorway ready for whatever.

Mrs. Davis walked over to him and rubbed his shirtless chest. "Jose, uh...we could do that...a little later..." She danced her fingers on his chest and he smiled liked a muthafucka.

Jabari knew what that was, she was still up to her old tricks. She was horny as hell, but Jabari wouldn't have mind tapping some of that ass his damn self.

"Jabari, what brings you out here?" Mrs. Davis asked as she grabbed ahold of his hand and directed him to the living room.

"I was in the neighborhood, so I thought, I'd stop by." Jabari looked around for the presence of another man or anyone else in the house and saw nothing except the half-emptied mini-bottles lined up. Jabari got a bead on a prescription bottle that sat on the mantle, O-C's...Oxycotine. "What the fuck is up with this chick?" Jabari mumbled under his breath.

They sat down on the couch and she crossed her legs. Her robe slid further up her legs and she smiled once she saw Jabari staring, she was damn near drolling.

"Wow, you've really grown up...haven't you?" she said admiring him like a lion watching a steak.

"Yeah." Jabari started rubbing his neck, getting uncomfortable. Mrs. Davis had Jabari feeling like a piece of meat. "I thought, I'd see what Double D was up to, that's it."

It was over just like that, her whole fucking demeanor changed. Worry marks appeared like rain clouds in a desert across her forehead and she dug in her robe pockets and took out a cigarette. Jabari reached for the matches on the table and lit it for her. After she took a deep breath, she sighed and ran her hands through her hair.

"He doesn't live anymore..." she began.

"Oh, well I didn't know. Did he move out..."

"Hell no, and go where? That little bastard stole everything I didn't have nailed down."

'What the hell is this nigga up to now?' Jabari thought.

He really needed to crash there for a while, but Double D had fucked that up. Jabari had to find another spot quick. He wouldn't have minded staying there with Mrs. Davis, but she'd fuck the shit out of him every day. He couldn't take that, besides he needed to get high on a regular just to function. So, it probably wouldn't have worked out anyway. As he looked at the way she pulled on the cigarette and started rubbing her arms, she was fiening right now, so the hell was he.

He looked over at her pill bottle, got up and grabbed it. Then he popped the top and walked over to her, handing her one. She smiled nervously and hesitated at first until Jabari nudged his hands towards her.

"It's cool," he said.

Mrs. Davis reached for one and Jabari handed her the bottle of Johnny Walker Red off the table by the fireplace, and she searched for a shot glass. Jabari brought the bottle up to his mouth and took a swig, then handed her the bottle. She grabbed the bottle from him and took two to the head, then handed him back the bottle and laid back. It was what it was, they were two goddamned junkies just from two different environments. She wiped her mouth with the back of her hand.

"He started messing around with that goddamned meth," she said.

Jabari was shocked, he expected to hear anything but that. He knew Double D did weed mostly, but he would've never thought he'd get involved with meth. But then again, a lot of white boys were caught up on that shit.

"Wow, meth, what happened?" Jabari asked.

"He met some girl from town and next thing I knew he was losing weight and shit. He'd even stopped eating." She reached for the bottle again and Jabari passed it to her. "He'd by up...wide-eyed for days. It was crazy!" She took a swig and passed Jabari the bottle. The more she drank and started acting like a drunk, the better she looked to Jabari.

"So, where'd he go?" Jabari asked.

"Somewhere in the country...the swamps, with some ole white trash..." She started slurring her words. Her mind drifted off and on, the pills had started taking effect. "I don't give a fuck, he just fuckin' left me, ya know. His own mutha...eff..." She dug into a drawer next to the couch, pulled out a telephone book and flipped through it. "Here's his number, it's a pager. When I need to hear from him, I page him, and he calls me right back." She scribbled down the number. "Takes about fifteen to twenty minutes or so."

Jabari reached for it, the area code was local, so he wasn't too far away. "Okay, thanks." Jabari looked over at the kitchen and peeped the Mexican headed their way, he pointed to him.

Mrs. Davis looked over her shoulder smiling. "Is it finished, Jose?"

He mean-mugged the fuck out of Jabari and said, "No, Mrs. Davis, ma'am. I need to look at the plumbing." He glanced at the stairway leading to the bedroom. "Upstairs?" He asked tugging at his tool belt.

She turned Jabari's way and grinned. Oh...the plumbing, that's right." She started straightening up her hair. "Yeah... that sound about, right. Make sure you bring the right...uh, pipe!"

"Oh...I have just the right size..." He shot back with his mouth fixed into a sly smirk.

Jabari had, had enough of the bullshit game they were playing. It was making him sick to his stomach. "Okay, look..." he got up. "...I'll page him and uh, see what's up."

Mrs. Davis got up and walked Jabari to the door. She hugged him again as she opened it, squeezing his ass. "Next time come by earlier." She whispered into his ear.

Jabari laughed it off and looked over her shoulder at the dumb faced Mexican standing behind them. "Will you be alright here by yourself?"

"Trust me, these guys service the whole goddamned neighborhood. You know what I mean? After they leave

here...they have another job. Isn't that right, Jose?"

Jabari knew exactly what Mrs. Davis meant, but he played along with it. "Another job? Damn, they stay busy."

"At some other's whore's house," she remarked then pushed Jabari out the door softly and blew him a kiss.

"I'll call you back later, anyway, a'ight," Jabari said.
"Alright, Jabari, love you!"
"I love you, too!"

The door closed and Jabari walked to the car looking back at the window and got a glimpse of Jose bending over her as she sat back down. She eased back in the chair with her eyes closed and Jose had disappeared out of view, probably on his knees, Jabari figured. Jabari looked at the number in his hand, he needed to head into town and find a phone to call Double D. He had to find out what the hell he was up to and where he was at. He definitely couldn't go back to Charleston, not right now, at least until he got in touch with Dondi again after a couple of days and found out what was happening.

HULIE STEPPED OUT ON the porch of the two-story walk-up on the north side of North Charleston called the Height. Walking over to the side of the house, he glanced over at his bike, the Suzuki, the beast. It had been a minute since he rode it. He didn't have no real loot on the streets just little odds and ends, enough to keep his face out there. He thought about doing some pickups later, perhaps, but he needed to get up with Diplite. So, he could find out what was going on in Liberty Hill. Besides, he needed to find out about T-Black's mom and whether it was true that she was still alive or not.

He chatted with some hustlas walking to the poolroom and they asked him if he wanted to hang out. He needed some rest, he was stressing and had been worrying a lot lately. Sunshine was fucking with his head. His cell phone went off on his hip and he twitched a little then checked the screen. It was Sunshine...again. He ignored it and it vibrated once more. He tried to pay it no mind, but it was just too damn persistent.

"Fuck it," he said answering the phone trying not to go ham. "Didn't I tell you, I'd get in touch with you later?" The voice was silent on the other end. "Yo' speak the fuck up!" "What did I do?"

He jerked the phone away from his ear and grimaced. "Damn!" He needed a break, it wasn't Sunshine it was Cleo.

"Oh, sorry 'bout that babe."

"You alright? I haven't seen you in a while...a good, long while!" Cleo was Hulie's main hoe on the side.

She tricked on the block where his traps were set up. She steered clientele and kept her ears to the streets. Letting him know if there was any other rock blockers out there or even if somebody was trying to tread on his zone.

"Been a minute," he said.

"You think? You can come pick me up, we can spend some time together?" Cleo paused, hoping he'd say yes.

Hulie had a quick temper and he'd spaz in a heartbeat. She also had some money for him and some information she thought he'd be interested in. Anyway, you put it, she just wanted to be with him. Even though he was rough with her, he was her type of man. A thuggish, ruggish ball. She'd do anything for him, even trick. Her brother Diplite hated it, but he didn't have a say-so in the matter. All he really wanted to do was pimp her out anyway and make money off her himself. He wanted her to keep the money in the family, all while rubbing his hand on her ass. He was one sick muthafucka.

"I'm over at the Pink Panther...if you want to see me. Oh, yeah, I got some money for you, too!" She wanted to sweeten up the pot.

Hulie smirked, all she was doing was paying for his service, he really didn't need the money she offered, maybe the info, but definitely not the money. It was chump change in comparison to the bread he made off the streets, but nevertheless, he took it anyway. He respected her grind, most times he'd let her buy an outfit or two from the mall, get dressed up and go out to eat somewhere, then maybe they'd go to the club. Cleo was a good-looking chick, and she was classy too. Having her on his arm made him look good, so she was like a main squeeze of sorts. She didn't want nothing of him, but his time and he was cool with that.

"A'ight, let me get changed and I'll meet you over there...bout half an hour," Hulie said.

"Cool, I'll see you then," she said and hung up.

Hulie walked into the house and peeped in his closet, moving around clothes on the rack. He checked out a RocaWear linen, casual outfit and laid it on the bed, feeling good. He walked back out the door and peeped out, then locked it and dipped into the bathroom and started running the shower. He got undressed and just before he stepped in, he heard someone knocking on the door real hard.

"Damn," he said under his breath. "Hope it ain't fuckin' ball." He grabbed a bathrobe and slipped it on then peeped out the side window. He didn't see no one so he glanced out in the street and saw the car, the all-white, red interior, Beamer and knew exactly who it was. He marched to the door, pissed off and swung it wide open. "Sunshine, what the fuck you want?"

She stood her bowlegged ass in the doorway, looking fabulous as ever, wearing a full length, silk, trench coat that showed off her vivacious curves, then popped open the one button that held it closed and it swayed open against the breeze that raced through the doorway. Underneath was a red, laced push-up bra and a matching thong. This held

Hulie's attention like a muthafucka and his knees buckled.

She smiled. "Just thought I'd stop by."

Hulie back up slightly, focusing on the dime-piece that stood in front of him. She was fine as all fucking outdoors, but also the snake that would eventually bite him in the ass.

He frowned up at the thought.

"Girl, what the hell you want?" he asked.

She pulled open her coat and struck a more provocative pose, showing that ass. "No, it's more like, what the hell do you want?"

"I don't want shit, I told you, I'd call you later, didn't I?"

She giggled as she peered down at his robe. His dick had gotten hard as a rock and came out of hiding behind his robe.

"I can't tell." She brushed past him.

Hulie looked out the door to see if anyone was looking, then slammed it shut. "I told you never to come here. Muthafuckas might think I'm snitchin' and shit." He closed the curtains and blinds then turned towards her, she was right up on him in his face.

He could smell the rose scented perfume she wore, and it hypnotized him for a brief moment. She brushed her long locks of hair over her shoulders and pushed closer to his body. "You mean...you really want me to go?" She teased.

Hulie's dick was just about to take control of the situation, but he had to pull it together and tighten up quick. He put his hands in front of him and pushed her gently away from him.

"C'mon, now, I got somewhere to go," he said.

She started a mock striptease as she took off her coat and tossed it on the sofa beside him then walked towards his bedroom door. "Yeah, right here in this room!"

It took all he had to say no cause he really wanted the pussy bad like a muthafucka. He walked over to her slowly, his dick tripping him up and grabbed her by the arm, roughly this time. He led her to the sofa and threw her down.

She smiled. "Oh, you want it rough? I'm down!"

Hulie shook his head, she just wouldn't let up and plopped down on a chair across from her. "Look, we need to talk."

She straightened herself up after hearing the seriousness of the tone of his voice. "Talk...talk about what? We can talk later, I want some dick, Hulie!" Her mouth pouted up and she crossed her arms like a spoiled brat, the reached forward and caressed his still exposed dick.

He pushed her hand away. "Damn, Sunshine, not today...I'm busy and tired. I need to chill for a minute and figure some things out."

Sunshine grabbed her jacket and tossed it over her already crossed legs, the propped herself up, all the while sucking her teeth. "Okay, then, let's talk. Matter of fact let's talk about this. Where's my fuckin' money, nigga!"

"Damn, girl...you ain't gotta say it like that!"

"You wanted to talk." She tossed the coat to the side and spread open her legs in front of his face. Her red pubic hairs did little to hide the fat, juicy pussy she flashed. "Since you don't want none of this. Then yeah, where's my fuckin' money?"

Hulie sighed then leaned toward her. "It's like this, I went to the spot like you told me to, where that dude Moonie had his stash. When I got there, there was somebody else waiting for him."

"I need to write this shit down or what?" she said, matter of factly.

"Naw, this dude was a hustla from his side of town, but he wasn't a major playa, just a hustla. He did his own thing to come up, know what I mean. Robberies, stuck ups...extortion, bullshit like that." Hulie sighed again then paused as she started digging for her cigarettes. "Anyway, he told me that the muthafucka owed him some money."

"Hold up," she said as she lit her cigarette. Focusing her train of thought on him, she propped herself against the arm of the chair, straightened herself up then reached for the ashtray on the small, round, wooden coffee table. "Okay...so what are you saying?"

Hulie looked off toward the window after she glared her piercing jet-black eyes into his face. He quickly turned back knowing she would be checking out his every move, his every twitch. That was the interrogator in her, looking for his lie, studying him.

"He said there wasn't any money there and I needed to come back later and get it from Moonie."

"Whoa!" She found the kink and was ready to exploit it. "But my detectives...said, they found some money. Why didn't he take that...or better yet, why didn't you get it yourself?"

Hulie wasn't slow, but he wasn't as quick as her either. Usually, he'd have her playing on his own court, with his dick in her, but now he was trying to tell the lie straight up and it wasn't working for him at all.

"I didn't see anything," he lied.

Sunshine giggled, she knew he was lying but she still wanted to know where the money had gone. She had a good idea he'd taken it, but she didn't want to actually accuse him without real proof, which she really didn't need much of. Besides she liked him, it was a sentimental type of thing. Hulie was her very first case, she'd just gotten out of law school and landed a good job in the DA's office based on her high-test scores on the bar, but mostly because she sucked the right dicks.

Hulie had gotten busted on a violation, for a domestic issue, it was enough to send his ass away on a third strike. She schemed up a plan to get him bail and have the charges reduced to disorderly conduct, but only after she had some people put the tim down on the girl involved, then invited Hulie over to her place. She'd heard about his notoriety in the streets and she told him about a sure-fire plan to finesse dope boys out of their money, legally. Deep down she wanted to make them pay for all the years they laughed at her albino skin, eyes and hair. For all the years they made fun of her nerd ass, she'd make them all pay now.

Most just like Hulie would come back and forth in front of the judge, pay crazy money to lawyers that didn't give a fuck and he'd serve them with twenty-five and thirty elbows. She had a better plan, a plan she put together with some nerd buddies that had become cops and was tired of the same shit...making no money. She couldn't stop the repetition and she didn't care too. She wasn't a politician but giving them all that time would still at the end of the day stop nothing. They would just be replaced with someone else. She thought that maybe if she could keep them on the streets long enough, then they could make money for her, she could make them pay her to eat and live. She greased a lot of hands and with the money she made, wiggled from being an assistant district attorney to become the DA in a very short amount of time.

It was sweet, but she had one thing she couldn't stay away from and that was the streets. She needed credibility, that's what she missed. Being that fine, ass chick everyone wanted that chick that would come into the courtroom and turn heads. The chick that would come up on visits in sexy, tight ass minis and get all the attention she always longed for. She put Hulie in on the plan and he bit. It didn't take much convincing because the one thing she did have was, blazing ass pussy.

Hulie figured he'd cut the competition out anyway, after all, he had an inside and reduced profit margin on the street to his favor. But now, Hulie was trying to work her, trying to flam her and she knew it, she also knew that it would only be a matter of time before she'd have to feed him to the wolves. Then pick up some fresh meat and some young dick.

"Man, look, Sunshine, I tried to meet with Moonie and get the money, but when I got there, he wasn't there, and that same guy started tripping." He started to ramble and tried to retrace his words and it wasn't working.

She sat in front of him not saying a word but taking it all in as she blew smoke rings in his face. "Uh huh..."

"I...I...I didn't shoot him."

"Really, well who did?"

"That dude on the TV...Jabari!"

The name was familiar to her, but she couldn't quite place it. "Jabari...Jabari!" Then she put her hand to her mouth. "Ooohhh...shit!" She had it. "Muthafuckin' Tangie's brother!

Oh, hell yeah."

Hulie looked at her curiously trying to figure out if he'd said the right or wrong thing. "Yeah...that's right." He didn't have a clue that she knew Tangie.

Her mind started spinning around the whole thing, putting together the plan to finally get rid of Tangie's ass.

"So...he killed him, huh?"

"Yeah!"

"You willing to...uh...testify?"

"C'mon now...you know I ain't no snit..."

She reached over swiftly and grabbed him by the mouth. "Look, muthafucka, it's either you or him and remember...you're the one with the fuckin' strike!" She let him go.

"Damn," Hulie said as he brushed her hand away from his face. Could it get any worse?

His thoughts were interrupted abruptly by a knocking on the door. He wasn't expecting anyone and slowly eased his way towards a closet set across the opposite end of the den. Thinking maybe it might have been jack-boys. He eased in, reached into a cubby hole inside the wall and pulled out a snub-nosed .38 special, then motioned for Sunshine to move slowly towards the bedroom. She picked up her coat, reached into the pocket and pulled out a shiny, silver .380.

Hulie gawked. "What the fuck you doing with that?"

Sunshine glanced his way and giggled. "You dumb muthafucka, I'm a goddamned D fuckin' A. I can do this!" She looked at the gun in his hand and the closet he stepped out of. "What the fuck *you* doing with that? I'm telling you, Hulie, don't let me have to have my people come over here and go through this muthafuckin' cave with a fine-toothed comb." He knew she wasn't bullshitting and said nothing. She peeped back at the closet door then added. "And you better

not be holding out on me, either."

The knocking got more intense until finally, they heard someone shout. "Hulie, I know you in there! I hear some bitch up in there, too! She better be trying to run out the back..." It was Cleo.

Hulie sighed and tucked the gun in his robe pocket, then rushed to the window and looked out. Sure enough, standing on the porch wearing a white and red, mini skirt jacket outfit and stilettos was Cleo, all five-foot-seven inches of pure fineness. She bent over to take off her shoes and stepped back tying her long, dark, wavy, silky hair into a ponytail.

"I'ma kick that ass, Hulie, I'm tired of this shit." She threatened.

Hulie walked to the door and opened it only after Sunshine had put on her coat and after some prodding fasten three buttons. He opened the door and Cleo busted through straight into the path of Sunshine, who was standing there with a smirk on her face.

"Who's this bitch, Hulie?" Cleo barked.

Sunshine cocked her hip to the side and glanced over at Hulie. "You need to teach your hoe some manners...*before I do*!" Sunshine giggled.

Cleo charged at her, with her nails out, gritting her teeth. Sunshine sidestepped her easily and kicked her in the ass going by. Cleo fell up against the wall and Sunshine turned around standing over her.

"Hulie, I'm telling you, you better talk to her. It's going to get ugly in here if you don't." Sunshine said matter of factly.

Hulie stepped in between them before Cleo bounced back up onto her feet and lunged at Sunshine. Hulie grabbed her and yelled at Sunshine. "Just get the fuck outta here...now!"

Sunshine mean-mugged Cleo then unbuttoned her coat and swung it open. "Bitch, this is what your man really wants...believe that!"

Cleo swung wildly at her and Sunshine reached into her pocket, pulled out her gun and walked with it out towards the door. "I think you're a smart girl." She turned to Hulie. "I'll be in touch!"

Sunshine walked out to her car looking across the street at the small crowd of hustlas that had gathered. They recognized her, but it wasn't a big deal. They had cases pending and needed deals, so they knew to keep their mouths shut. Sunshine smiled at them as she high-stepped into her car.

One of them mustered up enough nerve and stepped towards her. "Cuse me...miss uh, I need to talk to you 'bout sumptin."

Sunshine eyed him up and down, admiring his tenacity then reached into her glove compartment and pulled out a card. She rolled down the window and called him over. Feeling confident, his tall, muscular frame swaggered as he got closer. "What's your name?" she asked.

"Q."

"Well, uh, Q, what can I do for you?"

"I got this case..." Before he knew it, she had reached out and started fondling his crotch. He bent over and got closer to the car, speechless.

"Why don't you get in and tell me all about it?" Sunshine suggested.

Q wanted to damn near fly across the roof of the car, but he kept his cool and she liked that. He glanced over at the porch at Hulie still trying to restrain Cleo and shook his head. Then Hulie put up hands like, what the fuck. Sunshine leaned over, stared up at Hulie and blew him a kiss.

Q got in, leaned over and said, "I need some work..." He stared at her legs. "...done!"

She giggled and gapped her legs opened wider letting him gawk at her lace panties. "Me too...Q!" Her mind saw red as she thought about the stunt Cleo had just pulled. But looking over at Q, she said fuck it as she pondered on different ways to take her ass out and make Hulie's ass pay for it.

Chapter Eight

Diplite couldn't believe the shit Dirty-Red had told him.

Could it be true? He wondered as he walked over to the window and peeped out, still tripping at the fact that after all this time the money that he and Hulie flamed to get came dropping right in his fucking hands. Dirty-Red told him that Nikki had confided in him about what happened and that she needed help. He had no clue that he was involved and neither did she. He kept a low profile; the police had already questioned him several times and were watching him. He was a person of interest they said, so he didn't want his face out there like that. She never questioned why her son was killed in front of his trap. At least from what Dirty-Red had told him. Hell, she'd just now buried him so that was probably the furthest thing from her mind right now.

He put his foot up on a chair and dusted off his Jordan's, then froze.

'What if she did find out? Would she still want him to wash the money? What exactly did Dirty-Red tell her anyway and
what kinda deal did he make to put him in the car?'

Diplite had a thousand questions and no answers. He walked over to the closet and pulled out his favorite jacket, a black, leather bomber. Her put it on, then picked up his keys off the dresser and headed out the door. He was supposed to

156

meet them both at Dirty-Red's and go over the plan to flip the money, then find out what he knew about her son being killed. He had to come up with something to tell them to throw them off.

He thought about it over and over again. If he could just figure out a way to take out Hulie then he'd get it all and split the difference with Dirty-Red, but it had to be something smooth. Maybe, he'd blame the whole thing on him but if he did that and they confront Hulie he could just as well throw everything back on him and Nikki would back out for sure. It was just too much bullshit from her. Hell, she might even run to ball and then they'd both go away, for a very long time and that wasn't what he wanted, at all.

As he walked to his car and opened the door, he peeped up the street at her house, leveled to the ground in a heap of ash, blanketed at the top.

"Damn, Hulie, didn't have to do it like that," Diplite said to himself.

He never did get the chance to holla at him that night, but according to the way Dirty-Red described Nikki looked, it was evident that Hulie had tried to off her.

"Why the fuck didn't he get the money?" Diplite asked no one in particular.

He slid behind the wheel of his black Mustang, then backed out of the driveway and sped up the street, he was already running late. The only other person that could finger him that night as being involved was Jabari or Rip, and Rip was dead. He'd have to get at Jabari too, but no one knew where he'd disappeared to. The chick Rip and he stayed with had to know something, but he hadn't seen her either. Somehow or another he had to get with Hulie on the low-low and not let him know about Nikki or the money. He had to keep them separated at all costs. He needed somewhere to stash her, to get her out of the hood. He knew Hulie would come looking once he got word that she wasn't dead.

He made a left on the main street coming out of the hood off Montague Street. After driving by his trap house to making sure everything was good, it suddenly dawned on him...his sister. He could just stash Nikki with her somewhere and have his sister keep an eye on Nikki, the loot and Hulie all at the same time.

"Yeah, that sounds like a plan!"

Dirty-Red sat on his porch looking up the block as Diplite's car turned the corner coming his way. He'd closed down shop for a couple of hours so that he could handle the business at hand and sent Wood to the liquor store. Nikki sat close by watching as well.

"Dat him?" she asked.
"Yeah!" Dirty-Red answered.

"Damn." She leaned up and watched him as he pulled into the driveway. "I 'member when hem ben just a lil' ole ting." Dirty-Red smiled and said out o the corner of his mouth.

"Still is." Then he got up and dapped him. "Yo'...wassup?"

"Wassup?" Diplite glanced Nikki's way. "Ms. Nikki!"

Nikki got up and walked towards him. Diplite could see a slight limp and some bruises around her face, but she was still fine as all hell. He hated to have to fuck her over, but it was necessary, and all apart of the game.

"You okay?" Diplite asked as he hugged her, tightened his hands around her waist and pulled her closer to him.

His head was damn near swallowed by her titties as she squeezed. He got a hard-on and was hoping she felt some sort of way.

Nikki pushed him away slightly and looked him up and down. "How's Cleo?"

"A'ight."

"Good." She grabbed him by the hand, and they followed Dirty-Red into the living room.

On the table was a duffle bag and she walked towards it past Dirty-Red and emptied its contents onto the table.

Diplite was so shocked he gasped.

Nikki smiled. "Dis it!"

FINALLY, HULIE WAS able to sit back in the tub, relax and wash his ass...well, Cleo washed his ass.

"Uh, yeah, girl...the back...ahh, right der..."

Like a baby in her hands, she gently scrubbed him as sweat dripped from her forehead from the steamy hot water making her skin moist to the touch. Hulie peeped up at her and caressed her face as she soaked the soothing soft sponge.

"Damn, girl...you really love me, huh?" She looked into his eyes and smiled, then continued. Hulie got up and lifted her in one swoop, then tenderly kissed her face. "Take dem clothes off and come in here wit' me."

After letting her down gently, Cleo reached around her back and unsnapped the button on her mini-skirt causing it to fall softly to the floor. Hulie started unbuttoning the blouse she had on and unhooked her bra-strap. He looked her up and down as she moved about, ever so gracefully as she stepped back out of her clothes in one motion. Standing in front of him with just a thong on made

Hulie's dick rise and poke stiffly to the left like a banana. She stepped forward and stroked it then, played with the tip with her thumb until he purred.

"Don't tease me like this..." he said.

Cleo pulled her thong off, stepped closer to him and rubbed the head of his dick on her soft, trimmed pubic hairs and his knees buckled. His eyes fluttered as he stared into her kinky Chinese eyes that fucked him up every time. Her soft, cocoa-brown skin was nearly flawless as her long straight, jet black hair set off her look and made muthafuckas stop dead in their tracks. Her body was petite and slim, but yet full of perky titties that stood firm with thumb sized nipples and a dark-nickel sized ring around them both that almost made

Hulie cum just staring at them.

Cleo knew all of this, she knew she was fine and that men would do anything for her, but somehow, Hulie was different, maybe he just wasn't the average man. She never knew what angle he'd come at her with. He'd smack her up a couple of times, then make mad passionate love to her and afterward, cry like a little bitch. She shared that with her mother once and her mother told her point blank that he was sick, that he needed help and she'd better do something quick before he killed her. Cleo paid her mother's words of advice no mind, it went in one ear and out the other. She had no doubts in her mind that Hulie loved her and it would only be a matter of time before her peeps came around to seeing that.

Hulie watched, trying to figure out what to do to satisfy her seductively, horny ass. She'd been so used to tricking and at a hundred dollars and a better nut, muthafuckas would come up with all types of shit to get their monies worth. If not, they knew just by looking at her long enough, they'd cum quick and lose, then be assed out.

'Fuck 'em,' Hulie thought. *'This bitch belongs to me, I own this pussy!'* "Come 'er!" Hulie grabbed her arm and pulled her roughly towards him.

Submissively, she rubbed her hands across his broad hairy chest, tickling him and he responded by cupping her ass and pulling her closer, making his dick sit snuggly between the gap in her thighs, rubbing her clit.

"Oh, Hulie baby..." she moaned as he hoisted her up and angled his dick into her pussy, then bought her down on it.

Her head tilted back as he thrust the full length into her and pumped ravishly, like an animal, he lowered himself into the tub with her still on his dick and sat down. The soothing, heated water electrified them both as their senses exploded from the rush. Hulie leaned back and gripped the side of the tub.

Cleo lifted up her legs with both arms and spread them over his shoulders. Hulie looked at her like, *what the fuck,* his dick was fully in her and it felt good. she leaned back and balanced herself in his lap. Then with both hands, she grabbed the railing and started spinning herself in a 360-degree angle.

"Goddamn, girl!" Hulie yelled out. "Oohhh, muthafucka...oh, yeah!" She spun and stopped, then looked at him and

he hollered. "Please...please...don't stop!"

She moaned and continued to corkscrew her pussy around his dick until she felt him swelling up inside her. Then she turned facing him, let down her legs and eased up off him softly. He was sweating and breathing so hard he could barely speak as she started positioning herself in between his legs and lifted his waist out of the water enough so that his now huge dick flopped around like a small whale ready to blow. She opened her mouth and swallowed him whole down her throat and slowly sucked.

"Oh...God!" Hulie screamed out.

Cleo rubbed the head of his dick around her tongue and licked the tip of it like a lollipop and rubbed it around her face letting her wet hair tickle his groin. He couldn't take no more, he grabbed the back of her head and eased it down until he felt himself all the way in the back of her throat and she stopped resisting. He let loose and pumped until he started cumming, she swallowed his cum in one shot. He went limp on her tongue and she washed his head with it. His body shuddered as she kissed it, then he fell backward and closed his eyes.

"Baby...you alright!" Cleo asked.

Hulie opened up his eyes ever so slightly and said, "Yeah...I'm...a'ight!"

Cleo curled up in his arms as they both let the water sooth their bodies and looked up at him, then of into the ceiling and said to him, "Hulie...I love you!"

He stroked her hair and answered, "Believe it or not...I love you, too, baby!"

Cleo didn't even want to look up at him, she wanted the moment, for life. A grin appeared across her lips as she heard him snooze, then begin falling asleep.

"Finally, Mama, I told you he'd come around!" she said to herself.

Cleo laid snug in Hulie arms as he stared off into the abyss of the night. His mind wandered aimlessly. He stroked the back of her neck tenderly, occasionally looking down on her and smiling. They'd been fucking the better part of the evening. All in all, he really did like her, as much as his gruff persona would allow him to show. Hulie was smooth in some ways, but he was still a two-bit thug in every sense of the word, and he couldn't change that.

He tried wrapping his mind around the idea of taking her off the streets. He didn't need her money and so far, she'd proved to be a thoroughbred bitch. He just needed to get his money straight and his shit in order. He needed to find the money he was still looking for. A couple of hundred grand would easily award them the luxury of chilling somewhere South of the Bahamas.

"Maybe it might be good if she moved in, it's a good time to ask," Hulie said to himself. Then he turned toward her and shook her softly. "Hey, baby...wake up!"

Cleo opened her eyes as she yawned, then smiled rubbing cold out the corner of her eyes. "Yeah, babe...what's up?"

"I was wondering, well, actually thinking about making a move."

"What kinda move...you need some money?" She asked excitedly as she prodded herself up on her elbows. "I told you if you needed some money, I could..."

Hulie put his finger to her lips, shushing her. "Nah, it ain't like that. I mean..." He pointed out the window. "I need a change of scenery. I'm tired of this shit. I can't get no peace and hell, you see what the bitch did earlier."

"That hoe!" Cleo reached over, pulled out her cigarettes and lit one up. She was clearly still frustrated over the dispute she'd had earlier with Sunshine. "That bitch needs her ass kicked!"

"Well, it's comin'...one day."

Cleo turned his way. "If you want...I can do her a little something..."

Hulie looked at her and shook his head. "You talkin' 'bout...offing her ass?"

"Hell yeah...I can do it, Hulie, if you want me too!"

Hulie opened his eyes wide. *'Damn!'* he thought. This bitch would kill a muthafucka for me. "Damn, baby, suppose she was like a chick on the side or something?" He laughed waiting for her response.

She put the cigarette out in an ashtray and swung her legs off the side of the bed. "Well...I'd be real careful with that, ya know." She got up sucking her teeth and walked into the bathroom, leaving Hulie in bed with the answer he was looking for.

She would kill him, too. "Now I don't want this bitch to move in at all, matter of fact, she don't need to know shit." He said to himself.

"Hulie...what is it you wanted to know?" Cleo asked.

"Just thinking, uh, maybe we should start going to...uh

better clubs instead of those holes in the wall spots."

She peered her head out of the bathroom. "Okay, let's go downtown then. Meeting Street...I can wash up and put on my make-up real quick."

Hulie got up, walked over to the window and stared out of it. "Take your time, babe."

He thought about the bullshit from earlier and he definitely needed to eventually find a way to take Sunshine's ass out of the picture. She was becoming too much of a problem, but still, she was a DA and it wouldn't be easy. Somehow, he needed to figure her in on some shit, a flam...something she couldn't wriggle out of.

"Hey, Hulie!"

"Yuh?"

"Remember, I said I had something to tell you?"

Hulie sat on the edge of the bed, checking messages on his cell. "Wassup?"

"I heard on the block that Ms. Nikki is still alive."

"Who?"

"Ms. Nikki, she was the one who everyone thought was killed in the fire up in Liberty Hill! Remember? Hulie turn off your phone. The chick that was caught in the fire...T-Black's mother, remember he was found dead, too."

"So, they found his mother, uh...Nikki?"

"Ain't that some shit. Then on top of that, I heard she found some money or something too. Probably T-Black's stash, they said it was a lot."

Hulie was already at the bathroom door. "Found some money..."

Cleo looked up and tripped, he moved that quick. "Yeah, they said she had a lot of money or something, but so far it's just a rumor."

"You sure?"

"I guess, but you'd have to ask my brother. That's his hangout spot. He'd know one way or another."

Hulie scrolled through his voice messages and Diplite's name came up a couple of times. He'd been trying to get in touch with him.

'*Yeah, that's what's up,*' he thought as he put it behind his back as she came out of the bathroom with a towel on. "I'll find out something later. Come over here and hold me." He hugged her, stroking her long, soft hair.

"Oh, baby..." she cooed in his arms.

'*She did good,*' Hulie thought.

He'd have to get up with Diplite and find out if this shit was true and if it was. He needed to get his goddamned money before someone else did.

"SEVEN...EIGHT...NINE...ninety-six. Damn, that's a nice piece of change!"

"Damn, right."

"So, Dirty-Red, you my witness, right?" Diplite turned towards Nikki. "Ninety-six gees on the head, those the numbers?"

"Uh...huh!"

He sat down in the chair in front of a small oakwood desk where the money laid, looking over the bundles and rubbing the brow of his forehead. He knew Hulie was more than likely looking for it, and he'd have to act fast. At the same time, he'd have to careful not to bring any suspicion to himself.

"Check it out, the only way to flip this kinda bread is in the country." That was the same lie he'd told Hulie.

"The country...why?" Dirty-Red asked as he looked over at Nikki hunching her shoulders, trying make sense out of what was just said. He damn well knew it would be crazy hard to separate the money from her. Wherever the cash went,

she'd be right there. "Don' know 'bout that."

"Don't know..."

"Hem right. I go wit' dat money just case somebody tries..." She reached into the gym bag she carried around with her, then stopped when Dirty-Red touched her shoulder. She put down the seven-inch, stiletto switchblade she was carrying.

"No, need for that...it's cool!"

"Hell, me kno dat. I kno his people, but, I don't kno who hem kno...dats not good." Nikki remarked.

"You don't trust me, Ms. Nikki?" Diplite asked.

"Trust? C'mon now, who you kiddin'? You got more dem trap houses den tha law allow. You 'bout dat paper, dat's what's up. If you knew you could get dis from out my hand,
you would...na wouldn't you?"

Diplite sat back in the chair watching her body language as she spoke that good geechie shit to him. She knew his ass, and his kind, that's for sure. It was going to be difficult at best, but not impossible.

"You know, you're right. So, we move you and the money at the same time...didn't you say that someone was trying to kill you? How do I know that they might not try and kill me

too? No way in hell we do this in the Chuck..." "Cheraw!" Dirty-Red interrupted.

"What...what the fuck you talkin' 'bout Dirty-Red?"
"We can hide her in Cheraw...my hometown." Dirty-Red walked over to Nikki. "Nobody don' know you down there, right?"

"Ain't neh ben, not as I know."

"Then, it just might work. Hell, my cousin runs a club out that way and we can flip it from there. There's plenty of bread moving in and out."

Diplite leaned over looking at the both of them, contemplating to himself that just might work. "She needs someone else to be with her tho. We gotta make it look good, like family, kna-mean."

"Family...like who?" Dirty-Red asked.

"My sister, Cleo, she knows her. She can go with her and it'll look like mother and daughter or some shit, visiting from
outta town, and less suspicious."

Dirty-Red rubbed his deep red goatee. "Yuh...sounds 'bout right. But, what's up with your sister? Ain't she still fuckin' with that dude from the Heights?"

"I got that covered."
Nikki walked over to the table. "The Height...who?"
"I think his name is Hu..."
"Yo...I got it, Dirty." Diplite butted in.

He damn sure didn't want them to figure in on his connection to Hulie, not now. Or at least not until the money was handled and he got his cut, then it would be too late for them to do anything about it.

"Wha hem look like?" Nikki looked over at Diplite and he ignored her. She turned towards Dirty-Red and pressed him. "Wha hem look like, Dirty-Red."

"Big, husky...missing a tooth with a mouth full of gold..."

"Muthafucka, that's dat nigga who tried to kill me dat night!" She walked over to Diplite. "You kno hem, muthafucka?"

"Not really, he's just another hustler."

She leaned over and grabbed him by the collar, look him in the eyes and said in a raspy voice filled with hate. "Okay, we do it dat way...but den, when it's ova...I wan hem ass dead!
You hear?"
Diplite got scared and pushed her away. "Hey, I ain't got nuthin' to do with that bullshit. I was at the crib when your son was killed."
"Diplite, if I find out yu had something to do wit' me son's murder..."

"Man, fuck this shit, find somebody else!"

Nikki stepped in front of him as he stormed towards the door. "I'm gon go wit' yu on dis, ya hear. But 'member if I den finds out..."

"I don't know nuthin' except what you told me...a'ight." Diplite lied turning away from her.

She smiled, rubbing his cheeks. "A'ight...den do it." She knew he was lying. No one knew that her son was killed before the fire. She knew right then he would die. She leaned forward and kissed him. "Sorry, 'bout that, heh." He would be the one who would lead her to the man who killed her son.

Diplite reached into his pocket and pulled out his cell. "I need to call, Cleo.

"Yo' Wassup, it's me Dip."
"Boy, what you want?"
"Damn, sis...it's like that?"
"I'm in the middle of eating."
"So, damn, you can't stop to talk..."

"I'm at a restaurant with Hulie. I had to sneak into the bathroom just to take this call. You know how paranoid he is.

Now, what you want?"

Diplite cuffed the phone closer to his ear and walked off towards the back of the room out of earshot. Dirty-Red and Nikki sat at the bar sipping on drinks he'd set up and engaged in small talk. She turned briefly and glanced his way but turned back quickly once he realized she was staring. She leaned closer towards Dirty-Red. "You think we can trust em?" she asked.

Dirty-Red looked over at him. "Hell naw, I wouldn't trust that muthafucka as far as I can throw him," Dirty-Red admitted.

Nikki smiled. "Me neither...sumptin, 'bout him, ain't right."

They both snickered as Diplite turned towards them, then back to his conversation with Cleo.

"I need a favor, sis."

"What kinda favor, what is it...money?"

"Naw, I'm straight, I need you to..."

"Hold up." Cleo popped out of the stall she'd ducked into. Hulie had knocked asking if she was alright. I'm okay, I think my friend came..."

"Damn!" She heard him mumble as he stomped back to their table.

She closed the door slightly and hunched down. "C'mon now, he done came to my door with his nosy ass."

"I need you to go away for a few days."

"Go away, where?"

"Out in the country."

"The country?"

"Would you just shut the fuck up for a minute?"

"Aw hell naw." She got up. "You called me, remember.

Who the fuck you dissing?"

"A'ight...a'ight hear me out. I need you to go with Ms. Nikki to Cheraw for a few days. Just so she can stay out of sight for a while."

"Ms. Nikki, what's happening with her now? I heard she was almost killed or something."

"She was, we trying to keep her low for a while until he find out what's up."

"I dunno, Dip, supposed someone tries to kill me, too?"

"Naw, it ain't like that, besides you gonna be with Dirty-

Red's folks."

Cleo leaned back crossing her legs. "Hmmm...fine ass, Dirty-Red, huh? He'll be there with us? Okay!" She had dealings with him, very frequently and felt some sort of way. There was something about him that she dug. He was mysterious and very different from Hulie, he was more confident and everything. Even when she refused his money, he'd make her take it anyway, not like Hulie's grimy ass, he was just cool like that.

"If you want, I'll tell him to make the trip with you personally."

"Okay...okay, but what's in it for me? I know you getting

something out of it...you don't do shit for free."

"Right...right, okay, sis, you on point. I think I can

squeeze about two gees or..."

"Two-grand...please, I can get that..."
"A'ight, four gees, cash, and all the expenses paid, that's it."

"Hmm...sounds good. How many days again?" She started counting on her fingers the amount of money she'd make a day.

"Damn, Cleo, who the fuck are you now? Goddamned

police or some shit? You gonna do it or what?"

"How many days?"
"About a week, okay!"

"Alright, a week and that's it? Call me later and tell where you want me to meet you. Or do you want me to pick up Ms. Nikki instead...and of course, Dirty-Red."

"I got that, I'll call later...and sis!"
"What, I gotta go!"
"Don't tell, Hulie, jack shit!"

"I'm wrapping that muthafucka around my fingers, he wants me to move in with him. He didn't say it, but I know he does."

"Don't do it, I'm tellin' you that muthafucka ain't shit."

"You sound just like Mama! Let me live my own life, okay?"

Diplite knew good and damn well he couldn't let her do no dumb shit like that. Hell no, if he did, Cleo's ass would be in danger, but on the other hand, he'd know all Hulie's comings and goings and that shit might work in his favor. One way or another, he had to make a decision quick.

"If you make that move, I'ma tell Ma. He's beasting on you. How's that?"

"You wouldn't...I...I...I thought that was between us. Dip you said you was gonna talk to him for me. C'mon now don't
do no slip like that, Mama will raise pure hell."

"Then...don't do it! You heard what I said, at least sis...not right now. I'm serious, okay?"

"Damn, but you better have this Nikki...country shit together!"

"I will, later!"

"Bye!" Cleo closed her phone and walked over to the sink to wash her hands, partly drying them, like she had used the restroom.

She put on some fresh perfume, her game face and stepped out the door. She knew Hulie was gonna drill her about what was going on, so she'd have to come up with a lie...a damn good one. She made her way to the table and sat down.

She grasped at her stomach, groaning. "Baby...got cramps!"

"Damn, Cleo!" Hulie fumed. "You sick...you need to leave or what? Hell, I just ordered fuckin' steak!"

"No, baby...that's alright, I'll stick it out."

"A'ight, but if it gets any worse..."

Cleo reached over and stroked his hand. He wasn't shit, he really didn't give a damn about her. "I might be sick or about a week, tho." She said in her best Emmy Award-winning performance voice.

"A'ight...I understand. It's a female thing, no problem. Once we finish eating, I'll take you home. I can't get no pussy anyway!" he mumbled.

She managed to fake enough of a smile as she thought. *'Diplite better have my goddamned money!'* But one thing she knew for sure it would give her a chance to find out what really happened to Ms. Nikki...and get with that fine ass DirtyMuthafuckin'-Red's ass in the process...instead of the muthafucka that was mean-mugging in front of her.

He was in the game now, Diplite closed his phone and turned to Dirty-Red and Nikki. "Well, it's all done...what the fuck!" The money on the table was gone, bag and all, along with Nikki. He did a double take glancing around making sure she just didn't step out for a sec, but she was nowhere in sight. "Where the hell is, she... and the money?"

Dirty-Red was behind the bar wiping down shot glasses and peeped up at him, then smiled. "Naw, bruh, she's ghost gone!"

"Where the hell did, she go? I wanted to tell her..."
"She knows 'bout a week or so, right."
"Y'all was peeping in on my call?"

"Nooo...ain't like that!" Dirty-Red walked from around the bar over to a closet and pulled out some keys, then opened the door and snatched up a keg with a label attached around the backside in ink: *Anheiser Busch-Plant 9.* Dirty-Red was the biggest buyer of stolen kegs and cases in North Charleston. Ball could never pin him down because as quickly as he got them, they were gone, that damn quick. He grumbled something under his breath about having to get a couple more, then turned his attention back to Diplite.

"Yo' she moves like that. In and out, you never know when she's coming or leaving. I really don't blame her, err since her son got killed and she got caught up in that fire, she changed. She trusts people, but no way like she used to, not even me...I'm tellin' you."

So, damn, how the fuck am I supposed to let her know where to meet my sister and all that shit?"

"Trust me, cuz, either she knows already, or she'll see you real soon, like."

Diplite walked towards the door on his way out and turned back around. "Well, at least where's she staying?"

Dirty-Red put the keg down he was dragging towards the back of the bar and looked at his stupid ass. "Damn, you ask a lot of questions. Just lee' it alone." He shook his head then rubbed his goatee. "Besides her peoples is dem root workers. You don wanna fuck wit' that. So...if you plannin' sumptin'

stupid, I advise you to think twice about that shit!"

Diplite grabbed the door and swung it open. "Naw, it's cool, don't worry 'bout it, everything's a'ight. Then he let the slam shut behind him.

Dirty-Red stood there and watched through the window as Diplite got into his car and pulled off. "Homeboy...don' got it twisted, I'm not the one worryin."

TANGIE RUMMAGED THROUGH the box Dondi had given her. It contained old clothes, papers and a lot of stolen credit card receipts that were taken out of dumpsters, somewhere downtown. She sucked her teeth and sighed as she looked at them.

"Jabari's crazy this shit don't work anymore." She snickered, then flipped through some old photos of her, her mom, dad, Jabari, and she and Jabari together. There were a couple of photos she didn't recognize, with smiling white people in them and some freckled face young white hugged up on Jabari. She'd never seen him before, she picked up the phone and dialed Dondi.

"Hey, uh, wassup?"
"Hey, Tangie girl...wassup?"
"Damn, you sound too good, you alright?"
"Hell, yeah, I'm alright."

"Girl, look, the day when I left your hot ass, all you wanted to do was get fucked up. Now, you sound like some Dixie chick white girl or something at a square dance."
"Dixie chick white...where do you get this shit from? Naw, I'm cool, I just ain't been gettin' high. Been going to meetings and shit."

Tangie smiled and leaned back in her chair. "For real, girl,

I'm proud of you. That's alright!"
"Yeah, wanna get my shit together! Maybe I can't be like you, all smart and shit...and good looking, but I can be somebody."

"You can be whatever you want to be, believe that."
"So, what's up, you find out anything else about, Jabari?"

"Not really, I'm going through his things and I found some pictures I didn't recognize, though. Thought you might..." She picked up the photos off her desk. "...know why there are pictures of white people. Lots of pictures of Jabari and some white boy, that's tall and lanky, with freckles...ring a bell?"
"I asked about him, too. Jabari said some it's some dude he met in a foster home. Didn't say his name though...oh...no wait he did.

Something like Dory...Dee or something like that. You know them drugs done took all my little memory. I

can't really remember for sure."

Tangie laughed. "You crazy, just stay clean...it'll come back."

"That's all I know. Hey, would you like to go to a meeting with me? I'll be picking up a thirty-day chip soon and I'd re-

ally like for you to be there. I mean, you like family now!"

"Sounds cool, just leave a message or you know, call me. I'll be there!"

"Thanks, Tangie, sorry I didn't know more."

"No...you did good, catch you later!" Tangie hung up the phone and paged an intern. "I'm looking for some foster care

records. You think you can help me?"

"Sure Tangie, let me know what you need."

Chapter Nine

It wasn't as difficult as she would have thought. A couple of hours at best. She had dates, names, her brother's social security number which was a plus and then finally a lead. Martha Marie Davis, last known address, Boonie Doone Plantation. But it was her son's records that nailed it. He had marijuana busts, thefts, juvenile delinquency and finally foster care. He was in foster care the same years as Jabari give or take. At last, she had some history, a name, and a picture that was about to come up on her screen. Dunnington Doral Davis, The Third, no wonder he stayed in shit, who names their kid that, then on top of it, the third?

He looked the same as he did in the younger pictures, except scragglier. His last known address was the same as his mother's.

No..." She scrolled deeper and another address popped up.

He'd been busted in Colleton County on several occasions for theft, just recently. They had his address as being somewhere near Walterboro. She knew the place, it was right off of I-95. She had a few friends there that she went to school with, who was a sheriff, so she had access to the local police.

She gathered up the information she had on her desk and stuffed it into her briefcase, then got on the phone with

179

her assistant. "Missy, I'll be gone all next week. Could you reschedule everything I had pending? Give them continuance and let Brad handle my caseload, okay."

"I'll let him know, but it's better if you call. He'll ask a lot of questions and I don't have no answers."

"You're right, I'll take care of that, but everything else is the same."

"Everything alright, Tangie?"

"It's good, I just need to go out of town to check on some things...personal, you know. You, uh, know my cell phone number if anything comes up, right?"

"I got you, just be careful."

"I will." Tangie cleared her desk and picked up her jacket. It was a long day and she needed to go home, pack a bag, and hit Savannah Highway straight to Walterboro.

JABARI FINALLY CAUGHT up with Double D, after calling him about four times and spazzing out twice. Double D swore all the antics regarding his phone being answered by other people and Jabari being interrogated was just precaution due to bill collectors harassing him. Jabari gave Double D the best advice he could think of...pay them. After conversing for a while, Double D told Jabari to meet him on exit 68, right off the rampway of I-95. When he pulled up in a brand new, sparkling blue F-150, Jabari smiled.

Maybe he'd gotten his shit together after-all, but when he out of the truck and walked closer towards Jabari's car, doubts flashed around in Jabari's mind like lights. First of all, Double D kept looking around like someone was about to jump out of the bushes at any minute. Then he kept eyeballing Jabari, trying to figure out if it was really him or not and he was also spying inside the car looking for someone else.

He didn't walk to driver's side and get in like normal muthafuckas, instead he right past Jabari and straight to the trunk. He tried lifting it open when he couldn't get it up, he shook his head and smiled.

Then his demeanor changed, he crawled into the passenger side grinning. "Hey, what's up, dude? Ain't seen you in years. What brings you to the sticks?"

Jabari reached over, dapped him up and they hugged. "Good to see you too." Jabari got straight to the point. "Man, I need you..."

Double D pulled back towards the door and looked at Jabari oddly. "Need me, what...what do you mean?"

"Man, I ain't no goddamned faggot!" Jabari blurted catching on to his hint.

Double D sighed. "I didn't mean to say, or imply, anything like that. I mean you and me cool, whatever..."

"I'm on the fuckin' run, I need a place to duck for a few weeks," Jabari explained.

Double D took the cap he was wearing off his head and rubbed the beads of sweat into his already shined skin. It was starting to get humid and he insisted on keeping the windows up. he looked down, then back up at Jabari, all the while shaking his head. It looked more like a nervous tic than anything else.

"I don't know about that dude. I mean, I got a lot of shit going on. Shit, you may not want to be involved with..." He jammed the cap back on his head and dipped into the seat when he saw a state trooper drive by. "They...slowin'...down!"

Jabari looked up the road and the car had jumped on the rampway going North, paying us no mind. "Naw, what the fuck is going on? You in some sort of trouble?"

He eased back up and said, "Look, man, I'ma be real. You always been real with me, so I'ma give it to you straight."

Jabari moved in closer. "Okay, what's up?"

"I got this bad cold." Double D faked coughed. "I need to get some medication, quick. Follow me to the drug store, and help me out, then...I'll tell you more afterward."

Jabari looked at that muthafucka like he was fuckin' crazy. "Why can't you pick up your own shit?" Jabari grabbed him by his shirt. "You better let me know what's up!"

Double D pushed Jabari away. "Said I was sick."
"You ain't got that shit, do you?"

"Shit...noooo, I ain't got the virus." Double D looked at his hands, then rubbed around his mouth. A thick brownish plague was built up right about the gums, and his teeth looked bad, real bad.

'Damn,' Jabari thought knowing exactly what his problem was. "Oh, hell you on that fuckin' shit!"

"What!"
"That fuckin' meth, damn, D...your moms was right."

"Fuck her...that bitch! She don't want to help me none. Don't need her!" Double D reached for the door handle. "And if you don't wanna help he..." He turned off. "I don't need you, either."

Jabari felt like Double D had put him in a bad spot, just that damn quick. Here it was he needed a place to hide out, to be real low-key for a minute, and Jabari had gotten up with a fuckin' junkie. This didn't look good at all, but he needed a place, bad. He didn't have a choice.

"A'ight, where's the drug store? And you...you got any money?"

Double D peeped his head back into the window after he got out. "Money?" he snickered. "We don't need no fuckin' money!" He jumped back in his truck and sped off, with

Jabari right behind him.

They pulled in front of an Eckerd's somewhere downtown. It stood off from the main road and if the sign wasn't there, you'd miss it every time. Jabari followed Double D into the parking lot, and he angled his truck outwards facing the back entrance of the parking lot. Jabari did the same, somehow, he knew to expect something crazy, so he stayed alert.

Double D got out and walked over to the car and bent over inside of the window. "Alright, I'ma go inside with you

and show you where the stuff I need is at..."

"Why don't you just go in and buy what you need?" Jabari knew there was some bullshit in the mix, but he wanted to hear it from Double D's own mouth. Double D thought he was just going to use Jabari as a crash dummy or something.

'Naw he got life fucked up,' Jabari thought. Jabari knew he'd have to bring Double D's ass back to reality real quick.

Double D looked at Jabari all crazy. "Hey, dude you gonna help me or what? I told you I needed some..."

"Fuck what you told me, D, fuck that! Now you either tell me what's going down or I can leave your dumb ass out here to fiend, looking stupid. Fuck it, so, what is it, cause you wasting my goddamned time!"

A smile grew across Double D's face as he looked up at the doorway of the green, stuccoed building, then twisted his hat around his big peanut-ass head. The freckles on his face were dulled pink from whatever dope he was doing, but still, he was that same reefer smoking lil' ole white boy from back in the day.

"Okay...okay, you got that. Same old, Jabari!" Double D took a deep breath and said, "I need the Sudafeds...a lot of them. The last time I was in there, I almost got busted and I had to run off. I need you to throw them...keep their eyes on you."

"Won't they watch you? Hell, you was the one who tried to get..."

"To be honest, they gonna watch you simply cause you're black. It is what it is!"

Jabari shook his head, knowing Double D was right. "Okay, so once they zoom in on me, you just grab a couple and dip, right?"

"Something like that, but we have to play it by ear. If it ain't all good, then pull back, we can go somewhere else."

That somewhere else shit wasn't working for Jabari, he really wasn't feeling that. This was where it was going down, he didn't give a fuck about no place else.

Jabari got out of the car and walked through the door, and sure enough, all were on him. Immediately a small, petite, blonde white girl approached him.

"Sir, can I help you?" she asked.

Jabari looked at her and almost laughed, knowing that in the back of her mind she was really saying. '*Can I help you out the front door?*'

"I'm uh...looking for some medicine," Jabari lied, then sniffled like he had a sinus problem. His eyes were already tearing up from the cold ass A-C that pumped throughout the place, and had the chick's nipples hard as hell, but more so because he needed a good pill fix.

She directed Jabari t the back of the store to the Pharmacy and the shelf was sitting right behind the counter, with nothing but sinus pills.

"So, far so good," Jabari said to himself.

He didn't know exactly what he wanted so he stood there looking stupid. Then he heard the door open up front and there he was, Double D. The old grey-haired white man standing at the counter turned his attention towards him and started for the phone.

Jabari couldn't let that happen, so he said, "What are those?"

The guy at the counter put the receiver down and turned toward the shelf. "Which ones?" "Them." Jabari pointed.

"Which ones, son?" He turned around and pointed at Jabari. "Look, boy, don't play no games! Now which one you want?"

"I really don't know, something for sinus..."

"Oh hell, no, tell you what. Why don't you just come back later when you got it all figured out."

Jabari knew what that meant. He'd have the police waiting for his dumb ass if he did return. In this old hick town, an ass whipping was probably the norm.

On cue Double D, stepped between them and said,

"Hold up, what kind of symptoms you got?" "Runny nose...eyes are teary!" Jabari said.

He pointed toward a lime green box that read. "Sudafed's, that's what you need."

Jabari played it off, then smiled. "Thanks!" He told Double D.

The old man kept staring at Double D. he wouldn't let up, hen finally, "Ain't you that boy that was here the other day? The one we ran off? Yeah, you're him!" He went for the phone and yelled up front. "Joan, lock the door, that boy done come back! I'ma call the goddamned police, this time I got your ass!"

He thought he had Double D, but he wasn't even worried, Double D didn't blink an eye. Jabari, however, was ready to haul ass, but he stayed cool. I hope this muthafucka didn't have a gun, then it really was gonna hit the fan.

Instead, he walked towards the door and said, "Alright, alright, I'm going!"

The old white man was right behind him, taking all eyes off me. When they got out of view, Jabari jumped across the counter and snatched up two cases. He didn't know how much he needed, but this would have to do, for now. Jabari eased back around the side in another aisle and waited for the old man to get the fuck out of the way, then he'd haul ass to the car. Someone tapped him from behind, scaring the shit out of him. That was the same old white girl from earlier, he was busted.

She snickered at the look on his face, then pointed towards the stock room. "Go in there."

Jabari obeyed, the girl was right behind him and opened up a back door that led to the alley and let Jabari out. Jabari crept around the backside and waited until Double D finished showing out and got in his truck and sped off. Everyone out front finally walked back into the store with the old man pulling up the rear, talking shit, and silently unnoticed, Jabari got into his car and dipped. He didn't know where the hell he was going, so, he went down a side road that was flooded with trees and that's when he saw Double D's truck.

Double D pulled up next to Jabari and smiled. "Follow me!"

"Hey...what about the girl there, she won't say anything?"
"Yeah." He laughed. "How 'bout I suck your dick."
"What!"
"Trust me, you'll see that whore later...trust me!"

Jabari dumped the cases in the backseat and followed Double Dd out of town down a long winding road and thought about what he'd said about the girl.

"Yeah, that would be nice," Jabari said to himself.

A week had gone by and everything between Jabari and Double D was straight. Double D shared a double-wide trailer with a couple of dudes he quote-unquote, worked with, at least that's what he told Jabari. One of the dude's name was Smoak and Jabari thought his ass was crazy. He stood a little shorter than Jabari at about five-eight or so. He had long arms and sandy-blonde, scraggly hair with sad, sagging, bright blue eyes that made him look like Shaggy from Scooby Doo. He was a character, he had this wide ass smile that was inviting, but had a couple of teeth missing and some chipped up, mostly from fighting according to what he'd told Jabari. To Jabari, it looked like he stayed on the losing end.

Jabari often wondered why a guy that didn't seem to pose a threat would be fighting all the time? That was what threw Jabari off, but it wasn't long after that, that Jabari discovered the real truth. His M-O was popping and drinking moonshine, what a hellufied combination, it all made sense to Jabari after that. He stayed fucked up daily. Jabari had only seen him sober once or twice since he'd met the man. On the days he was sober Jabari would go hunting himself to find something for him to drink. Smoak suffered from manic depression and he was more manic than depressed. Jabari thought he was a borderline serial killer in the making, at best.

Double D and the other guys along with Jabari kept his crazy ass high, and of course away from any guns, but ironically Jabari later discovered that Smoak had the IQ of a genius. He'd sit down-high and would read books on Neuroscience. Then want to discuss what he'd read with Jabari of all people and debate about it.

'*A goddamned junkie, now ain't that some shit?*' Jabari often thought.

The other guy that lived there was a real old-school dude named Jason. He was a short, pink, white dude that talked real muthafucking fast and kept his eyes locked on yours when he spoke. If you looked off, he'd feel some sort of way about it. He did a total thirty-years in and out of prisons starting with Juvenile-DJJ, then eventually the CCI, Allendale, Lieber, Lee and all of the other compounds that State called institutions. If you stood around listening to him long enough, you found out that he had these crazy conspiracy theories about incarceration in South Carolina that was half-decent.

He had to get to know before interacting with him because he had a bad taste in his mouth for black folks. The ones who worked hard and did good and went to church were considered the good black folk in his eyes. Then there were the ones who sold crack, robbed white people, and made that goddamned nigga music crap that he hated. He called them niggers, and the ones like Obama and General Polin were considered African-American. This made Jabari keep his distance, he didn't want to be caught up in that racist ass shit.

Things got better though, one night when Jabari was feining for some pills. The man copped him half of bag full of Adams. He laughed like a baby as he watched Jabari choke them down like candy. He told Jabari niggers were easy to manipulate, he said pretty soon they'd be one for twoing their own shit. Jabari didn't really get that at first until he started jonesing for more and he made Jabari work for it. The best thing about the place as far as Jabari was concerned was that it wasn't too much traffic in and out.

Double D lived about a half mile off the main road. It was off of I-95 going into Walterboro, road 64, coming off of Savannah Highway out of Charleston and the subtle backwoods area they drove to was called Round O. When Double D and Jabari came from the store that day wit the case of Sudafeds Jabari had stolen. Double D had Jabari follow him on that, long ass, two-lane road until they got to his turn-off.

The first thing that hit Jabari's nose was the smell of old, stinky ass socks. He thought Double D might have been raising hogs or something. It made Jabari think back to the times when his old man used to take him and his sister out to the country. The smell seemed the same, just harder and raunchy. Jabari remembered that he and his sister would run around barefoot, chasing chickens, then every once and while his dad would come across a rattlesnake. He'd kill it and cut the rattle off, then chase him and sister around the yard. It sounds crazy, but those were the good days, Jabari was glad those days and hopefully, his days of encountering snakes were long gone.

Reality set in the minute they came to a clearing and Jabari saw the double-wide trailer on concrete footing in the front and brand-new fucking pick up trucks in the yard. There were no signs of chickens at all. Off to the side-chained up were two big-ass pit bulls that stared at Jabari when he got out of the car like they were starving Africans in a McDonalds. On other side was a barn with two dudes posted up out front.

One had a .45 on his side. There were a couple of cars parked in the front. They were all new models, Beamers, and a 300 Chrysler. To the left of the trailer was another driveway with a car trailer next to it. On the side was a nice suppedup race car. Directly off to the side of that was a road leading to a bridge going across a winding shallow creek. An R-V was parked on the road and Jabari asked Double Dd about it and he ignored him. All he said was there was another one that looked better than his. This confused Jabari because, from the looks of things, they were far from the poor white trash type of white boys.

The front door was damn near immaculate. The kitchen was straight, but the bedrooms were like pig-stuys, well all of them except Smoak's. He had an ass load of books all over the place. They had brand new plasma TVs with games consoles attached and plenty of cushioned, real leather sofas in the living room. AC buzzed through the place and Jabari could smell the steaks that were laid out on the table in the kitchen, along with the fruits, beans, and nuts. Jabari just kept his eyes on the steak, he hadn't eaten shit in a long while, and his stomach raised all types of hell from the varieties of aromas.

In the back of the trailer, there was a pond that came in off the creek and Jabari saw small platoon boats for fishing. Off to the side behind some weeds on a boat ramp was a twentytwo-foot cigarette boat, like the ones on the Miami Vice TV show. It was chromed, shined and ret' to go.

'*What they fuck these white boys into?*' Jabari thought.

Jabari knew they had something going on, maybe weed, but he didn't see any traces of it. Actually, he didn't even see a fucking ashtray laying around anywhere. But the smell that reeked throughout the house seemed to get a lot stronger towards the back. Double D pointed to a closed door and said, that was the room where Jabari was going to be crashing.

Double D opened the door to the room and Jabari stepped in to see a blonde, white chick bent over by a table, smoking something from a glass pipe. It was the smell he'd been inhaling since he arrived, Jabari knew it wasn't crack. When the white chick pulled back, she smiled at Jabari. Jabari grimaced because she was in desperate need of a toothbrush. Double D laughed a little when he saw Jabari's facial expression. Then he stepped out and shut the door behind him.

Jabari looked around, he didn't know what the chick wanted, but he damn sure didn't have any dope. She came closer to Jabari, timidly at first, then suddenly fell to her knees and started fumbling with his pants. Even though Jabari didn't know her, he knew exactly what she was about to do and he damn sure didn't put up any resistance. Her boldness and head skills made Jabari want to hold on to her.

AFTER ONLY BEING THERE for a few days Jabari was ex'ed the fuck up, smoking weed and then finally meth. The white bitch kept coming in and out, smoking dope and sucking his dick. At one point he'd tried to stop her, but she got on some freak shit. Jason the old school dude, talked him into fucking her while he watched, and she was down with it. Jabari was all jacked up and didn't give a fuck...that goddamned meth had him doing crazy shit. Then Jason went too far when he wanted Jabari to fuck her in the ass, while he watched. Jabari had been up for the past three days, so he was too weak to check Jason. Then Jason pulled out some pills, Jabari went for them and it was on after that, he felt straight played.

Double D checked in on Jabari from time to time making sure he was alright. Jabari needed to rest and eat something. He thought about the steaks that were on the table, uneaten. He finally realized why it was because everyone was too goddamned high to eat. Even if he didn't eat, he had to at least get some rest. When he finally woke up, he felt one-hundred times better. That meth shit, that was it, he couldn't do it anymore. He didn't understand how muthafuckas did that shit on a regular.

Jabari showered and walked into the kitchen finally haunting something to eat. The refrigerator was laid, with eggs, chicken, juice and more. The granola cereal caught Jabari's eye, so that what he went with. He was sitting at the table eating when Double D walked in.

"Yo' wassup...you alright?" he asked.

"Yeah, took me a minute though," Jabari replied.

"You'll be alright. I see you like that granola shit, huh?"

"It's alright, need to stay healthy." Jabari looked at the box then back at him. "I need to let you know what's going on, ya know."

"I feel you." Double D glanced out back around the house and turned around then smiled. "Pheeewww...hell, I need to do the same."

Jabari laughed. "For real, cause this some crazy shit you got going on."

"Yeah, well..." He smiled then stretched. "This is the life...for us. When you finish come outside and meet me in front of the barn. We'll talk."

"You sure it's alright? The dogs...dudes with guns..." "You straight." Double D promised.

The inside of the barn looked more like a make-shift office, not at all what Jabari was expecting. Double D nodded as Jabari gawked around at tables and cushioned chairs set up in the middle of the floor. A wooden desk was off t the side with an electronic scale on top and medium-sized plastic bags all filled with a powdery whitish substance. This really set it off for Jabari, at this point he had a good idea what was in them...meth. The windows were tinted dark and when he got closer, he noticed that they were clean and spotless. Double D said it was so they could see who was coming, clearly and no one could easily sneak up on them.

On another table, a crackling sound from a handheld receiver caught Jabari's attention. He walked closer and listened, it was a police scanner. A computer screen directly next to it showed images of satellite enhanced, area surveillance photos, shot in Google Earth. They had a scan of the whole muthafucking area. Double D came over and pressed a key and it flashed real-time images of the highway, the road in front and a place somewhere out in the woods that Jabari had never seen.

He pointed to the last one and said, "That's where you're going to be working."

"*Work!*" Jabari repeated shocked.

"Yeah, work, you got to do something while you're here. Hell, Jason's already complaining and 'sides we're short the help."

Jabari snickered. "Short the help? Fuck all y'all do 'round here is get high. Hell, you're high now and Jason...fuck that dude!" Jabari put up his hands and back away. "Naw, I don't want no parts of this shit. Meth too, we talkin' what twentyfive...thirty years...or even life. Naw, not me..." Jabari back into the pointed end of a rifle barrel. He turned quickly and Jason had an AK-47 pointed directly at his chest.

"Well, tell you what...if you don't...then, uh..." he looked over at Double D. "...we can't let you leave here." "Oh, hell naw!" Jabari screamed.

Jason slid one into the chamber. "It is what it is then. Hey, D, crank that boat up. We might need to take him for a little...swim, heh...heh."

Jabari looked over at Double D and he actually started to walk off towards the door to the creek. "Yo' man, you gonna let this go down," I asked.

Double D spun around, his face was all screwed up. "I ain't got no choices. You came here on your own. Said you was running from someone. You ain't said who, you might be the muthafuckin' man or somethin'."

"The man, you think I'm the man?" Jabari walked closer towards Double D and got in his face. "All the goddamned dope I smoked and shit, and hell...you know me. And you think I'm the fuckin' man!"

"Well, hell, 'Bari. You might be one of those informants or something. Looking to kill some time, we done had them types before."

Jabari damned raised his hands to slap the shit out of him, until Jason butted in. "Well, what are you here for?"

Jabari looked at them and they were both right. He had to tell them something. "Okay, y'all right." Jabari pulled up a seat and sat down in front of them, then he began explaining the whole thing from the beginning.

Jason lowered the AK and Double D just looked off out the window, then said, "Okay, okay, some muthafucka is lookin' for you because he thinks you might tell on his ass...snitchin' or some shit?" Double D sounded as if he had an attitude.

"Uh...yeah!"

Jason pulled up a chair and sat down with a look on this face that told Jabari he had a lot of fucked up questions.

"Hmm, 'bout thirty-grand...and four keys, lot of fuckin' money. But why'd you run? You ain't have nothin'."

Jabari rubbed both his hands across his sweaty face. "I got scared," he confessed. "Rip was killed, then the woman that was in the fire, I mean...I didn't have nothin' to do with it but try tellin' that to the cops."

"It be like that," Double D said. "You tell anyone you were coming here?"

"Hell, naw, I didn't know where you was at until you met me at I-95 in town. Your own mother don't even know where you're at."

"Now, you see why."
"I see, now."

Jason got up and tucked the rifle under his arm, then started walking towards the barn door. He turned around and looked at Jabari then at Double D. Jabari thought his life was over, he just knew they were going to kill him. He glanced over at a window thinking maybe if he dived through it, he could make a run for it. He'd be scratched and cut up, but at least he'd still be breathing. Jason studied where Jabari's eyes were going and started laughing.

"It won't work cuz. Okay, you can stay for a minute, but still, you gots to put in some work," Jason said.

Jabari looked over at Double D, Double D nodded in agreement. "Okay...okay, but I don't know shit about what y'all do here," Jabari finally said.

Jason glanced over his shoulders and said, "Hmph, trust me...you'll learn quick 'specially if I paid you with pills." Then he left out laughing.

"One day I'ma have to handle his ass," Jabari mumbled under his breath.

"Damn, Jabari," Double D said. "Don't see how you got caught up in that dumb shit, but, you're here now." He walked over to Jabari and pointed around the room. "This is where people come to pick up the dope."

"Pick up?"
"Yeah, we sell meth."

"Okay..." Jabari nodded, looking around the barn, seeing something he hadn't seen before.

"We sell it the same way muthafuckas sell crack, give or take. Ounces, half ounces, grams, hell even rocks of twenties.

But, one thing for sure, we sell it all. We got to get rid of it one way or another."

"A'ight, so this is the spot where everyone comes, huh?"
"Yeah."
"Suppose the man rolls up?"

Double D pointed Jabari to the computer screen, turned it around facing them and pressed some numbers. Images popped up on the screen, enhanced.

"This is out front, out back...hell, we got cameras on e'thing surrounding us, even the goddamned sky." Double D pointed to an electrical pipe leading up to the roof.

Sure, enough a small disk was mounted pointing outwards, Jabari knew one thing, it damn sure wasn't for cable TV.

"Yeah, we spends money, nobody ain't trying to feel the time if you get caught."

"I see you got those dudes out there with guns...ready!"

"We had to do something, oh believe me we done been tried before. So, Jason hired those two guys out front. They mind their business and they don't get high."

"That's good, must pay them pretty good, too?"

"Good enough, to put their asses on the line if they have to." Double D turned off the screen and walked Jabari to what normally would have been the horse stables.

Double D kicked some dirt and hay from around the ground and an o-ring appeared on the floor. He pulled at it and it sprang open, rather quickly. Inside were gun racks and cases of ammo from 9mms, .40s, then assault rifles and three M-14s. There were also bulletproof vests, they were dead serious about this shit. Double D pointed to the far left and showed Jabari a rocket launcher hidden underneath some canvas.

"What the fuck!" Jabari gasped.

Double D grinned. "Yeah, we picked that one up one night from some Arab boys. Fuckin' around with that same trick that be suckin' yo' dick."

"Hold up...hold up!" Jabari started tripping. "You mean to tell me they was getting high?"

"Hell yeah. They couldn't afford the shit either, after a while, next thing you know Jason's on some ole wanting to hang the muthafuckas type shit. He was fuckin' geeking up on them damn N'ratins." Double D started laughing and Jabari couldn't help but laugh himself. "Them muthafuckas ripped open the bottom of the SUV they were driving and
bam...rocket fuckin' launcher."

"Still shoulda hung them muthafuckas!" It was Jason, he'd brought his crazy ass back in, being nosey. "You shoulda seen

them muthafuckin' rag-heads haul ass outta here." "That's why Stacy..." "Stacy?" Jabari repeated.

"Damn, she's been suckin' your dick and fuckin' you for 'bout a week and you don't even know her goddamned name?" Jason said. "I see why nigga keep getting that goddamned shit...that's fucked up."

Jabari looked at the ground and kicked a rock. "Damn!" Jason was right, it was all fucked up.

"Her name is Stacy," Double D confirmed. "And she was the one who bought them here. Hell, it was a good deal though, we made money. I ain't mad at her, she ain't had no
place to go. So, she crashes here, steers customers to us, too."

Jabari looked at Double D and smirked. He knew her ass wasn't actually tricking.

"Trust me, she looks better after she takes a break from that shit." Double D assured.

"So, Jabari?" Jason approached him. "You know 'bout

everything about us. So, you in or what?"

Jabari extended his hand to him and nodded. "I'm in!"

"That's good, but don't get it fucked up. It gets serious and can get bad real fast."

"I'll stick it out, Double Dd can vouch for me..."
"He done did already."
"But, damn, you was about to kill me!"

Jason laughed. "Maybe...maybe not!" Jason closed the gun rack and covered it back up. Then he looked over at Jabari and cocked an eyebrow. "By the way, who's this fella that's trying to kill you anyway?"
"Some dude outta Charleston, I don't think you know him."

"Try me, you'd be surprised."
"His name is, Hulie."
"Oh hell!"
"What? Don't tell me you know him!"

"Do I know him?" Jason walked over to the side of the barn and kicked the door, causing dust to scatter all over the place. One of the men outside peeped in and asked if everything was alright. Jason waved them off, then looked over at

LOST BOY 201

ME. "YOU DONE GOT YOURSELF caught up with one crazy-ass nigga!"

Chapter Ten

The situation Jabari was in was unlike anything he'd ever seen. Sure, they made good money, but there was a lot of paranoia that went right along with that. Everyone got caught up with the thought that someone was the goddamned police even him. Normally according to Jason, it would just take two people to make meth. One person was needed to go to the store to buy or either steal the pills they needed, that would most likely always be Double D. Then they needed someone else to get the other ingredients. They would punish the hardware stores for Denatured alcohol, sulfuric acid, lithium batteries, and STP starter fluid. They put Jabari on that, because Double D had become a hot boy, and him getting caught up with pops in Ekherds didn't make it any better.

They had to be real careful that none of those items could be bought at the same time. Two or more could get you a manufacturing charge, easy. Then you had to be careful who was at the check out line with you. Jabari found out first hand that a lot of white folks fucked around with meth. They would end up following him to the truck, then cracking on where his spot was. Of course, Jabari played dumb, which wasn't hard to do because he were, and he was glad Double D

202

and them kept it that way. Anyone of them could have been the man.

The hardest thing to get and the most important was Anhydrous Ammonium Gas. Jabari tried going to a Welder's supply shop to get some, but they wanted some credentials, a business license or a Welder's certificate. Jabari had none of those and neither did Double D. It was a stroke of luck, fucking around the hardware store and casing it out. Jabari struck up a conversation with this older dude, who was a preacher. He'd preached around the same area where Jabari's old man grew up. In a small, one-stoplight only town called Ruffin. Anyway, Jabari told him he was visiting the area and he asked Jabari if needed a job.

"No, I'm alright," Jabari told him.

"Good, I don't you'd want to do anything like I do anyway," the preacher responded.

Double D started clowning Jabari, then for the hell of it, Jabari asked the preacher what was it that he actually did. The preacher worked on a fucking chicken farm.

"Oh hell, no, I can't be fuckin' wit' chicken shit all day long," he damn near screamed at the preacher, then turned to talk shit to Double D.

Double D had a gleam in his eyes like he'd just won the lottery. In a way he did, because farmers used the gas to fertilize their soil, and wouldn't you fucking know it, that's exactly what needed to be done. So, Jabari was knee deep in chicken shit. Double D didn't want to fuck his face up or cause any suspicion, being that the old dude knew people, so he laid low. Next thing Jabari knew, he was on his way to Moncks Corners in another town, this one was a lot bigger and he started working with the preacher for a few days.

Double D followed them and quickly and quietly scooped out the spot and eventually stole most of the shit they needed. Jabari felt sorry for the preacher. To make things worse he and the preacher had actually prayed for the thief who stole his shit. Jabari felt so bad, until later and he'd finally dove into a couple of pills. Then he was like fuck it, Oxycontin had that effect on people.

Once they got all the shit they needed together, they needed to show Jabari where it was going to be cooked. That's how he got to know Smoak, cooking the shit was Smoak's job.

HULIE FINALLY CAUGHT up with Diplite in Liberty Hill and met him up on Montague and Abraham Avenue, where he was watching tricks. Diplite had control of the small, drug-heavy community but every now and then he'd have a little show of force, to let folks know he was connected. All the big boy hustlas from the Chuck rode through. Hulie was one of the ballas that showed his face every now and then.

Hulie figured it was a good opportunity to pick his brain. He hadn't really kicked it with him since the time they rolled on T-Black. Diplite's sister Cleo had spilled the beans about T-Black's mother and Hulie definitely wanted to know more. He would have never thought Diplite had anything to do with the money that was missing, but he didn't put it past him either.

Hulie pulled up into the lot outside of the candy store across from him. He jumped out, checking out the area and scenery. Runners, small-time hustlas, and fast ass young girls came out of the woodworks trying to flaunt in front of him, hoping to tap in on the quote-unquote, small, pocket change he kept. Hulie was that dude, but right now, he wasn't concerned with all that. He had to stay focused on the bigger picture, Sunshine's money, if not his ass was gonna do hard time and the asses he would see there damn sure wouldn't be no young girls. He shivered at that notion.

"Yo...what's up?" he said as he reached out and dapped Diplite, then sat down next to him on a bench underneath an oak, shade tree, hiding from the low country sun while Diplite choked down peanuts and soda.

"What's up, ain't seen you in a minute," Diplite said.

"Been trying to handle some bis'ness, that's all."

"Yeah...what kind?"

Hulie smirked. "C'mon, now."

"I know, none of my business."

"Sum'thing like that."

"Well," Diplite threw some peanut hulls off into the dirt and turned slightly towards. "What's up with the other business?"

"Other business..."

"C'mon now, Hulie, we got two...well...you got two bodies on your hands and so far, as I know, no muthafuckin' money. Where we at wit' that?"

Hulie grinned and turned towards Diplite. Diplite had gotten straight to the point and Hulie knew he had something up his sleeve because his body tensed up and he normally squirmed whenever he was around. So, he played the game

Diplite had set up for him and went with it.

"Yeah, I got them bodies or at least your partners, partner...remember him? The one you put down...Jabari...he's got them, kna'mean."

"I know what you mean, but you ain't got Jabari, though.

And he could finger you easily, you know what I mean?"

"Finger me on what? Who else seen an'thing or even knows an'thing...except you? And, uh, I know you ain't saying an'thing...right?" He peeped out the corner of his eyes.

"Naw...but supposed that dude's moms..." Diplite fucked up that quick and had said too much already and Hulie caught it. Diplite stayed true to his character, a fuck up as far as he was concerned. He knew he shouldn't have known a damn thing about T-Black's moms except that she was missing and presumed according to the news. No one else would have known shit, except, of course, her. Like Diplite said, he hadn't seen him in a minute, so now he knew, she was at least still alive.

Diplite knew he had fucked up, but still figured he had all the cards in his hands, mainly Nikki herself, so he played them. "Well, I mean, suppose she spoke to someone." Damn, he'd fucked up again. He was losing, giving Hulie more leverage, more info than he wanted to. He had to somehow put Hulie in a position so that they could be on equal ground. He had to spook him in some sort of way and find a balance.

Still, Hulie didn't say a word, he just casually played it off, smiled and waved at some of the local hustlas that came through, occasionally winking at a trick or two. He turned his head slowly towards Diplite who was now handing on his every move, trying to feel Hulie out. So, far he was fucking up and Hulie knew it, now he had to play the game.

"So, uh...you seen your sister?" Hulie got on that emotional, manipulation shit.

Diplite didn't anticipate that question, he relaxed, maybe he thought he hadn't figured it out, yet. "I heard from her the other night. She said she was going to go see moms later..."

"No...not that." He was dead wrong, and he'd have to pay.

Hulie pointed towards the back part of the block, on Disco Street going towards the subdivision. "I mean on the hoestroll!" He shook his head. "Mom...naw, I don't get down like that. I really don't give a fuck. Hell, I just wanted to know why on this pretty ass day with plenty of fuckin' money comin' through she ain't out sellin' that good pussy." He turned towards him crossing his leg. "Kna'mean, oh, yeah that's right. I mean all this money, cuz, damn she could be suckin' pretty dick right about now...besides mine." He slapped him playfully. "But, yeah, I understand she gots to see mom-dukes e'er now and then...that's right." He started laughing, knowing that this was the dagger he was gonna stick through Diplite's heart. "Them lips gotta rest sometime...but you think after suckin' all that dick, she kisses her own mother when she sees her? That's just nasty..."

"A'ight...that's enough!" Diplite said about to go off.

"Whoa, my man, I didn't mean to offend you." He saw that he had him where he wanted and got up. "Look, I'll talk to you later on, okay." He pulled up the sleeve of his jacket and unsnapped a twelve-jewel encrusted, gold watch and tossed it at him. "Here you go, a little present, okay."

Diplite caught it and examined it. "Naw, I'm alright." He started to toss it back at him.

"No, no...keep it. It's cool! I apologize for what I said. Didn't mean to hit a soft spot, but..." He turned to walk away, then glanced back around. "Seriously, though, when you do see your sister, tell her..." He fixed his fingers into a phone and put it by his ear. "...to call me!"

Diplite sat still, fuming as he watched Hulie pull off. He was definitely feeling some sort of way and wanted to kill that muthafucka. He knew now more than anything he'd have to get that money from Nikki, one way or another. If she wasn't willing to do it voluntarily, he'd have to pry it from her cold, dead hands.

Hulie drove a little-ways down Liberty Hill towards the Height snickering to himself about how he played Diplite and how weak he was. Now, he knew for sure that the chick wasn't dead. She'd be easy to find, a little money on the street could do the job perfectly. He also knew that she must have had the money because Diplite knew about it. Hulie had never told him that he didn't get the money that night.

'*Punk, muthafucka trying to play me,*' he thought. "I got a trick for his ass."

He stopped by the Jamaican restaurant on River's Avenue after leaving Diplite. He stayed there for a good minute eating bean pies and drinking ale. He stepped out back at one point and smoked a blunt with one of his homeboys, it was good weed, too. When he got good and high, he dipped. It all seemed pretty intense as he turned off of River's Avenue on Reynolds past Spruill Avenue. He could see his house from a distance, beckoning him, calling him like it had been violated, something just didn't look right. He shook it off, placing the blame on paranoia, especially after the episode he had with Sunshine earlier, she had him shook.

He felt like he had no privacy. He glanced around and didn't see her car, but as he came down the block, all eyes were on him, or so it seemed to him, weed still had his head banging. Instead of the hustlas and runners standing on the corner down from him shooting the shit, which was the norm, they were across the street or gathered up the block. He pulled into the driveway, got out and from the corner of his eye, the store's owner walked out, with a broom in his hand, sweeping, checking him out. He wasn't sure, but he swore he'd seen a little smile on his face. Now, he knew something was wrong, that fat, lazy ass bastard didn't do no work, he usually let them crackhead broads do it for him, then he'd take them in the back, pay them and smoke up their dope. The muthafucka didn't like him cause he never gave him credit.

'*The police?*' he thought. '*They must be somewhere around, scoping me out? Ready to come out the bushes as soon as I get in the door and all these muthafuckas are ready to see me go down!*'

Hulie took out the gun he had underneath the seat and pulled out the clip. A felon with a gun was straight Fed time. When he got inside, he figured he'd go straight to his stash spot and hide it.

"What if they bust in while I am in there? They'll take my gun and everything that's not nailed down. Naw, that ain't gonna work," he said to himself.

He peeped his head out of the truck looking around for someone he could give it to. A crackhead maybe, it was risky, but he'd give up a cookie, easy. No one was close by, everyone was up the block, watching him.

"Damn, something's up!" he said.

He glanced toward the backyard. That's how he was gonna have to do it. He'd have to go around back and toss the gun and clip across the yard to the railroad tracks. He pulled a rag from underneath the seat and cleared off the prints carefully, then wrapped it up and stuffed it in his pocket. He moved cautiously, ready for anything. Once he got out back, he tossed the rag and gun, looked around to see if anyone was looking and headed straight to the back door, pulling out his keys all in one swift motion. The door lock was jammed, he looked closer and it was broken, and all busted up. He pushed at it and it opened slowly.

He eased in a little-ways and yelled out. "Who the fuck is in here...if I catch you, it's your ass!"

That was definitely wolf tickets cause he didn't have nothing on him at all, and if they did, he'd be the one fucked up. He needed something just in case, he peeped out back and noticed a bar that he used for weights leaning against the door. He grabbed it and started easing his way in again, this time with the bar raised, he was ready to swing. The place was dark, and he stayed still and low for a minute, waiting to hear if anyone was stirring. He hadn't heard shit, he felt for the light switch, gripped the bar and clicked it on.

"Aw, shit," he gasped.

The place was a wreck, glasses and dishes were broken. Drawers were pulled open and tossed to the floor. His refrigerator door was barely hanging off the hinges and the insides gutted. Whoever did that was looking for dope and money. Everything in the freezer was torn apart, they had to be on some old Jada Kiss freezer, popsicle shit. Insulation was all over the floor cut up. He looked up, they'd gone through the vents too. Pots, pans and everything in the kitchen was all over the floor, even the goddamned flour, grits, and muthafuckin' Jiffy mix.

Hulie stepped into the living room and it was more of the same shit. He rushed over to where his fish tank was and sighed. Whoever hit him up poured Clorox in the tank and all his fish were floating belly up.

"Bastards!" he screamed as he punched a hole in the wall.

His bedroom was the same shit, mattress ripped open, the closet was butchered up, and his clothes were cut up and thrown all over the place. That had to be just plain hate. He looked over on the dresser and his jewelry box was empty. He picked it up and threw it at a mirror, smashing it and scattering little pieces of glass all over. Hulie was pissed off, but he knew one thing for sure. The one place he knew was untouched, had to be his own personal stash spot. No one knew about it, he rushed into the living room and opened the linen closet. Someone had been there already, the faked-out rack holder insert, hiding the concealed wall paneling was pulled opened, crudely, with a pry bar. He got closer and looked, everything was cleaned out, except for a few papers here and there.

"Damn, what the hell...Sunshine!" Hulie remembered she saw him go in there. "It had to be her ass!"

He walked through the house kicking shit out of his way. Then said fuck it, and walked to the front door, swung it open, and stepped out onto the porch. Now, all of a sudden, a group gathered in front across the street, checking the whole thing out.

"Y'all know what it is, anybody see anything?" he hollered.

They all looked at him like he was crazy, then shook their heads no. No one saw shit, so they claimed.

"Bullshit!" he snarled. "Yeah...I know, but I'll say this. If I catch the muthafucka or even the muthafuckas that had anything to do with this bullshit!" He fixed his hand into a gun and pointed at them. 'Pow, you know what it is. You got this one...for now!"

They knew he meant that shit, too. He started to turn away, but there was a face in the crowd that caught his attention. That dude, Q. He left with Sunshine that day, maybe she said something to him. She mighta been looking for the money, thinking he was holding out, that was her M.O. He looked at him and mugged. Q looked off, talkin' to his boys, then they walked off, ignoring Hulie, playin' him out like a pussy.

Hulie nodded, he knew he had something to do with it.

He looked across the street up over the store and spotted what he was searching for. A window across the street in an apartment, with tan blinds, barely half opened.

Hulie grinned. "Yep...somebody know what went down!"

HE STOOD AT THE KITCHEN counter hunched over, his head bushy and grey. His brown eyes were strikingly bright white, with crow's feet around the corners. He'd seen a lot in his long life. Hulie was awestruck by his massive, broad shoulders, arms like Popeye the sailor and a tattoo on his right arm that read: *Mom!*

The old man turned towards him and sat down a cup. "This that der good coffee, hear me? My gran'baby got it from one dem 'xotic stores in New York City." He reached on his mantlepiece and picked up a picture of a big smileyfaced, young girl and beamed. "Luv dat yungen. Luv herself some pop-pop, too!" He put the picture down and picked up the cup of hot coffee in front of him and looked around the rather dimly lit, neat place. "Ya know, I been here at dis here

'partment for 'bout ten years now...since me wife died."

"Yo' pop...sorry to hear 'bout that." Hulie was genuinely sincere.

He'd met the old man a couple of times out back behind his house on the railroad tracks picking up cans. He offered him some money, but the old man turned it down and said he was alright. Hulie got used to seeing him and when he found out he liked coffee, he'd leave him a cup or two out back, and sure enough, it was well appreciated. They got to talkin' and he told Hulie he once worked at the Shipyards, but long time retired, telling him stories of the places he'd been and things he'd seen. He told Hulie he had a family, two girls, one was in Atlanta and the other left to go to New York recently. They got in touch with him on a regular basis, begging him to move but he wouldn't, because he was stubborn like that.

Instead, he took all the money he had saved, along with his pension and paid off his grandchildren's college tuitions. He swore they'd never have to work as hard as he did, ever. Hulie, respected him to the fullest. The old man eventually found out the lifestyle he was into, but he didn't judge him. He just told him more stories of hustlers gone by, years ago, and gave him tips and pointers like a grand-pops would. He told Hulie he'd watch the house for him when he was gone, and he did just that.

"T'was two of dem boys. One was short and stumpy with dem long braids or sumptin' in his head. What's dat name for dem?"

"Dreads..."

"Yuh, dat dem. That other was an ole tall boy, 'bout a little taller than you. He was skinny, tho...small thing. But he had a nice hair cut, real sharp der. Could tell he didn't get it round here." He laughed and Hulie smiled at him. His pretty white teeth and bright red gums spoke volumes. He was

Charleston...the real.

Hulie couldn't remember the old man's name, he probably told him at one time, but it didn't matter, he woulda called him Pops anyway. The old fella respected that. He also found out he had a passion for fishing. Hulie didn't hesitate to pull out the brand-new, shiny reel and rod he'd just gotten and give it to him.

"Didn't have to do that, son. I'da watched the place for nuthin'. Dem yung boys just can't be breakin' in shit, ya know. T'wasn't like that before."

"I know, I know, but I remembered you told me your old one wasn't holdin' the line like it used to. Hell, I'da brought it over anyway."

Pops picked it up and examined it. "Reallll nice...spent good money, too. Thank ya!" He got up and opened the closet door, checking out a brand-new fishing outfit he'd collected over time. It was a slickers fishing vest with a brand-new hat, and all the hooks he needed attached to it. He smiled, "Ya' know, maybe I should make that trip down Beaufort way now."

"Beaufort? You never told me you had people in Beaufort before."

"I don't." He closed the door and walked over to the pictures posted up on the mantlepiece and picked up one. An old black and white photo of a beautiful, full-haired, brownskinned woman with the prettiest, whitest smile he'd ever seen. "That's where me wife at. Been meanin' to go see her...gravesite and all. Who knows...might stay down der with, her?" He turned towards Hulie and smiled, then looked off out the window with the picture still in his hand. "Yuh might stay down der..." His voice trailed off into a whisper, he was gone.

His mind had left just that quick. Hulie wasn't mad at him, he'd gotten all the information he needed anyway. It was his cue to leave, he got up and crept toward the front door, but not before he reached into his pocket and pulled out thirty, one-hundred-dollar bills, placed them on the floor, then silently closed the door and left.

The old man walked back over to the mantlepiece and put the picture back down, then kissed it. Afterward, he went over to the door and locked it, then picked up the money and walked over to the table. He poured another cup of coffee and sat down. He reached for an envelope on the counter that had the name and address of a bank on it, then reached into his wallet and took out a picture of a bouncing, cute baby boy.

He looked at it and grinned. "Well, yungen...time for you to get ready for College, too. Don' have much time, ya know!"

DIPLITE HAD CALLED his sister, Cleo, she was out of breath when she answered the phone. "I did it!"

"A'ight...a'ight!" Diplite said. "Anybody see you?"

"No, I came up from around the back, behind the railroad tracks."

"You sound winded and shit. "I know you ain't do all the work, right? I paid them boys' good money to help!"

"I'm straight, oh I paid them an extra two bills a piece."

"Two bills? What the fuck...I thought you was supposed to just give them..."

"I sucked both of their young dicks. Shit, they were glad to get that, and the afterward, they tried to give it back.

Fuckin' suckas!"

"Crazy...but I hear you." Diplite picked up his head when he saw Dirty-Red's car come through. He had to take care of business with him, now. He'd already gotten under Hulie's skin, but it was his sister's plan to rob him, and she did good too. '*Punk muthafucka!*' he thought. "Trying to play! That muthafucka too stupid for that." Diplite got up and looked around. He'd seen enough for today, and enough people saw him for that matter, outside at the same spot. He had a good

muthafuckin' alibi, now he was out. "Hey, sis!"

"Yeah?"

"Keep the money, a'ight!"

"What...why?"

"Cause you gonna need it when you go outta town, anyway."

"Yeah...you're right. When?"

"I'm going over to Dirty-Red's right now. I'll call you later!"

Diplite hung up his phone and got into his car. He thought about the lick his sister made on Hulie, she'd got at least fifteen thousand. He knew pretty soon, Hulie would be calling him, wanting to get some get back on whoever and asking him for a favor. Diplite laughed, he was going to play Hulie again just like he'd done with T-Black, but this time he was gonna get all his money, that dumb ass, freak Sunshine's and if Dirty-Red slipped...his too.

Q PUT HIS FOOT UP ON some old chairs as he stood in front of the old Circle A on Spruill Avenue. He was waiting for a call back from Sunshine, finally, the phone buzzed.

"Yeah, what's going on, babe? You've been blowing me up."

"Trouble!"
"What?"
"Yeah, trouble."

"What kinda trouble? I can hear it in your voice, cops fuckin' wit' you, baby?"

"Naw, it ain't that." He looked around. "That dude Hulie just got robbed."

"No...really! That's good for his punk ass."
"Naw, that ain't good!"
"Why Q? You ain't never liked him anyway."

"True, but he thinks I had something to do wit' it. I know it!"

"Ooh, shit, be careful. You want me to have him picked up...brought in?"

"Naw, that's alright, I can handle me. We'll see how this plays out."

"Cool! You know who did it?"

"That's the strange thing, no one saw shit. I swear, they musta knew his crib because it was like boom, bam and they was gone. A couple of people heard some noise, but they didn't think nuthin' of it. Just thought maybe, he was beating that chick up like he always do."

"Know that's right, I wonder if they got any money?"

"Don't know, but...look, I gotta go, okay. I'll holler at you later."

"Will you be able to make it over to my place? I'm horny!"

Q rubbed his crotch, he knew what it was. He wanted to see her, too. She was putting it on his ass pretty regular and he was whipped.

"Yeah, I'll be there." He hung up the phone and stuffed it in his pocket, looked both ways and dipped back down Baxter Street out of sight, totally oblivious to the eyes that followed closely behind him.

Sunshine spun her chair around and stared out the window. She knew if Hulie thought Q was involved then she damn sure knew he thought she was too. One thing was for sure if she knew that spot, he had in the closet was holding she would've got the money, but maybe he didn't have it there.

Maybe he didn't have it at all. She banged her fist on the desk.

"Shit, I need to get this money! Put some pressure on his dumb-ass...or he's just gonna have to go to Prison for a long fuckin' time. Punk muthafucka, fuckin' wit' me. No...no, hell maybe Q might be of some use for me after-all. Instead of just being a stiff dick!" She smiled and spun back around. "I just

might be able to make this work for me!"

Chapter Eleven

Cleo laid back on her bed counting the money she'd just stole from Hulie. She was feeling herself, she had a little over ten stacks. Plus, the money her brother was going to give her for the trip to Cheraw. If she was lucky, she figured DirtyRed would also end up giving her a nice little chunk of change as well.

She was tickled to death as she rolled around her bed, playing with the money, knowing full well she could kick Hulie to the curb now and get herself a real playa, instead of some thug come-up like him. She stopped for a moment after she heard her mother call out her name, asking if she would be home for supper. Cleo opened the door and told her no. After all, she could afford to go out and eat now, easily. She did think about taking her moms out to dinner, but she knew her mother would only fuss about where she got the money and Cleo wasn't in the mood for that. Maybe, once she returned from the country, she'd take her out then, and tell her that Diplite gave her some money.

Her moms was the type to pry, but she was also in straight denial too. People would continually tell her that her daughter was out there selling pussy on the streets. However, Cleo denied it promising that she was just dating different guys and exploring herself. Her pops, on the other hand, was hardly

220

around. He stayed an active businessman and spent most of his time on the road. In all truth, he was out fuckin' everything he could get his hands on. So, it was like father...like daughter as far as Cleo was concerned.

Her moms would just plain old gossip over the phone when he wasn't home. Which was often, and every now and then when he was, she'd take a sip of Jack Daniels, then crawl into bed with him demanding a good fuck, telling him it was the one job he was good at. She thought more than once about getting a boy on the side, but the last time she made an attempt, Diplite found out about and beat the young man senseless. No one had seen or heard from the young man since, although Cleo's mom couldn't prove it, she swore her father had something to do with the young man's sudden disappearance.

Cleo figured it would be a good of a time as any to go through her closet and see what she needed for the trip. Then a shopping spree would definitely be in order. She turned up her iPod, put on her headset and started dancing to an old school, funky ass, reggae beat. She grinded her hips into a frenzy as she threw out of the closet across her bed. She stopped suddenly when the door popped open.

"Cleo, baby, some guy's downstairs at the door to see you," Cleo's mother said.

Cleo took the headset off and shot her mother a strange look. "*See me?*" she repeated. "Well, who is he? I wasn't expecting no one!"

Cleo's mother eye hustled the room and Cleo caught her scanning the place like a radar. She started for the bed where the money was scattered about, but Cleo rushed in front of her.

"What's that all over the bed...money?" Cleo's mother asked eyeing her sternly.

'Damn!' Cleo screamed aloud in her head. She made her mother head back toward the door and started rambling. "Just old crumpled up dollar bills. Me and some of my girls are going to a strip club."

"*Strip club?*" her mother asked for clarification.

"Uh...yes!" Cleo knew she should've come up with a better response than that, but she had to keep it going now. "A male strip club. They just opened it in Columbia. Remember, I told you I was going out of town for a week or so? C'mon now you remember!"

Her mom looked at her like she was crazy. She knew her ass was lying, but denial kicked in again. "I think I remember you saying something about it," she finally answered.

"And when I come back..." Cleo grabbed her mother by the hand, then walked her out to the stairs, but not before she closed her door behind them and locked it. "...one day I'ma take you there."

"You always say stuff like that."

"What? Oh no, you didn't!" Cleo stepped back and looked her mother up and down. "The only reason I don't take you out with me anywhere is because you look like my damn sister. I don't need no comp!" That was the one that did it for her.

Mom-dukes giggled like a baby with candy and they bounced down the stairs arm in arm toward the door. Then Cleo's mother cut off into the living room, feeling good and probably getting ready to call one of her girlfriends to talk shit about how young she still looked.

"As long as you ain't with that dope dealer boy...what's his name again?" Cleo's mother asked.

"Ma his name is Hulie," Cleo responded.

"Yeah, yeah...Hulie that shit. Sounds like some hoodlum to me. And how could I possibly forget that?" Cleo's mother said sarcastically out of the side of her mouth.

Cleo waved her off as she dipped, straightened up her hair and answered the door. Her face frowned up when she saw who it was, then she stepped outside the door, looking over his shoulder at the old Bondo covered hooptie.

"What the hell are you doing here?" Cleo asked.

The slim built young man who was in his twenties was well dressed as he stood there, with a bouquet of flowers in his hand and the biggest cheese-eating smile she'd ever seen.

"Thought I'd stop by and give you these..." he said.

"Thought you'd stop by...what the fuck! Are you crazy?"

He looked at her twisted then sideways. "I thought after what went down. I told you I was feelin' something for you."

"Look, you got to leave. If we get seen together by my old man. Shit!" She started to escort him back to his car.

He stopped and said, "Okay, I tried the nice guy shit. Fuck that!" He threw the flowers to the ground. "No, you look, fuck that nigga, Hulie, he can get it, too. Right now, I'm feelin' some sort of way about the way we got down...and to be straight up, I want some more. So, wassup?"

"Oh, hell no. You gots to pay for this pussy. Shit ain't free!"

Her moms opened the door and started eye hustling again. "Everything alright?" she asked.

Cleo gave him the look and he smiled. He had her where he wanted her.

"Yes, ma'am, she just dropped the flowers I was giving her, and we were just about to go out back and find a uh...vase."

He cut his eyes at Cleo. "Right...sweetheart!"

Cleo sighed. "Uh, yeah, ma!" She bent over and picked up the flowers.

Cleo and the young man walked off toward the side of the house out of view, then they stopped.

"Look, I'm not tryin' to take no pussy or nothing, a'ight. Just got out of prison and your brother called me to do the lick and fuck it. I needed the bread, but when I saw you...remember it was you who wanted to suck me and my man's dick. I ain't force you to do..."

"Okay...okay!" Cleo threw her hands up, knowing he was right. "What do you want? More money...because if you do,

you have to deal with my brother."

He pulled her by the arm and pushed her up against the house, then directed down the steps leading to the cellar. Once he got down there, he pulled his dick out.

"You know what it is. Now get your ass down here...tired of playin' games!" he growled.

"What...oh hell no..." Cleo didn't see the slap as it struck her hard across the mouth.

"Get down...ain't got much time."

Cleo got down on her knees and after stroking his dick she swallowed it in her mouth. The side of her face stung as he rubbed it softly, matching stroke for stroke as she sucked. Somehow, she had to get rid of him, quick. He was another Hulie in the making and she damn sure didn't need that. She continued to suck him off as his head looked upward toward the sky and his eyes fluttered in ecstasy. He mumbled something to himself, saying something about love and shit, but a hard dick could make a man say or do anything.

In the meanwhile, all Cleo had to do was step back a little and she would have easily spotted her mom's looking right dead at them. She watched as her baby girl sucked his dick, with one hand she wiped the window to get a better view and with the other, she started playing with her already fattened clit and masturbating. She wasn't mad at Cleo, after-all she was just like her mother and father a stone-cold freak.

DIPLITE CAME UP BEHIND Dirty-Red as he pulled into the driveway. He didn't get out of the, but he watched as he unlocked the chained linked fence and made his way to the door. Once it was opened, he waved at him to come in and Diplite was right behind him. Dirty-Red tossed his keys on the table and walked back out to his car, where the trunk was opened and wrestled with a big bag full of red party cups, then pointed and Diplite ran out and grabbed another bag full of chicken wings. He bought them in and asked was there anything else. Dirty-Red shook his head, grabbed his keys and opened his liquor closet and dragged out a keg. Diplite watched as he drug out three, after he was finished sat down across from him, pulled out a handkerchief and wiped his forehead.

"So, what's up?" Dirty-Red asked. "You got things in order or what?"

"Yeah," Diplite said as he walked around the counter and poured a cold one from the tap. "My sister's ready to go."

"Cool."

"Oh yeah... by the way..."

"Now what? I can tell by your voice, there's some bullshit coming wit' it." Dirty-Red smiled and reached out grabbing the mug Diplite passed him.

"My sister wants to..."

"Oh hell, knew it was sumptin'. What the fuck that crazy ass broad want now?"

"You know what it is, she feeling you like that."

"Well." He took a swig. "Tell the truth, she ain't a bad chick, for real, but that cat she fucks wit'...Hulie. He's a goddamned problem! Don' know how you let her..."

"Whoa, hold up, cuz. I can't make her do shit, she's grown!"

"You right, she grown. She can make her own decisions and all that shit." Dirty-Red got up after he spotted someone coming up through the back. "But, you gots to put her in a better position after all, so she can make better decisions knamean."

Diplite shook his head, Dirty-Red was dead right. Hell, it would be a better situation if Cleo was Red's girl. He needed a main squeeze anyway, but there was no more he could really trust. Cleo would fall right in line, long as she could make some money, shop and floss she was straight. Besides he and his people were tired of Hulie beating on her anyway. Who knew, maybe after this lick, if things went right, he'd finally get Cleo away from that no good, ass muthafucka.

WHEN DIRTY-RED CAME back, Nikki was right behind him dragging a large duffel bag. Diplite got up and hoisted it on his shoulders, then put it on the couch.

"There you go, damn girl, it's heavy as hell," Diplite complained.

"Coupla tings fa tha trip, that all. You spoke to your sista yet?"

"She just needs to know where you want to meet her?" Nikki looked over at Dirty-Red.

"Guess, right yer' be good," Dirty-Red agreed.

Nikki pointed to the bag and said, "The money's on top, it ain't no full ninety-six, though. Short about s'ree, I had to pay for room and board."

"That's what's up, it's cool. Shit trust me flipping ninety grand is a good payday. Right, Dip?"

"Hell yuh!" Diplite said trying to open the top bag, but the zipper attached got caught.

Nikki came over and tugged on it. "Sometimes it gets stuck, you gotta fight with it."

Diplite grabbed it and snatched until it popped up but not before Nikki jumped back and gasped. "Let me see that."

"What?" Diplite said as he started pulling out stacks and counting them. "You talkin' 'bout the money?" "No..." she pointed to his watch.

Dirty-Red grinned. "Yuh noticed that too...nice ass watch looks expensive!" Dirty-Red came closer and looked at it as it shined from the glitter off the diamonds. "Looks like a Rolex or something."

Diplite shrugged it off. "Somebody gave it to me."

"Who?" Nikki asked.

"Nobody important...somebody just gave it to me, okay."

Nikki pushed him out of the way and started grabbing the money out of his hands, stuffing it back into the bag.

Diplite tried to stop her by putting his hand on her arm. Nikki spazzed on him. "Don' touch me...ever!"

Diplite stepped back and looked over at Red, confusing the fuck out of both of them. Dirty-Red stepped closer to Nikki trying to figure her out. Nikki reached into her waistband. Dirty-Red could see the shine from the handle of the dagger she was gripping.

He immediately stopped her. "Hold up, Nikki. What the fuck is up?" Dirty-Red asked slowly backing away from her.

"The deal is off." She started backing away, slowly dragging the bag towards the door. "And don' try to stop me, or I swear..."

"Hold the fuck up, Nikki!" Dirty-Red raised his voice a notch. "What the fuck is going on...you flippin' or what?" "Sumptin' ain't right, hem know what!" Nikki pointed at Diplite. "That me goddamned..." She caught herself, thinking about what she was about to say and realized she couldn't really accuse Diplite of anything. She had to find out more or at least where he'd gotten the watch from. It could just as well have been a crackhead, instead of one of the muthafuckas that robbed her that night. "Need a few more days, that's all."

"Few more days!" Diplite yelled. "Hell naw, we ready to roll now."

She looked Red straight in the eyes, he knew something wasn't right. He also knew it had something to do with the watch, but he figured she'd tell him something later. Right now, he had to just go with it. He couldn't let this sweet a deal go.

"Okay, okay, but Nikki hear me out. Take some time to get whatever it is that's fuckin' wit' you outta the way. Then it's a done deal, a'ight."

Nikki wouldn't look at Diplite for hell. She had to set a trap, that's if a trap wasn't being set-up for her. She had to at least trust Red, he'd been straight up with her so far. The look in his eyes showed her was baffled. He didn't know nuthin'.

"Okay...okay, a few days that all. Got me reasons...spect that." She finally glanced over at Diplite and mean mugged the hell out of him.

"What the fuck did I do?" Diplite asked as he put up his hands.

Nikki walked over to him, ungripping the handled of her dagger and said, "Nothing...I hope!" She turned back towards

Red. "I trust you to put the money up. You do that for me?" Dirty-Red answered yes and asked Diplite to leave. "Yo' man I'll call you, a'ight."

"What the fuck?" Diplite groaned.

Dirty-Red escorted him to the door and watched as he pulled off in his car. Then he closed the door and turned toward Nikki. "Had sumptin' to do wit' dat watch, right?"

"Yuh!"

"A'ight." Dirty-Red pointed toward a seat and said, "Sit your ass down. You need to tell me sumptin'. Fuck the games, but straight up. Don't put me in no bullshit. Now, what's up with tha fuckin' watch?" Nikki sniffled as a tear gently ran down her face. DirtyRed handed her a napkin. "That been me son's watch. The muthafucka dat fucked me up dat night, snatch it from me house. He's wearin' it, he knows who did it, or hem might

have had sumptin' to do wit' it. I can jus feel it!"

Dirty-Red sat down contemplating on what Nikki had just said, she was right. He'd been on that same shit before with a muthafucka so he could feel where she was comin' from. He also knew for a fact Diplite was known for some sheisty shit and who knows he might have just as well been the one who set the whole thing up. He wouldn't put it past him.

"Hmm, okay...okay, let's give it a few days and I myself will try and find out about the watch. And...where he got it from, cool?"

"Okay!"

"But, Nikki, I swear this shit gonna cost..." He got up and walked over to the bar shaking his head. Nikki was right behind him, he was pissed, and she knew it.

"I'll give you whatever you want." She reached her hands around his waist in front of him and started rubbing his dick.

"Anyting."

Dirty-Red exhaled deeply, reached for her hand and stopped her. He wanted her, hell, she was chocolate mocha fine, but T-Black was cool with him, ever since he came into the hood. He couldn't disrespect his peeps like that, even though he wanted that ass.

"You don't owe me nuthin' like that. Me and you's bigger than that." He turned around and hugged her, then kissed her softly on her cheek. "But...thanks for asking." He pinched her

ass, causing her frowned up face to smile

Dirty-Red was now feeling some sort of way about Diplite. Could he be trusted or what? What kinda game was he playing? Damn, he knew he had to watch his back now.

Who else was watching, or tied up in all this?

The mood was interrupted as they heard a door opening up front. Nikki reached or her knife and Dirty-Red stepped behind the bar ready to grab his gun. Was it Diplite coming back on some ole bullshit? They were both ready for anything but that in particular.

"Yo-yo, what's up?" It was Wood. "Goddamn, what the fucks going on in here?" He said as he approached Nikki. "I see, you don't want my lil' bit of pocket change." He smiled at Red.

Dirty-Red shook his head, this dude was a straight character. He was for once glad to see him though. "What's up, Wood? You hear early!"

"Well, damn..." He grabbed Nikki poking fun. "We ain't

got to stop nuthin'. Hell, I can just like, uh...join in and shit."

Nikki laughed at him and her whole demeanor changed.

"Boy, you crazy...yanh."

Wood finally caught her and started caressing it. "Bout you, baby...bout you."

She giggled as she made her way to the door away from Wood's groping. Then said to Dirty-Red, "Be by, later on, tonight."

"A'ight."

Wood stood there watching her ass as it jiggled outside the door. Then his eyes cut at Red. "Yo' man, wasn't that Diplite that peeled up outta here?"

"Yeah, that was him."

"He was pissed. What's up...trouble?"

"Naw...everything cool," Dirty-Red said as he walked into the back room. "I was just about to set up for tonight. Be back out in a minute." He grabbed the bag and swung it over his shoulder. He walked into the bedroom and closed the door behind him.

Wood listened as he heard the door lock, something was up. He walked out to the front yard and looked over his shoulder again making sure Red or anyone else wasn't around. Then he pulled out his iPhone, then scrolled through some numbers and smiled when he found the contact, he was searching for...Hulie's.

IT WAS STRANGE HULIE kept thinking. 'Why would he try me? He was supposed to be cool like that, even fronted me a couple bricks here and there. And always paid me back on time!' Hulie sighed loudly as he peeped from around the side of the tan, bricked building with an old bulb lighted awning that read: Diane's!

Stretching his leg out, he shifted his body weight from side to side on his bike. He'd just finished smoking a blunt and felt nice but frowned just as soon as he looked over toward the Circle A, a convenience store across the street. He was out to get this muthafucka, fuck why he did it...all Hulie knew was that he'd done it. He fit the description to the tee of the dude the old man saw. He was tall, neat and clean cut. The other one, some ole dread headed dude, Hulie would find him later. Right now, he wanted the rat bastard that doublecrossed him and that to him wasn't cool at all. He'd been feeling some sort of way ever since.

He didn't answer any of his calls and they went straight to voicemail. Cleo, Diplite and some dude he utilized as a snitch, a flunky muthafucka by the name of Wood. Who was Dirty-Red's so-called right-hand man. He even sent Sunshine to voicemail, he was feeling that she knew something about the shit anyway.

'Man, fuck that broad,' he thought.

He tossed the blunt to the ground and outed it. His thick heeled 309 riding boots crushed it to ashes as the cool Chucktown breeze swept it away. He stopped, once he saw the dude coming out of the store.

"Got him now," Hulie said as he cranked up the bike and throttled down.

Q walked out of the store rummaging through the small, brown bag he carried. He was wondering if the chick at the cash register threw his Dutch's inside or not, he damn sure didn't see them. He turned around and saw her at the counter cheesing like a muthafucka with them his Dutch's in her hand. She'd cuffed them intentionally, just so she could get him to dip back into the store and grab the number she was flashing on a piece of paper with the other hand. Q grinned and started back into the store, then stopped abruptly as he watched her face turn from sugar to shit just that damn quick. Q reached for the door handle as she started to back away from the counter.

"What tha fuck is this psycho bitch on?" he asked himself about to open the door.

However, he was blinded momentarily by some glitter coming from the handle. He turned to see what it was and

mouthed the words, "*Oh shit*!"

Hulie was up on him, his bike laid slumped over on the ground where he'd jumped off. He didn't even put the kickstand down. The first punch he threw caught Q upside the head. His legs buckled and he was down quick. He peeped into the store and saw the girl from the counter running straight to the phone. Hulie flashed his gun and shook his head. The girl stopped dead in her tracks. Q was on the ground stunned holding his head. Hulie grabbed his leg and started dragging him to the side of the building out of view. Even though a small crowd had already gathered, this was the hood and just like Vegas. *What happened in the hood stayed in the hood.*

Q eventually regained his senses and yelled at him, "What tha fuck you doin'?"

Hulie didn't say anything as he got him near the dumpster and started kicking him in his head with the steel toe boots, he wore. Q put up his hands frantically trying to stop the flurry of kicks inflicted on his body. It was crazy, though, all he could think of was Sunshine. He should have listened to her. She told him Hulie's ass was unpredictable, dangerous but damn they were homeboys. He never dissed him and didn't have no reason to dis him at all.

Ever since he started fuckin' with her, she told him to keep an eye on him. Fucking hard, strong and long and every time it was the same shit.

She'd always tell him, "*Watch him, baby. Let me know what he's doing.*"

Every time like clockwork, he protested but when she squeezed those pussy muscles tight, he screamed like a bitch and like everyone else, obeyed.

"Yeah, baby anything for you," he'd always respond. Just like everyone else, he started spelling her name.

Hulie watched as he spit up blood, then started without mercy pouring blows to his ribs. Q rolled up into a ball trying to cover himself up.

Then Hulie went for his face again and said, "Bet you won't steal from no one else!"

'*Steal...damn!*' Q thought. '*This muthafucka seriously think I had something to do wit' that.*' Q put up his hands, trying to block some of the blows. "Yo' man, I ain't have nuthin' to do with that shit!" he yelled out.

That only made Hulie pissed, he figured he could of at least man up. "You did muthafucka, I had someone watchin'

the place. Matter of fact, where's the other muthafucka?"
"Don' know what tha fuck you talkin' 'bout man."

Hulie didn't let up as he spit blow for blow to his body. Q's face was swollen badly. He spotted a small electrical pipe coming off the side of the building and the crowd instantly knew where this shit was going...Five-O'clock news murder bulletin. Someone stepped up, his shadow was all that Hulie saw as he spun around with his hands up ready to swing.

"Tryin' to jump me?" Hulie asked.

"Hell, naw. Matter of fact, fuck you, but you don't want to beat him with no pipe. Might kill em and you don't need no shit like that. Look at em! He's already done!" Tree, a barber in the making stood tall, about six-ten, easy and was cool as all hell.

Respect was all that was given to him everywhere he went in the Chuck. It damn sure didn't stop here, Hulie knew him, well. Hell, he cut his hair. Hulie stopped knowing Tree was right. He leaned against the wall breathing hard and looked over at Q.

"I gotta make him an example or ee'r one'll try me," Hulie stated.

"Whatever...you your own man. I'm just tryin' to tell you something good. I'm out, this shit too hot for me." Tree turned around and dipped into the crowd, knowing full well that ball would be rolling eventually. He definitely didn't want his face to be seen around this dump when ball rolled up.

Hulie watched as he left and thought hard about what Tree had said. Maybe he was right, but Hulie still needed to find out some things. He turned to go wash up near a small faucet by the building and didn't hear the steps behind him.

When he did, he said, "Yo' Tree man, a'ight...you right."

He was floored that damn quick, stars and blackness followed right after as he struggled to fight the unconsciousness he was falling into. Blackness once again engulfed him as he felt a thick, metal pipe hit him upside his head, making him dizzy. It hurt like hell! He could see his attacker as he squinted through the pain. Q had recovered, gotten to his feet and started wailing the same pipe he was getting for his ass.

Hulie looked up at him as he yelled, "Muthafucka, I told you I ain't have nuthin' to do wit' that shit!"

Hulie could hear the faint sounds of police sirens in the background as the crowd started to scatter. Q's boys started pulling him away, but he was fuming and talking mad shit about killing Hulie's ass. But Hulie being Hulie just wouldn't let it go. He wobbled to his feet, reached into the dumpster and grabbed a bottle and ran up behind them swinging. Blood splattered all over the ground as he caught Q upside the head with a 40 ounce, then he staggered over to his bike, picked it up, got on it and hauled ass down Burton Lane behind the store out of sight.

One of Q's homeboys took off his shirt and wrapped it around Q's head, trying to stop the bleeding. Another one of his homeboys pulled up in a ride and opened the back door. The homeboy trying to stop the bleeding pushed Q inside and skidded off toward the hospital. Ball finally arrived...*late as always*. Blood was all over the place and they tried questioning people around about what had happened. No one knew shit, not even the girl at the counter inside the store. Frustrated Ball gave up and decided to leave the premises.

One of the officers an old, seasoned vet, walked over to his car and gave some dude a long ass glare, he knew the face, but couldn't quite place him. He stopped and stared for a while, waiting for him to rabbit or something but he didn't, he just kept his cool. The cop finally let it go and got into his car, he continued to stare as he drove by. The ole boy just smiled, then laughed at his dumb ass. After all, he didn't have nothing on him, he'd done his time. He stayed there for a minute as he watched the Police car turn up Reynolds Avenue then glanced over at the manager spraying blood into the gutter. He turned and dropped two quarters into the pay phone he was leaning on and dialed Diplite's number.

"What the fuck is up with you?"
"Aw, man, home...you'd be surprised."

"Man, fuck that homie bullshit! What tha fuck you doing at my peeps house?"

"Shieeettt...me and your sister, man, 'bout to be real close...brotha'n-law." The dude that called Diplite on the phone smiled as he looked around at his surroundings. A real cold pause came from the other end of the phone as he waited for old boy to collect his thoughts.

As he waited, he thought to himself that maybe one day he'd be able to control this side of town. All he needed was a little money which he already had, and a good start could get his foot in the door.

A nice piece of ass on his arm would also boost him up as well. Cleo, hell all the ballas wanted her, and now it was finally coming to him. After the fifteen years, he'd spent rotting in SCDC day for day, it was finally his time. Jesse Taylor-off brand, country boy, field nigga, ex-con whatever you wanted to call him. Nothing was gonna stop him now, except perhaps...Diplite.

"Don't ever go to my peeps house again. You hear me, nigga?"

"Naw...broth'n-law, you got it twisted..."
"*Twisted!*" Diplite yelled. "Mutha..."

"I'm gonna help you get it, right, though. For one, if you even attempt to make a move on me, that nigga Hulie'll know everything."

"Snitch ass muthafucka!"

"Two...I'm gonna see your sista. You hear me? And you ain't gonna do shit to stop me...and three, if you ever threaten me again...I'll kill you and your whole family!"

"Whoa...what! If you ever..."
"Fuck you! Tell your sister, I'll see her later, bye."

Diplite looked at his phone twisted and said, "This crazy ass muthafucka. What the hell did I get myself into?" He slammed the phone to the ground, and it shattered into tiny pieces. Just that quick he knew somehow, he had to handle this. This knucklehead was definitely going to be a major fuckin' problem. He didn't that type of shit to deal with, right now. He already Hulie to get rid of now this nigga was on his list as well. He had to think of something quick.

'*Wait a minute,*' he thought. "Cleo wanted to move in Hulie anyway. Okay...okay, maybe this could work. If she goes there, she'll at least be safe for a minute, until he figured out a way to take this nigga out, for good."

Jesse hung up the phone laughing about how he'd just played Diplite like a sucka. He dipped across the street and strolled down Spruill Avenue toward the Chinese restaurant. Then he dug into his pocket and pulled out some crisp twenties. After he'd finished eating, he figured, maybe he'd go to the mall and get some fresh gear, then pick Cleo up later on.

That sounded like a sure plan.

His old Chevy was parked in the bushes behind the restaurant. He didn't have any insurance, a license or nothing and it had to stay out of sight until he got a muthafucka to front their face and get all that paperwork he needed. He was thinking Cleo might do it, even though h might have to quote-unquote persuade her. His front end peered out a little more than usual from the wind pushing back the small foliage he used to cover it up.

As he walked over to take care of it, he glanced around at the old railroad tracks that ran next to the Navy Yard and saw some children playing and acting crazy. He stopped and looked at them. They finally found him, his so-called partner Dread. The one he didn't want to share the loot with. The one who got nervous when Hulie started spazzing on his front porch. The one who fucked Cleo much harder than he had, and then she felt some sort of way toward him. Hell, she gave him back the money he'd given her and kept his. The one he did the job with, the one he put on his knees and emptied the 9mm clip into his brain. Yeah, he was the one! The one whose body they'd finally found.

Chapter Twelve

Hulie chilled on his front porch watching his runners serve dope by the handfuls. Lately, North Charleston had been booming because of new industry migrating into the underdeveloped, impoverished hood. The Boeing airplane plant had its hand in a lot of it, and it helped out the unemployed and the small business owners, but it also came with a price. It fed the addictions of many that were already well hooked on dope before they even came. Now, once they provided them with a job, that helped the pockets of the dope dealers, Hulie's in particular.

He had his clipped .40 Caliber underneath the chair he was leaned back in. He also had another clip by the doorway going into the house, just in case something jumped off. He'd boarded up the back door earlier on in the week, cleaned the place up, gave his lookout *Pops* across the street a couple of stacks, then sent him on his way to some of his people's house in the country for 'bout a week or so. Hulie surprised him with a fishing trip, he'd fully paid for. It was well worth it though, Hulie was just simply returning a favor.

His money started to swell, he'd only put out a couple of bricks the other day, and he was already sold out. He kept business moving to his supplier, Deezo. Deezo noticed the increase, especially on Hulie's end. He suggested that maybe

242

Hulie should move. The spot was hot and if the Feds moved in on him, he'd rather them get the supply as opposed to the supplier. He was watching out for his own ass, and it made plenty of sense.

Hulie knew it made perfectly good sense, too. He started looking around for a couple of places. Upper scale neighborhoods were affordable but hard to maneuver. He could make the move easily, but it would cost him big trying to keep up a front. He liked the idea of living in a gated community, but he also knew they probably weren't ready for him or his kind. The suburbs seemed to be the most logical move for him.

He pulled his skully up and noticed some of Q's boys entering the store across the street. He slowly reached down for his gun. The owner still didn't like him, and he made sure Hulie knew it, but mean mugging him every chance he got, especially since that shit had gone down with Q. They looked over his way before finally going inside. He kept his eyes beaded on them, so far, he hadn't had any flack from them or anyone else since he'd fucked Q up. But somehow, he knew it the time would come, and he tried to stay one step ahead and ready at all times.

They walked back out after a while, jumped in their ride and hauled ass, not even looking Hulie's way. Hulie thought it was strange, but that only further confirmed that Q actually did robe him, and they probably figured he'd got what he deserved. His phone hadn't rung in a while. He hadn't heard shit from Sunshine's ass in a minute and because of that, he knew he was due. He frequently thought about Jabari but figured he was gone for good. He had to somehow make sure that was the case. The girl in the hotel would confirm that easily. All he had to do was give her a little dope, maybe some good old hard dick and she'd come around to seeing things his way.

"Hell, maybe I can clean that hoe up and put her ass to

work," Hulie said to himself. "Yeah, that sounds like a plan." Yeah, it was time to see that bitch anyway.

SUNSHINE TOSSED AND turned in her bed trying to wrap her brain around the bullshit that was going on in her life. Q was lying in the hospital on life support, the base of his skull was ripped to shreds by a bottle and no one would tell her anything. His boys said that there would be revenge, she wanted to handle the business now, her way! But they insisted it would be done in due time. The only thing they asked from her, was once the deed was done, they'd get full immunity and she agreed.

She kept asking over and over if Hulie had anything to do with it, but they wouldn't answer. They knew of her involvement with him, but she had that feeling though. This was the last straw, the money, the bodies the attack on Q...Hulie had to go down. She still wanted the money, but Q had convinced her that it wasn't worth the stress anymore. She was leaning that way, tightening up and going legit. But not until she got Hulie for his involvement in this.

She picked up the phone and dialed the hospital to check on Q. The nurse on-call told her he wasn't doing well at all.

His family had already gathered, and they were waiting for a preacher. She had really wanted to speak to his mother, but she didn't give in. Q and her wanted to surprise his mother with the relationship after it was solidified. But they never got the chance to and now it was too late. So, why would she even bother? She let it go and bitterly hung up the phone.

She sobbed softly for the rest of the day in her pillow, asking herself over and over amidst tears. "Why does shit like this always happened to me?"

CLEO WALKED UP THE driveway of Hulie's place, checking out the chair propped up against the door and thought it was weird. But she paid it no mind, she just figured Hulie was on some ole bullshit. When she grabbed at the doorknob, he came stalking from around the back of the house with his gun cupped in his hands.

"Damn, girl...make some noise or something. You almost got capped!"

She was right he was on some ole bullshit. She shook her head at him as he peered around at her car. His paranoia was in full effect, and the goddamned weed he was smoking didn't help matters. She gently grabbed him by the hand.

"C'mon...come inside," Cleo requested.

Hulie followed behind her like an obedient child. She was the only friendly, familiar face he'd been seeing lately. She was the only he didn't think was out to get him. Once they were inside Cleo opened up the curtains and walked into the kitchen and whipped up some canned roast beef and eggs, prompting him to eat. She could tell he'd lost weight, but he wasn't falling for it, not yet. She had heard something or another in the streets about what had gone down with Q, but she dared not ask lest he spazzed and she really wasn't feeling that right now. So, far, he didn't have a clue as to who really robbed him and that was what she wanted to find out.

"Baby...any word on what happened to your money?" she asked.

Hulie looked up at her out of his crazed daze. "Naw...but, something'll turn up...it always does." He pulled her closer to him, sat her down next to him and caressed her hair. "Baby, I need to move and find a new crib. But, uh...I need you bad!" Cleo knew he was sincere because Hulie never asked her for shit. "I think I might have found a place downtown. Remember, when we talked about us living together?"

Cleo smiled, it was about fuckin' time. Not only would she be able to avoid that sick ass nigga that was stalkin' her. At the same time, she could finally get paid. Hulie was finally making that kind of bread. Hulie, on the other hand, needed a new lookout. Somebody he not only could trust but put the tim down on when he needed to. Besides, he needed to keep dibs on her brother, Diplite. He knew from word on the street and his snitch, Wood. That, that bitch Nikki was not only still alive, but also still had the loot. He couldn't prove it, but he knew Diplite was in the picture some way or another. Keeping Cleo around would help him out big time.

He also felt that Cleo was good for him. Her schooling and her family's reputation would make him look a whole lot better in front of them rich, well-to-do folks. He just had to stroke Mom-dukes the right way, that might be his only option.

"I'd make you happy, Hulie. I wouldn't be in your way or nothing. I can cook, clean..." She stopped then thought for a moment. "But...I can't work no streets..."

He kissed her. "Naw baby...you ain't got to do that," Hulie said thinking about Dondi replacing her.

He needed to at least keep somebody out there on those streets so he'd know what was going on at all times. It was one of those things that worked for him.

"I got to go home and pack." She bounced up and rushed for the door. "I gotta tell my mother!" She blew a kiss at him as she rushed out. "I'll be back later on, I'll call you when I'm packed. You'll pick me up, right? I mean with a truck or something, huh?"

Hulie smiled. *'Damn, how much shit does this bitch have?'* he thought. "I will, but we still have to go see the place first, Cleo and make sure it's big enough." Hulie winked at her as she bounced down the steps into her car and sped off.

Hulie closed the door behind her and looked through the windows out into the streets in front of him. There were no changes, his runners were still making that money, but he did notice some dude in front of the store staring back at him...real hard. When he made eye contact the dude walked off, looking crazy.

'*Damn*,' he thought. "Hope that ain't ball, but if it is...fuck 'em. I ain't got nothing in here...no more."

He closed the curtains back and kept the blinds half cracked so he could still see outside as he sat back down on the sofa and started playing with his gun.

JESSE WATCHED AS CLEO jumped in her car. He thought maybe he had her to the point where she would cut Hulie off, but she didn't. The only way he figured to handle this shit was to take that muthafucka out for good. Then, all she would have left was him and that muthafucka's spot. He snarled up as Hulie stared his way, making eye contact.

"Yeah, I shoulda got your punk ass before, but now I won't make that same mistake twice," Jesse mumbled, as he dipped and became camouflaged by the crackheads and runners in the North Charleston sunset.

Cleo ran lights, two-three at a time on her way home. She fucked around and even took crackhead short cuts, dipping in and out of the torn-up hoods where tricks walked, and fiends stalked. The crazy thing was that she knew them all. As she gunned it down the street from her house, she happened to catch a glimpse of someone on the edge of the woods off to the side. Someone that looked vaguely familiar, was hunched over and crying. She slowed down and stared hard: it was Nikki, T-Black's mother sifting throughout the ashes and debris that was left of her charred home.

Cleo slowed down and looked over at her. They exchanged glances but no words were said. Then Nikki quickly dipped into the woods out of sight. Cleo started to get out of the car and call her, but because she was caught up in her own emotions. All she did was shake her head and make a mental note to call her brother later and see if they still wanted to do the Cheraw thing. Right now, she had to stay focused, on her own grind. She pulled into the yard, jumped out of the car and ran up to her mother.

"I told you, ma...I told you!" she said excited.

Her mother looked at her like she was crazy, and as far as she was concerned, she was. She never had a clue as to what Cleo was blabbing about at any one time. But she knew one damn thing for sure, it was never nothing good that she wanted for her. Like school, a good job, even a good man, hell a decent man for that matter.

"Ma..." Cleo called out.

"What child, can't you see I'm checking out this mail? Your father done fucked around and spent money..."

Cleo decided to just spit it out. "Hulie asked me to move in with him. He's got this nice place downtown."

"Move in...oh, I see..." her mother responded dryly and continued sorting through the mail. "So, when is all this supposed to be going on?"

"Now!" Cleo yelled, then turned on her heels and raced into the house.

"*Now!*" her mother repeated and stormed into the house behind her. "You kiddin' me, right? We don't even know him like that!"

"C'mon, Ma, we've been seeing each other now for a few years. You know that!" Cleo tossed clothes on her bed and started going through her drawers. "He wants to get serious." "*Serious?*" Her mother propped herself on the door. "What, are you crazy? He ain't never been over here to talk to me or your father. He's a two-bit thug and he lets you run the streets. Now, what kinda man is that, Cleo?"

"He's changed." Cleo reached underneath her bed and dragged out the two Louis Vuitton luggage sets and opened them up.

"*Changed!*" Her mother scoffed. "Is he still selling dope? What...no, don't tell me...he got saved or something!"

"Ma, c'mon, he's just making his paper like that to live comfortably just like anyone else. And you can't blame him for that. He ain't forcing no one to buy anything and it ain't like they can't get it somewhere else anyway."

Cleo's mother walked over to her very naïve dumb-ass daughter and sat her down on the bed. "Cleo, I know I haven't been the best mother. Lord knows I've made plenty of mistakes when it came to you, but I've always had your best interest at heart." She ran her hand softly around her face, then smiled. "I remember when you were coming up. You were so ambitious, we all thought you'd be an actress or something...even a model. You're so, so pretty, from a mother's perspective, I will say this child. If you move in with him...you'd be making a serious mistake. You hear me?"

Cleo smiled back at her mother, knowing that she was half-assed right and might as well come clean since they were having this...talk. "Ma, to be honest, I want to get some money out of him. Yeah, that's right, just like he does me...then, I'll cut him loose. I promise!"

"*Promise?*" Cleo's mother shook her head. "A man like him don't let a woman like you go until they're finished with you. And no one else wants you. Trust me I know!" She did, her husband was the one man that used her. So, she returned the favor as best she could. To show for it she had a house, her own business and plenty of her own money in the bank.

"I know you want yours, but at what price...girl?"

"C'mon, Ma, I ain't gonna be like you...damn!" Cleo looked off. "I'm sorry!"

"That's alright...I understand...but, I'm straight. It cost me a lot though, remember, you're living in my paid for house."

"Please let me travel this road on my own...this one time.

I know what I'm doing."

"I'll let you go, but remember, he's got one time to fuck up and I find out about it..."

"No, Ma, it ain't like that."

"I ain't blind, girl, I see the bruises. I hear things...like I said, from this point on...one time!" She leaned in to kiss Cleo. "One damn time!"

"Okay, ...you got that!"

"Well, then...what all you taking? And where y'all going downtown?"

"Uh, I don't know exactly where..."

"You what!"

"Ma...you promised."

"As soon as you find out let me know. Me and your father want to come visit and make sure you're okay."

"Okay, but...I'ma need a bedroom set...if you don't mind."

"Damn, Cleo, he ain't buying furniture or what? I

thought you said he had money?"

"He does...living room, too..."
"Oh, hell no, fuck that!"
"Ma!"

"Damn, but I want my shit back in one piece." She got up and walked toward the door. "He must be hustling backward or something. You better bring it back, Cleo or I'ma come get my shit my damn self. You hear me, girl?"

"Yeah...yeah, Ma." Cleo watched as her mother huffed and puffed her way downstairs. "Why wouldn't Hulie want a woman like me?" she asked herself. "Hell, he's the one that be bullshittin', I could easily find another man. But I'll be cool for now, once I show him how to spend that money, and take him places where he can be seen with a fine ass bitch like me. Then, I'll find that dude I'm looking for, and with plenty of time on my hands to do it and money to spare...his. I'ma cut Hulie's ass loose so goddamned fast it'll make his head spin." Cleo laughed a little louder than expected.

"What the hell you laughing at?" Cleo's mother yelled back upstairs.

"Nothing, ma, not a thing!"

SUNSHINE HAD FINALLY gotten herself together. Q's death and funeral had taken a toll on her. She did manage to, however, eventually pull herself together long enough to speak with his mother, swearing on her own life that she'd bring his killer to justice, swiftly. His mother responded by telling her, she'd hold her to that. At one point she tried in vain to pick his homeboys brains, but they still weren't giving up anything. All they said was they'd handle it in their own time, their own way. She was trying to be patient, but word on the street from her informants was that Hulie had something to do with Q's death. She didn't know exactly to what extent, and sadly no one would dare put themselves on the line to tell her anything, knowing full well that he had dealings with him in the past and knew how he handled snitches.

It had been a minute since she'd heard from Hulie anyway. He'd stopped calling and texting. Sunshine felt some sort of way about that, knowing that something was going on. But she couldn't quite put her finger on what it was, and besides, he still had her goddamned money. She glanced up from her tear-soaked bed and stared at herself in the mirror. She frowned, lines of worry and discontent stared back at her mockingly. She felt that everything was all her fault and it probably was. She needed to get her ass up and the only way to find out what the hell was going on was to hit the streets herself.

She groggily got up from her bed and drug her ass to the closet. She started rummaging through different outfits that all looked the same. A low-cut cleavage, hoochie mama blouse with tight-fitting jeans to match caught her eye. She tossed them on the bed with a half dozen different set-ups, she'd thrown together. She ruffled through her shoes and picked out a pair of four-inch stilettos that matched.

"This'll get me some attention and some answers for sure," she said to herself.

She took a deep breath, then bounced into the bathroom and turned on the faucet for a nice, hot, steamy bath to get herself right, then she laid back into the tub.

"Yeah, muthafucka…you want to play…then let the muthafuckin' games begin!" she told herself with a loud giggle.

HULIE DROVE INTO THE Motel 52 on Rivers Avenue, peering slowly around the corners of the drug-infested slum. Runners scampered out of rooms like roaches. Or they were posted up on their respective spots, like soldiers. Hulie liked seeing his money at work, since they were after-all, hustling his dope. Tricks also came out, slowly, geeking trying to get a peep of the balla they'd all heard of, but never seen. The balla whose name was synonymous with ass whippings and now...death. They were just being nosy cause they knew for sure there was no way in hell they'd ask him for a bump even though, they damn sure wanted too.

One door, in particular, stayed closed as he pulled up in front. He honked the horn a couple of times and a curtain at the window was pulled back. He waved his hand and the door opened slowly, then wider. Dondi's small, petite frame had filled up nice since she'd stopped getting high. She was still knee-high to an ant as she stood in the doorway sucking her teeth, with her arms folded. She shrugged her shoulders, then spoke real slick with an attitude. "What you want me for? I ain't in the game no more. Look elsewhere, nothin' happenin' here no more!" She started to turn and slam the door behind her.

"Heard anything from, Jabari?" Hulie yelled out.

That was enough to stop her dead in her tracks. It had been a minute since she's heard his name or even heard from him for that matter. He was supposed to have been got back in touch with her at least a week or so ago. She was wondering what was going on with him now. She knew about Hulie's rep from the streets and from Rip.

"Perhaps he knows something," Dondi said to herself. "He damn sure ain't here to trick or get high on any crack. So, why would he just come up in this rat hole of a joint looking for me? Maybe, Jabari, sent him?"

She turned around and waved him inside. Hulie got out of the car and walked through the door, but not before looking back behind him both ways, making sure his runners were still on point. He didn't have to say a word, but someone was damn sure gonna keep an eye on his ride.

"So, what is it you want?" Dondi asked.

She motioned over for him to have a seat. Hulie sat down and crossed his legs. Then he looked her up and down taking in every detail of her fine, luscious, well-defined body. Her curled locks were now a reddish hue with blonde streaks, and it looked like she'd just had it done. Her nails were manicured, she nervously uncrossed her arms and looked away from his stare. Her long, natural eyelashes fluttered as he stared her down. Hulie had that effect on people and it always seemed to put him in the driver's seat.

"Well, uh, just thought I'd see how you were doing. Since, uh, Rip's gone and Jabari...left. Kna-mean?" Hulie finally said. "You heard from, Jabari?" she asked.

"Not since the last time he spoke with you. Why?" Hulie threw that one out. She really had no clue that he'd never actually spoken to Jabari, but she couldn't have known that. The day in question was the day he spent spying on them from across the street in the first place. Now the game definitely was on.

"He said he'd call back, but so far...nothing." She eased over to her clutch-bag and pulled out some cigarettes.

He made her nervous, she pulled a cigarette out, then searched around for a light. Hulie stood up quickly, he knew he made her uncomfortable and he played on it. He reached into his pocket and pulled out a lighter.

"Here you go." He was up on her before she knew it and as she pulled on the cigarette, he coped a quick feel of her round, fat ass, testing her.

He was too close for comfort, Dondi felt his dick getting stiff and backed away. "Said, he'd be back in town soon."

"Well, uh..." Hulie thought he might as well try again. He was gonna get the information he was looking for one way or another. "I wanted to give him a couple dollars." He reached into his pocket and pulled out a small stack of hundreds. "But since he left and went to..." He trailed his voice off on purpose and flashed the money in front of her, watching her eyes as she followed.

Granted it had been a while since she'd tricked, some things never changed for a girl like her. She went to meetings faithfully, kept clean, stayed looking like new money, as they say, she'd even gotten her teeth fixed. But still she needed some fast money to keep up with her newly developed maintenance and she had no other job skills except lying on her back with her legs behind her head.

"I think he's still out in the country. Least that's what his sister told me when she called," Dondi admitted.

"Oh, yeah, the country...hmmm!" Bingo now they were getting somewhere. He figured he'd keep going to see what else he could get out of her. "Maybe I should put him in touch with my man from Beaufort." Hulie didn't know where the fuck Beaufort had come from at first. Then he remembered the old man and his fishing trip. "Damn, Hulie calm down...hell...it's too late now," he scolded himself silently.

"Whatever." She still stared hard at the money, in a trance steadily puffing on the cigarette. "That's not too far from Walterboro."

"Walterboro, yeah...it's not." ,Finally, he'd found out where Jabari was at. Now he needed an address or something. "He's staying there with, uh...damn, what's his name?" Hulie snapped his fingers as he continued to wave the cash in front her face, as he spoke, flaming like he was trying to remember something.

"Some white boy…Dee, I think that's his name." Dondi sat down on the edge of the bed. "You, uh…gonna take that to him?"

"What?" Hulie said as he peered out of the window. "You mean this?"

"Yeah, the money."

"Why?" He checked to see if the door was locked and

then walked over toward her. "You need something?"

"I mean, I ain't got no job yet, and I'm running out of the

money Jabari left me. Rent is due…"

Before she could finish that last statement, Hulie threw the money to the side of her on the bed. Then he gently stroked the side of her face. He ran his fingers softly through her hair and kissed her lips gently. He let his tongue wrestle with hers and she melted like butter. He softly grabbed her hand, guided it to his manhood and let her tease his dick as it became hard as steel.

"We all got needs!" he breathed lustfully.

Dondi eagerly and hungrily fell to her knees. She swallowed him whole, with one hand she played with his balls and picked up the money from the side of the bed with the other hand.

Hulie looked down at her and smiled. "That's it, baby, I got you. We'll go see, Jabari, later on, and make sure he's alright…okay?"

"We going today?" She finally asked after pulling back from his dick. Then she motioned for him to get on the bed.

"Naw, baby," Hulie said. "Not right now! We got some…uh business, right now…kna-mean?"

Dondi eased up on the bed beside him and started coming out of her clothes. She knew what it was, but she reasoned at least she wasn't getting high. Besides, this was one of the biggest ballas in

Charleston. Hell, if she could just throw that pussy him right, she could easily get on his team. She'd been there before, it was nothing new. She needed some dick anyway, it had been a minute and clean or not, she was still a freak. She eased up and pulled him down closer to her and started kissing his earlobe.

"Yeah, baby...got work to do," she cooed.

An hour or so later, Hulie rinsed his face in the sink then stared in the mirror, profiling as Dondi laid still in bed sleeping, the recipient of a good fuck. He quickly glanced over his shoulder thinking, I still got it, then he cheesed like a muthafucka. He thought about a quick shower after smelling himself, he was supposed to pick up Cleo from her Mama's house. He damn sure didn't want to smell like pussy when he saw her. This was business though, she didn't want to walk the streets anymore, so he had to pick another hoe. If she got too crazy, he'd put it down like that and kill all the drama.

He figured he'd let her sleep just a little while longer, then drill her about Jabari later. If he went to Walterboro, he had to be flippin' money. Why else would he dip out like that? Well, at least when he caught up with him, he'd have a nice piece of change to take from his ass, money he'd keep...fuck Sunshine. She could get dummied up like that muthafuckin', Q, too. He shook his head as Dondi finally started coming around. Yeah, she'd have to get it, too bad though, she had some good pussy. Granted it would be a waste but maybe something could be worked out between them before it came down to that.

"Hey, baby!" Dondi finally woke up.

She stood up in the bed yawning, then rubbed her babylike eyes. She was pretty and Hulie was digging her. She just looked good like that. She definitely would bring in some serious money. He started to get a rise looking at her, but he had to tell maintain and get back to business. He walked over to the bed and kissed her, then stroked her neck softly.

"Was just about to jump in the shower...wanna come?" Hulie said.

Dondi's lil' ass crawled from underneath the covers then glanced over at the window. "Damn, it's almost night. What time is it anyway?"

Hulie looked at his watch on the table. "Bout a quarter to six."

"Damn, Jabari was supposed to call me at six or so, but he always says that shit." She shrugged her shoulders and jumped in Hulie's arms. "Shoot, I got something else going on lover.

Fuck him!"

'No...no...no,' Hulie thought, that damn sure wasn't the direction he was going at all. He'd played this one hand out, but right after she washed and got her self together. They were gonna wait on that call, whether she liked it or not. "Yeah,

whatever...let's just take this shower."

He gently and ever so slightly guided her still half sleep ass toward the bathroom, then stepped back out and made sure the phone was still on the hook. This was the one call he didn't want to miss. He stepped back in and she was bent over, running water. Her ass was shaped like a cocoa colored heart, like Kisses candy without the wrapper, inviting him in and he accepted. They fucked more than they washed and

Hulie started talking that good shit in her ear.

"Damn, baby...if I could just find that muthafucka, Jabari. We could live...eat good!" Hulie was spitting her his own bullshit.

"Why?"

"Shit, I gave him some money for me to flip and..."

"Oh, so that's why he ran to Walterboro, huh? That no good muthafu..."

"Whoa baby, don't let the dick slip out. Yeah, put it back in, right there. Uh...now all we got to do is find him and I can get it back."

"I said he was in Walterboro."

"But you have to come with me. I mean, once he sees me,

he might try to haul ass. But you can draw him out."

"I...I...don't know."

"C'mon, now girl. You know deep down he ain't shit. He was the one that got your old man killed anyway. You know

good and damn well he don't give a fuck about you."

That stung, maybe he was right. It had been a while since he'd called. Why didn't he take her with him when she asked? He never sent no money and when he called, he always acted like he was living the life while she stayed in rat-hole hotels barely making it. On top of that, he never did send Rip's half like he said he would. She glanced behind her at Hulie, slowly, holding on to the rail so he wouldn't miss a stroke. He was all up in her ready to bust and that was all it took.

"Yeah, I'll do it baby!" she finally agreed.

Chapter Thirteen

"S**O**...okay, okay." Double D got up, walked over to the window and looked out, then stared back at Jabari.

"You want to bring this chick, uh..."

"Dondi."
"Dondi...out this way. For what again?"

Jabari looked up from his plate but then went back to it. Those pancakes were just getting good and he was punishing them. They were oozing with that good country syrup.

"Jabari...for what?"

"Yo' man calm the fuck down." Jabari knew it was going to be a long shot, but he figured if they could let Dondi come down there for a few days. He could get her out of Charleston.

He was doing pretty good there with that meth organization. He was damn near at cooking level and the motherfucking money was starting to swell. He had a couple of grand easy, that was enough for him to get one of them double-wide trailers out in the country.

He'd start distributing for himself from there. He had people he'd met from around town that was willing to support me and besides he could get his supply from Double D. Everybody was cool with it so far, until he brought up Dondi. They were top of the line paranoid. Jabari wasn't mad at them though.

262

"Remember, I told you about, Rip? Well, she was his girl and I want to make sure she's alright."

"Sounds to me like you tryin' to fuck something," Double D said.

Jabari looked away from him. He came and sat on the other side of the table across from Jabari. "Yeah, well, maybe I do feel some sort of way, but still, the bottom line is that I owe her."

"You do...not us."

"True." Jabari got up to go to the sink, his appetite was all fucked up now. "Look, I was only supposed to be here a few weeks, anyway. Figured I might as well get ready to dip."

"But, damn, what about Stacy?"

Jabari looked at his crazy ass. "Man, she was just a trick. A piece of ass, that's all." Jabari looked behind him and to his surprise she was right there at the doorway of the kitchen, looking at him with her mouth dropped open. "Damn, hey, Stacy sorry 'bout that, but you know it's true, c'mon now."

She brushed right past him toward the refrigerator and took out some juice. Then poured herself a drink and looked his way. "Yeah...that's all...you right, just a trick."

That was fucked up and Jabari knew it. They'd been fucking around with each other the better part of a month now. She was starting to feel some sort of way. She'd even tried cleaning herself up and stopped getting high, giving up pussy and all that. But Jabari owed Dondi and Rip, he was damn sure going to take care of that...debt.

Stacy finished drinking her juice and started to walk off, but then she turned back and got in Jabari's face. "Oh, yeah, your things will be in the hall...bye!"

Double D shook his head. "Well, that's over with. Now what?" he smirked.

"Guess I gotta sleep on the floor for a few days until I get Dondi...then I'm out." Jabari sat down next to Double D.

"Still got a job, right?"

"Yeah, you put in the work. Jason likes you and all, now he feeling some sort of way about you leaving, but he'll never admit it."

"You got that right."

"Okay, but when you gonna do this?"

"Probably tomorrow when I come in from town picking up supplies. Is that cool?"

"Cool!" Double D got up and walked toward the door.

"I'll let Smoak know."

"No...no, I'll tell him myself."

"Alright, suit yourself. I'll be in the barn, got some customers in a few. Smoak's got another slab coming, right?"

"About four bricks...coupla kees."

"Cool, might need it, big boys, from out of town. I think gonna be a big score?"

"A'ight, I'll let him know when I go back there."

"Alright, then it is what it is. See you later!"

"Peace." Jabari got up from the table and walked down that hall. Damn, sure enough, his clothes were thrown all over the floor. He sighed then started reaching down to pick them up and underneath the door, he spotted a shadow. It was her, he put his ears to the door and could hear her crying on the other side. He started to say something, but there nothing he could say. Maybe once he got straight, he'd come back and get her, too...*maybe!*

SOON AFTER THEY FINISHED washing, fucking, sucking and fucking again, the phone finally rang. Hulie was dead on it, he made Dondi wait a few extra rings before answering so he could school her.

"Be cool, girl, let it ring one more time."
"Why? I don't understand, why you actin' crazy now!"

Hulie wanted to spazz out, but he had to keep his cool to make his plan work. "Everything's cool. We want to get paid, right?"

He was talking her language now.
"Yeah," Dondi answered eagerly.

"You want to be with me, right and have some money? Go buy some new clothes, get your hair done and live the good life, right?"

"Yeah!"

"Well, we gotta play it cool. We gotta put him in a position to not say shit like he ain't got it. He gotta go get it, dumb shit like that."

"You right, he might even try to play me," Dondi agreed.

"Like he been doing, but I'm here so that he can't." Hulie caressed her face softly and kissed her gently on the neck.
"You trust me, right, baby?"

Dondi moaned and purred like a kitten with every touch.

"I do...baby!

"Okay, then...pick it up now."
Dondi picked up the receiver and said, "Hello."
"I just got out of the shower. Who's this?"
"Jabari! Damn, it ain't been that long...has it?"

Dondi seemed distant towards Jabari but she had every right to be. He was supposed to have called her at least two days ago. But it had taken him that long to convince Double
D, Jason and them that she was straight.
"Hey, look, I'm sorry 'bout not calling, I had to make sure things were cool."
"That so?" she responded dryly. Hulie was coaching her and persuaded her to ask, "When are you coming to get me?"
"Well...uh...that's a little problem, right now," Jabari stuttered.
"What...wait, you changing your mind?" Dondi asked raising her voice a notch.
"No, it's not like that. I just don't have access to a vehicle, right now. I was thinkin' tomorrow morning'll be good."

Dondi looked over at Hulie and covered the phone's re-

ceiver. "He wants to get me in the morning."
Hulie shook his head. "Tell him you got someone that can bring you to him."

"I got a ride." Dondi quickly replied.

"A ride! You bought a car?"

"Naw, I got someone that can bring me out that way tonight."

"Who?"

"His name is..." Hulie put his hands to her mouth and shushed her, then whispered. "Don't tell him it's me. Tell him it's a trick or something."

Dondi nodded and continued. "I got this guy and he's

willing to drop me off up there, now."

"Dondi, you tricking again. Damn...you still gettin' high?"

"No...no...he's just a friend. Well, Jabari, I needed some money. You never did send me any remember?"

She was right, Jabari had got caught up. He'd meant to send it, but things got hectic. He'd meant to make up for it another day, but as the days slipped by, he just plain ole forgot.

"Okay...okay, but who is he?"

"He's cool."

"I can't let him know where I'm at. So, uh...meet me in

Walterboro off I-Ninety-Five."

"Tonight?"

"No..."

"Why not? I can't wait another day, Jabari. These people want their rent."

"Look, it's got to be morning, I can't help that."

Dondi looked over at Hulie, he told her to go with it.

"Okay, then! What time?"

"Bout nine in the morning. That cool?"
"Yeah!"

"Tell, your...uh...friend or trick, I'll pay him when I see him, okay."

"C'mon, Jabari, he's a friend, but okay...I will."
"So...uh, you okay?" Dondi looked over at Hulie and said.

"Tryin' to get there?"
"Well, uh when you here, I got some things to talk to you about."

"Like what, Jabari?"

"Things, we'll talk about tomorrow. I'll call around eight or so to make sure you're ready."

"You want me to bring my things?"
"Yeah, pack up, you gonna be with me from now on."
"You? I'm confused, Jabari!"
"Trust me, I'll make it all clear tomorrow. Okay?"

Dondi looked at Hulie then back at the phone, and he waved his hand at her before she hung up. "Ask him exactly where to meet him at."

"Where do you want us to meet you at on Ninety-five?"

"I'll tell you in the morning. I'm not quite sure, just be ready."

Dondi shrugged her shoulders, and Hulie did the same.

"Okay, then I'll talk to you in the morning."

"A'ight later."
"Bye!"

Dondi hung up the phone, but Jabari could hear something in her voice that was different. He was hoping Dondi wasn't back to her old tricks, getting high because back here is no place to have a serious habit and Jabari knew that all too well, but all he could now was just wait and see.

Hulie reached over and kissed her. "Did good, baby!"
"Hulie?" Dondi asked. "Everything's cool, right? I mean, ain't nothing fucked up about this. And I'ma be your lady, right?"

This was where he had to be crafty and just downright lie. "Of course." He started putting on his clothes. "I'm going to the crib now to make room just for you. Fuck this hotel shit.
You can move in with me, alright."

She smiled. "Okay!"

Hulie kissed her then stepped out of the room heading to his car. He called one of his runners over and said, "Don't let no one near her room. You hear me?"
Then he got in and drove off. He thought about tomorrow as he dipped through traffic. He needed to bring some heat with him, he knew Jabari wasn't going down without a fight. He knew he'd definitely have to take him out. He was sure hoping Dondi would be cool with that. Because if she wasn't, she could get it too. Then that would damn sure be a waste and even more money lost.

THE ALL WHITE ROSE-colored exterior BMW swung the corner of Grayson Street and North Carolina Avenue as Sunshine whipped past on her way to Hulie's. She raced up in the driveway noticing the front porch was filled with fallen leaves and very unkept. Then she snatched her shades off getting a closer look. The place was completely locked down, the windows were boarded shut and as she glanced around back, the fence to the yard was chained up. Not that he had a whole lot of shit that a regular home would have had anyway, but there were things only exclusive to Hulie and the old piece of beat up Chevy in front was one of those things. It was left abandonment to rot and wear, the hood was shut and chained down also-seemingly held hostage.

"Damn," she grumbled. "What the fuck...where the hell is this muthafucka?"

She glanced across the street and noticed a couple of runners hanging out in front of the store and decided to get out and let her outfit do some talking.

Heads turned abruptly and at attention as Sunshine walked her tight jeans wearing, tittie bouncing ass across the streets. Her stilettos were punishing the game. It was a little breezy this time of the year and she killed it by wearing a long leather coat that swayed in the wind each time she stepped. Sexy didn't come close to what Sunshine was at the moment.

She picked her mark, a fresh colored new to the block, handsome, young boy and asked him. Where's Hulie?"

His buddies snickered immaturely all they wanted were laughs.

"Uh...uh don't know. Why you wanna know?" he asked, looking at his boys in an attempt to man-up, but he had no idea who he was fucking with. He also didn't have the slightest as to who Hulie actually was or he definitely would have known about her.

Sunshine was bored already, so she decided to have some fun. She reached her hand down between his legs and whispered softly into his ear, close enough for her to kiss his earlobe and blew a soft, sultry kiss.

"Damn, awe fuck is he dead?" Sunshine asked, shocked.

The young man couldn't take her teasing any longer and it caused him to faint. His buddies clowned as they woke him up. Sunshine was definitely too much for him, now all he had was that one embarrassing moment he'd live out over and over again...forever. Sunshine giggled at that time the owner walked out.

"Lucky young man!" the owner said.
"He'll be a stunner when he gets older, if he makes it,"

Sunshine replied.
The owner smiled and shooe'd the boys off. "He left a couple of days ago. He packed his shit and a U-Haul came later, and he was gone."

"Gone?"

"Nobody knows where least they ain't saying but..." The owner looked around to make sure he wasn't being watched.
"I heard he was staying downtown..."

"West Ashley?"

"Something like that, him and that chick but you ain't get it from me! Ya hear?"

"Chick?"

"Brown-skinned...pretty...like you, of course." The owner moved in closer and slid his hand under her coat copping a feel of her ass, awaiting a backhanded slap, reprimand or something but it never came.

He mustered up the nerve and said, "You know, uh...I won't faint..."

Sunshine smiled and pushed him inside the store. She had to give him that, he had balls. He ran everyone out and locked the doors behind them. Sunshine stood in front of him with her coat open, then reached in her blouse and pulled out both of her girls. The owner sat down quickly and calmly, took out his dick and started jacking quietly. Sunshine smiled, while she licked her nipples and began rubbing her clitoris. She was ready to reward him.

"And tell me what else you saw?"

SHE DIPPED OUT OF THE Makin', looking behind her in the rearview, knowing that the next time she saw this neighborhood somebody was going to jail. It was over with, Hulie's leaving took the protection along with him. She'd had her fun now it was time to move on. Right now, she had bigger fish to fry and that was to find Cleo. So, she could find out exactly where Hulie was living at now. She thought maybe she'd just get with Hulie and that would be simple enough, but now plans had changed. Instead of slow grinding info out of him like she used too, he'd went and got himself another piece of ass.

"Smart move," Sunshine said. "I shoulda capped her ass like I started too, then I'd lock her dumb-ass up."

She pulled up in Liberty Hill and turned up Lester Street like the man in the store had told her earlier. There was no way in hell for her to be low-key, her Beamer killed all attempts of that. So, now, she'd have to make another entrance. Right in front of the house, she pulled up like it was her shit and got out, with a wide-legged stance, flossing on some ole Pam Grier shit and struck a pose.

Cleo's mother was out in a flash like a Cougar protecting her territory and looked up and down the street at her neighbors also peering out their double door, being nosy.

"What the hell is this...and who the fuck are you?"

Sunshine pulled out her card and handed it to Cleo's mother.

"Okay...DA! Someone in trouble?"
"Where's your daughter, Cleo?"

"Damn!" Cleo's mother said as she turned away. "Now, what?"
"She's not in any trouble. If that's what you think I just need to talk to her."

Cleo's mother noticed her pink and green keychain and said, "Hmmm...A.K. A...you on point, I see."

This was her way in. "Sista...I just need to talk to her, about the company she keeps."

"Sista...okay, okay...I see. You know, girlfriend, I've been telling her he ain't no good...nothing but trouble. What did he do...murder...rape?"

"Let me talk to your daughter first, then I'll holla back at you, okay."

"I'ma get her, right now. Come on inside, these nosy-ass muthafuckas starin' and shit."

The curtains in the window closed shut as they both approached. Cleo started to run out the back way, but it was too late. Fuck it, she didn't do nothing anyway, but if this bitch tried her like she did before, she was definitely gonna have to kick that ass, or hit her with something she thought. As she looked her scary-ass around the room for something to swing, the door opened and they both stepped in.

"Cleo, baby, someone's here to see you."

Cleo turned and mean mugged Sunshine. "And you've seen me...later."

'Hold up, just hear me out...let me talk. Straight up!" Sunshine raised her hands. "No bullshit."

She looked at her, realizing that she really wasn't no threat. Not much older than herself, a very attractive woman, but still a spoiled child at heart. Her mother didn't make it any better. It wasn't her fault she acted the way she did. Hulie brainwashed her, maybe if she could find out what was going on with him, she might spare her grief, that she'd one day go through by fuckin' with his ass.

Cleo looked Sunshine up and down, still leary. "Just for a minute. Looks like you got to go to uh, work or some-

thing...on somebody's corner, huh?"

Sunshine blushed shamefully as she glanced over at the steely, frowned eyes, you know better was written all over her face. "You got that."

Cleo's mother directed them to the living room, and they sat. Cleo stared at her hard, then Sunshine broke the ice.

"Look...you know it's about, Hulie," Sunshine said.

"Damn, girl...I know, all you want is my man," Cleo shot back.

"No...sweetheart...it's much more...complicated." Sunshine pulled out her cigarettes and motioned to her mother

to see if it was okay for her smoke

Cleo's mother came over and got one herself, then she sat down and crossed her legs getting comfortable.

"Ma...you need to leave..." Cleo sneered.

"No...it's okay," Sunshine butted in.

Cleo's mother took advantage of the situation and pulled out a bottle of Bourbon she kept around just for special occasions. She knew that this was gonna be one of them, with three glasses, she started pouring.

Sunshine reached for her glass. "Ladies bottom's up, I do believe after this, we'll be...much closer." Sunshine giggled and went on to explain thing in further details.

"So, you're telling me..."
"Us!"

Cleo shot a look at her mother, pausing waiting for her to interrupt her again, then sucked her teeth and continued.

"Like I was saying, Hulie was supposed to have been in-

volved in some sort of robbery. That's what you're sayin'?"

Sunshine took another swig of the Bourbon she was sipping on and sat her glass in front of Cleo's mother.

"Please...just a tinsie bit more...if you don't mind."

Cleo's mother picked up the glass and eyeballed her, so far this had been her fifth tinsie glass.

"More like a damn shot," Cleo's mother said to herself as she poured. "But what the hell, it's worth it." So, far, Sunshine had told them one hell of a story. Cleo's mother handed Sun-

shine's filled glass back to her. "Here you go."

Sunshine swirled the glass around watching the dark brown liquid maneuver it's way around the glass in a spin, but not enough to spill out over the lip, then looked up at Cleo and smiled. "That's what happened."

"Well, how do you know...did he tell you that?"

"Look, sweetie." She smiled dryly and matter of factly, the sat back and crossed her long, smooth legs. "You know him like I do...right? Now, you know when he get's, uh...good and

sexed up, he starts talking. Well, ...he talked!"
"Damn...that shit is deep," Cleo said.

"It gets even deeper, sweetie. I know you heard about the guy that was beat up over on the Makin'?"

"Hell, yeah I heard about that. He just died, right?" Cleo's mother said as she leaned forward.

She'd heard about it on the street and it was good gossip then, but now she had an inside source, making the gossip even sweeter once she got back around her friends. "I heard that...you were...involved."

"Naw not really." Sunshine frowned and took another swig.

She just knew if it was buzzing all over the streets, then it was definitely buzzing in her office. She turned her head away from them, not wanting to see the sore spot it made on her face and took a deep breath.

"He was a nice guy, I mean. I thought he would be like...a thug or something. But he was different, so, I uh dated him. He knew all about, Hulie, but it didn't fuck wit' him. He kinda knew he had me...wrapped...and it was a matter of time before I'd leaned his way." She snickered as she reminisced about

Q. "Hell...it didn't take no time at all."

Cleo poured herself another drink and butted in. "Damn, I'm still trippin' off the fact that Hulie was dealin' with that both of us...at the same time."

"Yeah...that kinda worried me."
"Worried you?"

"Hell, c'mon girl. I know what you were doin' out there in them streets..." She stopped herself and shut up cutting her eyes at Cleo's mother, who was all up in her mouth. "...you know what I'm saying."

Cleo nodded, the cat was out the bag she might as well had fessed up. "Ma...I, uh...been wantin' to tell you some...things."

Cleo's mother took a drink, then looked at her and put

her hand on her thigh. "Cleo...I been knew." "What?" Cleo was shocked.

"What you do is your business...always told you that. Even tried to school you." She got up, went to the curtains and peered out. "Of course, it was an embarrassment. But what could I do?" She walked back over and sat down. "I just made your brother promise me that he'd look after you."

"*Look after me!*" Cleo shrieked. "Hell, he damn wanted to pimp me..." Out of nowhere, Cleo was slapped hard across the face.

Cleo's mother looked her dead in her eyes. "But...never, you hear me? Never bring that shit or even that language in this house again...ever!"

Cleo rubbed the side of her face, stunned, but knowing it was a slap if there could ever be one out of love. "Yes, ma'am." she slowly answered. "We'll talk later, another time, but..." she glanced back around at Sunshine like she never missed a beat.

"So, what's gonna happen with, Hulie?"

"Well." Sunshine leaned forward and put her still half-full glass down. "We could make this work to our advantage."

"How? People have already died, you fuckin' kiddin' me or what? It's evident...he's a fuckin' killer. You should lock his black ass up!"

"I could, but he wouldn't be locked up for long. His money is what always gets him out. So...we eliminate the money, put him in a position to own up, then...we got him."

"Yeah, that shit sounds easy, but I'm the one living with him now. Maybe I should call him and move back in..." She looked over at her mother.

Sunshine shook her head. "Keep doing what you doing so he doesn't have a clue. I'll keep my eyes on you...you have to trust me on this."

"I don't know...you know how he is..."

Sunshine put her hand out and grasped Cleo's, rubbing them gently and assuringly. "Trust me."

Cleo's eyes locked in on hers. She sounded sincere, but, if Hulie ever found out she had something to do with him being robbed and then knocked.

'*Oh, hell no, I need an out*,' she thought. "When this is over, I want to leave town." She glanced around at her mother, then back at Sunshine.

Her mother said, "That can be arranged."

"Hell, if it all goes down right. You'll have your own money to go anywhere you want. I know people all over...me and your mother."

"Shit...all the time...sista."

"Well, I need to say something..." They looked at her with *now what* written all over their faces. "You might not like it..." "What baby?" Cleo leaned closer toward her mother.

"I did something..." The doorbell rang.

Started her mother jumped up and peered out the window. "Cleo, it's the guy you were seeing."

"Guy...who, Ma?"

Good and tipsy now her mother looked back over her shoulder and smirked. "The one you deep throated on the side of the house...remember?"

Cleo's face turned two shades red and she screamed out.

"Ma! You was watchin'?"

"You're good, but...hmmph...we'll talk." She walked into the foyer to the door.

Sunshine got up. "Relax your moms is good people. You just need to talk to her sometimes...woman to woman. But, hey, I gotta go. I'll call you either tonight...or tomorrow." Sunshine dug into her bag and pulled out her phone. "I need to change my number, so if he picks up your phone, he won't know it's me." She bent over and hugged Cleo, then left out the living room, leaving Cleo speechless, and very embarrassed.

"I can't believe she muthafuckin' watched...oh my, God!" Cleo mumbled to herself.

Sunshine walked to the door, the side-stepped Jesse on her way out and eyeballed him up and down like a piece of meat. Then she winked at Cleo's mom and did the tongue in cheek thing. They both started giggling leaving him clueless.

His dumb ass had to say something. "Uh... is everything alright?"

Her mother pointed him towards the living room. Sunshine waved before jumping in her car, looking back at the door.

"Seems like I seem him before...or know him from somewhere," Sunshine said to herself.

She took a photographic picture of him in her memory back so that later one, once she returned to her office, she'd go through some mug shots. She shook her head and cranked up the car, knowing good and damn well that had to be where she knew him from.

Jesse hunched his shoulders as he closed the door behind him. he knew her, he didn't have to guess. The fuckin' D.A. that sent him up the road. "What the fuck business does she have with, Cleo?" He asked himself.

Cleo was feeling the same way as she watched Sunshine peel off. He probably was thinking some sort of way, so when he came in and sat down. Off the top, she said, "No...I wasn't snitchin.'"

Her and my mom are sorority sister. Just had a couple of drinks that's all...girl talk."

Her mother came back to the door and said, "Y'all...uh, want the rest of the Bourbon?"

Jesse looked down at it. "Yeah...for sho."

She smiled and tipped her drunk ass out, bouncing upstairs all fucked up. Cleo pushed the bottle over to Jesse. She wanted him to feel good before she told him she had moved in with Hulie. But she had a plan for his ass. A damn good plan that definitely involved making another lick. Something that would make him okay with her being there and an ace in the hole in case Sunshine dropped the ball. She knew one thing for sure, if she called, he'd come running. She leaned over and kissed Jesse's on the cheek. She knew what to say and do, to make it work for her.

"Drink all you want, baby."

SUNSHINE DROVE OVER to Cooper River Bridge punching numbers into her cell, but no one was answering.

"Shit, where the hell is this muthafucka? I've been to all his little spots and no one ain't seen shit. Tried calling informants...my people on the streets, cops and...nothing!" She threw her phone into the seat next to her. "Damnit!"

She'd left enough voice messages that he'd eventually call her back. She was thinking seriously that perhaps he was hiding from her all this time. Maybe, he did do that shit to Q. Damn, she started thinking, if he did, then he'd be locked up for a long time, if not the rest of his life. If Q's boys didn't get him first, but first, she had to get her money back.

All the shit going on in her head, it was like having an Angel in one ear and the Devil in the other, fighting. One side of her mind said fuck it, let it go and just send some of her people at him and let the system do the rest. Without her help, he really couldn't do shit anyway...except snitch her ass out. That's where the other side of her mind kicked in. Take his ass out, but who, who would have the balls to do him in?

She pulled into the lane going toward the condos that sat on the edge of Cooper River. She was home, finally, it seemed like forever. She continued wrestling with her thoughts as she pulled into her private drive and thought once more about, Cleo. Something was going on because she didn't have a clue about Hulie's dealings and he damn sure wasn't trying to fill her in on shit. He had to move her in, he needed to look good and clean up his act fast. What was he planning? Whatever it was, was big. She thought Cleo did the move, but hell, all the time it was Hulie. She was and is just a front. Her phone lit up as she parked.

> It was Cleo, she immediately picked up. "Hello!"
> "Yeah, it's me..."
> "Why are you whispering?"
> "Because he's in the other room."
> "Okay, okay! So, what's up?"

"Hear me out! He's packing a bag to go out of town...I don't know where. He did mention somewhere in the country. Said it would be for a few days but wouldn't tell me noth-

ing else. Except that he'd be leaving early in the morning."

"Good...good, can you meet me..."

"No...no, gotta go...bye!" Cleo hung up the phone quickly.

Hulie must've been walking up on her. Sunshine kept the number in her memory and speed-dial in case she called back. Then she'd know who it was. She needed to call a good friend of hers she'd been thinking about lately. Mark...aka, Muslim. He set her up with that dude that did Moonie G in the jailhouse. Maybe, he could find her someone to do, Hulie. Yeah, just in case shit went south, he'd have to be murked quick.

She got out of the car and walked up the walkway to her spacious, two-story home. Not being able to shake Cleo from her mind, wondering what was up with that Jesse dude? Maybe he might want to make a quick dollar, she grinned. The Devil that whispered in her ear was winning the battle and winning easily. She was obviously, oblivious to the fact that Jesse was the one Mark used to murder Moonie G and also, the reason why Q was dead...totally oblivious...to the fact.

Chapter Fourteen

Tangie couldn't understand for the life of her, why her assistant was cutting her eyes like she was, with her lips poked out. Of, course, it had nothing to do with the fact that she'd been running back and forth to Walterboro for almost a month now. Or the fact that every time she left or returned Tangie would say: "Missy, please look over this case for me...girlfriend."

Yeah, the girlfriend thing was what did it. Missy didn't mind looking over cases since she was going to Law school anyway. So, it was good hands-on training, all Tangie had to do was show her ass up in court. But Missy was starting to feel like she was blindly helping out. Then there was just plain old getting used and Missy now knew she was getting played.

Tangie shuffled through some papers on her desk and said, "Missy...I thought I told you to find me the Davis case out in Edisto..."

That was the last straw that almost always broke the Camel's back. No one ever knew what it looked like, but it always sounded like this.

"Fuck that, Tangie! I ain't you goddamned slave and shit. Find it for yourself!"

Tangie's eyebrows crashed together like a bad car accident on her forehead. She needed to vent too, so she said fuck it.

284

"Hell, I might as well, but damn, I thought I had an assistant to do this shit for me. Look, if you don't wanna work here...shit can be arranged."

"Arranged...arranged, oh hell no!" Missy dropped some papers to the floor and stomped over to her desk with both hands pounding down and said, "You don't think I know that. Hell, any Lawyer worth their salt would jump on me in a fuckin' heartbeat. Hell, Tangie, I damn near been handling your caseloads for a minute. And I will say, my goddamned approval rating is off the fuckin' hizzy. So, if you want to run around handling shit you ain't got a fuckin' clue on or no goddamned control over...Miss control freak...then fuck it. Yeah, fuck it...cut me loose and I'll be working for the same goddamned Prosecutor bringing your ass up on Misconduct and Ethics charges. I tell you what, I bet you, I'll have the paperwork then. You got that?"

Tangie looked up at her and her mouth started to quiver. Then tears flooded her eyes and just like that, she hung her head and cried like a baby. "I'm s...s...sorry...Missy! I'm s...s...sorry..."

"Damn!" Missy said, sucking her teeth.

She felt for her, after all, they were friends. It was Tangie who suggested she go to Law school anyway and it was Tangie who'd brought her on as her assistant, giving her free rein over the office. It was Tangie who helped her out with bills and groceries when times were hard on the boulevard. Tangie had even put her husband in rehab, bought her twins presents for Christmases and Birthdays. It was Tangie...and now she needed Missy's help.

Missy walked around the desk and hugged Tangie. "C'mon now, girl...I'm sorry, too! Don't cry, we'll work this out...like we always do."

Tangie looked up at her. "I just want to find my brother. He's all I got, Missy. I know he's in trouble, and I ain't never been there for him. I'm sorry!" She lowered her head. "If you want to go...I understand..."

Missy reached into her desk and pulled out some napkins, then wiped Tangie's reddened, wet face. "Girl...I ain't going nowhere. You hear me? We gonna find your old big-headed brother, and when we do...I'ma kick his ass!"

Tangie smiled and said, "Maybe, I should just let it go..."

"Let it go...let it go!" Missy stood up. "You better not let it go. Not after all we've been through together. You ain't never said let it go when it came to me." She stomped in front of the desk and snatched up the papers she'd dropped, then stormed toward the door, opened it, and looked back over her shoulder. "And I won't let it go...when it comes to you, either." She turned, facing her, and balanced the papers in her arm. "Look...I got those files somewhere on my desk. I'll get them in a minute, we'll go over them and see what we working with."

Tangie smiled, she always knew Missy was a good friend, but never knew on what level. She would have been there for her anyway, she was loyal like that. But Missy proved one thing to her...best fuckin' friend forever...BFF, and another fuckin' F.

'*Now ain't that some shit?*' she thought as she answered back. "Okay!"

Missy closed the door partially, then swung it back open. "Girl, clean up, that fine ass Sheriff from Walterboro is out here waiting on you." Tangie got up and started racing around, this caused Missy to smile. "Your makeup kit is in the top drawer...left-hand side. A fresh blouse is hanging up in the closet toward the back and of course, the toothpaste and lipstick is in the bathroom. Damn, girl...what the hell would you do without me?" Missy laughed and closed the door.

Tangie looked at her as she walked off, talking to herself more than likely saying some shit about her and smiled. "Don't know...really don't know!" she replied then started rushing around in the order Missy had told her, cleaning herself up.

The Sheriff from Walterboro flipped through the scanner in his car as he waited for Tangie to come downstairs. What started out as give me a couple minutes, I'll meet you downstairs, ended up being a half hour. Tangie had decided to damn near get a full makeover as far as he was concerned. He personally came to Charleston to pick her up and she had the nerve to take her time like he didn't have nothing to do.

'She's always been like that,' he thought, even when they were in college together.

He had the nerve to try and date her, but he was much too clumsy of a young man for her. She liked the athletic, jock, brutish types, but never the less, they still became close friends. Tangie always asked him why he never went into the practice of law instead of public service, he was smart like that and real quick. He would always explain that policing was just another aspect of the law. Amidst heavy debates, she agreed and even respected his decision. He definitely was no dim light at all, he graduated with a GPA of 4.5 easy. He was damn near at the top of his class. He made different choices with his life after graduating and getting married early and having kids was a choice, he'd made that Tangie didn't.

He really didn't mind at first, entertaining her thoughts of finding Jabari, but now, it was damn near becoming work. Interrupting the heavy caseload he had also, but she was his friend and he too, was loyal. He tapped on the steering wheel impatiently as she finally scampered out of the door to the car. He leaned over and opened it, feeling like spazzing out, but the wait was well worth it. She was fine...a dime piece and if he wasn't happily married with two beautiful daughters, he definitely would have made a move on her, a long time back when she'd first came to town.

"Damn, girl...what took you so long?" He asked like he didn't already know.

Tangie smiled apologetically. "You know...girl stuff." "*Girl stuff*?" he repeated.

"C'mon now, Bobby. You got three women in your household...don't act like you don't know."

"But damn, Tangie! I came all the way here on a flam. I, the goddamned Sheriff, transported a prisoner here just so I could pick you up. Hell, that's why I got deputies. You know how that looks or how it will look when I get back?"

Tangie leaned towards him and stroked the side of his arm. "C'mon now, Denita ain't having none of that foolishness."

He frowned and poked out his lips. "Yeah, but even she

thinks that you might be pushing it a little."

"Maybe..." Tangie leaned back. "Okay, this one last week and it'll be over."

He snickered. "Yeah, you said that three weeks ago." He put the car in gear and headed to Highway 17 towards Walterboro. Halfway there, after a little silence and small talk 'bout his girls, he said, "Look, Tangie, if your brother is in Walterboro and he's mixed up in anything illegal. I got to do my job...and you too."

"Yeah...I know, but at least I might be able to get him some help."

"Sometimes a man don't want no help. Then what?"

"Bobby, I guess I'll have to cross that bridge when I get there."

They pulled into a gas station a little way out of town and she started stretching her eyes again, looking for any signs or clues of her brother. She stared at people, watching them.

The Sheriff came out and pulled her to the side. "You're making people uncomfortable," he whispered. "And they're complaining. C'mon now I got my people out looking."

She blushed. "I'm sorry, but I saw him that day, right here.

Just thought maybe I'd get lucky, that's all."

He opened the door to the car, and she hopped back in.

"Good police work requires no luck," he commented.

She smiled. '*Yeah, that's something, Bobby would say*,' she thought. '*Always on that Mister Goddamned Cop shit.*'

They pulled off again and he suggested maybe they should cruise downtown on Main Street.

Tangie nodded in agreement. "When we finish, I need to get a room also. You can just drop me off."

Bobby laughed. "Oh, yeah, those rumors. My wife loves it, she goes to church, and they tell her that the Sheriff was seen dropping a woman off at a hotel. Then she plays along with it, you just wait until I see him...yeah, she loves that shit!"

Tangie laughed. "Tell Denita I'm sorry. Promise I won't hold you forever."

"No...you can tell her yourself. She invited you over or dinner...again."

Tangie playfully punched his arm. "Oh, so you don't want me over. Wait till I tell, Nita."

"Please don't do that...I got enough problems."

They shared the laugh as Bobby cruised downtown, mostly near drugstores in hopes of spotting, Jabari.

JABARI'S MIND WASN'T there today, anxiety had him damn near ready to cut and run. Why? He didn't have the slightest idea. It was weird like that, ever since he'd spoken to Dondi. That was all he could think about...hauling ass. It seemed like he was about to move on to bigger and better things. He had at least five gees saved up and he was ready. *For what*...he didn't have a clue!

"Maybe I might or we...me and Dondi might catch a bus out to Cali somewhere. Or slow drive and get to know each other like that." Jabari said to himself.

The more he thought about her, the better it all seemed to look, but every now and then the reality of it all popped into his mind. He was nothing but an orphaned, dopefiend and she was no better, she was a two-bit hooker. Where could they go? Who would want to be around them? Oh yeah, those questioned danced in his head regularly. But he never shared them with anyone.

"Naw, fuck that!" he said.

He went on a couple of websites and checked out a few places, far away, across seas, with a lot of white people dreaming. They seemed to be more understanding.

"I guess that's why I sort of clicked with Double D and them."

They realized one thing about themselves, they were, what they were and they didn't blame no one for it. Jabari had a little while to go to get to that level. He figured maybe this Dondi thing might his second chance. Hell, even if they didn't make it as a couple, they'd still have a chance to live out their lives a whole lot more comfortable than they were before. Or at least afford better dope. He knew one thing for sure, Rip would've been damn proud of him for getting his shit together.

"Damn, I miss that dude."

Jabari glanced over at Smoak, still in conversation, talking to him. Normally, Jabari would've been right there listening since Smoak usually had some good shit on his mind. He gave him a hands-on of the business, at least the business of making meth and one damn thing he always fucked with Jabari about, was the one thing he wasn't doing now...listening. Jabari looked back at him, he didn't miss a beat, he was steady running his mouth.

"...you can also grow ice using gun blue lithium strips and red devil lye...but, either way, you make it...you got to clean it when you done making it with ether. You got that, Bari?"

Jabari was lost. Normally, he'd have him repeat it, but he wasn't gonna use this shit once he got away from there anyway. Hell, with his luck...he'd blow his ass up.

"Yeah sure man, I got it!" Jabari replied.

There were many times when Jabari paid attention to Smoak because Smoak knew his shit that was a fact and in this ,game, you had to. They were already in the HydrogenSudafed mix-stage and was starting to smoke it like a ham, to get it good and crystalized. The gas tank was wide open and all of a sudden, Jabari felt his pants vibrating.

"Damn cellphone!" he griped. He had to hurry up and cut it off.

Hell, with all the vapor that was in the air, and with the gas wide open, any sudden spark would blow their asses sky fuckin' high. He back off slowly, looking toward the door. He figured he could step out real quick and fast and catch the call.

"It might be, Dondi." He back up slowly.

Smoak was still running his mouth. "...anhydras is the name of the gas we using, Bari. You see, you get the 'fedren out of it...along with the Sudafed...that's where the speed comes from..."

Jabari made a move and opened the door a little bit, and a slight breeze blew through. It had just rained, and dew was still on the ground. The moisture, that's what caught Smoak's attention and he turned Jabari's way with his face twisted.

"What the fuck are you doing!" Smoak yelled.

"What..."

"Close the fuckin' door! Don't you know that moisture in here will fuck around and blow this whole fuckin' area like a goddamned space shuttle? I told your ass that shit!"

Jabari eased back in, Smoak's hands were in the tub crystalizing the ice and he could see the hairs on his arm literally burnt. Jabari rushed toward him.

"No...no stay there!" Smoak looked at the gas. "Ease over there and...oh hell no! What is that? A fuckin' cell phone...are you tryin' to kill us!"

Jabari was had, Smoak was spazzing on him. Jabari really couldn't blame him. He was already up, cutting the gas off and mumbling something under his breath about Jason kicking both of their asses...if not killing them. They'd fucked up a batch...costing fifty grand easy that was invested to make at least close to a quarter mil. That was a lot of money.

Smoak looked his way disgusted. "Just get out quick with that damn phone. I got this!"

Jabari slid out of the door quickly and all he heard was Smoak cussing his ass out. He was in for it, it was one thing to help out and shit, but it was another to break rules and fuck up money...that was huge. He knew he'd fucked up big time. He peered over at the ATV and figured he'd just get his money and dip. He looked at the numbers on his phone and sure enough, it was, Dondi. It was about a half hour or so past the time he'd given her to call him. He hopped in the ATV and headed toward the house.

Smoak busted out of the door. "Wait up!" he yelled.

Jabari hauled ass, once he got to the trailer, he ran in the back and snatched up his clothes. They were all bundled up in a duffel bag along with his cash. Double D was on his way out of the barn.

"Damn, I'ma have to kick his ass," Jabari said to himself.
"Yo...Bari...wait up," Double D said.
"Fuck it he probably knew already. Hell, man up,

Bari...least hear him out." Jabari told himself.
"Yo' if you going to town. Pick up a case for me, okay. Got some people coming in, ya know."
Double D didn't have a clue. Smoak didn't call him, for some reason, he didn't call.

"Damn, I shouldn't have left him back there," Jabari said.

"Okay...I'll be back soon, we got to talk anyway."

"Okay, cool...you a'ight, where's Smoak?"
"He'll be here."

Double D started to turn and go back to the barn and said, "Going to pick up that chick? He looked down at Jabari's bag.

"Yeah!"

"Cool, see you when you get back then. My keys are underneath the floorboard."

"A'ight."

Jabari got in the truck and peeled out up the road watching Double D as he headed back into the barn.

'*Damn,*' Jabari thought. '*Once Smoak gets here and tell Jason what happened, he's gonna wanna kick my ass.*'

Jabari couldn't worry about that, right now. It was getting later, so he dialed Dondi's number.

THE SHERIFF WAS ON is A game, establishing his presence. He did everything but kiss babies. Walterboro was growing fast, not the small hick town from years-gone-by. I-95 went straight through and it was fast becoming a haven for layovers, truckers, and even tourists. The Sheriff knew that, and he also knew that elections were not too far around the corner. Keep the business happy, the people safe and the money flowing...not necessarily in that order, but the biggest problem he had was drugs. He used a third of his staff on a task force for the gangs that pushed the dope, then another for task forces for burglaries and robberies as a result of drug usage, and the rest for patrolling what got him elected in the first place, the people's safety, from the drug users. It was a lot, granted, but he was quite the politician and he winged it well.

It was getting close to the time for Tangie to check into a hotel. Still early in the day, but if she caught the eleven o'clock check out hour. She could get a pretty good rate. She seemed more interested in the traffic that flowed in and around the street, trying to catch a bead on her brother, than she was a room. It wasn't a good hot minute when they finally received the call she'd been looking for.

"Sheriff!" The radio was scratchy, but he adjusted the frequency and it cleared up a bit. "Hey, uh, I got something you might be interested in."

"Bring it on." It was Randy; one of his task force lieutenants that worked undercover in the field. "I spotted a truck, that burgundy one you told us about. Souped up with the big rims and shit."

"Yeah, been trying to get up with that. The driver...is it..."

"Naw, man! Strange though...some black dude is driving

like a bat outta hell...reckless. Think I should stop him."

"Well, hmm...might be stolen. Follow him...but not too

close so he'll spot you. Maybe he could lead us to..."

Tangie butted in. "Brown-skinned, wavy hair...like a white boy!"

"Think so...yep, that's him. You know him?" Randy asked.

She looked at the Sheriff wide-eyed and said, "That's him...that's Jabari!"

"Okay, Randy...good work. Keep an eye on him, I got to

drop off someone and call for back up, ya hear."

"Ten-Four...out."

Tangie looked at him and said, "Oh, hell, no. You're not dropping me off. I'm going with you!"

"Damn, Tangie, you can't! Suppose something..."

She grabbed at the steering wheel, making him pull over. "Look, that's my brother. I want to be there. If something goes down, I might be able to talk to him...help out." The Sheriff frowned his face and she continued. "C'mon now, I've been

trained too. I know how to get out of the way...please!"

He banged the dash and said, "Okay...but be careful, ya hear? If it gets ugly, stay out the way. Don't need no goddamned headaches!"

She nodded her head. He called for back up and called back Randy. Who'd told him the truck was headed toward

I-95.

DONDI DIDN'T SAY A word as he sped down Highway 17 doing eighty-five easy. Dondi had just called him about twenty minutes earlier. Luckily, he was in the process of checking his voicemail when he got the call, or it would have been well into the day before he got it. Cleo was crashed out, but she was in the process of waking up when he left out. He'd told her earlier he was leaving out of town, but he wasn't quite sure when. He packed a small overnight bag just in case things drug out longer than expected.

He packed a couple grand, a change of underwear, clothes and another .40 Caliber gun with three clips in case shit got ugly. Cleo didn't ask any questions and he wasn't giving up any answers anyway. He left her with a couple of dollars and a credit card, just in case she needed to handle any business or just go shopping to kill time and she gladly accepted.

He felt awkward kissing her as he left out. Made it seem like they were a couple and after all, to him it was really just a business arrangement. So, now, here he was on his way to Walterboro to either do one of two things. Kill Jabari to keep from being a snitch and telling the cops what went down that night. Or, get the money from Jabari that they was supposed to have gotten that night. Either way, the first thing seemed a lot more feasible. He'd already heard a little something-something from his snitches about that chick Nikki getting out of the fire. How she did? He didn't have the slightest clue, but he knew he was slippin'. He'd also heard she might have had the money, but he never got around to calling his main snitch, Wood, to find out.

If that was the case and she was being protected by that muthafucka Dirty-Red like he'd heard, then it would have to be an all-out war getting his hands on her. Dirty-Red didn't play no games, and Hulie couldn't go at him just any kind of way. But before he could even think on that level, he had to handle this Jabari business once and for all.

Dondi, on the other hand, didn't know what to think. She thought they were going to pick up some money, then she'd be on the way back to Charleston to move in with him. At least that was what his mouth had said. She had a hunch though, something wasn't right. It all seemed too smooth, and one thing she knew from dope boys, smooth wasn't always good. But she still had Jabari to fall back on. Maybe, he did have some money and they were going to haul ass somewhere. The more she thought about things the better that plan sounded, but right now, she had to play her role in this whole mess she was already in. She glanced at Hulie after about twenty-miles of straight silence.

"Baby...you know where you going?" she asked.

Hulie looked at her like she was fuckin' crazy. He couldn't believe that shit. Here it was, she was the one who'd called his ass up, packed a bag, hopped in the car with him, and didn't say shit for damn near thirty minutes. When she did it was to ask if he knew where he was going.

"This is truly a dumb bitch!" Hulie mumbled under his breath. "And to think she wants to be my main squeeze." He almost spoke out loud, he had to get her ass out on the track quick...with her stupid ass.

"There it is...I-ninety-five," she said pointing toward a turn-off.

He looked over to his right and she was right. In the distant, a sign off the side read: Off-Ramp, caught his eye. Only a couple more miles to go now. "Okay, exactly...where did he say to meet you at?"

"Over by a store...gas station...BP. Going away from town!"

Hulie slowed down once he got to the highway.

"Okay...over there? I see it!"

Dondi nodded her head, and Hulie pulled into a cut, out of view and stopped. "Okay, this is where you get out."

"*Get out*! I thought you said..."

"C'mon now...remember the plan. If he sees me, then he might dip, and we won't know where the stash is," Hulie explained.

"He might have it with him," Dondi replied matter of factly.

The whole thing about Jabari having a stash of money seemed far fetched and she really wasn't buying into that bullshit at all.

Hulie frowned, he was losing her quick, he had to turn it up a bit. "Picture that." He moved over and stroked her face, then kissed her. "C'mon, girl, remember what we talked about. If you keep wasting time, we'll never get back to

Charleston so you can move in."

Dondi's smile was twisted and forced. "Yeah...sure!" She opened the door and started to get out. She thought about it, then reached back in and grabbed her bags.

"Why you grabbing all your bags?" Hulie asked.

"Like you said, don't want him to get suspicious, right...baby?"

"Oh yeah...now you thinkin.'"

Dondi grabbed her bags and dragged them off to the side of the road. Hulie didn't lift a finger to help, then started walking down the road toward the store. Halfway there she spotted Jabari standing on the side of a bright burgundy truck. She looked back and Hulie was gone, nowhere to be seen. All that did was confirm that he was on some old bullshit, but still, she wasn't sure of what quite yet.

"For once stick to the plan, Dondi," she coached herself. "At least see where this is headed."

THERE SHE WAS, SHE looked good, better than the last time he'd seen her. She looked like she'd gained weight, got her hair done and had even got around to getting her teeth fixed. Or she was wearing dentures, either way, she looked good.

"Okay, she spotted me. Damn, I don't see...why the hell is she walking? Let me see what's up." Jabari said to himself as she approached.

"Hey, baby...what's happening?" Dondi said from behind him.

Jabari spun around and looked her up and down, then hugged her. Her grip was tight around his neck and as she looked in his eyes, she seemed like she was sad. He could tell from dealing with her, even when she was with Rip, he always knew when something was up.

"What's going on, baby?" Jabari asked.

"My bags...they're on the other side of the highway," Dondi sais, then looked off avoiding eye contact.

"We'll get them. What happened...did that dude you told me about kick you out or something?"

"Yeah, basically...told me to find you best way I could," Dondi lied.

"Damn...sorry, 'bout that baby. Hell, I thought he was going to drop you off."

"Don't worry about it."

They hopped in the truck and Jabari drove to the other side of the overpass and sure enough, three bags were on the side of the road. He got out and put them in the truck, then looked around, he felt like he was being watched, he shook it off and got back in.

"I'm probably just being paranoid," he told himself. Dondi was all smiles. "So, how you been, girl?"

"Been alright."
"You look good as hell."
"Thank you!" Dondi smiled.

Jabari rode through town, picking up the case Double D had asked for and was turning on Highway 17 heading out of town.

"So...what did you want to about, Jabari?" Dondi asked.

Jabari wasn't expecting her to just jump the gun that quick. But oh well there no time like the present. "Look, Dondi, I got a few dollars saved up and all and I figured we could go out of town and get a fresh start somewhere." Jabari kept it real with her.

"*Fresh start...me and you!*" Dondi was shocked.

"Yeah, me and you. What's wrong with that? What I ain't good enough for you..." Jabari was starting to spaz out.

"No..." Dondi grabbed his hand softly. "It's not that...am I good enough for you?"

"What you talkin' 'bout, Dondi?"

"C'mon now, Jabari. I ain't nothin' but a hoe...admit it...straight up."

"Naw...you've changed...right?"
Dondi looked off out of the window and said, "I make

meetings, I got a little time under my belt, but still..."
"Look, Dondi, I ain't no better. At least we can try, and...if it don't work out. Hell, you'll still be clean..." Jabari fumbled with his words trying to find the right ones to say and couldn't. "...and I'll still be..."
"Jabari...sweet old...Jabari." She smiled then snickered making him feel a whole hell of a lot better. "Well...so far...sounds good."

"So, far, huh?"

"DID HE SEE US?" TANGIE asked as she peered her head up from behind the dash.

The Sheriff was slumped down right next to her behind

the wheel. "Naw...don't think so."
"I can't believe Dondi would lie to me! She told me she didn't know where he was!"
The Sheriff got on his radio and told his Deputies he'd spotted the truck and was following closely behind it. "So, you know the girl?"

"Something like that."
"And..."

"She was a person of interest...in a double murder..."

"What!" Bobby was shocked. "And you didn't say this before, because of what?"

"She was involved, Bobby. I had spoken to her already,

hell, that D.A. bitch Sunshine tried to damn near kill her."

The Sheriff pulled the car over and turned toward her.

"Hold up...anything else you want to tell me?"
"No...you know everything. I'm sorry, I didn't tell you about her, but she's the last person I would have expected to see. Anyway, why don't we just stop him..."

"No, he's gonna lead us to the owner of the vehicle."
"Who?"
"They call him, Double D."
"Yeah...I spoke to his mother..."
"Damn, Tangie...really! Anything else...really!"

Tangie kept her mouth shut, even though, she was tempted to tell him that everything he knew, she knew, and it only took a week or so to get it. His office needed an upgrade bad and she made a mental note to thank Missy for hers when she got back, but right now, she tried to stay focused and composed.

"So...what happens when he gets where he's going? Do you know where he's going or what?"

The Sheriff glanced over at her and said, "Hopefully...he's taking us to a meth lab."

"*A meth lab*!"
"You said you wanted to ride."

"Oh God...please, Jabari...don't be involved."

"Yeah...for his sake."

The Sheriff continued to follow close behind Jabari, at least three cars behind, not realizing at all that the car in front of his was Hulie's. "What the hell..." Was all the Sheriff could get out of his mouth. The shit happened so quick, the truck turned abruptly and sharply down a dirt road off to the left. He was right behind it, he noticed underneath the tops of the trees was burnt, brownish, and dead looking, and this crazy smelling odor came from the area like bed socks in the heat of the sun and stunk like all hell. He knew from his training and experience, that it was a trail leading to a meth-making operation. Why didn't he spot it from the air when SLED came through with the Helo? He didn't know, but when he looked toward the back end of the road and the sides around him, all he saw were acres of top, heavy oak trees, camouflaging everything in sight.

"Damn good cover," He said to himself. "No wonder we

never knew where to find it."

The car in front of him turned also, and that's what threw him off. What the hell was going on now? He followed this same car from town, maybe, it was a set-up. He stopped at the front-end of the road and got on his radio. In between crackling, scratching sounds and bad frequency, the only audible words that got through were: "This is the Sheriff...halfway up

Highway 17...gonna need back up...and a lot of it..."

Tangie stared at the truck trying to keep an eye on Jabari as it rambled down the winding dirt road, then suddenly, it screeched to a halt. Halfway up the road, the car in front of them stopped too. The Sheriff reached in the back for his shotgun and told Tangie to stay low. She did, but not before she got a peep into the car in front of them and had a clear view of the driver and recognized him.

"Oh shit! Where'd the fuck did he come from?" she asked.

"Who?" The Sheriff inquired.

"The car in front of us...the driver is bad news."

"Shit...the whole damn thing is bad!"

"Naw...this guy is fucked up, trouble...from outta Charleston. His name is, Hulie."

The Sheriff got back on the radio and started babbling off. "C'mon people...it's about to get real ugly out here!" Evidently, he knew Hulie also.

Chapter Fifteen

Jason picked up the call from a cheap, old scanner he'd bought from Walmart for little to nothing, and the frequency, he got that off the internet. The Sheriff's call for backup came through as plain as day as him and Double D scrambled around shredding paper, mostly addresses, receipts and phone numbers. Then, suddenly, a high-pitched whine went off in the speakers in front of the barn, a wire had been tripped up the road, Ball was on their way in. Jason looked over at Double D and they both knew it wasn't going to be good. Stacy came running through the back door with an arm full of large Army duffel bags.

"Okay, D, load the fuckin' bags with as much cash as you can get in it!" Jason told Double D.

Double D was on it, right along with Stacy. They stuffed fists full of cash into the bags, then Smoak came rushing through the door right behind Stacy.

"Dee, your truck is in the middle of the road!" Smoak yelled. "Is that, Jabari in it?"

Double D looked up, he'd completely forgot about that.

"Hell yeah...tell him he's got to move..."

"No...no!" Jason said. "Keep the truck parked there, matter of fact, block the road. It'll slow down the police when they come."

306

"A'ight...I'm on it." Smoak ran out to the truck and Jabari was just getting out.

"What the fuck is going on?" Jabari asked.

Smoak pushed him out of the way and jumped in the truck. He put it in gear and angled it sideways, blocking the road.

"It's a raid...a big one. You might want to get your things together! Get ready to haul ass!" He turned around and started to race back to the barn, then stopped and looked past

him. "The girl, too!"

ALL HELL HAD BROKEN loose. Tangie was in the back seat of the car in a state of shock, crying and shivering like a scared child. The Sheriff was bent over toward the side door, trying to get closer to it. His arm had blood all over it, leaking out of a small hole near his shoulder, he'd been shot.

He glanced over at Tangie and yelled out, "Snap out of it! Now listen up, try to go out through the side door once I open up this one over here and run like hell toward the highway and stay low!"

"But, what about you? You're bleeding...I can't leave..."

"Damnit Tangie, I ain't got time for that shit, right now! I'm okay, just do what I told you."

The Sheriff reached into the glove compartment and pulled out some more shells, then reloaded the shotgun. His handgun was still in his holster, he never got a chance to pull it out with all the shooting going on. He angled his body around and braced the side of the steering wheel then kicked the door open. Tangie opened the back door and jumped out, then took off hauling ass up the road.

"GODDAMN!" HULIE STARTED telling himself. "How the hell did this shit happen? Got a Sheriff in back of me...motherfuckin' crazy ass white boys shooting at me in front and I'm fuckin' trapped in the middle like a fuckin' rat."

Bullets whizzed past his head as he looked both ways for an out and found none. He thought about jumping out of the side of the road where the foliage was thicker, but he didn't have any idea where to go from there. He damn sure didn't want to get trapped off in the woods, but fuck it, that seemed to be the only way to go right about now. He'd already tried to make a run for it, a little while ago, and ended up shooting at the Sheriff. He shot at someone in the car, didn't know exactly who, dust was all over the place, but it didn't matter anyway. With his luck, it was all the same, bad...probably a stinkin' cop. He damn sure didn't need that along with the rest of the bullshit he was already going through.

IT WAS CRAZY, JASON came running out of the barn with an M-14 and someone on the other side of the road must have seen him cause all that happened right after that was straight gunfire. Jabari and Dondi ducked down as bullets tore through the truck and shattered the windshield, never been, but if Iraq was like this...then damnit man. Jabari pointed toward the clearing in front of the trailer and she shook her head, letting him know she understood what he was saying and where he wanted to go. Jason was full ham on the M-14, pouring out rounds quicker than a fuckin' slot machine in Vegas, screaming out like a madman.

"Fuck you, muthafuckas!" Jason yelled.

Double D's crazy ass was right behind Jason, giving Jabari and Dondi cover fire as they stayed close to the ground. Then, he fucked around and pulled out the rocket launcher.

"Damn this shit is gettin' serious...fast," Jabari said.

Double D called Jabari over to him and said, "Look, jump in the ATV and go to the inlet. Get the boats ready! Help Stacy, load the duffel bags...ya hear!"

"Yeah...but what about y'all?"

"We got this. Gonna blow the barn, trailer, and the lab..." Double D pointed to the rocket launcher and smiled, then glanced over at Dondi. "Sorry, I didn't get a chance to talk to you, get to know you, but this guy here...loves you."

Dondi looked at Jabari and nodded, then said back to

him, "I think I love him, too!"
"Think?" Jabari said under his breath. "After all this shit...she think?"
Double D pushed Dondi gently toward Jabari and pointed to the barn. Jabari ducked down low and was already sprinting toward the door. Jabari thought Dondi was right behind her, but she'd doubled back to the truck.

"Where you going?" Jabari yelled after her.
"I gotta get my bag!" Dondi yelled back.
"Fuck the bag, you can get another one."

She wasn't trying to hear that shit. She ran past Double D and Jason and slipped into the truck and came back out with a small clutch bag. The one Jabari had gotten for her long before all this dumb-shit went down. She smiled at Jabari, waving the bag, then her eyes bulged wide, almost like they were being pushed out of her head. Blood squirted out of her mouth and she collapsed to her knees, then fell face down first to the ground. She'd been shot, Jabari rushed toward her, but the gunfire was much too heavy for him to make it.

Double D had to hold Jabari back. "C'mon, let me go!" Jabari yelled.

"It's too late man...she's dead! You gotta go!"

Jabari yelled out Dondi's name at the top of his lungs, but of course, she couldn't hear him. It was all too surreal, everything was at a slow-motioned pace, like the movies and shit. Jabari looked past her, trying to find out which bastard had shot her and all he saw was that muthafuckin' Hulie with the gun in his hand that shot her, still smoking. He looked at Jabari and snarled, then pointed the gun at him and Double D jumped in front of Jabari and pulled him down to the ground hard, laying right on top of him. After a while he wouldn't move, and Jabari had to go, so he pushed at Double D.

All that time, his eyes were still open. "Hell, I just thought he was being cautious or something, but he'd been shot in the head," Jabari said. He was dead, too. "Damn...Double D...fuck!"

Smoak picked Jabari up off the ground and out of the clear blue gave him the rocket launcher. "Man, it's on you now. You gotta blow the barn...everything!" Jabari was still in a daze until Smoak slapped the pure shit out of him. "C'mon, man snap out if it. It's over with...Double D's dead...your girl...do it!"

Jabari shook his head out the funk he was in, picked up the four grenades and hauled ass toward the barn. He was on a mission.

Stacy was just coming out of the barn with the last of the duffel bags working up a sweat as she drug them across the ground to the ATV. Jason was laying out lead all over the damn place, painting the road and police cars with bullets. Stacy helped Jabari load the damn thing, it was heavy as hell. Jabari aimed, then squeezed the trigger, and it fired almost blowing him back into the woods. It was like a baby missile, which was all it really was. The barn went up like an inferno, the noise damn near deafened them. Jabari aimed at the trailer and the same shit happened. It was over with and time to go.

Stacy had already cranked up the ATV and had it ready to go. She spun around and grabbed the bags. Jabari hopped in along with the launcher and they drove to the side of trailer ready to haul ass toward the back, then she pulled over and yelled at Jason to come on. He and Smoak were all over the place with M-14s, .40 Calibers...keeping the police cars that had gathered, at least a dozen of them, at bay. They knew pretty soon though, they'd send in a 'copter overhead. But, for some reason, Jabari just knew they had something for that too.

Jabari fucked around and looked up the road and that's when he spotted her. He stared hard to make sure...his sister. They looked directly into each other's eyes and held it for a minute. Why was she there? Stacy rudely snatched him out of his trance and back into reality, telling him that Jason and Smoak said they'd meet them in the back and told them to go. They hauled ass toward the trail and Stacy snatched the rocket launcher out of his arm and threw it over to them, with enough time to toss one grenade. Damn, who the fuck was this chick...fuckin' Ms. Rambo or something?

Jason smiled, and winked at her, then said to Jabari, "Gotta love this type of shit, huh?"

That was the last time Jabari saw those two crazy ass white boys...Jason and Smoak.

A COUPLE OF DAYS HAD gone by quickly since the shootout. Hulie finally made the decision to cut and run through the woods. Two helicopters had passed overhead, a couple of news reporters flying too low, and with everyone concentrating on that fuck up, he hauled ass through the swamps and didn't let up until he got close to Walterboro. He made some calls, got himself a change of clothes and eventually a ride back to Charleston. He reported his car stolen and used Cleo as his alibi, but oddly enough no one came looking, no questions were asked...nothing. He didn't sweat it, but still decided it would be in his best interest to lay low, real low for a minute, and just stay around the house and observe Cleo every chance he got, and she hated that.

He'd been by the Makin' a day or so ago and that's when he heard about Q. He felt the stares as he drove through, they were real cold and hard, but he kept his cool. Despite knowing that Q's boys were known to be notorious. They had to be paid off just to keep from moving in on dope spots and shit. Hulie's was no different, he just paid them off in his own way. Moving his dope from corner to corner when they came through was one and when they caught him slippin' he didn't say a word, he just charged it to the game...another pay off of sorts.

Q was that dude, that did small jobs on the side and probably could have taken Hulie's ass down easily, but hell, he wanted to back off, cause he didn't want no beef. He made more money than robbing a freakin' house, B&E just wasn't his thing, there was no money in it. Hulie should have been figured in on that, but his bull-headed temper wouldn't let him and now it was over with and too late.

After some thorough hood-type investigating, he finally came to the conclusion that Q was not the one who'd robbed him. Now he had to make good by his people. That's if they really wanted to do that. They might want it in blood, or his life even. He had to try though, after all, he didn't need any more enemies than he already had. He had to call Sunshine, Q was seeing her, so she had to know something, and that might be why no cops came around looking for him. She's probably pulled them back, laying in wait for the right moment to do him. Yeah, now that sounded more like her M.O. He needed to call her quick.

He made the call quick...fast and in a hurry and she seemed eager to meet him, a little bit too goddamned eager, Hulie thought. He gambled with it, he wanted to pick her brain and see what she was working with. He told her to meet him at his new place, so she could see what was going on with him. He wanted to make it seem like he'd changed and gone legit. All he was really trying to do was play her, like old times sake, but with all the shit that had gone down lately, the game had been changed. It was just too bad that nobody informed him.

"C'mon, baby, stop trippin'...I live here."

Sunshine looked around the marvelously built, 1950s old Charleston, but state of the art, bricked townhouse. All eighteen hundred square feet of some serious living space. It had three bedrooms, all with full baths, a dining room with a baby light chandelier, nice sized sunken living room with a fireplace, gas, of course, high arched ceilings. A huge deck out back that was large enough to hold a picnic table and grill.

'Damn,' she thought. 'How the hell did he get this? I mean, I'm the goddamned elected prosecutor for this whole fuckin' city and I don't live this well. I live good, but still, a two-bit dope dealer like him. What the hell?" She turned on her heels and looked at him.

His face was smug, arrogant and sign of him definitely smelling himself. He knew she was feeling some sort of way, especially when he brought her to the bedroom, and she saw

Cleo's things. She was jealous.

He shook his head approvingly, with a wide smile on his face. "Yeah...those rugs...Persian, I think. Cleo picked them out. Woulda gone with carpet, but she wanted to show off these Brazilian hardwood floors, kna'mean."

"Uh-huh...I see." She looked out the window at the view overlooking the water coming in off the inlets.

This was definitely money, more money than he normally would be bringing in. Hell, he wasn't pushing that much dope on the streets, or she would have known something about it. It had to be some other type of money. Or maybe he had his claws deep in someone's back. She turned around and smiled, then started giggling.

'*Yeah her fuckin' back,*' she thought. 'The muthafucka had her money and this was what he was spending it on. With some other bitch and she was supposed to be okay with that.

Oh hell, nah!'

It was time to put it on the table, she figured. Their romance, money, arrangements, friendship...all that bullshit was over. He'd fucked it up. "Put it out there and get it over with." She silently coached herself. "Hulie, did you kill Q or what?"

That threw him, he wasn't prepared for that and as always, his character when he was off-square, he started stuttering.

"K...k...ki...kill..."

She had his ass. "Yeah, k...k...kill! You stuttering muthafucka because the word on the streets and at my office downtown is that you did. Now, what's up with that?"

'*Her office?*' Hulie thought. 'Okay, now think.' Hell, if she really knew that much, his ass would be in jail. "I heard too, but, uh...anybody could be saying that. Nothing but rumors, muthafuckas hatin'. I mean if that was the case, I'd be locked up, now, wouldn't I?"

He wasn't biting, go another route Sunshine, that's all. "Yeah, you're right, Hulie. Besides didn't you say you were out of town for a while? Maybe...perhaps even in Walterboro? Uh-huh, well, uh you know there was a crazy shoot out up that way. A meth lab, I think. Two white boys killed...crazy! Some crack head girl...from here, Charleston...North Charleston to be exact. She was killed, too. I think you knew her...uh, damn, now what was her name again." Sunshine shrugged her shoulders, then snapped her fingers. "Dondi, yeah, that was it. I mean, I heard it was real ugly, a Sheriff was shot and all. Uh..." She walked past him toward the bar and poured herself a drink. "Did you hear about that one...Hulie?

Or was that just...rumors?"

Hulie slowly walked up behind her, carefully and quietly. The blinds were open, and a slight breeze blew through. No one could see inside, he was sure of it. He could kill her easily and bury her dumb ass out in the swamps somewhere. Then maybe haul ass to Cali or sumptin' with the money he did have. She was starting to be a royal pain in the ass. She knew too fuckin' much of his business.

Sunshine watched his reflection and every move he made off the side of the bottle as she poured. Her other hand was already fastened on the butt of the .380 holstered to her thigh underneath her skirt. If he tried anything, she'd cap his ass. Then she'd tell her people he was trying to turn his ass in, and he called her to his apartment for help. That he'd confessed to Q's murder, yeah, she had it planned out to the dime.

"Fuck it, take the loss girl," she told herself. "Then press Cleo's dumb ass for a bank account or something and get what she could.

She stood up with the pistol cuffed in her hand. "So, uh...what did you have in mind?"

Hulie sneered as he crept closer toward her. He didn't see the gun, but he knew she had something up her sleeve. But he'd be up on her quick enough to distract her from making a move. Then wrap his python-like arms around her neck and snap it in two...easily.

"Yeah, this bitch is toast," he told himself, but then his pocket started buzzing...his fuckin' cell phone. *'What the fuck?'* he thought. *'Now what?'*

He stopped and pulled it out, wanting to turn it off so he could finish what he'd planned. But he fucked around and checked the number. It was Wood, his fuckin' snitch and lately, he'd been on a roll with the info.

"Yeah, what the fuck you want?" Hulie answered.

"Yo' man, remember that shit I told you about with that broad Nikki?" Wood said.

"Yeah, why?"

"Man, they about to make a move. Yo' they got a lot of money, a goddamned duffel bag full. I seen it, I guess they thinkin' 'bout flippin' it in the country somewhere."

"Country...where?"

"Don't know, your boy, Diplite was with them. I do know for sure it's someplace Dirty-Red set them up with."

"Okay...cool! Be up that way shortly, keep an eye on them."

"A'ight later."

Hulie hung up and stared at the phone. Sunshine had turned around enough so that he finally saw the gun in her hand. It was what it was.

"Okay...so this is it," she said and slid the hammer back.

Hulie shook his head, he didn't have no wins, then put his hands up and said, "You still want your money or what?"

"Money, muthafucka, you just tried to kill me. Fuck the money!"

"Right now, I know for a fact where the money is."

"You've been saying that for...months!"

"Yeah, a'ight, you got that, but right now..." He showed her the number. "I know where it's at and to tell you the truth, I'ma get it." He turned his back to her and said, "You're gonna have to kill me...to stop me."

"Just like you killed, Q, huh? Sneak 'em...fuckin' coward!"

Hulie spun around and lunged at her. "Fuck you!" He caught himself and stopped then rubbed the sweat off his forehead after staring down the barrel of the gun pointed directly in his face. "Okay, I was wrong...I fucked up! Ain't been the first time, probably won't be the last. Yeah, it bothers the hell outta me and I'ma make it right, but Sunshine..." He put his hands out towards her pleading. "...I need to do it with money. Gotta get you out my pocket, then leave town...for good."

"How you know I'ma let you leave?"

He looked her square in the eyes. "Cause I know too

much...about you...your office..."

"I could kill you, right now."

"Yeah, you're right, but you're not prepared to take that kind of risk...and lose. Now, are you?"

She lowered her gun, turned and swigged the drink she had in her hand down, in one gulp. "Hulie...one more time to try me, ya hear? One mo' goddamned time!"

He picked up her car keys. "Now, look, I'm on my way to a liquor house owned by a dude name, Dirty-Red. Your people probably know the name, I'm sure...y'all know everything

else. I'll call you when I get there, a'ight."

Sunshine put the gun away and walked toward the door, then turned back around and looked him dead in his eyes.

"Yeah...I think you better do that."

Hulie locked the door behind him after he left out. Feeling paranoid he nervously looked over his shoulder. He had the feeling he was being watched. Maybe, Sunshine had her people following him. She hauled ass out of the driveway before he could ask. He continued to look around, up and down the block. No cars had moved, nobody was around...nothing.

He shook it off, jumped in his ride and dialed Cleo.

"Yo' baby, gotta make a move! I'll pick you up later."

Cleo hung up the phone and right after it rung again. This time it was Sunshine. "Cleo...whose name is that place in?"

"You were there? Aw shit, I thought you didn't want him anymore..."

"Cleo, whose name is the place in...yours or his?"

"What...mine! Why?"

"Okay...okay, it's nothing..." It was just as she thought. It was all a front. "...look it's about to get real ugly, he's fuckin' outta his mind. You might need to stay with your mother for

a few days, okay. If anything goes down...call!"

"Okay...no, he's supposed to pick me up later on. What happened?"

"Shit happened, Cleo...shit happened!"

"HEY, COCKY...YOU THINK we should get at him?"

"Naw...let him ride."
"Still followin' him, right?"

"Oh yeah, we gonna do that. You see...a cat like him always thinks he's safe, ya know. He always takes things...the real small things for granted...punk ass muthafucka!" Cocky stretched his large, calloused hands, opening and closing them. As he watched Hulie's car race toward highway I-26.

His Benz was right behind him. He couldn't wait until the day he punished him for what he'd done. Cocky was Q's homeboy, he wasn't in town the day Q was jumped by Hulie, and he felt real fucked up about it. After all, he and Q were boys, his right-hand man. They were side by side, had always been together, except for that one fucked up day. Cocky knew of Hulie, but he never thought about whether or not he liked him. Now that was no longer his concern, him and his boys made enough money in the extort game so that Hulie didn't make a difference one way or another.

The Makin' was their hood, born and raised. They swore no one from the outside was ever gonna hold it down in their hood except if they let them and they stuck to that. It was a generational type of thing, and Hulie, Hulie was a fuckin' offbrand as far as they were concerned. What made Hulie stand out this one particular day, and al the others since Q's death, was that he killed his homeboy. His face muscles tremored as the anger coursed through his veins. The more he thought about it he was hurt, and damned angry. Yeah, he'd sold Sunshine that bullshit, ass dream that they were gonna do it their way and all that, which they were, but she wasn't going to know a damn thing about it.

Hell, she was a D.A. and dirty on top of that, then she used to fuck with Hulie's ass. So, of all people, how could they trust her? Q had mentioned her to him once before, but nothing enough that concreted a real relationship. After all, he was known to have several other women, all the time so she was no different. He did sort of slow down with her, but he figured he was going at an angle, trying to make something happen, although he never said what his motives were.

"Yo' Cocky...look like he's headed for Liberty Hill. What's up with that?"

"Don't know, stay on him and try to stay low key, a'ight. I want him to sweat a little bit...coupla days or so."

"I feel you!"

If Sunshine got in the way, he'd have to take her ass out, too. But one thing was for sure, Hulie was going down, but killing a muthafucka like him was much too good for his ass. Cocky wanted him to rot, he wanted to make him suffer like

Hulie made Q's mama suffer watching him never come out of that coma.

"Yeah, I'ma make him suffer like that," Cocky admitted.

He was going to set his black ass up, that's the direction they were going. So, they had to watch him, know everything about him then get 'em. After getting him get all his loot, cars, home, and even his pussy...everything...every muthafuckin' thing he had that gave him all of what he took from his boy's life day for day.

"Hey, uh...you got Dirty-Red's number?"

"Yeah, think so."

"Call him, see what he knows about that dude being in Liberty Hill."

TANGIE PULLED AT HER hair frantically and nervously. Her body was still freaked out from the other week. It was fresh in her mind that she was almost killed. She could barely sleep at night and the pills she was taking weren't working at all. She was fucked up, but not so much from the shooting than from the many questions that ran through her mind. The main one being why was Dondi with Jabari? Why didn't Dondi at least tell her? Maybe she woulda later, but Hulie shot her down in cold blood like a dog before she could say or do anything. He'd damn sure pay for that shit, she swore.

She ended up burying her body right next to Rip. She was sure that's where she would have wanted to be. No one came to the funeral, except for a handful of people. That looked like some of her folks from Narcotics Anonymous and she was glad, actually proud to tell them that she was clean until the end.

"You go, Dondi," Tangie said out loud.

The Sheriff was doing much better. The shot to his shoulder made his movement limited and stiff, but he still made time to play with his kids. Matter of fact, it was so close a call, he cherished it. She called him up and told him that she was finished with Walterboro. He laughed at her, then still invited her to dinner.

"Scary ass," he called her.

She told him not to hold his breath, but deep down, eventually she knew she'd come see him. After all, he was a friend and the reason she was still alive.

The 5th Circuit Solicitor's Office in Charleston got some of the details but not all, from what Missy was telling her.

Sunshine was asking a lot of questions.

"Hell, she seemed more interested than Walterboro's people," Missy informed.

That dude Hulie had to b the link, and she was gonna expose it and bring her dirty, giggling ass down, if for nothing else then for Dondi.

Still tense and nervous, she jumped slightly when Missy knocked on the door. "Yes...come in," she answered.

Missy walked over to her and rubbed her hands. "Feeling cold...you sick?"

"No...don't think so."

She reached over and placed the back of her hand on her forehead, checking for a temperature. "Hot...you need to rest."

"No, got too much work to do here," she said as she shuffled some papers on her desk.

"Look, girl who you kidding? I can take care of all that. I'll call, keep you posted. I know what you're stressing about, go home."

She was right as usual. Tangie did need rest, and yeah Missy could take care of it all herself, hands down. She gave

in. "I need you to call a cab, then...I can't drive." "No...I got someone that can help you home." "Home...who?" Tangie asked.

Missy walked to the door and opened it wide enough for her to see the man on the other side. He stepped through.

"Oh, my God..." she said as she jumped to her feet and ran into his arms awaiting a hug, and it came, finally it came.

"Jabari, I'm so glad to see you!"

Jabari looked deep into her eyes, they were searching, searching for something. What he didn't know and up until now, didn't even care. She had this crazy-ass smile on her face that seemed so...so, for lack of better words, dumbfounded. Like a child that had just picked out a puppy from a pet store or something...crazy. Possibly looking for a link between us, being his blood just wasn't good enough for her Jabari guessed. She wanted to find out...things. These things, Jabari couldn't help her with. He'd made his bed a long time ago.

"Okay, sis, you're way...way out there...weirding me out here," Jabari said softly.

"Wha..." she noticed she was staring and had made Jabari uncomfortable. She quickly averted her eyes. "I'm sorry...I didn't mean to..."

Jabari felt her pain, it was written all over her face. He reached over and touched her chin with his fingers, gently turning her face toward his, like their father used to do.

"It's not your fault. Things...just happened!"

"But I should have been there for you. Shoulda said something...shoulda..."

"Shoulda what, Tang?" Jabari was tired of it already.

There wasn't anything else to say anymore. They were both grown and what was done was done, even now.

"You can't hold yourself responsible for what our parents did. You just can't...or, you'll be like me...crazy," Jabari said then got up, walked over by the window and stared out at nothing in particular.

Tangie came up behind him and stroked his back. "Yeah, we can't but we also can't let their mistake...be ours...Jabari," she said softly.

Jabari grinned slightly, that was sort of what he wanted to hear. Then he toward her, thinking maybe she was right. He needed someone in his life, he was tired of being alone, or the odd man out. He wanted to at least give her half of a chance.

He started copping deuces. "Look...I'm not perfect. I'm not this big, righteous...do right kinda guy...no, not me. So, don't expect..."

Tangie hugged him and started sniffling in his arms. Since he'd come through the door, it seemed like she felt at home there, like that's where she wanted to be. He hesitated at first, like when they were kids, but now, it had become his nature. He hugged her back and squeezed her, tight, finally a tear came down his eyes. She was his big sister and for the first time in his adult life, he didn't feel so quite alone and for some reason, he didn't want her to feel that way either.

After a while of talking, well Tangie did most of the talking. She talked about old times and asked where he'd been, told him where she'd been, and all of that. Her assistant Missy came into the room giving Jabari those crazy, googly eyes.

"Man, oh man, they sexy as hell," Jabari said to himself.

He couldn't keep his eyes off of her. Her long natural eyelashes, chinky eyes, full lips and the fact that she looked half Filipino.

"Damn, if she wasn't married with kids and all that other bullshit, she could get it."

Jabari was scratching and feeling antsy, he hadn't been high now in about week and he was wanting a fix bad. He needed pills, weed, anything right now wouldn't have mattered. Tangie watched him as he moved, squirmed and paced around. He knew she knew something but was holding back.

"Maybe I should say something to her about my...problem...come clean with her or whatever." He told himself, then

thought against it just as fast. "Hell naw, fuck it."

Tangie and Missy were going through some papers, and Jabari sat down on her couch trying to figure out his next move. It seemed to him as he checked them out like they were both trying to read him or something. Either that, or he was crazy or fuckin' paranoid, perhaps a little of both. It didn't help much when they both looked his way, got up and sat down with iPads on their lap in front of him.

"Now...what happened that night?" Tangie said.

'*Night?*' Jabari thought. '*Hell could be a thousand god-*

damned nights for all I care. They were all fucked up lately.'
"Rip...Nikki's son...Carl?" Tangie asked.

Okay, now she was being a little clearer for Jabari. He wondered who'd told her about Rip, but then he remembered Tangie telling him she'd visited Dondi at the hotel a few times. He was quite sure they'd talked about him of course, and she probably mentioned Rip. Hell, she probably ran from there, running her mouth he more than suspected. He turned toward them and gave them his full attention, crossed his legs and got on some old interrogation room, CSI bullshit.

"Okay, so, you know a little something. Know what, how 'bout y'all tell me what y'all already know? And I'll just fill in

the blanks. How 'bout that, ladies?"

Tangie wasn't trying to feel that shit, and she didn't watch CSI either. Jabari had to admit she was good, she'd read right through his condescending, dopefiend ass, off the muscle.

"You kiddin' me or what? Okay, just to humor you...I know enough. That, hmm, okay, how can I put this? If you weren't my brother, and this case dropped in my lap. I'd be fighting to get you out of an elbow...easy! That good enough? I mean...really...that good enough, Jabari? I mean, you know, what an elbow is, right? *Life*!"

"Damn, sis..." Jabari shook his head. '*Smart ass, now I see where I get it from*,' he thought and almost laughed.

"Oh yeah...what kinda drugs you doing?" she added.

"Here were go with the bullshit, knew that shit was comin'," Jabari grumbled to himself. "Why is that your business? You ain't my mother, I'm grown," he fussed.

"Yeah, true, you are but...you're in one hell of a predicament. This is real serious, and I think you need to be sober...uh, focused. Jabari, your life may as well be on the line."

She was right, but Jabari didn't know how to stop or at least how to stay stopped. "I can't help it, Tang. I'm jonesing like a muthafucka, right now...sorry 'bout that, but you know what I mean."

"I can put you in a detox for a minute and then we can go from there. You'll be safe and outta sight. I got you, okay?" She turned toward Missy and they scribbled down some stuff on paper. They meant well, but Jabari was tired of being treated like a patient though. Hell, he'd come there to see what she knew about that dude Hulie, that was all. He wasn't looking for no goddamned family reunion or therapy session. All he wanted to know about was the dude who'd killed Dondi.

"Naw, fuck that, let's get real then. What's up with that dude, Hulie? Hell, you knew him from back in the day, least that's what he said."

"Okay...let's go there then. Dondi, said that you said he had something to do with killing Rip, right? Okay, my source tells me that, that night, also, Nikki was almost killed, and your name just happens to come up. You see, this is all of what the D.A. knows and so far, bro, that's enough to take you to a Grand Jury looking at Murder indictments, easy. So, I believe, you need to let me know what's what and you need to listen

to me, so I can help you. That's real talk."

"Like I said, you know that dude Hulie better n' me. Why don't you ask him yourself?"

"What the hell are you talking about, Jabari? Hulie...I never dealt with him. Damn, you must be talkin' 'bout when I was in high school or something. He took me to a movie or something, then tried to make a move, cop some feels, and I dumped his ass...that's all. Yeah, he called me some names and shit, spread rumors, but fuck him! I never fucked around with him!"

Jabari's eyes widened as he looked at her demeanor. She was feeling some sort of way. Damn, Hulie had played him off the rip. He'd played on his emotions from the start.

"Well..." Jabari said hanging his head. "...he said different-

ly."

"And you believed him?"

"Hell, I didn't talk to you much...deal with you..."

"Jabari!" She got up, came over to him and kneeled down in front of him. He was already feeling like shit and hoping she wasn't about to make it any worse. "Trust me...just, trust me. Tell me everything and we can go from there. I'm not gonna get you any drugs, tell you that, right now. Okay...okay, I'll get you some cigarettes, that's all." She nodded at Missy and Missy left the office, probably on her way to the store. "We gonna get you out of this shit, I promise...and then start from scratch, together, the right way, okay."

This time Jabari looked deep into her eyes. They reminded him so much of their mama's and he fell right in, like a little child, a mama's boy.

"Okay..." he said.
"We gonna get them both."
"Both...who else?" Jabari asked.

"Hulie...and that damn Sunshine...can't stand her ass..."
"Yeah...that's the D.A. chick, her name? Heard him mention her. Matter of fact, he had her card."
Tangie nodded. "Yeah...get them both, and you're the key."

"A'ight...well, it was just a regular job for us..."

"Hold up..." Tangie ran to her desk, picked up the tape recorder and she noticed Jabari grimace. "Trust me, Jabari...trust me." Then she ran back over and sat Indian-style next to him.

Jabari frowned, but he trusted her, so he continued. "He said, it had something to do with money. A lot of it...close to a hundred grand."

Chapter Sixteen

"O let that muthafucka get away wit' that shit. Hell kay...I see, naw I ain't know that. Hell, yuh, we can't

naw!" Dirty-Red scanned around the now packed liquor house, observing folks, smiling at some and staring equally hard at the ones he didn't know trying to figure out just who they were, making sure they were spending money and drinking, trying to spot ball if he could.

He also looked for Wood, it shoulda been a lot easier. Hell, it was his job to scope out the joint anyway, to watch his back, and from the call he'd just got, he damn sure needed him to be on it.

"Yuh, Cocky...I got you. If I see that muthafucka, I'll call you."

He stuffed the small cell phone back into his pocket, looked around again, then threw his hands up and said to himself. "Damn, where the hell is this mutha..." Someone tapped him lightly on the shoulder and he spun around abruptly, ready to straight ham, but it was Nikki.

"Wassup, Red?"

"Nuthin' Nikki, can't find that goddamned Wood for hell, that's all. He supposed to be somewhere in this muthafucka. I pay him good money to watch the place. Where the

fuck is, he?"

331

"Something wrong?"

"Naw, not really, just got some word on a muthafucka, that's all." Dirty-Red finally spotted him, in the parlor like always up in a woman's face, tricking and probably beggin'. "Yo' Wood!"

Wood paid him no mind at first and ignored him. It was only after Dirty-Red hollered out his name a coupla times, that Wood finally responded.

"Wassup, Red?"

Dirty-Red was already up on him, with Nikki close behind, spazzing. "Yo' man, you supposed to be watchin' eer'thing. You over here fuckin' wit' the pussy. Wassup wit' that?"

Wood looked behind Dirty-Red at Nikki and said, "Naw, wassup wit' that?" He turned facing Dirty-Red, sizing him up. "Man, you've been bullshittin' me. You thinkin' 'bout leavin' town and shit, with this broad, ain't said shit to me 'bout nuthin'. Now all of a sudden you worried about shit up in here." He pointed his finger in Dirty-Red's face. "Fuck that,

you look after this muthafucka your damn self!"

Dirty-Red looked at him like he'd lost his goddamned mind. Usually, that same look woulda been enough to back Wood down, but not this time.

"So, what...you feelin' some sort of way, Wood?" DirtyRed turned toward his room, laughing it off, thinking maybe he had too many drinks, but Wood stepped in front of him with his hands on his gun.

"Yeah...I am," Wood admitted.

The place started clearing out quickly as Wood and DirtyRed stood toe to toe, eye to eye, neither one backing down. Nikki backed up a ways herself, ready for anything. Dirty-Red looked around him, then smirked and slowly back away.

"A'ight...you got that," Dirty-Red said. Wood took out his gun all the way this time and Dirty-Red nodded. "Naw, don't worry 'bout that. You ain't gotta go there. It's cool! You this one, Wood, uh...huh, but I tell you what. You need to get your shit and go. Don't come back, got that son?"

"That's what it is, but not before I gets my cut." He looked back over Nikki. "Yeah, I heard, shit everyone knows.

Where's my money, Dirty? Since everyone gettin' theirs!"

"What the fuck you talkin' 'bout, your cut?"

"I know she's got some money. A couple of grand plus some dope. Now, let's do this civilized and just let me get a couple grand and we'll be straight. Just like old times, forget about it huh. I can still work the spot here and..."

"Muthafucka...you done lost your fuckin' mind for real!" Dirty-Red stepped toward him, his face was flushed red and he was pissed the fuck off.

Nikki stopped him. "No...no, let hem say wat he want."

Dirty-Red looked at her like she was crazy too, and she continued to push him back.

Wood snickered. "Yeah, you heard the chick...give me, me."

Nikki turned around and said to him, "I got the money 'round back. We can give yu a cut, 'kay."

She started easing back toward the doorway of the parlor with Dirty-Red by her side. Dirty-Red remembered the .38 he had tucked under the bar and glanced that way, but so did Wood.

"Don't try to go for the gun either, I'll blow both your asses away," Wood spat.

Nikki turned up at him, then said to Dirty-Red. "Giv' it to hem...coupla gees don't worry, 'bout it."

"I ain't givin' that muthafucka shit! Hell, I give him enough as it is now!"

Wood put the gun up in Dirty-Red's face. "Keep runnin' your fuckin' mouth!"

"Man, fuck you, Wood, you ain't shit anyway!"

"What...what, oh, I ain't shit...huh? Okay, then..." He felt some cold steel by his earlobe and froze, then looked it was

Diplite.

"Muthafucka, you, breath hard and I'll put a hole in your head. Now, put the goddamned gun down!" Diplite demanded.

Wood looked back over at Dirty-Red and Nikki, then back at Diplite. He ain't have no wins. He slowly started lowering the gun and copping pleas.

"Yo' man, Red, just bullshittin'...heh...heh!"

Dirty-Red smiled, looked around the room, then peeped into the back. It was empty, everyone was gone. He sighed, then out the fuckin' blue backhanded the shit outta Wood.

"Muthafucka, just bullshittin', huh?" He kicked him in the mouth. "Uh-huh...just like me...kickin' your ass!"

Nikki pulled Dirty-Red off of him, but Wood still got up talkin' shit.

"You know what it is Diplite. Don't know why you actin' crazy. Hell, you had something to do with this Nikki bullshit, anyway. That nigga, Hulie gonna make sure you pay...either in

money...or blood. Real talk, my nigga!"

Diplite pointed the gun back at Wood and hollered. "Get the fuck outta here!"

"Wat hem talk 'bout, Diplite? Hulie...s'cond time his name done came up!" Nikki said.

"Yuh, Dip...what's up wit' that?" Dirty-Red yelled over at him. "Got this muthafucka actin' crazy."

They took their eyes off of Wood for a minute, long enough for him to pick up his gun. Diplite was too busy arguing with Dirty-Red and Nikki, mostly Nikki trying to come up with something to tell them. Or else this muthafucka Wood was about to tell it all, at least what he knew anyway. Wood fucked around and pointed the gun at Diplite and squeezed off. Diplite ducked and the bullet ricocheted behind him hitting Dirty-Red's big ass seventy-five-gallon fishtank. Water exploded all over the place, Wood hid behind the door and fired again. Nikki and Dirty-Red dove for cover on the wet floor, as Diplite started firing back at Wood.

One of his shots caught Wood in the arm and he screamed like hell, then turned and took off running outside the backdoor into the woods. Diplite was right on his ass until he got right to the tree line of the woods, then pulled back and started calling him a hundred pussy muthafuckas. As he squinted his eyes in between the trees trying to get ahead on him. Wood ran through the trees towards the old school house, his face was scratched the fuck up from the branches and shrubbery hitting him upside the head. He'd fell at one point and pumped his arm, it hurt like all hell and throbbing. The bullet probably broke a bone, he didn't care, all he knew was that Diplite was still close behind him and on his ass. He pulled at the trigger of the gun and all he heard was click...click...click, damn it was empty.

Somehow or another he had to get up with Hulie and let him know what was going on. Luckily for him, he spotted Hulie as he came out of the cut running, tired, bleeding and breathing hard.

He hailed at him. "Hulie...yo' Hulie!" He kept looking behind him, holding his blood-soaked arm, he was scared.

Hulie got out of his truck and as he came closer to Wood, he said, "Whoa...hold up! Don't get all that blood and shit on my truck. What happened?" He examined his arm and looked into the woods behind him.

"Man, that muthafuckin' Diplite shot me!" Wood yelled.

"Shot you!"

"Hell yeah, I was at Dirty-Red's trying to find out some more shit. You know, about that chick, Nikki."

"Keep your voice down. What'd you find out?"

"That muthafuckin' bitch got the money, said she was

gonna give me a coupla gees and shit."

"Damn, no man..."

"Yeah, but when I mentioned your name..."

"You mentioned my name? Damn!" Hulie turned away from him and punched his fist into his palm. "Thought I told you not to?"

"It slipped...sorry 'bout that, but they still don't know nuthin.'"

"They know about me...and you, and that's not good." He opened the truck door, reached in and pulled out a rag. "I understand though, come here. Let me clean up that blood for you. Damn, Wood, you might need to go to the hospital or something."

Wood rubbed at his arm and grimaced in pain as Hulie tied a tourniquet around his arm.

"This'll stop the bleeding. Hey, uh...look in the back seat, there's some bandages."

Wood opened the back door and peeped in. "Where at?"

"Look, it's somewhere."

"Naw, don't see none...ackkkk!"

Hulie had his massive arms around Wood's neck, squeezing tightly. As he tried gulping for air, Hulie held him against the truck so he couldn't move. As he did so he kept looking around for anyone, making sure he wasn't being seen. He angled Wood's body inside and squeezed until he heard his windpipe breaking. Then he finally stopped beating the side of the truck, stopped kicking and resisting.

Hulie said to him tauntingly. "Yeah, that's it...let it happen, go to sleep. C'mon, now...you fucked up, letting them know I knew what they were trying to do. You know this was coming." Wood's body trembled. "Stop fighting, muthafucka...let it go...die. Man, up, Wood...you's a liability...besides, I got all I needed from you anyway."

Wood tried to struggle one more time as all the life left his now limp body. Hulie pushed him into the backseat and covered him with an old blanket, then slammed the door shut and looked around again.

"Good," he said. "No one saw me."

He jumped into the truck and rummaged through the bag he had packed for the Walterboro trip the other week, pulled out a fresh shirt, stuffed the blood-soaked one he had on in it, and cranked up the truck. He was just about to pull off, and then he saw Diplite come running out of the woods. His gun was tucked down in his waist and he walked slowly to the truck once he realized it was Hulie.

Hulie lowered the window. "Yo' wassup, Dip? Damn, where the fuck you coming from?"

Diplite glanced into the back seat, then at Hulie who tried to shield his view. "Nowhere special," Diplite said. "Had to handle some business, that's all."

"Really...like what?"

"Look...let's cut the bullshit. You want me to help you get rid of him or what?"

Hulie grinned out the side of his mouth, then shook his head. "Naw, I'm a'ight." He nodded one more time as he put the truck in gear.

Diplite back away as he started revving up the gas. "Oh...by the way." He looked into the back seat again. "Am I next...or what?"

Hulie snickered. "I don't know, Diplite...I mean, you know how these things happen," Hulie shot back. "I know one thing...bitch better have my money..."

"Talkin' 'bout, Nikki?"

"Let the chips fall where they may, but all of it better be there, kna'mean?"

Diplite stood there looking stupid as the truck backed into the street and sped off. He looked back into the woods toward Dirty-Red's liquor house.

"I gotta get back and clean this shit up." He knew Hulie was feeling some sort of way. Wood snitch's ass told him all he needed to know. "Dumb muthafucka, shoulda kept yo' fuckin' mouth shut, and you'd still be breathing. But damn, I wouldn't have chocked you out, though!"

STACY STARED OUTSIDE the window of the small, inconspicuous shack up from the pier. She'd been at it now for a little over a week. The same thing, every time she heard the roar of an engine from the trucks and cars go by, she peeked. She and Jabari had finally made it to the back road, right after they up the meth lab. Then cranked up the boat and waited. Jason or Smoak never came. They waited until it was just about time for the sun to set to leave for cover. That was also when SLED finally figured out the road they were on and started making their way with the dogs. It was time to go!

They were loaded down with a duffel bag full of cash and a damn rocket launcher. Jabari cleaned it off with his shirt and they tossed it into the swamp. They definitely didn't want to get caught with it in their possession. The smoke from the fire was getting heavy and it had a real putrid type of stink to it. The chemicals mixing and they couldn't afford to stay much longer. At any time, ball would probably shoot another helicopter overhead to figure out just where it was coming from, either way, they couldn't stay.

Smoak and Jason never made it back to the boat landing, so they had to assume they were busted or either dead. Considering all the police, SLED and muthafuckin' F-B-fuckin'-I, it was damn near impossible for anyone to make it out. Anyone, true, but not that fuckin' Jason.

"*C'mon, now, Stacy he ain't coming.*" She remembered Jabari telling her.

After she dropped Jabari off in the Red Top section, a small fishing town that set off of the inlet. She went to the spot where they'd planned to meet up later on that week. After the heat had died down a bit, and there he was, Jason. He said he didn't know what had happened to Smoak. He'd said some shit about him running up the road shooting. But the real deal was that had given Jason enough cover to haul ass.

Smoak thought he was coming behind him, but when he found out he didn't, it was much too later, his bullet-riddled body proved that much. Jason didn't give a fuck, he wanted to chase behind the money. That's exactly what he did, he basically said *fuck, Smoak*. As far as he was concerned that was one less muthafucka they had to split the money with.

"He said he'd be here?"

"Hell, he ain't even called. Now..." Jason walked over to her and rubbed her back assuringly. "...you've given him enough time...damn good time, but Stacy...we gotta go. It's gettin' too hot for us to just sit...and wait, especially in South Carolina."

Stacy turned toward Jason, tears had welled up in her eyes. She started crying for the umpteenth time. "You think he got caught?"

"Can't rule it out," Jason informed.

"Okay, ...you're right." She let out a deep sigh, then stepped into the bathroom to clean up and put on the disguise she'd made for herself.

The period of mourning was over, she'd already cut her hair and dyed it. But the teeth she had, were optional, with false eyelashes and contacts to boot, she looked like an entirely different person. Jason stood by the window looking up the pier himself. He'd hope Jabari wasn't caught. He knew too much about them and the whole operation.

"He should have at least called, but he didn't, something has to be up," Jason to himself. "Fuck it, no time to dwell, we've given him enough time already. Anymore would fuck us up. It ain't personal, it's just time to go. Maybe one day, I'll find out what happened, after all, I do sort of owe him my life."

Jabari was a real trooper. It was just a crying shame that his girl was killed like that, but that was life. The fucked-up part of it, the part Jason knew, all too well. Stacy stepped out of the bathroom and Jason's eyebrows raised. She looked damn good, she was glamorous like a baby light movie star or something. She hadn't gotten high in a while, and her skin had cleaned up, her body was starting to fill out. If Jabari did show up, fuck it, Stacy might be Jason's prize worth fighting for.

"You ready?" Stacy asked.

"Yeah...time to go. I'll go crank the boat up." Jason looked over his shoulder at her and noticed the blouse she had on was thin, and her nipples on her titties poke through it hard. "You might want to put on a sweater...gettin' chilly outside."

She smiled at him. "Sures!" She glanced one more time up the pier, then shook it off. She grabbed her bags and Jason loaded them up on the boat and tied them down. They had purchased another much bigger boat to make the trip to Mexico. Especially around the Gulf where the waters were vicious this time of the year. If was a ride that had to be taken. Stacy closed the door and locked it shut behind her.

"G'bye, Jabari," she said softly under her breath.

Jason shook his head approvingly and cranked up the boat. Stacy hopped aboard and they pulled off.

Under her breath she mumbled, "Mexico sounds damn good..." then she put her shades on and smiled as the green spray tickled her face.

There was a muffled sound heard inside the room after they left, buzzing underneath a blanket. Stacy had left her cell phone, she'd forgotten all about it. She had an automatic speaker voicemail gadget installed, just so she could scan her calls. After the fifth ring it automatically, picked up and the voicemail became audible. Like an answering machine of sorts.

"*Stacy...Stacy*! Where are you? It's me, Jabari. Where you at? I still want to meet you...damn...hey look, when you get this call, hit me at five-four-seven-nine-two-three-five! I'll be at this number for a minute. Okay, hey...uh love ya!"

It was something she told Jason about. She figured if Jabari called, well, anyway...Jason understood, so he definitely didn't remind her that she'd left her phone. Too bad for Stacy, because it was too much, too little...too late.

HULIE STEPPED OUT OF the shower admiring the light fixtures and tile on the bathroom floor. It was immaculate, you could tell it cost money. The walls had smooth paint jobs, and no peeled back wallpaper like in the hood. He walked into the walk-in closet, picked up a towel off the rack and nodded approvingly. Cleo had picked up some fly ass towels from Bath and Beyond that were off the chain. They were fluffed up, folded, different colors and pretty cool.

She had good taste for a diva on a budget. He wondered what else she'd done with the money she saved him. He'd definitely have to look into that later, he couldn't let her keep it all. He snickered at the thought. He walked into the bedroom and sifted through racks of clothes searching for an outfit. He wanted something casual since he wasn't planning on going anywhere today. He'd done enough shit the other day, getting rid of Wood's body itself was a headache.

He had to cut it up, stuff parts into a couple of barrels, then take the barrels out to the islands near Beaufort to drop them into the swamps. That was a lot of work, but at least no one could track them back to him. Wood, poor sucka, shoulda kept his mouth shut, but still, that damn Moonie G wasn't no better, but it was a little easier takin' him out though. He sat down in the living room and started watching TV, or at least the TV watched him. He thought about ways of getting up with Q's homeboy, Cocky. Who was a mad thug dude from the Makin'. He'd heard from his snitches that he was following him around town, planning on making a move on him.

He'd have to get to him first to make plans of making amends for Q. It was a hood thing, nothing personal. He thought had beat him, he damn sure didn't mean to kill him. Cocky would have to understand, it's not like it never happened to him before. Cleo had come in from shopping and called him into the kitchen. She had a bag full of snacks, fruit and all the things he'd like. He lovingly kissed her on the forehead.

"This chick ain't half bad," he said to himself.

He looked out the backyard at the swimming pool and smiled. He needed to find someone to help him clean it out and then fill it up.

"You know...there's a service for that," Cleo said.

"Huh," He spun around quickly, not knowing she was watching. "Really, thought I'd have to get a crackhead or something to help me."

Cleo smiled, then walked over to him. "Naw...don't need no crackheads knowing where we live." She grabbed his hand.

"This place is private."

"Yeah, I guess you're right. It'll be my luck he'd come out and help me. Then come back later and rob me, along with the rest of the neighborhood. That wouldn't be good! But that's my luck, huh?" They shared the laugh and he grabbed some ice cream and walked back into the living room turning on the massive eight-inch TV he'd just gotten and plopped down onto the sofa. "Damn...know the game is on...somewhere."

Cleo came in and sat down next to him. "You don't want to watch a movie?"

"Naw..." He flipped through the channels. "Tryin' to catch a game..."

Just then the phone rang, and Cleo answered it. "For you, Hulie." She handed him the phone, sat down and picked up the remote.

After about a couple of minutes or so, Hulie hung the phone up and sat back down. "Found it yet?" he asked.

"Tell you the truth, really wasn't trying to find one..." Cleo admitted.

He snatched the remote from her. "Told you, I wanted to catch the game."

"Hey, don't be so mean. Ain't nothing but an old stank ass game."

"See where you going..."

She sucked her teeth and crossed legs pouting. Hulie looked her way said out the side of his mouth. "You still trickin'?"

"What...what the hell are you talking about? Hell no!"

"Hey, don't bite my head off. I mean, someone just called and told me..."

"Goddamn snitches. You gonna get tired of them muthafuckas yet!"

"Hell, you was one too..."

"The hell with you, Hulie!" She started to get up.

Hulie held out his hand stopping her. "Hold up, look, someone said they saw you with a dude that just got out of prison. Heard he was a hot boy, that's why they called me. All

I want to know is who is he and how you know him?"

"I have no idea who you talking about. You sure they saw me?"

"Yeah...sure!"

"What he look like?"

"Clean cut, short, cropped hair...damn sounds like the dude that pops said he...anyway, something like that." He tossed the remote on the end table once he found the game and leaned back focusing on it, but not giving it his full attention.

He was still trying to figure out who she was with. She finally figured it out, that goddamned Jesse. But where were they seen together? She had to come up with something.

"Hell, you talking about my cousin?"

"Cousin?"

"Yeah, ...he came into town for a minute. We hung out a little, that's all."

"Hmm...cousin...what's his name?"

"Darryl...yeah, cousin Darryl...from the country."

"Where at in the country?"

"Damn, you sure are asking a lot of questions. You don't trust me?"

"Naw...I trust you, but you never mentioned no, Darryl. Where at in the country?" He was coming on strong and she couldn't get her lies together for hell.

"Cheraw." Damnit, Cleo couldn't you think of something better? Her mind screamed, but that's what she came up with, probably from a conversation with her brother.

"Cheraw..." Hulie thought back to what Wood had said, that Dirty-Red was talking 'bout taking Nikki to Cheraw. It didn't quite add up, she was holding back something. "Hmm...whole lot going on in Cheraw." He leaned closer.

"Said, they saw him talking to your brother, too. Maybe I should ask him..."

"For what, Hulie?" He was all up in her face.

Cleo became rattled. "You act like we can't have family and you don't know everyone we know."

"Hold up, don't bite my head off. I mean, I got the call...that's all. They told me to be careful."

"Who?"

"Don't worry about that. Look, later on, you...uh, show me who he is. Damn, Cleo, as much as you want to protect this spot, and us. Hell, you shouldn't even be trippin' like this."

She sucked her teeth, picked up the remote and turned the channel.

"What the fuck you doin', didn't I tell you I was watchin' the game?" Hulie snapped.

"Seems like you questioning me more than you watching the fuckin' game," Cleo barked.

Hulie snickered, then eased over to her. "Damn, girl, it ain't that serious..." He kissed her on the neck. "You know ever since I got robbed, I need to watch my back. Still, don't know who did that!"

Cleo kissed him back. "You got a better situation here, baby. Hell..." She pointed to a picture frame hanging off to the side of the steps going upstairs. "...you got two safes here, no more holes in the walls...or linen closet, picture that." She laughed. "And the vent can really be used for getting some air...know what I mean."

Hulie backed up a little, that threw him. "Yeah, getting air..." Hell, no one knew his dope was in the vent. That's why the muthafucka was clogged up. He ain't never told no one, 'specially her and her big ass mouth. She couldn't hold fuckin' water. "Heh...heh, linen closet..." He damn sure didn't mention nothing to her about the money he had stashed, much less in the linen closet at that. On top of all that both spots were got. Hulie started feeling some sort of way now.

"Damn," he said to himself. "This bitch was the one who muthafuckin' robbed me, or she damn sure knows who did!"

"AAHHH!" DIRTY-RED SCREAMED out as the paramedics lifted him onto the stretcher. "Told y'all I don't need
to go to no goddamned hospital."

He'd caught a bullet to his shoulder, and it wouldn't stop bleeding. Even after a couple of attempts were made to clog it. Someone suggested that he go to the hospital and that the bullet might have hit an artery. It was either that or Nikki was gonna go to the root doctor. He bitched and moaned for a while then decided the root doctor was out of the question. "Hey...hold up. I need to do something real quick." He motioned for Nikki to come over to him. "The police'll be here looking for shit, thinking it was gang-related or something...clean up the dirt for me...knamean...please!"

"Come na...you know I's got that...I got yu."
"Pass me my phone quick."

Nikki grabbed his cell phone and handed it to the paramedic as they loaded him into the ambulance. She kissed him on the cheek and disappeared into the house to take care of business like he'd asked her to. She started moving weed, boxes of bootleg, old kegs, and anything else that the police would be sniffing as illegal. Even though, ball knew it was a liquor house, if they came, they would have no choice but to act if they saw anything of the ordinary.

Dirty-Red smiled at the female paramedic who was taking his blood pressure. "Hey, uh, pass me my phone. If you don't mind?" She passed it to him. "Whoa...put your number in, too...a'ight." She did that, too. Then he dialed Cocky's

number. "Yo' man, got shot up."

"Yeah, I heard," Cocky replied.

"Damn, it just happened."

"Tell you, I got my sources. I sent my boys over to your

place to give the girl a hand...cool with that?"

"I'm cool with that, but hell, is she?"

"Think she'll be alright. She knows my people, never did no dirt to her or her son."

"I hear that. Hey, look, try to find that muthafuckin' Wood. And when you get him, holler back. I think he knows something 'bout that shit that went down with T-Black and

Nikki."

"Yeah, your man was a snitch for that dude, Hulie."

"Kinda figured that."

"Think Hulie had something to do with that fuck shit, though."

"Wouldn't doubt it."

"Check it out, you get better, then we'll take care of the business when you get out. Might be about a day or so, they'll probably want to keep you. I got that chick Nikki's back, so don't worry about that."

"A'ight man, I'll holler. I'll have my cell with me."

"Got you, believe that." Cocky closed the phone and stuffed it in his jacket, then glanced over at his boy. "Plans changed, now we go to war. Don't think that dude, Hulie will go down without a fight."

WHILE ALL THAT WAS going on, Diplite peeked from out of the woods. Right after leaving, Hulie looking at the back of the house. He thought about going inside but figured he'd just play it cool first and keep a low profile. He watched as Nikki and a couple of dudes he recognized from the Makin' took boxes and kegs out back and hid them. Then he saw one of the dudes come out with a big satchel bag and dip through the woods opposite where he stood, with Nikki right next to him.

"It is what it is," he said to himself as he crouched down so they couldn't see him.

The Cheraw run was definitely off, he'd just have to take the money. But he needed help, cause it seemed like DirtyRed had help, too as he thought about it. He might have been onto him. He knew he'd have to put Hulie down now, but he also knew he'd have to take Dirty-Red's ass out, too, once the deed was done. It'd be an easy set-up, he'd call Hulie and tell him that Q's boys were looking for him and that Dirty-Red was trying to make a move on him because of Nikki. Then he'd say that Dirty-Red hired Nikki to take Hulie out. Sounded good enough to Diplite, it was just the thing to throw some salt in the game. Diplite didn't even think Dirty-Red knew that it was his gun that had shot him.

It was fucked up, Diplite really tried to take Dirty-Red's dumb ass out, then that bitch Nikki, and get all the money. He kinda figured he had it in the house somewhere, but damn, that muthafuckin' Wood got all in the fuckin' way. It was cool, though, Diplite just had to go another route and be patient.

Diplite sneered as he watched ball go into the house to look around. It was time to go, he dipped toward the street and circled around the back. Then got in his car and hauled ass. The only thing he had to figure out now was, how he was going to get Nikki to come out of hiding with the money and the dope, together. Maybe he'd work the dope angle first, then tell her that he needed to help work it.

"Yeah, that sounds half ass right," he said. "One way or another, it's going down."

If Diplite had been paying any mind to his surroundings he would have noticed the eyes that peered down hard on him...Nikki's. She has spotted him the minute she came out onto the back porch earlier. It was her idea to snatch up the duffel bag and take it into the woods, but it was only a flam. The bag was filled with rags and old papers. The call had already been made to Cocky, and he was going to pick up the real loot later, with her blessing of course. She needed to go into hiding, but she was never one to run from a good fight. She figured she'd keep an eye on Diplite and see what kinda sheisty ass move he was gonna make next. But truly, straight up according to Cocky it would be his last move.

Diplite pulled in front of his mother's house and sat in the driveway. She peeked out and he waved at her.

"Be in, in a few!" he yelled to her.

He promised her earlier that he'd stop by to talk to her. He figured it was about Cleo, and him keeping an eye on her. It was cool, he didn't have a problem with that. He needed a way to get in Cleo's business anyway. Considering all that was going down, it was dangerous. She needed to stay clear of, Hulie. The trap was being set at that very moment. He dialed Hulie number. "Yo' Hulie, wassup?"

"Damn, cuz just finished talkin' to you. What's up? I'm busy, right now!"

"I just spoke to one of Cocky's boys. They want to talk to you, and it's serious. The way the brother told me they was trying to get at you on some revenge shit for Q. And, I think that muthafuckin' Dirty-Red got something to do with it, too," Diplite lied.

"Oh yeah...hmm, alright, good looking!"

Diplite hung up the phone and snickered. "Yeah, punk muthafucka, go to the cheese, you fuckin' rat." He glanced out of the window and saw his mother peek her head out again.

He nodded at her. "Be there in a few, ma!"

Somehow the call didn't seem quite right for Hulie. Why would Diplite wait, and say something about that now? He'd just left him not too long ago. He needed to meet and talk with Cocky his damn self. But maybe some of that shit Diplite had said was right. Supposed it was a trap or something. He knew what to do. He pulled out his phone and speed dialed Sunshine, betting anything that she knew.

Chapter Seventeen

Hulie stared over at Cleo, barely paying any attention to the game now. She sat with her legs across the armchair of the sofa swinging it, doing her nails. It was harmless, innocent boyfriend-girlfriend type of shit, but Hulie wasn't looking at it like that. He'd already called Cocky and tried to straighten things out, but he could tell by the way Cocky was acting over the phone that he wasn't really feeling no type of money retribution. Which was the only thing Hulie was offering. Hulie understood because had he been in Cocky's position somebody definitely would have to be taken out. Or at least get one of hella ass-kickin'. But things were reversed, and he personally wasn't trying to feel that shit, at all.

Diplite had been acting crazy, Hulie had a good feeling that he was up to something. But what? Hulie couldn't put his finger on it. He knew he'd been calling his sister quite a bit since the time he spoke to him about Cocky. That's about the last time Hulie had seen him. Hulie called Sunshine and she wasn't even in, either she was getting his calls, or something was up. Hulie was at least glad no one knew where he was staying, to the best of his knowledge.

He was so 'noid, he didn't even check his dope-spots. He had Deezo's people doing his pick-ups. It cost him big money, but he had to stay low, things were getting dangerous and

354

he couldn't afford to be careless. He was on the shitty end of the stick now, and as he stared at Cleo. He was thinking quite seriously that she had something to do with him getting robbed. The bullshit that started the fuckin' ball rolling, yeah, he definitely felt some sort of way.

It had been building up for quite some time now, he just needed a breaking point. He watched her glance over his way, lean forward and pick up the remote control. She turned the channel, then toss it back over to him.

"She got a lot of fuckin' nerve," Hulie mumbled to himself. Because of everything that was on his crazed mind, he picked up the remote and backhanded her with it.

Cleo toppled backward onto the floor and looked up at his crazy ass. "What the fuck!" she screamed.

"Bitch, I know it was you who robbed me!" Hulie barked.

"What the fuck are you talking about, Hulie," Cleo still tried to play dumb. "I don't know shit," she screamed as she backed away from him.

"I'ma give you a chance to come clean, okay. Just tell me who did it..."

"I don't know..." she screamed louder.

"Alright." He walked over to her slowly and started cracking his knuckles. "I see where this is going. How the fuck did you know where my stash was?"

"You told me, remember?" she lied.

"You got that, but still no one knew about the fuckin' vent!" He bent over her. "Now...who the fuck did it? You or what!"

Damn the vent, she knew she was busted for sure. That shit had slipped out easily, but she couldn't come clean...no way. He'd kill her for sure. She didn't have no choice but to dummy up. she couldn't replace the money, dope or anything and she really didn't want too. Hell, it was hers as far as she was concerned.

"Fuck it take an ass whooping..." she coached herself

silently. She closed her eyes and said, "Do what you do!"

"Who did it, Cleo?" Hulie asked as he raised his hand. "You know you've been wanting to this anyway..."

"Damnit, Cleo, I'ma kick your ass. Why'd you do it?

Wasn't I taking care of you?"

"Just like Mama said...gotta take your lumps. I'll take

them today, Hulie. But this'll be the last..."

He didn't even let her finish her sentence.

A WEEK LATER, CLEO came out of the hospital. She was wearing shades to cover the bruises to her eyes and bandages were on her ribs where Hulie had broken them. Hulie tried to pamper her, so she wouldn't say anything to the police. She was unconscious for about two days and by that time, he'd already told ball that Cleo was cleaning out the gutters and fell off a ladder. He'd even staged the whole thing when they came by. He cleaned everything, put her body on the grass by the sidewalk and set up a ladder, too. Then told the paramedics that he didn't want to move her until they arrived.

She'd robbed him and was spending a lot of money. Hulie guessed that money came from what she took when she robbed him. He felt bad about whipping her ass later, but, shit muthafucka had died because of that dumb shit. He still had to deal with Cocky, this week at that. For all he knew, maybe he'd helped Cleo. He didn't know the whole story, and Cleo still wasn't saying shit. So, now he was having a cookout for her and her family to try and smooth things over.

It wasn't working though, they were pissed. Her moms went to slap Hulie, Cleo's pops wasn't even trying to be around. He and Hulie had already scuffled in the hospital. Her pops told him that he didn't know how or when, but he swore on his life, he'd get Hulie. Diplite played it off the best he could, trying to keep shit quiet. When she regained consciousness Diplite told Cleo that he'd pay her to keep her mouth shut. They even made plans to do another lick, but this time Hulie would have to be taken out. Cleo was game and all the way in.

Her mother would leave the house when he came over. Hulie tried talking to her, buying her things and making promises he couldn't keep. All she ever said was after he left and under her breath. *"I'ma get you muthafucka if it's the last thing I do."* She wasn't trying to come to no goddamned cookout. She told Cleo after Cleo damned near begged her. *"I'll never come over there and let him put out into the street. Hell no!"* She tried her damnest to convince Cleo to get off the lease, so she could put his ass jail, take the condo and put a restraining order on his ass. Cleo, however, had other plans.

Her mother got tired of the bullshit and did the best thing she knew to do, she called Jesse. She told him what happened, and she got what she was hoping for. Jesse was hot as hell, he said he was personally gonna kill Hulie. Then, she fucked around and called Sunshine. Sunshine told her some shit about being patient, but she wasn't the one that was beat the fuck up. So, that went in one ear and out of the other.

Cleo's mom threw a soro charity event for some neighborhood kids. Hulie made the big mistake of trying to fit in. He had a couple of bags full of candy and started throwing them around like a big shot. He was also flashing money like a big man. Cleo wasn't there, so her mom tried to send Hulie on about his business. Hulie wanted to show his drunk ass in front of her friends like he was legit. She grew tired of it and him.

She remembered he had taken some pictures, fucking around trying to be family friendly. She took them and went straight downtown to the DA's office to see if she could get something done and get a restraining order. It was there that she bumped into Jesse.

SUNSHINE WAS ON THE phone flipping through messages on her desk. She had several messages from Hulie and Cleo's mom.

"Now what the fuck is going on?" She sighed. "It's like they're going at each other out of spite, just for the hell of it." She thought about how feisty Cleo's mother was and how she definitely wasn't trying to let Hulie walk all over her tiny ass. Sunshine giggled then suddenly the person on the other end that she was on hold for finally picked up.

"Yeah, who dis?"
"Sunshine!"

"Damn, girl...long goddamned time. Wassup, you your mind about me? You wanna get with a real playa or what?"

She giggled. "Another time, baby."

"Aw, hell, I can tell this is business, huh? Damn, I can never catch your ass when you's horny."

"Another place...Mark."

Mark was a childhood friend, one out of the handful she actually had. He was a nerd, like most of them, but he'd turned gangsta. He'd learned the business of dope, specifically trafficking and laundering and profited well from it. He always cherished Sunshine more than she cherished him. Every now and then, he let her in on some of the goings on's in the dope business. In exchange for some pussy, which he never got. Mostly, they just talked shit about people and old school mates. He already had his own connects, judges, cops and lawyers. So, he really didn't need no favors from Sunshine so far. He liked her, a whole lot, but they were on separate roads that every now and then crossed.

"So, what's going on, babe?" Mark asked.

"Trying to figure somebody out," Sunshine replied. "Seems familiar but I can't quite put my finger on 'em. One
thing I do know for sure is that he's crooked."
"Well, we'll find out who he is." Mark had an office in the back of a neighborhood back shop run by Muslims. He had converted to Islam and invested heavily in the Charleston community. He was considered a renegade of sorts though, because he wouldn't give up his hustla lifestyle, but yet his money was always accepted. So, he never ostracized anyway, and it really didn't bother him. "Let me go online...okay.
Now, give me something to work with."
"Damn, Mark, you got your gangsta friends online and shit?"

"Sunshine...with Facebook...damn near."

"For some reason, I believe that. ,Anyway, his name is

Jesse, just got out of prison..."

"What he look like?"

"Tall...quite handsome...brown-skinned...oh yeah, he had a scar on his neck..."

"Damn girl, you don't know who that is?"
"No...who...what?"

Mark swung his legs up on the desk and leaned back in his chair. He finally had one up on her and was going to exploit it to the fullest. "You gonna have to handle me for this one." "C'mon, Mark, stop playin'..." she whined.

Mark's voice got serious. "Naw, fuck that, when I tell you who this muthafucka is. I'll be over your crib this week...knamean!"

"You're serious?" Sunshine was feeling some sort of way. She liked her men forceful and figured she'd role play this out. If that's what he wanted, but he better have the answer she was wanting to hear. "If that's what you want me to do..."

"Yeah, that's what I want you to do. Tired of this shit! I want that ass...you hear?"

"Okay...Mark...sweetie. Don't be so mean!"

"Yeah, that's it, and damnit...Muslim, my name is Muslim now."

"Okay...Muslim. Who is he...baby?"

He chuckled, he had his hand deep down into his pants. He thought about pulling out, that's how good it was going to be once she heard this. "The same cat you paid me for...for offing that dude Moonie G."

"*What!*"
"Yeah...that was him!"

"Oh shit, I knew I recognized him..." She paused. "Friday night."
"Friday night...what the fuck are you talking about? Don't fuck up the moment..."

"That's when I'll see you."

Mark almost fell over in his chair. "Hell yeah...what time!"

"When you get here."
"Okay...okay."
"But Muslim...baby...sweetie..."
"Huh...huh?"

"Remember, I'm gonna be the one to fuck your brains out, alright!"
"Sure, the hell will. By the way...you looking for anyone else? I need to stay one up on you."

Sunshine giggled. "Boy...you's crazy. When I finish with

you, one is all you'll need, bye!"

"Damn, can't wait till Friday!"

Sunshine's grin was ear to ear. She finally found the right muthafucka to take Hulie's ass out. But now, she had to find him. Her phone kept blinking and vibrating, somebody was blowing her up.

"Hello!"

"Sunshine, I've been trying to reach you all day!" It was Cleo's mother.

"Been busy...sorry," Sunshine said, but really hating that she even answered the phone. She really needed to find dude, so she sounded cold.

Cleo's mother didn't give a damn, she wanted to take Hulie down, too. "I'm in your building here, downtown. I need to talk to you!"

"Sure, come on up." Might as well hear out, Sunshine sighed.

"But, I'm with someone and he may have to come up, too."

"Damn, probably her husband," Sunshine said to herself. "Ain't in the mood for this shit." She swung her legs back onto the floor and said, "Who?"

"Jesse...Cleo's friend, the one we met the day you came by."

Sunshine's grin grew so damn wide she looked like a wild albino female version of the Joker. Her fuckin' demeanor changed with that one name. She answered back quickly. "Oh, hell yeah, I'm right here waiting for you...and I got a little bottle for you, too...girlfriend." She pressed the intercom on her desk to her receptionist up front. "They'll be someone coming off the elevator to see me. Point them my way, please. And uh, hold all my calls, appointments, meetings...till tomorrow, okay."

"Yes, ma'am."

One-half bottle later, they all came to one conclusion, and that was that Hulie had to go. Now, how, that was another thing.

"Look...I got you if you get caught. I can make arrangements for bail. I'll tell them you were afraid for your life..." Sunshine was explaining to Jesse.

"No," he said as he got up from his chair. "I can take him."

Cleo's mother sat there sipping on her drink, observing the whole scenario. She didn't care how it was done, as long as her hands didn't get dirty in the process, and her daughter was finally free of that monster. Jesse, she could easily handle him, after all, she already was.

Sunshine's intercom buzzed and she answered with an at-

titude. "Didn't I tell you I didn't want to be disturbed?"

"Yes...you did, but I think you might want to take this call."

"Alright...put it through." She took the phone and walked over to a corner of the room out of earshot. "Who is this?"

"It's me...Muslim."

"What's going on? I told you Fri..."

"Naw...that ain't what it's about. Look, I got a call and that dude, Hulie, is going to meet Cocky, at a club in the Makin'." "And, this is my business..."

"I got word from his people that shit is going down. They're thinking about taking his ass out. Thought maybe you might want to know since you felt some sort of way about

dude and shit...least warn him."

Sunshine spun around and looked at Jesse. This was her window of opportunity. The perfect chance, she had to act on

it. "Thank you, baby...gotta go!"

She hung up the phone and looked at Jesse. "Jesse, I just got a call from my people. Hulie's in the Makin'...by himself. I

think this might be a good time..."

Jesse had already grabbed his jacket and was headed out the door. Sunshine grabbed hers too and glanced over at

Cleo's mother. "Think we might have this problem licked." She knew Cocky wanted to take Hulie out from day one. Why Hulie wanted to go to the club to talk to him, she didn't know and didn't care. She just wanted to be there to see this go down. She figured if Cocky fucked up, Jesse sure as hell wouldn't. Anyway, you put it, her Hulie problem would be solved today at least she knew that for sure.

Cleo's mother dropped Jesse off on Spruill and Reynolds Avenue, right up the street from the club. He told her he'd call her later, to pick him up. He needed an alibi, and along with Sunshine's advice, she agreed to be it. Sunshine herself waited on River's Avenue listening to handheld scanner she had, waiting for the ten-twenty-five call, shots fired, for shit to go down. Then she would pull up the rear, as though she was just riding through the hood or something. Make sure Hulie's ass was dead, that's all she cared about.

Jesse stalked over toward the pink and black club near the entrance of the Navy Base, waiting in the cut for Hulie to show. He looked over and spotted Cocky's truck outside the club. He didn't want no parts of him, or his people, they were too much for him. He figured he'd confront Hulie before he went in, put the tim down, then leave it at that. Fuck that bullshit Cleo's mom and Sunshine was on about killing a muthafucka unless they were gonna do the elbow he'd get for it. He wasn't no fool, specially theirs.

He came around the corner on his bright money green Suzuki was Hulie, and he waved him down. He damn near jumped in front of him and he pulled over.

"Who the fuck are you?"
"Name's Jesse..."

"You need to get the fuck outta the way, I got somewhere to be," he said as he looked over at the entrance to the club, watching as Cocky's boys peeked out the door checking
things out. "Move...gotta go."
"Naw...you need to holler at me." Jesse reached into his jacket and pulled out a snubnosed .38. "Pull the bike over and walked with me."

Hulie looked at him like he'd lost his mind. "Boy...you, robbed me? You know who I am?"

Jesse pushed him toward the side of a building with the gun stuck in his side. "The nigga that beat my girl up, punk ass muthafucka!"

"Aw man," Hulie said to himself. I know that bitch ain't hire this muthafucka, a crack head at that to try me. "Look, man, that's personal. I don't even know you partna. But look here, if she hired you to try me. I'll pay you double, cool?" He snickered as he reached into his pocket, pulled out a stack and started to peel off bills. "I don't want no trouble, a'ight. I gotta go...but on the real, though, I ain't trying to whip that girl's ass on no regular. It's a headache, trust me. It ain't like that...shit just went down...that's all. Here you go!" He handed Mark five crisp one-hundred-dollar bills. "This cool?"

Jesse looked at the money and shook his head, then

looked back up at Hulie. "Damn...you really ain't got a clue?"

"What?"

"I don't need your money. I'm straight...hell, I already got your loot. Laugh that shit off..."

"What the fuck you talkin' 'bout?" Hulie got off his bike and walked up on him with his hands out. "Look, I ain't got no gun and shit. You got something you want to tell me?"

"Hell yeah! But, uh...you don't even remember me, do you?"

"Naw man, fill me in. I really ain't got a lot of time either. I'm willing to hear you out." Somehow, Hulie knew he knew something, either about him being robbed, Cocky, Cleo something. He could at least give him half a minute.

"You remember that dude, Moonie G?"

"Yeah...and?"

"I was the muthafucka you paid to take him out."

"Okay...yeah, so that was you, huh? Look, Muslim put me on to you. What's up...he paid you right?"

"Everything's straight, but...I was approached by someone else...about you this time. I mean, I needed the money, just got out the joint. They told me it was a quick lick, so I put my

boy down and said fuck it, but I didn't anticipate the girl."

"Girl?"

"Yeah, I didn't think she would be in on the deal...it threw me. The dude that put me down said she was just going to show us where to go."

"What dude?"

Clear out of the clue, Diplite's car skidded out of control and bounced off the curb right next to them. Diplite came flying like a bat outta hell, waving his gun around.

"Alright partna, put the gun down!" he hollered.

Jesse looked over at him. "I was just tellin' him..." "Too fuckin' much...lies too!" Diplite cut him off.

"What the fuck are you two talkin' about?" Hulie asked, still shocked at the way Diplite had driven up. It was crazy, and stupid something like that wouldn't do nothing but draw attention.

"Yo' Hulie, back up, I got this. This muthafucka's straight up trouble. He's been stalkin' my sister like some sort of pervert."

"Naw, it ain't like that..."

"Hell, yeah it is. Feeling some sort of way about you seeing her, too. Hulie...muthafucka knows where you live!"

"Man, she told me she loved me," Jesse babbled, he started losing control. Exactly what Diplite he would do and wanted him to do.

"What...love!" Hulie laughed. "That's crazy.

"Look, man, that's the muthafucka that put me on to you." Jesse pointed at Diplite but with the gun in his hand.

Diplite just knew he was about to tell Hulie all about the robbery, the truth. Diplite said fuck it and shit him, he damn sure didn't want him talking. The bullet caught him in the stomach, and Jesse doubled over in pain holding his gut. He raised the gun at Diplite who pumped, faked like he was trying to shield Hulie and he shot him again. This time he caught him in the chest. Jesse dropped to the ground on his knees and looked up at Hulie as he tried to catch his breath and the life that started leaving his body.

"H...h...him." Jesse tried pointing at, Diplite but it was no use, he passed out.

"What the fuck was that crazy shit all about, Diplite?" Hulie asked as he watched Jesse gasping for air in the gutter.

Diplite walked over to Jesse's body and shot him point blank in the head. Making sure he was dead, then he kicked him. "Man, muthafucka been talking out his mind since he met Cleo at the mall, tried to get her to trick and she wouldn't...she was scared. Moms too, crazy ass muthafucka!"

Hulie shook his head and looked around, no one had heard or seen anything at least he'd hoped. He picked up his bike and glanced over at Diplite. "Funny...she didn't mention shit to me about it. Anyway, that's you and Cleo's crazy as shit. Hell...I thought he was your, uh...cousin. But fuck this, I'm supposed to meet, Cocky...clean this mess up. I'll get with you later."

"I got it," Diplite said as he waved him off.

After he left, Diplite pulled Jesse's body across the railroad tracks and left it there. He figured a train would be by later and it would run over the body, then make it look like an accident.

"Fuck him...snitch ass nigga," Diplite snapped.

He scuffled up some dirt to hide their footprints, threw some shrubbery and bushes around, then spit on Jesse and left him to the dogs.

Just like that, Jesse's life, Sunshine and Cleo's mom's plan, was over...than damn quick. Right up from where his body laid was the same place Jesse had left his partna, Dread. It was the prime of example of how hellufied of a bitch karma actually was.

DIRTY-RED GROANED AS he picked up the phone by the side of the bed. His arm was bandaged up with fresh stitches and itched every chance they got. His arm was swollen a bit but was starting to subside, finally. He was tired of it already, the smell of the hospital was making him sick. One thing at least, he had his girls from the liquor house bring him some good food, most of it he shared with the other patients though. He needed to call, Cocky to let him know what happened with Wood. If he's seen him around and if he did, to hold him.

He didn't have no way of knowing that Wood was dead, and he probably didn't have a clue that it was Diplite who'd actually shot him. Anyway, you put it, he needed to touch base with Cocky and tell him that the Cheraw run was definitely off for a minute. Nikki would just have to wait until all of this foolishness was cleared up.

He dialed Cocky's number. "Yo' Cocky, wassup?"

"Wassup, how you feeling?"

"Like shit, but I'm ready to get the fuck out of here."

"They finished with you?"

"Hell, ain't too much more they can do. They already removed the bullet and stitched me up. The bone in my arm was fractured but fuck it. Hell, the bullet just went in and stopped. Doctor told me I was lucky it didn't ricochet into my

lungs, then I'd really be fucked up." "Hell yeah," Cocky said.

"Ain't no need for me to stay here anymore. Cops came around asking questions and shit. Probably why I'm still here...they been watchin' me."

"True...check this out, though. That muthafuckin' Hulie called me, said he wants to meet with me to talk."

"Say word."

"I ain't got nuthin' to talk to him about. If he fucks around over this side of town, he might be a corpse before the day is over."

"Still think he had something to with Nikki?"

"I can see that..."

One of Cocky's boys came running through the door, breathing hard like he'd just ran a mile. "Cocky...man, shit is wild!"

"What the fuck?" Cocky put his hand over the phone.

"Hold up, I'm on the phone, right now."

"Yo' that dude, Hulie, and his boy just killed a man, right across the street."

Cocky took his hand away from the phone. "Dirty-Red, call you later."

"Hold up...I'm on my way over."

"Man, ain't you still fucked up?"

"Trust me..." Dirty-Red had already made it to the closet and started laying out his clothes. "...I'm alright, be there in a minute."

"A'ight." Cocky turned toward his boy. "What happened?"

"Man, that dude Hulie pulled up across the street and some dude approached him. Think it was that dude that just out of prison, can't call his name. Anyway, he approached Hulie and points him over into the cut. Hell, the only reason I went over there was because we don't deal dope near the club. I figure it was some old crack head type deal, and I wanted to check him."

"Cool...then what?"

"Next thing I know that dude from Liberty Hill, Hulie's boy Diplite came driving up in his ride. He damn near drove on the sidewalk, then he jumped out of the car and ran down into the cut behind them. You know, right, next to the railroad tracks. Then next I see flashes coming from a gun, didn't hear no shots, musts had a silencer on it."

"Dirty muthafucka mighta tried to set us up with a body, I bet," Cocky said as he thumbed the top of the bar with his fist.

"And that dude, Diplite dragged the body onto the railroad track and dips. Then he went into the gas station up the street on River's Avenue and used the fuckin' payphone like it was nuthin'."

"Payphone...oh hell yeah! It's a set up for sure, he's calling po-po to report a body, I bet." Cocky turned toward one of his enforcers. "Get the heat, it's going down."

SUNSHINE TRIPPED AS she watched in horror at Diplite as he spit on Jesse's body. "What the hell is going?" she asked. "Jesse's dead, aw hell, this is off the fuckin' chain. I can't believe I just witnessed a murder. I can't do this, got to call it in. Damn, who am I kidding? I'm the one who set this whole thing up. Damnit can't back out now. Okay...okay, girl, calm down...think." She picked up her phone and dialed. "Cocky, it's me baby, Sunshine."

"Would you believe that muthafucka is out here looking for trouble? He damn sure found it," Cocky said.

"Well, he's a loose cannon, now. Remember what we talked about...protection?"

"Yeah, you said if we offed that muthafucka, you wouldn't prosecute if any of us got caught. That's what I remember...you?"

"Yeah, Cocky, that's what I remember, too."
"Good...I gotta go."

Sunshine shook her head and shed a slight tear not for Hulie, but for all the money she'd have to let go. One thing she figured as she watched young boys post up on the street selling dope though. There's more where that came from, easy come...easy go. Then she cranked the car up and giggled. But she just couldn't let it go that easy, she'd holler at Cleo, one last time, then say fuck it.

HULIE PUSHED HIS BIKE around the side of the building, took off his helmet, and put his kickstand down. He took a long, deep breath then walked around to the front, keeping his hands in his pocket. His gun was in the palm of his hands. Cocky's boys were out front, deep. He approached the doorway and just like he thought, he was stopped.

"Yo' man what's up?"
"I'm here to see, Cocky. Tell him it's me..."

"John...John...go inside and tell Cocky," He glanced over at Hulie then said, "...that dude Hulie is out here."
Hulie knew then for sure that they were expecting him. He eyeballed the guy in front of him trying to figure out exactly where his arsenal laid. He noticed a bulge inside his pants. Old boys, eyes glanced down to his side then he parted his jacket and flashed his Desert Eagle.
"Damn," Hulie mumbled, as he looked at the rest of them, noticing big boy bulges, too.
They were ready for war. They knew he was coming, and they were prepared for a fight, not peace. Cocky was taking a while, too long, something was up.

Hulie back away and said, "Tell him...I'll be back..."
Cocky's boy knew what it was. "Yeah...I'll do that."

Hulie was feeling some sort of way. It was on, nothing was said, but that move right there spoke volumes, it was going down. Hulie had to respond one way or another and end this shit, fuck it. Time to go to the stash house, get his shit and let it do what it do. Damn he needed help, fuck it, Diplite was gonna have to ride it out with him, he owed him that. He hopped on his bike then looked up after he put on his helmet. Cocky's boys were posted out in front, watching him.

He cranked up and dipped around them into the street, stopped, looked back at them, then revved up his bike, and

snarled, "I'll be back muthafuckas, I'll be back."

Cocky came out right as Hulie had jetted up the street and told his boys. "That muthafucka is definitely coming back, so be ready. Post up on top of the building and put a

couple across the street. Be ready, he's sneaky."

"But damn..." One of his boys said. "...he's only one man."

"True," Cocky answered, then glanced up the street as he watched Hulie's bike turn on Rivers Avenue going towards

Liberty Hill. "But he's Hulie...don't ever underestimate him."

A LIGHT BLUE NORTH Charleston cab pulled up in front of the club, it was Dirty-Red. His arm was wrapped up in a sling and every time he moved, he cringed.

"Where's Cocky," was the first words out of his mouth.

Cocky boys wasted no time getting Cocky. He was glad to see Dirty-Red alive. He filled him in on what was going on and Dirty-Red made sure that he told him what he knew about Nikki, which wasn't much. He did kinda figure that

Hulie was in on killing her son, T-Black.

"Why would he do that?" Cocky asked.

Dirty-Red explained to him that it was about money, a lot of it. Money that Nikki now had in her possession. He couldn't quite tie Diplite into the equation, but he'd find out in a minute that he was one dirty no good snake.

An all black Excursion skidded off of Spruill Avenue on Reynolds coming straight at them. The windows were tinted heavily, pitched black and now they were slowly rolling down. Cocky yelled over at his boys. "That's him!"

Multiple shots were fired as the truck skidded in front. Hulie kicked open the door and started letting out with Street Sweeper, pointing at Cocky as he tried to run back into the building. It was sweet, Hulie started pulling the trigger every time he jerked a hole the size of a football opened up on the side of the building, painting an ugly, grotesque picture like they were in Iraq. Only stopping when it met its mark...Cocky. Where Hulie got that type of arsenal, Cocky didn't know, he knew Hulie was unpredictable, dangerous even, but damn he didn't know it was on this level. He may have paid for underestimating him with his life.

The passenger side door opened and Diplite was out. He ducked around the side and came up firing Glock .40s across the street. Eight bullets whizzed past Cocky's head later, and three of Cocky's boys came tumbling out riddled with bullets. Dirty-Red managed to dive out of the way and tried to hide around a parked car. Diplite saw him and aimed.

"Oh, shit...you down with this muthafucka!" he hollered out.

"It is what it is Dirty...now come out...don't run." Diplite reached into the side of his pants and grabbed a .38 Revolver

and tossed it at him. "I'll let you go out like a man, use it!"

Dirty-Red looked at the gun then Diplite then Hulie. He had already killed what was left of Cocky's man on top of the building. He glanced over at Diplite. "Make it quick!" He started back to the truck.

Diplite pointed his guns and aimed, Dirty-Red said fuck it, it hurt like all hell to move his arm, but he dived at the gun anyway, picked it up and rolled over by a cut near the side of the building. A bricked-in corner used for dumping grease. He aimed also, both guns were shot at the same time. Dirty-

Red grimaced as the bullet hit his bandaged arm.

"Damn!" he shouted out in pain.

Diplite staggered and Hulie honked the horn at him. "Come on, ball will be here in a minute!"

He turned and Hulie saw the hole in his shirt. He cranked up the truck and Diplite grabbed the side of the door and pulled himself inside before he pulled off. Dirty-Red squeezed off another round, this one caught him in the back, then he fell to the ground, listening as the sirens got louder and louder. He prayed to God, Hulie wouldn't run over his ass with that big ass truck.

He didn't, instead, he burned rubber back up Spruill Avenue going toward North Charleston. He figured he'd dip and dive into the hood, losing the police in the process. He glanced over at Diplite who bled all in the truck and was losing consciousness quick.

"Dip...best I can do is drop you off at a gas station or something! Least somebody..." He knew he was about to bleed out and there was nothing he could do for him.

"C'mon Hulie...hell, after all, we been through! Get me to a doctor."

"Man...ain't got time. You gonna fuck me up, I mean least you'll live..." He pulled over to the gas station, jumped out and ran over to the door, then opened it. "C'mon, Dip...hurry up."

"C'mon, Hulie...don't do this to me..." Diplite screamed at him.

Hulie picked up the guns Diplite dropped on the floorboard and pointed them at him. "Man, Dip...don't make me."

Diplite looked at him like he was crazy. He couldn't believe that his muthafucka came and got him to help his ass out, to keep his ass from getting killed. Now, this was what he was going to do. He didn't even want to take him to the hospital. A tear came down from his eye, he knew he was gonna died.

"Man...drop me off at my mama's house, at least do that." Diplite closed his eyes, blackness overcame him. He didn't care anymore, it was...whatever.

Hulie took aim, then shook his shook. "Diplite, don't do this to me...damn!"

Chapter Eighteen

J abari tried his damnest to stay clean, but them damn pills were hell to kick. You'd think maybe crack even meth was a muthafucka, but those E-pills were a bitch. Jabari stayed in rehab for about two weeks, then he couldn't take it anymore. Once his body had gotten clean, it wanted to pick up on something else. His emotions were off the chain, every time he came to visit he spazzed out, then smoked cigarettes like he was a fuckin' chimney. He finally got fed up and checked himself out.

He went to the only spot he could think of to score a hit immediately and that was Liberty Hill. He knew some people that hung out there, it wasn't too far anyway, it was right around Rivers Avenue or so. Everything was smooth, everybody was cool, all he heard was, *"Jabari, where you been?"* He was good, he got high and fell right back in. He knew his sister was probably trying to find out where he was, but once he got his hands on some money, he'd call her. That was no joke, he needed money. He'd fucked up the little piece of change he had, getting his fix. He couldn't think of anywhere else to go, except for a spot he remembered from a few months ago. It would be a risk, but he'd be in and out quick. Yeah, he'd heard that before, but it sounded straight at the moment.

378

HULIE PARKED UP THE block from Diplite's mother's house, off of to the side around the corner, trying not to be seen. But he didn't give a fuck, he wasn't the one who'd killed Diplite. He kicked him out of the truck into the yard as he drove by. But not before he stopped by an alleyway briefly. He had to get some things off his chest. He told Diplite he had a pretty good idea that he had something to do with the robbery, he just didn't know it for sure. Granted, he'd thought maybe he was the one who put Q in on the mix. He eventually realized how wrong he was, but the one thing he was dead on about, was that goddamned Jesse. His people had already told him they'd seen Jesse talking to Cleo and Diplite. Then Cleo ran that bullshit about him being her cousin. He knew something was up. Then the way Diplite just shot and killed Jesse, confirmed it, easy, it was like putting two plus two together, he was down with them.

He didn't want to have to take out Cocky, but he knew he would continue to be a headache. They'd never see eye to eye, so shit had to go down. Now, all he needed to do was lay low for a while, go out of town, maybe someplace out in the West. He knew he was going to hear some shit from Cleo but fuck her too. He wasn't the one who'd shot her brother, so she really shouldn't have no beef with him.

He'd done what Diplite had asked him to do and dropped him off at his mama's house. Let them take care of him, he was probably on his way to the hospital now anyway. That was a whole lot better than what he really wanted to do...kill him. Later for all that, right now, he needed to know where he stood as far as the shootout was concerned. It had to be all over the news by now.

He pulled out his phone and dialed Sunshine's to find out. "What's going on..."

"You know what the fuck is going on! Another fuckin' shoot out, Hulie! And someone murdered...again, c'mon, damn!"

"I ain't have shit to do with no muthafuckin' murder. That was, Diplite. Hell, all I wanted to do was talk to, Cocky."

"You just couldn't let it go? Well, I guess, you said fuck it and killed him, too...just like Q, huh?"

"They started it."

"You're really off the chain. I don't think I can cover for you anymore."

"Say no more...that's why I called anyway." Hulie started to hang up.

Sunshine shouted, "Hulie, don't hang up on me!"

"Why not? I gotta go, you probably done put the man on me anyway."

"No...actually, not yet! I'm at Cleo's mother's house now, the ambulance just left with her brother's body."

"He dead?"

"Naw...but pretty fucked up. He lost a lot of blood. Someone said a big, black truck just came by and threw him into the yard. Guess you don't know anything about that either?"

"Doesn't matter, least he ain't dead."

Sunshine walked out to the street and looked over her shoulder making sure no one was watching. "It's real hot over here. Where are you?"

"Why?"

"Might as well be straight up. What's up with the money, Hulie? Damn, I mean...don't you have a stash house or something with shit put up?"

"Here she goes again," Hulie mumbled under his breath.

She was still trying to be slick and shit, he was tired of her bullshit. She knows too goddamned much already. He wished he knew how to take this bitch out...wait stash house. He remembered and said, "Yeah, I gotta spot."

"Okay, where?" Sunshine's greedy ass took the bait.

"Not too far from where you're at." Hulie cranked up the truck and took the back way to the house where he had his guns.

His plan was to get her to his stash house, take her ass out right there, throw some dope over her body, and make it look like a fuckin' drug deal gone bad. She was dirty, anyway, they wouldn't do too much of an investigation. They'd probably be glad she was dead anyway. Then he'd take his ass to the crib, pack up some money, get on his bike and haul ass. It was too goddamned hot for him to stick around, it was time to go. He'd give Deezo a call and tell him to wire the rest of his money to him once he got settled, maybe in Mexico.

HULIE PLANNED ON MEETING Sunshine in the back of a house where his guns were stuffed in wall panels, abandoned and boarded up with trespassing signs in an attempt to keep people away. It stayed for the better part and remained secluded. Every now and then, he'd go by and check things out, just to make sure no one had broken in, trying to make a miniature shooting gallery and crack house of some sorts. He paid lookouts good money just to watch it, and even once or twice had to kick some ass, on G-P, so no one even bothered, it wasn't worth the hassle. It just stayed empty.

The last time he was there, was earlier, he dug behind the wall and pulled out the street sweeper he used on Cocky and them. Then went into the floor, got the ammo for it and rushed out. Now, he peeked over at the cracked door and realized that was why it was still partly open. He'd rushed back and forgot to close it. It was cool, though, hell, from the looks of things no one had been around plundering anyway. So, now, he waited for Sunshine to show up. he gave her directions, the long way around, but it still shouldn't be too much longer now. He slouched in the seat and pulled down his hat, then peeked over the dashboard and waited.

It startled him at first, maybe it was a dog or something, a bird by the window...hold up, not with a fuckin' flashlight. Somebody was inside. Damn, Sunshine wasn't there yet, but he still had to go see who the hell it was. He didn't have a lot of money inside, just small change if that, but the guns alone were worth a lot, specially on the street. He didn't want nobody fuckin' with that, he'd unload them all later, probably to Deezo for a fairly good lick.

Damn, he wanted to take Sunshine's ass out and he damn sure didn't need no witnesses or distractions for that. Fuck it had to go see who it was. He reloaded his Glock that sat underneath the seat, tucked it in his wallet and got out, closing the door quietly. He jumped over the fence and tiptoed to the back door that was half cracked. He peeked in and hunched down, then pulled out the gun. He heard sounds of someone pulling at the panels where his guns were at. He picked up his pistol and crept around the corner slowly, then spotted the intruder.

He stepped lightly behind him but fucked up and stepped on some trash and it made a noise a lot. The intruder turned around and Hulie tripped out.

"It can't be," he mumbled, after all, he'd been through.

"God damn...look what the wind blew in."

Jabari stood there frozen in time it seemed. As he looked down the barrel of the gun, then Hulie. Damn, this wasn't what he needed right now. Hulie walked up on him, looking him up and down, then glanced over at the wall panel that he was pulling on, and peeked inside. His guns were being neatly tucked inside a bag Jabari had by his side.

Hulie shook his head. "Hmmm...trying to rob the shit...huh?"

Jabari didn't have no wins, he figured he might as well come clean. "You caught me..."

"Yeah, so I did. You know..." Hulie got in his face. "...I've been trying to catch up with you for a long goddamned time."

Jabari back up. "I know, but you know what...why? Why the hell yo been fuckin' wit' me?" Jabari figured he didn't have anything to lose. He might as well put an end to this bullshit, right now. "What do you want from me! I ain't go nuthin'..."

"The hell you don't!" Hulie hollered back. 'You got fuckin' money you owe me!"

"Owe you! What the fuck you talkin' 'bout?" I ain't got no goddamned money and I don't owe you jack shit!"

"Muthafucka, you remember that night."

"Yeah...I remember that night real good. The night you killed a muthafucka in cold blood. The night you tried to kill his mother...burned the house down and everything...then left me to die. Yeah, I remember that!"

Hulie's lips twisted into a frown, he didn't like that shit. He turned and walked to a window, looking out. "I ain't make you..."

"Fuck that, Hulie! Fuck what you made a muthafucka do...fuck all that shit! You killed, Dondi! She ain't have hit to do wit' nuthin!"

Hulie turned to him. "That two-bit...hoe...she wasn't shit to me!"

Tears ran down Jabari's face now, he was pissed. He held his anger back, with a little help from the gun Hulie had in his hand.

"Just like Rip...like T-Black...everyone that you can't...maneuver around! Fuck it just kill 'em, huh? Well, I'm tired of it all...running...drugs...I'm fuckin' tired! Do what you want." Jabari fell to his knees and put up his hands. "Come on, muthafucka...do it!"

Hulie walked over and put the gun up to his head. "Least I know you won't snitch..."

"Hulie!"

He spun around, it was Sunshine. She had a gun in her hand, too and it was aimed right at him. "Put the fuckin' gun down," she ordered.

Hulie didn't bat an eye. "Look...this muthafucka tried to rob me."

"So...you just kill everyone that crosses you, huh? Well, you've killed enough people already. It's gotta stop!"

"Oh, so now, you want it to stop? You don't want no dope money no more? You don't want no more muthafuckas to set up...extort muthafuckas, so they pay you not to go to jail?"

"Hulie! Shut the fuck up, lease I ain't no murderer!"

"No murderer? Every muthafucka I killed was because of you. You just as guilty as me." He pulled the gun back and lowered it to his side. "Not unless you want to tell that to your people...or what?"

Sunshine kept the gun aimed at him, he was right. She was in deep. Hulie could easily fuck her all the way up and so could Jabari. She had to make a move. Hulie was the only one with the gun and now he had it lowered. Jabari didn't have shit. She could easily shoot them both and come up with the Okie-doke, bullshit that they had kidnapped her or something.

"Yeah." She grinned, she'd make it stick. "Just throw the gun on the ground, Hulie...right now!"

Hulie knew what it was, he did that math too. He fucked up and already had his gun lowered. If he pulled up or even flinched slightly, she'd definitely shoot. He had to work his way out of this one, slowly. "Look...baby, why we acting like this toward each other? This cat here knows where the money's at. All we gotta do is

go get it and still split it. Whatta ya say?"

"This is crazy," Jabari grumbled to himself. Hulie was standing right next to him, ready to kill him, and that crazy ass chick wanted to kill them both. "Damn this fucked up!"

He finally could put Sunshine to the name on the card Hulie had given him. She was the broad T-Black had mentioned before he died, or at least before Hulie killed him. The money, hell, Jabari couldn't believe Hulie was still looking for that shit, after all this time. Jabari thought about telling something, but honestly, he really didn't know anything.

"I gotta do something," he coached himself silently. He really didn't have nothing to lose anyway. He had to know why they were trying to kill him. Especially when he didn't have shit to do with any of this. "Hey, aren't you the chick TBlack wanted to give the money too?" Sunshine's head twisted in Jabari's direction as she focused in on what he was talking about. Jabari had her ear, so he continued. "That night, he said he had some money for you. Said Hulie gave it to him, said he tried to flip it..."

Hulie put the gun back up to Jabari's head. "Shut up!" he yelled. Then looked back over at Sunshine. "He don't know what he's talking about."

Sunshine kept the gun up, but it was starting to become heavy. She also needed to do something. She wanted to know what happened with the money, too.

"Hulie, ain't gonna say it no more, drop the gun!" Sunshine twisted her head slowly back toward him and took aim.

Hulie noticed she wasn't bullshitting so he kneeled down and laid the gun in front of him. Not too far, he figured he might still need it, and wanted a chance to get at it.

"Okay, okay...calm down."
"What's he talking about?" Sunshine asked.

"Hell, I don't know, some dumb shit," Hulie lied. "Why you listening to him?"

"He was supposed to flip the money with that dude, TBlack. Then get a cut, he was gonna tell you it got stolen and keep the money and shit you out of the rest. That's why he killed, T-Black. To make it look like he was trying to rob him," Jabari blurted out what he knew.

"Shut the fuck up. You don't know what you're talking about!" Hulie looked at Sunshine and said, "Dude was supposed to flip the money, granted but it wasn't my idea. That goddamned Diplite said he knew what to do. I wasn't gonna

shit you out of nothing. Hell, he was trying to shit me!"

"No, he wasn't! He had your card, he would have called you. All he wanted..."

Hulie backhanded Jabari and he fell back against the wall and he shouted at him. "Didn't I tell you to shut up!"

"Naw, muthafucka!" Jabari was definitely feeling some sort of way now. Hulie was going down. "It's too late for that! You killed Rip...Dondi, now you want to kill me! You even got bodies out in the country...Walterboro! You ain't no hustla, you ain't nothing but a two-bit thug."

Sunshine back up a little-ways leaning against a wall. Somehow, Jabari had to work her. "Again...where's the fuckin' money?" she asked as she mean mugged Hulie, then turned toward Jabari. "You, I don't know your name. Finish what you were saying."

"Name's Jabari."
"Hold up...Tangie's brother?"
"Yeah."

"Ain't this a muthafucka. Okay...okay, so what happened?"

Jabari stood up and eased away from Hulie. "I was with him that night. He told me and Rip that we were just supposed to put the tim down on a dude and get paid. He didn't say how much until after he killed ole...dude and went after his mother. Tried to burn us both up."

"I remember that...damn, Hulie, why didn't you just come clean with me? It was only about what...fifteen grand? That's ain't enough money for all these bodies..."

"Fifteen grand!" Jabari screamed. "How about ninety

fuckin' grand and what...twelve keys."

Sunshine looked at Jabari like he was crazy. She was shocked, her eyes opened wide and she stammered, "Ninety...ninety grand!" she looked back at Hulie with enough venom in her eyes to kill. "You muthafucka...no wonder. So, what was you gonna do...kill me, too? No better yet...I'm gonna ask you one more time, or I'm gonna shoot you right where you

stand! Where's the goddamned money?"

"Me...nah got da money!"

I was like, what the fuck? It was like a ghost or something, I hadn't seen her since that night. Wow, she still looked sexy as all hell...posted up with a shotgun in her hand long hair brushed back in a ponytail and a bowlegged stance that made her look like a fuckin'

Chucktown Foxy Brown. She aimed the gun over at Hulie. "Why hem look so shocked, huh? Ain't

'spect to see me nah, boy...hem look lost, huh?"

Hulie was really having a bad day but fuck him; these two chicks wanted to off him because of all the dirt he did to them. "

"Who the fuck is this? What the fuck is going on?" Jabari asked no one in particular.

"Look like he's about to piss on himself."

'More pussy...I never seen her before, hell, she's fine, too. Damn, Hulie how many enemies you got?' Jabari thought.

Hulie stared down the barrel of a shotgun and just smirked like he wasn't the least bit fazed.

"*You just threw my brother in the yard like he was a piece of trash...after all, he did for you?*" Cleo yelled.

He stood up straight and looked around at all three of them. Guns were pointed from every direction. After checking out the situation, he turned Jabari's way and snickered.

"Fuckin' women...can't live with them...and you can't live without them," Hulie said.

Jabari was thinking Hulie was a trip, but one thing about him, though. He was cool as all fuckin' outdoors. His composure itself was large enough so that it keeps them at bay. Not knowing what he was capable of, threw them and pretty much everyone who fucked with him, even Jabari. Hulie knew that and worked it to his advantage.

"So...what is this? Kill Hulie, day or something?" He laughed out loud as he looked over at Cleo. "Your brother

told me to drop him off, he didn't say how, though."

"So, fuck it, you throw him out of a moving truck," she shot back.

"Look..." He pointed at her. "...I'll deal with your dumb ass later. You see, I talked to your brother about y'all stealing my shit. Ain't cool with that at all! By the way, he handled your little, uh...what he say his name was, Jesse? Yeah, that's it, your Jesse problem. You remember him, right...your cousin...from outta town?" He started laughing. "Your brother just sent him home...oh shit, home...I like that!"

Cleo's mouth dropped open. '*Damn,*' she thought. '*He knows!*'

She faded back behind Nikki and shut the fuck up.

Jabari looked closer and it almost seemed like her bottom lip was quivering. Hulie had one less problem to deal with now.

Next was Nikki. "And you...you finally came out into the light, huh?" Hulie said looking over at Sunshine. "I suppose you can ask her about...the money!"

Sunshine looked at her with all the attitude she could muster. She even had the nerve to cock her hip as much as she could with one hand and the other hand still gripping the gun.

"Who her...who the hell is she?" Sunshine asked looking over at Nikki and rolled her eyes. "Need to take her fisheating ass back downtown or something." Sunshine giggled.

"Know what I mean, Cleo?"

Cleo wasn't trying to say shit, matter of fact, she backed away a little from her. Nikki looked at Sunshine like she'd just fucked up and from the look on her face, she did. Hulie glanced Jabari's way and winked, it was on.

"What? Nah, me kna know yuh don say I tink you, fa say." Nikki said.

"*Me-nah...what*!" Sunshine repeated. Look, sweetie, how 'bout you back the fuck up and walk on out the door and make sure no one comes in, okay?" Sunshine turned back toward Hulie. "Now, what that cunt got to do with anything..."

It was quick and vicious, Nikki had taken the butt of the gun and chopped Sunshine upside her head, dropping her right where she stood. She bent over her and casually picked up the gun she'd dropped, then put it to her head. "Now...uh, what yu say again?" Nikki asked.

Sunshine was still dazed as she looked up at her. She was on her knees helpless trying to regain her senses. When Cleo ran over to her and helped her up. "You alright...you don't want to fuck with her, trust me," Cleo warned.

"Oh, hell no!" Sunshine screamed. "I'm gonna kick that bitch's ass!"

Nikki pointed the shotgun at her. "Look, yah...tis ain't your fight nah. My beef ain't wit' you...so g'won nah."

Sunshine wiped the blood off the side of her mouth and groaned when she felt the knot upside her head. Jabari looked and it was easily the size of a fuckin' handball. It was also all red...blue and shit. Jabari frowned and Sunshine must have seen it because it made her hot.

"You put the gun down and I'll kick your black, ugly ass, bitch!"

"Yu got one lass time to call me butch, huh." Nikki low-

ered the gun down a bit, then squared up. "One lass time..." Sunshine put up her fist. "Fuck you...and the word is...bitch!"

Nikki tossed the gun behind her toward Cleo and said,

"Keep yah eye on hem...hear?"

Cleo picked the gun up and nodded. Then Nikki placed the shotgun against the door and started peeling off her jacket. Sunshine did the same. Jabari couldn't believe how in shape and fine Sunshine and Nikki were.

Nikki put up her fist too. "Come yer," she said.

Sunshine was on some old Karate shit. She got in one of those stances and did a Matrix type of thing, then prompted Nikki with her hand.

"No...you come..." Sunshine said.

Nikki moved in with the jab, it looked until she missed with the left. Sunshine moved out of the way, then spun around and came back around off a spin into a roundhouse kick. She caught Nikki dead in the gut. Nikki fell back against the wall and grunted, it looked like the fight was about to be taken out of her.

Hulie started clowning. "Damn...know that hurt."

Sunshine ran at Nikki with another kick and Nikki sidestepped her, then came up with a right hook that caught Sunshine square in the jaw. Sunshine staggered, her shit swelled up again. Nikki took full advantage of the way her legs wobbled and stung her two times in the eye. It closed quickly, that's all it took, and Nikki was on her toes dancing like she was fucking Ali or something.

Jabari tried to keep his cool, but he couldn't help himself. "Damn girl," he said quietly.

It wasn't quiet enough because Sunshine heard him and charged at Nikki with all she had. They clinched up and started wrestling. Shirts were ripped and titties were all over the place. This was the best-goddamned fight Jabari had seen in years. Nikki grabbed Sunshine by the hair and flipped her over onto her back to the ground, she kept pulling until she handful of red hair. Jabari knew that shit had to hurt because it hurt him just to watch. Sunshine retaliated by grabbing on to Nikki's leg and biting down until blood gushed out between her teeth. Nikki screamed out in pain like a muthafucka.

Jabari and Hulie didn't do shit. What could they do? Jabari was inching toward Cleo who wasn't paying him any mind. He saw Hulie's eyes focus on the shotgun. He couldn't let it go down like that. So, he ran over toward Hulie and lunged at him. Hulie tried shaking Jabari off his back and Jabari started beating the back of Hulie's head with his fists. Cleo looked over and ran toward them. Jabari thought she gonna help him out, but she took the gun and knocked Jabari upside the head.

"*Dumbass...hoe!*" Jabari yelled out.

Hulie finally grabbed the shotgun and pointed toward the two women, who were scuffling on the ground.

"*Okay...enough!*" Hulie yelled.

Both women, Jabari was still rubbing his head from the pain. Hulie pointed toward Cleo. "Thanks, baby!" She smiled and he smiled back her, then out of the blue, he shot her.
"That's for robbin' my shit."
Cleo's eyes were as big as quarters as she held her stomach and slowly fell to the ground. Nikki ran over to her, then looked up at Hulie.

"Why you done dat, boy?"

"Fuck that bitch, her and her brother was gonna try me again...kill me this time. Yeah, that's what they planned. I didn't tell her, though, that I tortured his soft ass before I
kicked him out. He told me everything."
Nikki shook her head then looked over at Sunshine who spotted the gun laying on the ground like she was gonna try and make a move.
Nikki turned to her and said, "Yu wan da money, I'll git it fa yu!"

Hulie smiled at her. "Now...that wasn't hard now was it?" He walked over toward where the gun laid and kicked it away from Sunshine, then pointed the shotgun at her head. "Damn...she just saved your life." He looked over at Nikki.

"You've got ten minutes to get back with the money." "*Ten minutes...what?*" Sunshine screamed.

Hulie smacked her. "I suggest you get up and haul ass before I change my mind!" he barked at Sunshine, then turned back to Nikki. "Nine minutes and forty-three seconds..." He started counting down. "Forty-two...forty-one..."

Nikki turned toward Sunshine. "Take yah coat and put it to her stomach...stop da blood. I'll be back!"

"And remember...you better come back...alone, or I'll kill all of them!"

Nikki got to her feet as fast as she could, turned towards Jabari, then looked back at Sunshine shaking her head. Jabari could tell by the way she looked, that she knew she had a choice in the matter. She could easily say fuck it and let Hulie kill them like dogs and walk away. Especially, after all, that was done to her, but for some reason, she wasn't built like that. Deep down she was good peeps. She'd just been dealt some fucked up cards. Jabari could kinda relate to that, but today...right now, was her moment.

She wiped her face off and limped out of the door. Hulie looked over at Jabari and told him to move closer toward Sunshine and Cleo. Sunshine had her blouse over Cleo's stomach trying to stop as much blood as she could.

She looked up at Hulie. "You gonna pay for this!" she said bitterly.

Hulie laughed. "Yeah...yeah...maybe one day, but just not today. Today...I'ma get paid!"

Tears ran down Sunshine's eyes as she stared at Hulie. She knew he was gonna kill her, he had to, and a part of her whipped up on herself for not killing him first, instead of playing around. She knew entirely too much, and he was never gonna let her get any of the money, anyway. It was all game but fuck it, she'd played it, too. This time there was nothing she could do. Jabari could see the pain in her eyes, it looked so familiar. Jabari moved slowly over toward her and put some pressure on Cleo's wound. He pulled her hand away gently giving her a break.

"It's gonna be alright...don't look like it, but, it will," he told Sunshine.

Sunshine just looked at Jabari and smiled, then said,

"Tangie...she is just as good...okay." "Just as good?"

Sunshine rubbed the side of Jabari's face and smiled. "Y'all look so much alike. Baby, she'll know what it means."

Jabari knew that Sunshine was gonna try and go out with a bang. What it was though, he didn't have a clue. Truthfully as he looked over at Hulie, he wasn't mad at her.

IT HAD SEEMED FOREVER to Jabari, the longest fuckin' eight minutes that he'd ever experienced in his life. Beads of sweat popped on Jabari's forehead as Hulie kept checking his watch, announcing the time.

"One minute and fifty seconds...left." Hulie played with the slide of the shotgun and whistled.

Jabari didn't know what was worse, him pumping the slide and hearing it pop. Or, the fuckin' whistlin', it was killing Jabari. Hulie peeked out of the window, looked around back and came in the room where they were holed up. They had moved Cleo's body into a room that had a mattress and tried to keep her conscious. She was in and out of consciousness, half of the time mumbling then going back out. The mattress was soaked with blood and it really looked like she wasn't gonna make it.

Jabari felt bad but not as bad as Sunshine. She kept talking to herself, blaming everything on her. She prayed and asked God for forgiveness, then, she started doing some real weird shit. She started pulling off her nails, which were fake, and pulled her eyelashes off, which were also fake and her weave next. Jabari watched her, hoping like hell, her teeth weren't next, even still he thought she had a pretty look about her. A more natural look now with everything off. She dug in her eyes and Jabari shuddered.

"Damn, not an eye," he mumbled to himself.

Sunshine plucked out her contacts. Jabari could see why she was called Sunshine. It wasn't because of her being so fine, but because she was so Albino. Her eyes were pitched black and her skin was so bleached.

She turned toward Jabari with snot running down her nose and sniffled. "We couldn't afford anything to keep the sun from burning my skin. So, my people kept white toothpaste on my face all the time. God, I couldn't stand that. I wore these dark, blind man shades...my teeth were bucked, and I wore baggy clothes that covered me up. I would look out of the window at the other kids and touch the glass...knocking. Hoping they would come and ask if I could go to the playground, but they would run from me. They called me a ghost, but all I ever wanted to do was play...*in the sunshine!*"

That fucked Jabari up. Hulie heard her and started laughing.

"Yeah...I remember that she was a ugly lil' ole thing. You shoulda seen her."

He laughed harder and the child in her head appeared just that quick. She tucked her head between her legs and cried, just like when she was little. Jabari pulled her closer to him and hugged her.

"How did you know my sister?" he asked.

Sunshine smiled. "Believe it or not, she's...my friend."

Jabari didn't know what Sunshine meant, but he damn sure made a mental note to ask Tangie next time he saw her. If they ever got out of that mess, they were in.

The door creaked open and Nikki came through, dragging a duffel bag behind her. She tossed it in the front of Hulie. "Take dat dam mon'ny...g'won frum ya!" She looked over at Cleo and Sunshine motioned to her that she was still alive. Nikki screamed at Hulie, "*Kna go!*"

Hulie pulled the money closer toward him, looked in and grinned. "Yeah...that's what's up!" He sifted through and picked up some clear bags with white powder, cocaine. "Cool...dope, too!" He closed it back and tossed it over to the door opposite us. "Preciate that. Really do...you did good." He turned, then spun back around and pointed the shotgun at us.

"But I still have to kill y'all. Y'all know too much!"

Jabari stood up. "Man, look, you got the money! Damn, you been looking for that shit damn near forever! You won, fuck it...let it go. We ain't gonna say shit, hell, if we do, we'd be just as fucked up." Jabari pointed over at Cleo. "Let us get her to a hospital man, be fuckin' human...for once."

Hulie nodded his head a little and started lowering the shotgun. Jabari thought he'd gotten through to him.

But then Hulie said, "Naw...killin' y'all sounds much better. This way I ain't never gotta worry...look over my shoulder, kna'mean?" He took aim.

Jabari started copping mad deuces, all the bitch came out of him. "Please, man...please...I don't wanna die!"

Nikki calmly took out a bottle she had in her back pocket and opened it. Then started sprinkling the liquid onto the duffel bag, she took out some matches and lit one.

"Fi'gah yu'nah say dat..." Nikki tossed the match on the bag and it exploded in flames. "Spend da mon'ny...in Hell!" She dived to the ground as Hulie shot in her direction and missed. She motioned to me and pointed toward the window.

Hulie couldn't see because of the flames and smoke, so he shot wildly at the doorway. Sunshine got up and ran to the door.

She looked back at Jabari. "I wish I would have met you earlier...Jabari!" She giggled, then raised her hand. "Hulie...Hulie...Hulie, listen to me! It ain't gotta go down like this..." Her other hand she put behind her back and pointed toward the window.

Nikki got up and looked. It was just low enough for them to climb out. It was their only chance. Jabari picked up Cleo as gently as he could and carried her to the window. Nikki hopped through first, then Jabari picked Cleo up and lowered her down on the other side. He ran to the door to see about Sunshine, she was still talking to Hulie, moving closer and closer toward him.

Hulie looked over his shoulder and spotted Jabari. "Oh shit...they're getting away!" he said.

Sunshine grabbed him and wrestled with the shotgun. "We can still be together like we planned," she told him.

Hulie finally wriggled the gun out of her grip and back away from her. "Hell no! Look, at you, I don't want you! Just like no one else wanted you when we were kids...you's a freak!"

All Jabari could see was pain as Sunshine looked back at him. she was gone and there was no coming back. Jabari reached out for her, but it was too late. She threw herself on Hulie and his shotgun. Jabari heard it go off twice and saw her body propel upward from the force of the blast, like a ragdoll being kicked up from the ground.

"Nooo!" Jabari screamed.

He was tired of all the killing. He was numb and his feet wouldn't move. Hulie looked at the body as it laid folded up in front of him in a bloody heap. Then he looked at Jabari and pointed the gun his way. Jabari wasn't really the religious type, but all he knew was that when Hulie did that, flame whooshed in front of his face, making him back off. When Jabari came back to his right mind, he heard Nikki calling him. So, he ran to the window and she was telling him to come on. He could also hear the police sirens in the background. He never thought he'd actually want to hear them.

He also heard Hulie in the background yelling out his name. "Jabari, I'ma get you muthafucka!"

A shot exploded and the side of the door shattered. Jabari wasted no more time. He dove through the window and fell on top of Nikki. They could hear Hulie coming through the door pumping the shotgun. Jabari picked Cleo up, put her over his shoulder and followed Nikki through the wood. Jabari didn't dare look back, but he could hear Hulie still hollering. "*I'ma get y'all!*"

Hulie ran back into the room. It was filled with smoke and the flames were climbing up the walls. He stomped on the bag with the money trying to out the fire. Then tried taking out whatever bundles he could. He heard the sirens too as they got closer. He knew he didn't have much time, he couldn't get any more, most of it had burned. He stuffed what he had, which was quite a bit, down his shirt and ran to the window. He looked both ways for anyone spying, then jumped out and dipped toward the street.

The building exploded shortly afterward and started popping like fireworks from all the gun and ammo Hulie had hidden inside.

Hulie came out of the bushes and spotted his truck. He reached through his pockets then realized he'd left the keys inside.

"Damn!" He grumbled. "Fuck it!" He tossed the bag over his shoulder and jogged through the woods toward Highway 26.

He had enough money to hitchhike back to West Ashley, pack his shit, get on his bike and haul ass. He'd finally got the fuckin' money, well at least most of it. Now, he could retire from the game and just chill or so he thought.

THEY WERE JUST ABOUT to hit a clearing, Jabari could faintly see some buildings and hear the sounds of cars and trucks. He had no clue where the hell they were. They came to a trailer park that sat underneath Highway 26. He'd heard about the area, but never ventured out that way, he thought it was too dangerous. Nikki knew the area very well, though. She didn't let up until they came to a brown trailer with an old tattered deck out front. Jabar looked around the front and it finally became familiar. It was a root doctor's house.

Nikki knocked and the door opened, a short, grey-headed man opened the door.

He shook his head. "Knew you were coming." He pointed toward Cleo. "Bring her in, quickly."

The inside had damn near hundreds of jars filled with different substances. Mostly roots and plants, but toward the corner of the room, there were old, dusty books and in the far back, a skeleton. Jabari didn't know if it was real or not, but the skull on the table in front made him not even want to ask. Jabari was freaking out, he respectfully stepped back out, with the blessing of the root doctor. A couple of minutes later, Nikki came busting through the door. The older grey, haired man was right behind her.

"I g'won git hem!" Nikki said.

She had a gun in her hand and was working up a full head of steam...she was crazed. He tried to pull her back in, but he couldn't. He glanced back over his shoulder, to handle his business with Cleo "Nikki...I need help with her!" The root doctor said.

"No." Nikki shook her head. "Tired this yeh' shit!"

Jabari really didn't want to intervene cause he was tired of it too. Actually, he was just about ready to go. Hell, he stepped in front of her anyway. "Where you going?" He asked. "Why don't you help him out with Cleo? Try to get a ride so we can get her to the hosp..."

"Whut, yu wen try to kill me again boy! Burn me up like tha lass time?" She spit at Jabari as she held the gun in her hands shakingly.

"Look...I tried to save you! I ain't got nothing to do with, Hulie!" Jabari said.

"You's jus as guilty boy, yu no stop hem!"

She was right, he didn't try hard enough. Jabari was just as guilty. He sighed, the spotted a chair and sat down.

"Fuck it, I ain't got no wins," he said. "Do what you want to do. Hell, I think I did enough good for today, anyway. Ain't got no friends...Rip dead...Dondi dead...Double D dead... man, fuck it!" Jabari grabbed her hand with the gun and

pointed it o his head. "Do it!"

Nikki looked him into his eyes deeply and tears came down her's. she mumbled something under her breath.

"I shoulda been home...a good wife...me husband. I tried to dem boys outta trouble...I failed...dem." She broke down crying.

Jabari pulled her into his arms and let her cry and he broke down crying as well.

The root doctor opened the door again. "Nik-

ki...please...go get the car. We need to get her to the hospital." "Will she live?" Jabari asked.

"God only knows best," he answered back solemnly.

Nikki got up and ran behind the back pulling up shortly afterward in a car and beckoned Jabari to get Cleo. But not before she called Jabari over.

"Maybe...you ain't so lost boy, yah!" she said.

Jabari smiled then turned and went to get Cleo. Jabari asked the root doctor if it was okay for him to use his cell phone as they rode to the hospital. The root doctor didn't mind, Jabari needed to make the call he'd been avoiding.

"Hello, Tangie?"

"Jabari, where the hell you been? Don't you know I've been looking for you? You had me worried!"

"You were worried...bout me?"

"Boy...you just wait until I see you. I'ma go upside your head!"

She sounded just like their mom. She actually cared about Jabari and loved him after all his bullshit. She really did...now that was family. Maybe he needed to give her a half-ass chance, then he thought hell maybe he should give himself a chance too.

He looked over Nikki and nodded. "It's over, Tangie...it's finally over," he said.

HULIE LAUGHED AS HE made his way to the highway.

After all the dirty, rotten shit he'd done, he knew without a doubt that people wanted him dead. But fuck them was his thoughts, then he smirked. "*Sometimes the bad guy just gets away!*"

Epilogue

A couple of years had gone by now, Jabari ended up getting five years. But actually, did about a year and some change in a rehab. He'd also caught some of the backlash behind the Walterboro incident. They couldn't find Stacy or Jason, so someone had to pay. Jabari wasn't mad at them, his sister eventually made him plea out to a misdemeanor drug charge. He'd gotten off light. Jabari didn't mind he needed a place to get himself together anyway, and he did just that. Eventually, Tangie shined so well she was asked to run for the State Solicitors office. However, she said to hell with that and ended up doing private practice, Civil Rights cases.

Cleo was paralyzed from the waist down, she's alright with it though, because at least she was living. She started school and stayed at home with her mom. Her mom had ended up divorcing her pops, so it was just the two of them now. Diplite wasn't so lucky, he eventually died. Cleo and them said they didn't want a funeral cause he looked so bad. Also, because he really didn't have any friends for a memorial service except for thugs and they were tired of them already. Liberty Hill had changed drastically, it was no longer the dope infested area it once was.

Nikki was doing well, she'd rebuilt her house, then gave some money to add on to it. Jabari had driven by one day and

405

stopped the car and they talked for a little while. She told him she was still seeing Dirty-Red on the low. He hadn't changed, either. He still ran the liquor house. The biggest thing going on over there was the lottery he had out for the day when Wood came back.

Don't know whatever happened to Hulie. Nikki said the root man had put a curse on him. Couldn't tell you what kind of curse, Nikki just said he wouldn't get too far. Anyway, Jabari didn't know whether to believe that shit or not. All he knew was that he wasn't lost anymore.

TIJUANA, MEXICO WAS known for gang cartels, prostitution and some of the best weed on the planet. The women there were exotic, sexy and plenty to choose from. Hulie had got connected with a cartel that served dope to the whole Coastal Region from Mississippi to Virginia. A lot of money was being made and Hulie's cut came out to at least forty percent. A good half a mil every four or five months. He was living large, had everything he wanted at his disposal. He'd told one of his Mexican cartel buddies one day, fuck them niggas in South Carolina. The best thing they could do was buy that good ass dope. He'd fucked up, leave it to Hulie to run his mouth.

You know, one thing about the Mexicans or anyone Latino was that they were painfully loyal, especially when it came to their la Familia. So, when you fucked your family over, they always, regardless of how much money was involved, looked at you some sort of way and with distrust. This definitely played to your off brands too, Gringo...Negro. They'd heard about some of the things Hulie had done.

So, as Hulie laid in front of the large Olympic sized pool in the back of his mansion. Overlooking the pretty blue water of the beach coolin'. It came as no surprise when the smooth, catlike figure eased up next to him and pointed the .22 Caliber with the gassed, carbon silencer to his head.

All Hulie could do was light up the chocolate Cuban rolled blunt, take a good pull, and say, "Finally, found me...huh."

"Yeah...well, you knew it was coming." She pulled the trigger, then wiped the blood splattered tip on his shirt. Then she reached into his pants pocket, pulled out his phone, dialed some numbers and waited for the person on the other side to

pick up. "It's done," she said. "I'll be home soon."

Taking a towel that sat by the lounge chair, she tossed it over Hulie's head and leaned back watching the waves slam into the rocks off the sandy white coastline. "Damn, this is nice."

The groundskeeper came over to her with a black body bag in hand and asked, "Senorita, is there anything else?"

"Naw..." She pointed at the body. "Just get him outta here."

"And...your things?"

"Might as well move them in...for now." She glanced over. "Mansions unoccupied."

"Yes, ma'am." He moved toward Hulie's body, then peeked his head up. "Senorita, sorry to bother you. What

name do I put on the door, after I, of course, remove his?"

She grinned, then reached over and picked up the blunt Hulie was smoking on. "Cocky..."

"Cocky, what?"

"Just...Cocky." She crossed her legs, puffed on the good Mexican weed and uttered under her breath. "Q's people...he'll be down soon."

Nikki had finally gotten the revenge she deserved for her son T-Black and the burning of her house and brutal attack that night. It came in the form of a nickel plated, Kevlar bulletproof vest, worn by Cocky the day Hulie tried to waste him and the .22 Caliber, gold bullet to his brain she'd just delivered.

So, Sunshine probably did get the last laugh...or, giggle!

~The End~
More from Dean Hamid LLC:

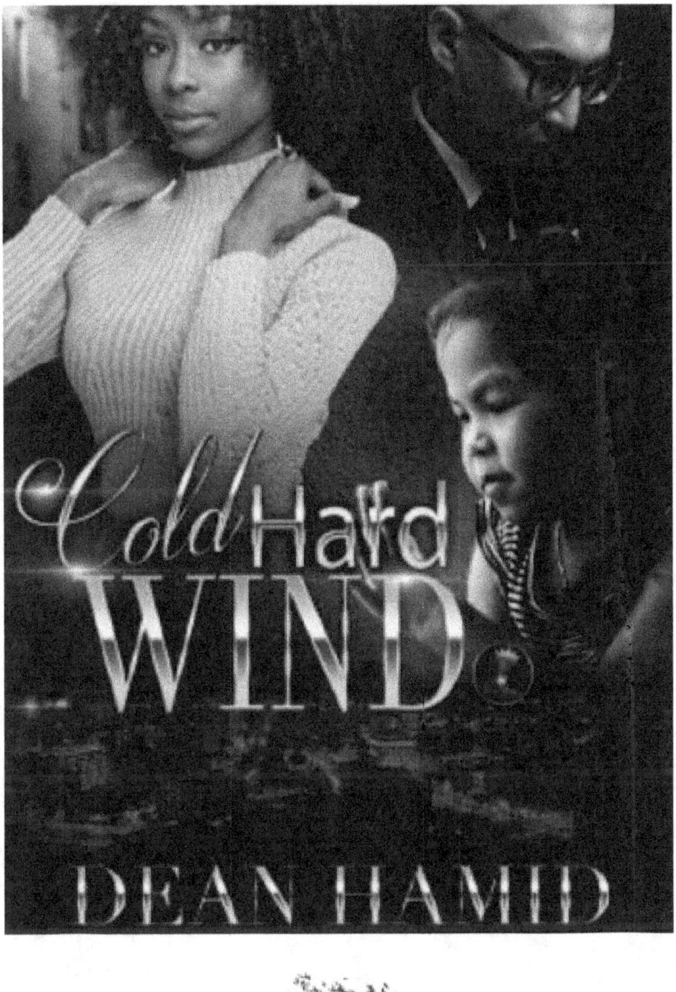
Cold Hard
WIND
DEAN HAMID

Don't miss out!

Click the button below and you can sign up to receive emails whenever Dean Hamid publishes a new book. There's no charge and no obligation.

Sign Me Up!

[1]
https://books2read.com/r/B-A-UOGI-JIPDC

BOOKS 2 READ

Connecting independent readers to independent writers.

---

1. https://books2read.com/r/B-A-UOGI-JIPDC

Don't miss out!

Visit the website below and you can sign up to receive emails whenever Dean Hamid publishes a new book. There's no charge and no obligation.

https://books2read.com/r/B-A-UOGI-JIPDC

BOOKS 2 READ

Connecting independent readers to independent writers.

Also by Dean Hamid

Part One

Epidemic 7.3k[1]

The Bushwick Chronicles

Dunya! The Do or Die[2]

Dunya! 2 Rasheed's Redemption[3]

Standalone

Hell has no fury[4]

Lost Boy[5]

Also by Dean Hamid

Lovin' Safari Series

Lovin' Safari / Lovin' Safari II: Gunzz and Roses

Part One

Epidemic 7.3k

The Bushwick Chronicles

Dunya! The Do or Die

Dunya! Rasheed's Redemption

Standalone

Hell has no fury Lost Boy

Cold Hard Wind

[1]. https://www.draft2digital.com/catalog/976746

[2]. https://www.draft2digital.com/catalog/932155

[3]. https://www.draft2digital.com/catalog/932192

[4]. https://www.draft2digital.com/catalog/594205

[5]. https://www.draft2digital.com/catalog/977037

Also by Dean Hamid

Lovin' Safari Series
Lovin' Safari

Part One
Epidemic 7.3k

The Bushwick Chronicles
Dunya! The Do or Die
Dunya! Rasheed's Redemption

Standalone
Hell has no fury
Lost Boy
Cold Hard Wind